2021-01-12 W9-BWE-566
50690011228738
Bear, Greg
The unfinished land

VALLEY COMMUNITY LIBRARY
739 RIVER STREET
PECKVILLE, PA 18452
(570) 489-1765
www.lclshome.org

The Unfinished Land

The
UNFINISHED
LAND

Greg Bear

A John Joseph Adams Book
Houghton Mifflin Harcourt
Boston   New York
2021

Copyright © 2021 by Greg Bear

All rights reserved

For information about permission to reproduce selections from this book,
write to trade.permissions@hmhco.com or to Permissions,
Houghton Mifflin Harcourt Publishing Company,
3 Park Avenue, 19th Floor, New York, New York 10016.

hmhbooks.com

Library of Congress Cataloging-in-Publication Data
Names: Bear, Greg, 1951– author.
Title: The unfinished land / Greg Bear.
Description: Boston : Houghton Mifflin Harcourt, 2021. | "A John Joseph Adams book."
Identifiers: LCCN 2020004939 (print) | LCCN 2020004940 (ebook) |
ISBN 9781328589903 (hardcover) | ISBN 9781328592361 (ebook)
Subjects: GSAFD: Historical fiction. | Fantasy fiction.
Classification: LCC PS3552.E157 U54 2021 (print) | LCC PS3552.E157 (ebook) |
DDC 813/.54—dc23
LC record available at https://lccn.loc.gov/2020004939
LC ebook record available at https://lccn.loc.gov/2020004940

Book design by Emily Snyder

Map by Carly Miller

Printed in the United States of America
DOC 10 9 8 7 6 5 4 3 2 1

For Chloe and Allison:
Brave Voyagers

THE NORTHERNMOST ISLE OF

TIR NA NOG

SE

GREAT

AGNI MOST FOUL

KRATER

FIRST QUARRY
OF SOULS

WESTERN
SPINES OR
RIDGES

ZODIAKO
(SOUTHWESTERN SHORE)

ICE CAVERN
OUTFLOW

THE RAVINE

OLD FORT

"To gain a fact is to lose a dream."   — OGMIOS

"A legend is entitled to be beyond time and place."   — COCTEAU

But not beyond words . . .

Far to the north, west of dream and east of knowledge, there lay a great ring of islands where life and time began, known to some as the Atlantides, and to others as Tir Na Nog. Still others remember them as the islands of Queen Hel, the most radiant but difficult of aspect, and name them the Fingers of Dis. But Hel hath not been seen for thousands of years . . .

There is no history before these islands. Here, surrounded by a thick, constant mist, are the seven navels of thought and soul, where linger the origins and the shaping of all we know and love, and all we hate and fear—for the Earth and its sheltering sky, despite their seeming age, are deceptively young.

The Unfinished Land

Broken Armada

REYNARD SHOTWOOD, no longer a boy, not yet a man, had pushed the last of his dead shipmates overboard two days before. Rubbing crusted salt from his eyes, he tried to say another prayer for them and for himself, but his lips were broken and his tongue filled his mouth so he could not make the words.

His uncle and the crew, English fishermen from the coastal town of Southwold, had been cut to pieces by grapeshot from a Spanish galleass. Except for one finger, missing its tip to the knuckle, Reynard had not been touched. But now, a week or more later, he was parched and starving.

Unfamiliar currents carried him through a thick, night-gray fog that looped and writhed over the toppled mast and the shredded sails like a sky filled with maggots. He had spent long, numb hours watching the bloodless, broken bodies of his uncle, the uncle's partner in the boat, and the partner's son bump and bob against the timbers and upper step of the mast, caught in eddies that seemed to mimic the whorls in the fog, the bodies rolling now and then to show their faces — if they still had faces — and stare blankly, resentfully, as if he should help them climb back aboard and resume their duties.

Yare, fast away! He could almost hear his uncle's cry as their boat tried to flee the Spanish, but it was only a patting breeze and waves slopping through the scuppers. Now the bodies were gone, sunk or grabbed by sharks, those snapping dogs of the sea — but the fog still turned the sun into a cold moon and shaded the moon as dim and gray as death itself.

The sloop-rigged hoy, once as hardworking a boat as ever harvested the sea, managed to stay afloat even with its larboard a mass of wrenched decking thrust through with broken timbers. The starboard, rising a few fingers above the dark, lapping water, likely held a bubble, but soon that would leak away and the wreck would sink and no one would ever know how long Reynard had been out here, alive, alone — but of course not afraid. Not now. The worst had happened, other than dying, and fishermen often died. Their names were carved into boards nailed on the walls of his family church — a good Protestant church. But dead all the same, and so many.

And now many more.

The great battle off the coast of Flanders had been long and fierce. Boats from Southwold had left their dozing harbor to serve the English fleet, at the command of Lord Walsyngham and the Queen, though the fishing season was but half done and many families might go hungry — but the desperate need of Elizabeth and of England against Philip's devils overcame village sense.

With the awful memory of the seaborne power the English ships had faced, it was easy for Reynard to imagine the Duke of Parma's soldiers filling the streets of London with forests of muskets and half-pikes, crested steel helms thick and shiny as shingle on a beach — and row upon row of great bronze Spanish cannons rolling, flaming, and bucking, blowing up homes and churches, intent on punishing all who followed the faith of Henry and Elizabeth and not Mary of ill regard. Maybe there was no home to return to.

Not the best sailor or apprentice, he had never wanted to go to sea, and yet had never found his place on land. His mother, a once-lovely woman who had withered early under the toll of being a fisherman's widow, lamented her son's pointless fascination with bushes and birds, ferrets and mice, snakes and turtles — more interested in studying the insides of fish than catching or making them ready for market. He could see her now, a sallow-faced, gray-haired figure, with a perpetual half-smile — though she was no idiot, and had taught him letters early on — pounding out washing or packing oysters and lobsters into barrels, graced with slimy, odorous seaweed, for sale in any of the five larger towns nearby, or even in London after a night journey, to avoid the heat of the summer sun.

Reynard was too numb for regrets, though he suspected that if he lived much longer, an unlikely prospect, he would have many. Could he regret not being more grateful for a home and a roof — though a leaky roof, thatch unchanged for years — or regret not being a better nephew, which he did not, not yet, and not much? Perhaps he could regret not having planned a way to keep the hoy clear of the galleass. His mind worked that way, regretting the undone and impossible, not the undone but doable. He preferred contemplating inventions and miracles, not plotting and planning actual work. He preferred reading to playing but had neither books nor companions, since his life was spent in service, mostly, to his uncle, with barely a day off in a month.

In what was left of the hoy, Reynard had recovered a cask of salt cod and two butts of water. One butt had been holed, and the second, poorly coopered, had leaked dry. The hoy had been meant to convey stores to the Queen's great ships, but the promised supplies had not arrived in Southwold by the time the boats put out to sea. There should have been more victuals for the English fleet, from the shore, from the Queen, before they engaged — so his uncle had complained. Only Reynard had lived long enough to suffer for it. His uncle was a hard man, a tough master, but fair enough and smart, and despite everything, Reynard had loved him as a grizzled, thick-browed, heavy-jawed, masculine mountain in his young life.

Maybe now, pulling his feet from the water and going through these memories, he could find his regrets. But for the nonce, sharks were of more concern. Their low triangular fins popped up here and there, swishing, probing; they no doubt remembered they had found food around this wreck before. He did not want to further flavor the ocean with his toes.

He rose on wobbly legs, feet wedged against the gunwale to see any change in the flat gray sea. No change. In the days since the battle, the fog had tempted with its promise of moisture. He had carefully gathered the remains of the spritsail and knuckled a dip in the canvas to catch fog and rain, but the fog did not condense or drip, and there had been no rain since the easterly winds and violent storms had broken up the Spanish fleet.

Reynard stared at the barrel of salt cod. At his present level of thirst, the thick white flesh, hard as wood, was worse than useless, with no water but seawater in which to soak it. Salt from either could drive him mad.

Having been fishing and delivering freight for only three years, Reynard had not yet had time to absorb all his uncle's sea lore, but he suspected—he felt, in a strange way—that the currents which drove the wreck were carrying him north and west. For most of a day, he passed through a slightly brackish flow, probably out of the Baltic, where shoals of herring and mackerel, along with sturgeon and fat bream and plaice, drew out English boats to compete with the Basques, the Dutch, and the French. On their first fishing expedition, his uncle had dipped a ladle in that water and offered it to his lips, to let him taste it, to remember the flavor of its source and learn how to find his way by tongue as well as eye. Now the sea was colder and saltier. That did not seem to match any currents his uncle had taught him, not for this time of year, when the North Sea warmed.

Perhaps the great battle, with its flashes and cries, its explosions and whistling shot, had frightened the sea into its own madness.

By morning of what he was sure would be his last day, Reynard's cracked skin was streaked with blood and salt, and a long gulp of seawater seemed a good, a *necessary*, option, if only to soften his lips and relieve his parched throat. Still, perhaps in honor of his dead uncle, he had so far resisted, knowing that he would shortly thereafter follow his shipmates to the bottom.

Reynard's head lolled. He tried to stay awake night after night and was now losing that struggle. Even as something powerful bumped his foot, he could not open his eyes, until abruptly he heard deep thumps and great splashes. He pulled his feet up tight against his butt and blinked until he saw, across the half-submerged deck, that a long, silvery-gray shark had pushed up to get at him and was stuck —unable to thrash free and back to the sea. Now it twisted and tossed its long scimitar tail, and gaped the most frightful open-jaw threats inches from his ankles and toes, its deep-sunk eyes intent on either dining or causing the ship to break apart. Reynard was already soaked, but rolled over the gunwale aft and grabbed for a splintered rudder bar. Without thought of the danger, so close was he already to death, he braced his feet against the broken planks, leaned out over the deck, wedged the bar under the shark's heaving middle, then hunched along on his knees and fairly lifted the great fish, teeth and dead eyes and all, back into the sea.

After crawling aft to the only dry patch that remained, he leaned back, felt his toes to make sure all remained, and continued his shivering and weary watch. The sea, gray and uniform beneath greenish-gray sky, resumed its boring mien.

Scrawny at the best of times, with a knife-cut shock of thick black hair, by looks and attitude Reynard favored his mother's side of the family, who claimed descent from the ancient peoples who had built the great stone circles. "Stone folk," his grandmother had called them, "and specially the men."

His mother had taught Reynard how to notch sticks or boards in ogham, or sign secretly on his arm with his fingers, called *rankalva*, which she explained had been taught to humans thousands of seasons before by great Ogmios. On occasion she dropped into a speech called *Tinker's Cant*, a kind of bastard Irish sometimes heard on wagons offering to do light blacksmithing, knife-honing, and scythe-sharpening — gruffly spoken by dark, black-haired peoples, women wild, men quiet and shrewd, jacks of all trades traveling horse-and-sheep-pounded pathways across Britain. His grandmother had once belonged to those folks, and his mother still proudly boasted of her girlhood, and of how women survived and even prospered in that life.

But Reynard had since his father's death felt there would be no prosperity or fortune in fishing with his uncle. Worse, he dreaded the sea. His fear of water had brought out a cruel streak in his uncle, who did his best to shock it out of him, and nearly succeeded. Once he had tied a rope around Reynard and dragged him along behind the hoy for several miles. The fishermen had watched closely to make sure he was not drowning, and he did manage in a way to learn to swim. But what appeared to follow — acceptance and a better attitude — masked a bitter hatred, strangely not of his uncle, but of the source of all their livelihoods — the sea, that forced them into such a desperate existence. So desperately sad had he become for the brusque, brawny man who had been his father, as the years passed and his memory faded, and so anxious had he become for novelty and wider fields, and to get away from the water and the smell of fish, that at age twelve he had run away from the coast and walked west across fallow fields and over hedgerows and along farmers' lanes until nightfall, surrounded by birdsong, light airs, and a boundless, floating sense of weary accomplishment.

On that first moonless and starless night, hunger had replaced his floating ease and cold had set in, along with guilt. He had huddled within sight of quiet shade-wrapped cows in a long wicker enclosure, observed with envy the goings-on and passing candles of a farmer's house, and finally snuck into the low, decrepit barn and wrapped himself in dirty, unturned hay, sour and wet, trying to sleep and not succeeding, until cock's crow and a pale sunrise.

There was nothing for it but to beg at the farmer's door or return to the coast, back to Southwold, the boat, his uncle, and his mother. He decided against begging. On his way back, he encountered a half-drunken press gang reeling over the road near Aldeburgh, alternately singing and calling out, hoping to fill the Queen's own ships of war. Reynard's black hair helped him hide in the shadow of a hedgerow. "Sir Frauncis Drake's ship," a sailor cried in a voice sharp as a billhook, "built in this very town of Aldeburgh, demands *thee!*"

Here was Reynard's chance to flee a life of fishing and village monotony! But as much as Reynard admired Drake (and what Englishman did not?), this would still be a life at sea and not for him. He did his best to stay silent as he observed through a screen of cow parsley, grass, and hawthorn six sailors and two soldiers, swaying saps and cudgels from their broad belts, and towing two skinny, sad-looking lads bearing badges of resistance — bruises on faces and arms, ropes binding their wrists. Reynard did not wish another and stupider set of masters.

And yet now, three years later, here he was anyway, lost at sea like Oxenham's men in his uncle's tales. He had no idea what had happened to Drake's ship in the engagement with the Armada, after the famed captain had captured a Spanish galleon and brought it to London to strip it of shot and gunpowder. Maybe Drake was dead or lost as well. Maybe he was alive and nearby, and soon they would meet, and the hero would rescue Reynard . . . What a tale that would be!

He tried to bring up some spit, but there was none to be had. Dry, rough tongue scraping cheeks brought only blood.

After the press gang had passed, Reynard had fallen asleep beneath the hedgerow, and then awakened to a strange black hand, streaked and lined with thorny white, reaching through the hawthorn to shake him. With a start, he had scrambled out of the thicket, brushing away leaves and twigs and dirt, and stood before a man who might have been older than he, or younger — hard to know, with his strange color and demeanor. Like an unholy spirit, the man had watched Reynard through eyes whose whites were black and whose pupils were a pale purple. Even in bright morning light, he appeared blacker than night, his skin blackest where touched by sun, yet brighter pale green-gray in the shadows. This bizarrely reversed fellow wore a ragged black and silver coat and breeches — and his hair hung elfin white streaked with green and blue.

"Thou must reach the island," the dark visitor had told him. "Get thee swift to sea and find thy way to where the Crafters scrub and moil. That will be thy true beginning."

"Who are you?" Reynard had asked in a trembling voice.

The dark man with purple eyes then faded, leaving Reynard on the road beside the hedgerow — alone and frightened. Later, the most memorable part of that odd vision had been that the man's shadow was itself white. He had cast a white shadow.

The nearer Reynard had come to Southwold, the less he had felt comfortable with the dark man's memory: dream or sorcery, trouble either way! And so he had tried to forget about him and told nobody, not even his mother, to whom he sometimes confided his dreams. He still had no explanation. But it was apparent he might not need to drink seawater to lose his mind.

◆　◆　◆

Waves sloshed over his legs. Reynard stared at the worn fingers of his right hand, lifting them one after another, testing their flexibility. First he rearranged and retied the filthy, bloody tag of cloth on his little finger, serving as a bandage. The tag fell off and he saw that the old clot had closed over the exposed knuckle, making the bandage little more than a cushion. But he pushed it back over the wound and held his hand in closer, under his arm, moaning softly. After a time, he took out his hand and laid the fingers as straight as he could along his left arm and arranged, by folding and extending, a series of ogham symbols, engaging in *rankalva* — spelling out letter by letter old Irish words, as his grandmother had taught him, and as his mother had on occasion signed to him when she wanted chores done. "Do not show this to thine uncle," his mother had advised. "He is unhappy with my side of the family. Oh, he is an honorable man, comes to that, but not ripe for such heresies ..."

The letters and words, dancing from the fingers both injured and raw, brought him comfort. He could still shape the necessary letters, even though his hand throbbed. Somehow, that seemed important, though it was a skill he had never found useful after his grandmother's death.

His uncle had been no-nonsense, straight as a staff and just as blunt in his opinions — unlike Reynard's father, his brother, who married, gambled, drank, had a son, and then died, leaving the uncle to take up the family and feed and find work for Reynard, who had always borne a distinct resemblance, black hair and all, to his grandfather, also a tinker, ne'er-do-well, and gambler — so his uncle had claimed, with quiet dismay at how life plagued and challenged sensible men.

He closed his eyes briefly, then opened them and saw nothing changed. But his fingers had a life of their own.

Old Goidelic words now danced on them, spinning a silent tale of the Anakim, powerful giants who had once lived in the Holy Land, vexing Moses and Joshua, and upon being pushed out of those countries, had moved to Ireland and Scotland. There, many centuries before, they had married into the dark Picts and other tribes and had acted as scouts and beacons for the even darker Roma, their distant cousins — according to his grandmother. "Stone people, and big," she had confided. "I met one once, long ago. Handsome and very large. Thought I to marry him, but mine own mither would hae none o' it."

Reynard had once asked the dotty old priest of Aldeburgh about the Anakim, and the priest had scoffed and suggested he read his Wycliffe. "Or seek'st thou a dark grammary, to learn magic? Thou hast that evil, Gypsy look, I wot."

Neither his uncle nor his mother possessed so expensive and rare a thing as a family Bible. And besides, through lack of books, Reynard's reading skills were haphazard, though he was swift enough with ogham and the finger-forms that spelled out words to those who wished to hide them.

Still, his grandmother's secret signs had not satisfied. He had wished to read about and learn of all the places and histories and fables and other glorious things that book-words described. Four months back, one cloudy spring afternoon, he had used his one free day to venture out of the small fishing town and, unannounced, knock on the door of a man known to be a tutor in Aldeburgh. The external beams of the instructor's two-story, half-timbered house were painted pink, and the door was set with purple stamped-glass windows in leaden frames. Reynard had knocked several times, at first light raps, then heavy bangs, on the thick oaken door, and asked the small stooped man who answered if he had books. Dubious, baldheaded, wearing a sagging, great-shouldered coat over a long gray gown, the instructor had looked him over briefly for weapons, then shrugged and led this strange boy inside. In a dark-shelved inner apartment, away from windows and sun, by the smoky light of a brass candle, Reynard had stared in green envy at the instructor's shelves of vellum-bound books, dozens of them, spines pale gray or tan, with titles calligraphed on their spines in sepia or black ink. The instructor had held out a clutching hand, rubbed his fingers, and with sucked-in cheeks and pinched lips studied Reynard.

"How much money doth your family possess?" he had asked.

"I come from fisherfolk."

"So ... very little?" This made the man's face turn red as a slice of beef. Unable to pay, Reynard had been shown the door, with a kick on his bum for farewell.

As he had made his return to Southwold through the gloaming, the same press gang, minus sad boys, almost caught him a second time, but he escaped through a half-overgrown wicker gate and fled through a copse alive with bird screeches. At least there had been no dark man with a white shadow.

With his fingers, he shaped more of his grandmother's words, concluding stanzas to ancient songs he did not understand, filled with nonsense lists and riddles and begging equally nonsensical answers that nobody had ever explained — then sighed and folded both hands into fists. The bandage fell off again. This time, he did not replace it.

All of it was nonsense for a fisherboy, nonsense as useless as salt cod in a barrel. Would that the Anakim could rise again and vanquish England's enemies! But they did not, and would not, ever. This was no longer such a world.

For months now, all England — and certainly the northeast coastal towns — had experienced a numbing terror inspired by actual threats, but promoted by the Queen's own henchman: agents of

Walsyngham and whoever could be encouraged or commanded to cry in the village squares or carry alarming handbills from town to town. Weeks before the battle, dire warnings had been posted at inns and around wells and on the docks. Each village was asked to help the effort against the Spanish by contributing ships and boats. Some villages demurred, made excuses; bet against the Queen, some said, a dangerous treason if the Spanish were defeated. Reynard read well enough to feel concern, but understood better the fear his uncle had expressed that not to give over the use of their hoy would bring down the Queen's anger. Beloved as the Queen was by most not Catholic, no one wished her servant Walsyngham's disapproval, and so South- wold had eventually compelled twelve boats, nine pinnaces and three hoys, to join the fleet.

Farmers as well were reluctant to donate crops and animals to supply the navy or the coastal defenses. Rarely traveling more than ten miles from their land, these yeomen and landowners had dif- ficulty imagining, in their inland fastnesses, a broad, wet ocean. Such, his uncle said, was what it meant to be English these days — surrounded by devils, and the farmers and highborn on shore caught in tides of ignorance and stingy greed.

"For which God willing I'll soon die," Reynard murmured, then cringed as his lower lip split, and not for the first time.

The fog! The cursed fog filled the sky with weird shapes. Devil's fog, devil's war, devil's time — and his life had scarce begun.

He could no longer keep his eyes open, even knowing what he now saw might be the last he would ever see.

The salt crusting his eyelids crackled.

He dropped into dark misery.

Somehow, the visions would not leave him.

"Wilt thou tak'st these signs to some who wait?"

Reynard did not bother to open his eyes. He was raw inside from the knotted string of memories and visions, with no way of knowing which was what. There was nobody and nothing beyond his eyelids to see, he knew that already. And besides, he did not need to open his eyes, as the lids themselves had become clear as stamped-glass panes, useless to block such specters.

And yet . . .

A well-dressed gentleman stood before him, shoes set solid on the sun-touched water. At least his coloring and figure were not reversed. A fancy ostrich plume adorned his well-shaped and expensive hat. Reynard, who seemed to watch from all around, saw the gentleman's pleasant smile and knew that something more was wanted of him. This was a man of privilege. Even for a vision, being so well-dressed showed money and power, and so he must needs be polite.

"Noble sir," he murmured.

"Fine lad!" The beplumed gentleman leaned in and stretched out his arm. "I have summat to teach thee about the heavens and their ways. I have studied long, and think thou needest guidance on such matters, even now, before thy moment of being born."

"I am already born," Reynard said, wondering if the man was an idiot, or truly a ghost.

"Nay, thou hast not even a name, yet."

"And what is your name, sir?"

"Frauncis," the man said. "Thou'lt know me better in time." His fingers tickled Reynard's palm in patterns he recognized, letters leading into words, words forming a kind of poetic sense, of which he translated a crucial few: *The First Mother . . . the First Word . . .*

The First Star in the Sky.

Was that the stand of it?

A far metal peal interrupted.

Reynard lifted his chin.

The man collapsed like folded paper.

Reynard looked for the source of the clang that had roused him. Had it been a swinging bell? Bump of blocks against an anchor? After a short, dark time, he thought he heard other voices — not English voices, but not dreams, either — and craned his neck to find their direction, muffled as they were by fog, like every other sound — but real. He looked down at his fingers, but could recover nothing from the strange dream of the feathered man except his smile and the arch of his plume.

Again Reynard tried to stand, and nearly fell into the water. Words from across the lapping waves came flat and clear to his ears — Spanish words, and not from spirits. Dare he cry out in answer? What choice? To keep to this drifting pile of sticks meant a sure and drowned death. Could the Spanish do worse?

Walsyngham had insisted they could.

Reynard made his choice.

"Ahoy!" he tried to yell, but the call came out a dry, weak croak. He tried again, and once more, with no better result, then leaned on his elbow and stared into the gloom, cheeks puffy, eyes stinging with salt.

There it was! A great shadow pushed through the lower grayness, huge spritsail dragging under a boom big as a tree. The sail passed over his wreck, and the hoy hard-bumped a keel and swung slow about, grinding and spinning along a massive, bulged black hull. Above, from as high as the sky, more cries drifted down. He knew little Spanish, but these were words he could almost understand — nautical words. They had seen the wreck and were discussing it, he was sure.

Reynard rose to his knees to hold out his arms and reach for a ladder or rope, something to climb or cling to. Whatever the origin of the huge, potbellied ship and its crew, they were alive, it was afloat, and together offered at least a thin hope.

But nothing was lowered to his grasp, and the wreck kept grinding and spinning.

And then, suddenly, shouts and cheers from above, and a huge, dark mass plunged from over the rail into the water, just feet from the wreck of the hoy. Bubbles greened the sea, and a sad hump surfaced and rolled to show a long head, folded and broken legs —

A horse! A dead horse. With such a feast, the ocean would soon be thick with sharks. The words from above grew louder. The wreck had beat along about a third of the galleon, wrenching against solid oak and splitting the frame. Reynard was awash to his waist when a thick line uncoiled like a snake from the quarterdeck. He grabbed it and held tight. A grizzled old sailor leaned over the rail, scanned the dead horse and the wreck's submerged tangle, then waved his arm and pulled back. A few seconds later, the old sailor was swung out again and down, sitting on a slung board, such as might be used to paint the hull or transfer sailors.

The old one laughed as if this was a joke and he was paying off a bet. He had very few teeth left. "*Muchacho!*" he said. "*¡Oye, tú! ¿Eres inglés o castellano?*"

Asking if he were English or Spanish. Reynard understood this much. But again, he could only croak.

The old man looked him over with a yellowed, doubtful eye. "I think *inglés.* Do not move. Thou art fast sinking."

A great voice boomed from the forecastle, arguments broke out along the rail, and the old man was pulled up. Water slopped into Reynard's mouth and he tried to swim, but his muscles knotted. The great ship moved on. He was sure that would be the last he would see or hear of any of them, but moments later, the old man descended again and flung him a second rope. "Tie it on!" he urged, and pointed to his own skinny waist. Reynard had enough strength to do that, and soon he was lifted like a sack, the old man keeping him steady as they both were hauled aboard the ship, passing gun ports, thick sheets of tar and hair to help repel shipworm, black steel spikes to discourage boarders — which could skewer them like fish on a hook.

But the men pulling from the deck swung them about, and the old man, with surprising strength, pushed the boy up over the thick rail.

Reynard sprawled on his back, gasping, and the sailors and soldiers — dozens of Spanish soldiers in full battle gear — formed a solid wall, like a stand of brutal flowers. A great net had been slung above the deck, and hammocks still dangled from its squares. The soldiers carried half-pikes and halberds and wore crested helmets and bulge-breasted cuirasses, and they were bearded, brown or olive with sun and warm-climed Spanish blood.

They circled around Reynard, curious, disdainful. Some spat. Some moved in with short swords drawn, ready to dispatch this useless English wretch, until the old man cried out, "*Santa Maria, madre de Dios!*" and pushed them back. The soldiers rewarded him with grating laughter and what sounded like insults.

The old man leaned over Reynard and whispered to him, "Speak truth! Speak lies! But say thou canst tell us where we are."

Reynard croaked and pointed to his mouth.

The old man lifted his gaze to the soldiers and curious sailors and called for water. The sailors grumbled, the soldiers parted and wandered off, but water was brought in a bucket by a frowning boy much younger than Reynard, and the old man ladled him his first drink in days.

"Not too much," he advised. "Thou wilt heave on *el maestro's* bloody deck."

The water was sweeter than fresh apples and gave Reynard back a whisper. "What ship?"

"A mighty ship," the old man said. "*El Corona Royale*, thirty-one guns! Sad boy, *niño inglés*, thou shalt surrender to the imperial navy of King Philip and the Duke of Medina Sidonia, and tell us where we sail!"

"*¡No hay viento!*" cried a voice forward.

"No wind," the old man translated. "No wind anywhere."

A man of great dignity and fine clothes came down to the middle deck to inspect their catch. He knelt beside Reynard and regarded him sadly. The old man, in oft-patched rags, with a rope for a belt, was a sorry contrast to this splendid fellow, whose gray-specked beard had been neatly trimmed, and whose enameled scabbard depended from a belt on a silver chain. His eyes were like emeralds, and his hands were pale and smooth — a young woman's hands, untouched by the wear of rope or oar.

The old man bowed low. "This is *el capitán del mar y de la guerra* Jorge Cardoza de Vincennes, very powerful. Say something. Name anything — an isle thou know'st, a spit, a reef."

"Where the sea doth strangle the wind," Reynard rasped, sensing he would be tossed back into the water unless he said something, however stupid.

"*Donde duerme el viento,*" the old man said to the gentleman.

"Ah," the gentleman said. "*¡Él sí conoce el nombre!*"

"Know'st thou this place?" the old man asked Reynard, with a sparkle of suspicion. "Or make cruel jest?"

Reynard tried to remember where he had heard the phrase, where the notion had come from. It might have been from his father before he died ... but that would have been when Reynard was little, no more than three or four years of age. "My father told it to me," he said, then put fingers to his mouth for more water and for food.

Sadly, deliberately, the gentleman in the fine clothes came off his knee and stood his full height over them — about five feet six inches, shorter than Reynard's uncle and slighter, more delicate.

"*¡Norte-noroeste!*" cried the voice forward.

"How doth he know?" the old man muttered. "For days, the compass guideth not."

And so it was. The Spanish were lost, too. The fog obscured the tops of sails and masts like a billowing blanket, dividing and reshaping into worms and wisps — but also hiding some of the damage the galleon had suffered in the great battle off Gravelines. Ragged sails hung, ripped and holed, rigging cut as if by shears, the ends tied and lifted for fidding and rejoining later, spars hanging but also tied away, bumping in dejection against the great masts.

The old man followed Cardoza, *el capitán del mar y de la guerra*, forward and up onto the forecastle. Two other boys, also younger than Reynard and curious about the prisoner, brought him more water. The oldest smiled, not in the least afraid. They were not unkind, he saw, not cruel — and he had heard many times that the Spanish tortured their own children when they were bad, that they flensed and ate fishermen and merchants for breakfast after breaking their necks in the noose. More grog tales, no doubt, but effective at keeping an air of menace about those who threatened the Queen.

"The Queen's a fair tease when it cometh to Philip," his uncle had said. "But now the old king's dander is up and we are all put to it. If only the dander flaked from a worthier head. Philip will be their bloody ruin!"

The sailors knew a little English, and as they led him to a cage under the overhang of the stern castle, followed by the youngest boy, they tried out their few words, as if seeking his approval of their pronunciation. "Bastard, asshole, thou donkey — thou monkey dick!"

Reynard nodded and smiled.

After the sailors locked the cage, the old man brought him a bowl of lentils and vegetables soaked in oil, not butter. He ate with his fingers. The old man went away again, and now sailors crowded around.

"I know thou is good lad," one sailor attempted.

"*Él es rubio*," said another, with a cackle. "*Él prefiere los pelirrojos.*" His puzzlement set them back and forth with each other until the old man returned. Despite his rags, the old man seemed to be respected.

The sailors, bored, left them to talk alone.

"They remark thou hast red hair," the old man said.

"My hair is black," Reynard said.

The old man shook his head. "Sea-bleached, then. No doubt from terror. Mayhaps it will grow out black. I have told *el capitán* thou'rt son of a fisherman and know'st the waters north to Iceland. Make me not a liar!"

"I know some of the coasts and waters off France and Flanders, and some of Ireland," Reynard said as he ate. His stomach was giving him pains.

"Hast thou fished with Basques? With Dutch?"

"My uncle fished with Basques off Flanders and Portugal," Reynard said. "No Dutch."

"Thou speak'st Basque?"

Reynard made a face.

"French?"

"No."

"Gypsy? Roma?" the old man asked, doubtful.

Reynard shook his head, unsure — his grandmother had never liked the name or judgment of "Gypsy," assuming as it did an origin in Egypt and a clannish, outlaw nature — but was not Tinker's Cant touched by Roma?

"English!" the old man concluded, with a wry twist of his lips. "Well, *el maestro* is afraid, and *el capitán* saith little but frowneth much. We have wandered at sea ten days without wind. And even before the battle, we were stuck in this wallowing tub of shit for over two months! Thou seest plain our galleon is sad. The soldiers never chanced to get ashore. The battle, the storms, the currents . . ."

"Your guns sank my boat," Reynard said. "You killed my uncle and our crew. They knew the sea better than I."

"Many ships and sailors now grace the Lord's deep," the old man said. "I think maybe the planning not so good. But say nothing of this to *el maestro* or *el capitán*."

Reynard's strength was slowly returning, and with it things he had tried to forget — wild winds and pounding waves, shots and fire, screams as his uncle and the crew tried to keep the hoy behind the galleons and away from the guns of the swift Spanish pinnaces. The hoy had been built for cargo, not war, and her four old guns had been mounted in all the wrong places, while a galleass, fierce in the dark gray light of that horrible noon, as the tide reversed and all the Spanish ships seemed to flee in their direction, came abreast and let loose with the scattered shot that put an end to everyone but Reynard ...

He lay back, shoulders against the rough bars, caged like a bear. It was said that the Queen liked to watch stags baited by dogs, and bears as well. There were dogs on this ship — big dogs. Reynard could hear them barking and growling. Mastiffs, he thought. Perhaps they belonged to the gentleman, el capitán.

But what kept his eyes from closing was fear of the living fog that had dropped no water into his sail and now followed all these sailors and soldiers northwest — to where?

Slowly he pieced together fragments of those long-ago tales his father had told him, of haunted seas and strange lands, and of the ring of seven islands at the top of the world. "Your grandmither, bless her and all she knows, tells me they are called Tir Na Nog, and they are places where mortals can live forever, and where gods, goddesses, and monsters roam according to their own laws. I have never been there, thanks be to God, but old fishermen who have, and told tales in mine youth, as I tell you now, spake of a slow, relentless storm that pulls and pulls, like a snake of wind and water, sweeping them north and west until there is no escape — all the way to where the wind goeth to die, and sailors with it. Some would say the nearest isle is a great land hidden beyond that storm, that none but demons should visit! So they say, and your grandmither as well ... But we are sailors, and know teat from twaddle, do we not, boy?"

And he remembered, as if his father were alive again, him dandling a much smaller Reynard by both hands, and the large man's laughter, the sweetest sound, silent now for seven years but alive in memory.

"But remember this, all respect to our kin and the good people they know!" His father had cackled, lifting him high. "Old seamen fart loudest on shore. Keep your wits, lad, and leave the dead to find passage to where the wind sleeps, for only they are allowed to fish there, and they catch nought but monsters — and there be no market for monsters in Southwold."

The old man brought him a small bowl of peas and sodden biscuit, this time with a slice of half-cooked carrot. Reynard was grateful for anything.

"I had a boy of mine own," the old man said, sitting beside the cage and watching him. "A son, a wife, and a daughter. They gave me joy and solace for twenty years, in the Philippines. All dead now. I am far too old, boy."

The look he gave Reynard was strangely hopeful, but then the old man reached into his own mouth and wiggled a tooth.

The day darkened into night. Only then did the fog part, but beneath the upper deck's overhang, Reynard saw little but a black wedge interrupted by a sliver of moon.

As morning painted the sky gray, the old man opened the cage door. "Come. El maestro says that, having fished here, thou may'st tell us what sort of animal doth follow our ship." Then he looped rope around Reynard's chest and neck, knotted the two loops, and led him to the hind castle and up two flights of steps to the far jutting peak of the poop. Here, three sailors and a soldier clung to the rail with white-knuckled fists, watching the ocean behind. All four crossed themselves.

"There," the old man said, pointing down.

Reynard looked into the gray-green churn swirling around the rudder. He shivered, as he always did looking into the deeps. "I see nothing."

The sailors pointed and jabbered. As the morning brightened, the old man said, "Water here is fresh. No salt. Are we at the mouth of a river?"

"I know not," Reynard said. The sailors started jabbering again and pointing, and now Reynard did see something beneath the waves, pale green, patterned like the wash itself, undulating, serpentine — neither fish nor shark nor any whale he had ever heard of. His first impression was that it had a pair of arms, and he thought it could be a mermaid — though he had never believed in such — but then, as it swam to the surface and, after thudding against the rudder, vanished with a splash, he saw the "hands" at the ends of the arms were more like claws, the long tail was segmented like a lobster's, and what parts he saw stretched at least fifteen feet.

The old man said, "It would board and eat us. The sailors hath piked it twice and shot it with a crossbow, *sin efecto, sin hacer daño.*"

Reynard shook his head and bit his lip. What did he know about lobsters that tried to board a ship? Nothing. But curiosity had taken over his fear. He was almost eager to know what this thing was capable of, and what it meant. He stared down at the waves, with an expression half grimace and half grin, trying to see below their wash and curl. The sailors watched the shape with wide, unhappy eyes. Then it slipped aft in the ship's wake and vanished in rocky breakers to the starboard side.

Lookouts called that they were passing small islands jutting from the sea, capped with shrubs. The old man repeated in English. One larger island to larboard boasted a decent tree, some kind of twisted conifer with dangling cones as big as a man's head.

Now Cardoza, *el capitán* himself, joined them on the afterdeck, accompanied by a harquebusier and two musket men. He finished strapping on his sword and cast a side glance at Reynard, then asked the old man, *el viejo*, if the boy was of use. Before the old man could answer, one soldier with a musket called *el capitán*'s attention to the island's lone conifer. A skinny, twisted sack hung from the middle branches, as long as two tall men, striped and spotted red and black, catching sunlight like dark silk and reflecting sparks of gold. All observed in silence. One harquebusier said that in the New World, Indians hung their dead in trees. Another observed the same was true in the far east, where other sailors had been, though not him. The old man translated, but, like his mother, Reynard was quick at languages and already had the sense of their words. Truly the Spanish empire was vast, though likely Drake or Hawkins had been to these places as well.

The bigger island fell behind. There were no people visible on it, and the waves pounding the sharp rocks around its base were fierce, cutting and roiling the water and spraying up to land on his lips — fresh water indeed, whatever that implied. A low fog closed behind, but the watch cried out there was land *justo delante* — dead ahead. At the jagged, echoing clash of breakers, more sailors scrambled into the rigging, struggling to bring the ship about, to slow or stop its headlong plunge.

Reynard was distracted and only heard part of what the old man was murmuring to Cardoza. "*Es posible que él puede ayudar con las lenguas bárbaras.*" Did the old man mean that Reynard might be useful as a translator? That was even less likely than his talent for geography. But his grandmother's words came back again, words so familiar . . .

And then the great hull slammed to an abrupt halt. Men flew from the rigging and the masts, onto the deck, overboard.

And a horse screamed, then another, not far behind him, perhaps in a stable or a cabin.

Back to the cage he went, tied up and left alone while the ship became frantic with activity. The galleon could not get free — it had beached itself, and waves seemed to drive it farther onto the shore — waves and something the sailors were calling, yelling it out, actually: "*La tierra respira.*"

They thought the land was breathing.

Reynard drew up his knees. The breezes that reached him were chill and smelled of forest. His pulse quickened.

¿Irlanda o Islandia?

THE OLD MAN returned an hour later, wearing a greatcoat too large by half for his thin frame — a greatcoat and a sort of crested watch cap that made him look like a scrawny gray cat. "They say we are cursed," he muttered. "What think'st thou? Curse or blessing?" He smiled, revealing the few rotten snags left on his gray-pink gums. "I shall inform *el capitán* thou hast true knowing."

"I know nothing!" Reynard cried, angry now that it had all come to this, that, Earth's trembling aside, they must have come to the Irish coast, or at the worst a French beach, and that he would soon be shot or cut to pieces or hanged. "I do not wish to be here!"

He did not add, *I am afraid!* Because in fact, strangely, he was not very afraid. This place had aspects of a dream, and perhaps it *was* a dream. In which case, he would soon awaken.

And if it was not a dream, he felt the possibility of a new chance, a new place not to fear, but to explore and hope to understand! Away from fish, away from Southwold, from his uncle's tasks — but perhaps closer to his grandmother . . .

"Not a wish I can grant," the old man said, and gave him a look that might have carried irritation — but also a touch of wonder. He opened the cage and untied the ropes. "But I can share a little more freedom."

Reynard got up, legs cramping, and stumbled onto a deck criss-crossed by men carrying boxes and barrels, and one leading a horse — a fine horse, a gentleman's horse, caparisoned as if for battle, with a forehead shield and side plates that would no doubt drown it had it to swim.

The old man led Reynard under the net, now being rolled back, to the rail, between weaving lines of frantic sailors and soldiers. By now, two more horses had been brought up on deck, rearing and spinning, screaming, adding to the crowd and confusion.

The ship had grounded on a long beach of black sand and shingle. The crests of the ocean waves were touched with gold by clear morning sun as they rolled between far-spread headlands topped with curling trees, so far off they seemed like bushes. The air was cold but not freezing. How far north had they come?

Dozens of soldiers and sailors had lowered themselves on ropes and a climbing net and were already walking around the ship, calling out that there was damage — a wide hole in the larboard hull.

The old man tied a rope around Reynard's neck. "Stay by me. I am th'one who hath heart for you."

Reynard gripped the rope in both hands, twisted it until it burned his neck, and for a moment, considered how he could escape from the Spaniards and even from the old man, to escape and discover this place on his own!

And to die thyself unfinished.

That inner voice again, not quite his grandmother — and not quite the man with the white shadow.

"My head is truly haunted," he murmured.

The old man heard this. "I share that concern," he said, and raised his wrinkled hand. "Stay alert," he advised, "and do nothing rash."

Cardoza seemed to want to stay and explore. The gentleman's

horse had had its armor removed and was fitted into a leather sling. A dozen soldiers and sailors rigged a crane and slowly, jerkily, lowered the unhappy beast over the rail to the beach, where it whinnied and scuffed, scattering pebbles and sand. As it was loosed from the sling, several more soldiers held its tack and tail, but it kicked free and ran for a time on its own, then turned, looked startled, reared, and trotted a fancy circuit of the cove.

Reynard thought he saw trees on a headland shiver as if in reaction to the horse's spirit, though it might have been wind. He stayed close to the old man as three brown dogs, almost as large as ponies, with leather muzzles, were also slung and winched down, but these were not set free. Instead, a single small man in pantaloons and a leather jerkin held tight to their ropes, as they seemed eager to leap and attack any and all. Fierce dogs. Dogs that wanted to fight and kill. Now would not be a good time to break free and run. The Spanish might enjoy such sport.

A long ramp was run out over the rail, and then another, aft of the first, and more soldiers scrambled down to the beach, where they flanked the boards and prepared to steady them. Reynard and the old man descended now, single file. On the beach, the old man squatted slowly, knees popping, then sat. Reynard settled down beside him and resumed his study of the land and the ship, the soldiers and sailors and boys.

Small crabs raced the waves and picked along the rocks. The rear of the beach, inland from the black sand, was shingle of a type he had not seen before — mixed rocks and polished pebbles, brown and gray, even pink, all shiny as glass. Now they jostled and rattled like dice. The great ship complained, groaning, creaking — making alarming reports like gunshots. Reynard had heard of trembling ground before, in Iceland ... Volcanic. With earthquakes. Maybe they had reached Iceland!

Or Reynard had died, and was now being punished.

"You are not dead," the old man said, as if reading his thoughts. "Nobody returneth from that country, so how could we?"

Sailors and soldiers crowded the rails, eager to see, but not so eager even now to go ashore. How many fully armed soldiers were there? Reynard wondered. At least a hundred, and as many sailors.

How many had died at Gravelines?

"You begin here," the old man said. "Or, like me, start over."

They watched young boys, *los grumetes*, as the old man called them, trying to shove through the crowd to the rail.

"The young are still curious. But most sailors, and smart soldiers, are less so. This is a strange land, and the ship is familiar, however much its bilges stink, however infested with lice and fleas."

Both had already found their way onto Reynard but, strangely, were either dying or dead. He had already plucked and tossed a few of their small, familiar corpses. "You have been here before?" he asked.

"Not for decades," the old man said. "I know not what hath changed. The sailors wish to return to sea with the flood," by which he meant the tide. "But *el capitán* is eager for conquest. And so his mare." He turned his head and pointed to the galleon. "*El maestro.*"

A very fat man climbed onto the forward ramp, then stepped down delicately to the beach, face pale and sweating despite a steady breeze that blew up the cove. He was soon followed by the gentleman, Cardoza, *el capitán*, who whistled and called as he descended, until his fine mare trotted to him. Soldiers in armor brought down an ornate tooled saddle, and soon the gentleman rode tall over to the fat man.

Then Cardoza and *el maestro* called for the rest to descend, all but a small crew to tend the ship and bring out weapons, and a guard to watch from the remaining crow's nest.

The old man prodded Reynard. "Get up," he said. "They have need of us."

Cardoza dismounted and led his mare over to them. Reynard knew horses from his uncle's stable, where, between fishing voyages, they had tended a fair number of Southwold's draft and work animals. Cardoza's mare was of mixed Arab blood, brown-eyed, with a concave forehead, strong despite the hardships — magnificent and nervous and very tired of being cooped up on the ship. No doubt her hooves would need tending, and soon, if *el capitán* planned to ride her about on these clattering shingles — as he seemed eager to do.

"The old sailor hath skills sharpening swords and repairing locks," the captain said, "but he saith thou know'st the needs of horses. Is this true?"

Reynard patted the animal's neck until it seemed to accept him, then got down on one knee, lifted its foreleg, and studied the horse's hoof. "Too long she stands in wet and piss," he said. "She wants a good trim and new shoes. Hot shoeing will be best. I can do it."

"We had twenty horses. Ten died. Thou wilt prepare the shoes from ship's stores ... And from a barrel of special shoes for my beauty." *El capitán* said a forge would be set up and an anvil would be brought down later. The old man said he would return to the ship to retrieve clippers and files.

El maestro was a bulky man, maybe fifteen stone, with thick arms and fashionable but worn clothing. In appearance, with his mottled, pale face, he resembled a stage clown, a marked contrast to *el capitán*, but a formidable presence nonetheless — in command of the galleon's day-to-day operations, but going where *el capitán* ordered. From a seaman's perspective, *el maestro* was the real captain.

Reynard never did learn his name.

"Where are we, boy?" *el maestro* inquired in English, taking advantage of the old sailor's absence. Until now, Reynard had kept his head down and focused on the horse, but this question was direct. Reynard wondered what the Spanish would do if they discovered his ignorance. Would they punish both him and the old man?

"*¿Irlanda o Islandia?*" Cardoza asked.

The old man returned with surprising speed, carrying a small bag of tools, and stood near Reynard. He stooped and picked up the rope again, cap in hand, not to interrupt.

"Come we to *Irlanda*, boy?" *el maestro* inquired, staring critically at *el viejo*.

"No, *señor*," Reynard said. "The trees and wind are wrong, and there be nought of Queen's soldiers. And neither is it Iceland, 'cause I heard we ply too far north, and not so far west." He knelt and bowed his head. "*Señor*, the horse's hooves are damp and could split on these rocks. You should not ride far till they be trimmed and shod."

Cardoza observed him critically, then turned to the old man. "I will see what is near and a threat—and then thou canst do thy work. Unless thou wish'st to discourage me?" *El capitán* chuckled. "*El viejo*, this boy is either a cunning fraud or a spy."

The old man inclined his head. "Spies know much, lord. And he knoweth horses."

"And of this land, thou say'st correctly, I know little. We will stay awhile, look about, give my beauty a brief run in the sweet air, curry and shoe her, and let her crop sweet grass."

"After so much time in the galleon, she should not eat her fill of fresh grass," Reynard advised. "She will bloat."

"*Conozco a los caballos, muchacho,*" *el capitán* said shortly. But then he called for hay and the last of the oats to be sent down the ramps.

El maestro's bark of a laugh irritated Reynard, who wondered why there was amusement, but the bulky man's attitude was neither aggressive nor angry—not yet, though *el maestro* then scowled, perhaps more worried than *el capitán*. *El capitán* seemed eager to learn the ground on which they found themselves, restless, Reynard thought, to conquer someone or someplace, having been unable to face an enemy for so many days.

The old man again jerked his rope, but Reynard growled and yanked it from his grasp.

"*Rescataste un cachorro, Manuel*," Cardoza said with a curl of his lip.

So that was the old man's name!

"*Sí, señor*."

"*Gitano*, as thou art?"

Manuel made the most elegant and tiny of shrugs.

El capitán smiled. "Keep him quiet till we have use of him, *o córtale la garganta*."

"*Sí, señor*." Manuel, for Reynard's sake, ran a finger across his own throat.

"And watch that he tendeth well my horse."

"*Sí, señor*."

Manuel gripped Reynard's rope and led him back up the narrow ramp to gather more tools. Two other horses were being calmed on the quarterdeck before also being winched to the beach. Reynard could not understand how such animals could be kept from sun and field, in tight wooden stalls no doubt, without exercise . . . for weeks or months. Horrible planning.

Soldiers on the shore were ordered to gather wood, and others helped convey an anvil down to the beach as Manuel and Reynard, on the galleon, descended steps to plunge deep into the stink and noise of the hull. Other soldiers were clanking and shouting, still removing weapons and armor, as if preparing to besiege the land they had found; this then was the business *el capitán* alluded to. Having left the battle for England behind, outcome unknown, the Spanish would now explore, fight, if necessary, and bring this place under Philip's rule, for that was what the Spanish did. Reynard found nothing unexpected about this effort, this prospect, though he was surprised he would be allowed anywhere near *el capitán's* fine horse.

"Are you Roma?" Reynard asked the old man as they opened a crate filled with iron shoes and boxes of nails. They were so near the bilges that Reynard clenched his teeth not to gag.

"*Esto es lo que soy. Gitano*, from Madrid," Manuel said, his yellow-outlined shadow moving about in the scant light of his one candle, backlit by whatever echoed from several decks above.

"And think you I am Roma as well?"

Manuel raised his candle and shrugged.

"I am not," Reynard said.

"Do not deny in haste," Manuel said. "Here, methinks there be advantage." Manuel handed him the box, a long iron file, and black iron clippers. "*¿Sabes cómo usarlos?* — how to use these?"

"Yes," Reynard said. "Unless the Spanish follow other ways."

"*Caballos son caballos*," Manuel said, and with a wrinkled expression of disgust pinched his nose. "*Alejémonos de este olor y regresemos a la playa.*"

They climbed out of the lower deck and made haste to the ramp. Manuel stopped them halfway down to the beach, and pointed along the curve of the shingle, southwest, toward an advancing shadow — like a small cloud crossing the sun. Trying to keep his balance, Reynard looked up and shaded his eyes. All he could see was the flash of a rainbow-colored triangle, then another, with a long dark line between, vibrating, rising — and then gone.

Manuel looked at Reynard, glanced over his shoulder, and continued down to the beach. On the sand and shingle, the men seemed frozen in attitudes of listening, of fear. They murmured to each other until Cardoza rode back from the northern curve, shouting orders, telling them to get the horses and dogs under cover.

"Giant eagles!" he cried. "Guard thyselves!"

Reynard did not believe what he had seen was any kind of eagle, nor any bird at all. The triangles, if they were wings, were like panes of glass from a cathedral window, and about as big — and the bodies had been slender and long, too long, four or five yards. As well, the shapes had vanished too quickly, flying too fast. He had once seen a peregrine dive that fast, but never ascend.

He stood beside Manuel on the beach. Soon the sailors and soldiers had all been told to spread out and cut down the trees that lined the shingle, and to bring from the galleon what little lumber and rope remained after repairs at sea. The forward spritsail was cut loose and slung like a tent over the animals, held by six men in a tight, restless bunch — the dogs growling at the horses and the horses scraping the shingle and kicking at the men and the dogs.

The weather along the beach grew sharp, and more maggoty clouds swooped in low, obscuring the promontories and the forest along the ridge that lowered over the cove, shadow upon shadow, until the men themselves and the constructs they tried to erect cast no shadows at all.

Cardoza's personal cook, a small, stout man with a leather apron and a bandolier of cleavers, knives, and spoons slung around shoulders and paunch, waddled at last down from the galleon, followed by three boys bowed under casks and bags. The cook ordered *los grumetes* to gather wood and set about making a cooking fire, personally gathering rocks on the beach to bank the heat. It seemed certain his efforts would not benefit the soldiers, but only *el capitán* and perhaps *el maestro*, who were now exploring the beach and the verge on foot.

Another fire, banked, bellowsed, and hotter, was lit between the anvil and the shelter of the sail, and Manuel and Reynard prepared to forge the shoes and repair the hooves of the horses, which had spent too much time in their stalls aboard ship, mired in sour straw and their own dung and piss.

"The wood is not happy," Manuel observed, lifting a branch, leaves dead and dry, but still difficult to grip, as if its twists and flaking bark were part of a serpent. Manuel pushed it in with the other embers, where it hissed but at last caught and crackled.

The fire hot enough, they took to their blacksmithing. Reynard inspected and rasped, Manuel tried a selection of horseshoes from *el maestro's* cask, special-made for his horse, and saw that some would also fit the other two. The horses twitched their flanks and withers, but seemed happy at this familiar ritual, for the human contact, for feeling once again sure of foot and free of the creak and sway of the ship.

The solid thud of their hooves, bare and then shod, and the gentle clang on the stones as the shod hooves swung right and left, drew in the other men, who stood around the fire, the tent of the sail, the familiar animals, rank upon rank of soldiers, still in their armor, watching, squatting, whispering, cleaning harquebuses and adjusting crossbows, sharpening daggers and swords — and nobody sleeping.

Reynard thought of the food his mother might be preparing right now: haddock and pease, buttered bread, wheat gruel. His mouth watered. As he and Manuel combed the other horses, and then Cardoza's splendid and nervous mount, a pair of *grumetes* brought them bowls with moldy rice and a few chunks of dried fish, and with this feast, they made do, wetting it down with sour and watered wine and an unexpected swig of island rum.

That at least was familiar and welcome.

"We arrive at lands none such as they have seen, on a ring of islands far north, very far north," Manuel murmured to himself. He lay beside a sleeping mastiff, then closed his eyes. The dog sighed but did not growl. "And those were not eagles."

A deepening dusk followed swiftly, without stars or moon. The soldiers tried to replenish their scattered fires, but wood from the forest spat and hissed as if wanting to speak, and burned with much smoke and little heat. In the gloom, soldiers and sailors held each other like young monkeys clinging to a stick in a river, group by staring group, as the great *maestro* carried his sputtering torch around the camp and muttered prayers to the Virgin, but also oaths, promising all he had, all the ships he had ever sailed, the riches of Philip himself were they allowed to again see the sun and survive these hours of black nothing.

Reynard crept off a few paces from the tent that covered the horses. The freedom and trust showed him were illusory — nobody in their right mind would attempt to flee through this enveloping night. He curled up on the sand, away from the forest and the fires, where the sailors and soldiers would not bother him, and somehow managed to sleep, if only for a few minutes.

Not quite dreaming, but with his thoughts fluid and unsure, he felt thin, cool fingers with sharp nails play about his face, his cheeks, brushing and then trying to comb his hair. A face seemed to flow into view, just a blur he saw through lids almost shut: thin and faintly aglow, like a candle behind a block of ice. Deep in the face's black eyes appeared sharp glints, like flints struck in a cave. Reynard rolled his head and saw pale figures glide between the sailors and soldiers, murmuring like waves on the beach — using words he almost understood.

After soft-raking his skin with sharp nails, like cat's claws, another strong hand grasped his chin and swung his head around. A second face swam out of the darkness, this one female. She used the same strange-familiar language to tell him something, as if out of concern for his well-being, and then backed and flitted off like a moth. If only he could remember enough of his grandmother's speech to understand!

After that, sleep came heavy, as if to blot out all he had seen.

Valdis

VALDIS HAD LEFT the Eaters' Ravine and stabled her horse in Zo-diako, the southwestern shore's only human town. She had moved through the darkness with the pacted Eaters, down to the wide scimitar of beach, and there they had found sleeping Spaniards and done what was necessary to remain Eaters, not so different from what these men themselves did to stay alive — steal time from ani-mals, a long chain of thievery back to when Hel was young and the Crafters first shaped their brutal tales.

In appearance Valdis still kept a semblance of the adolescent girl she had once been, five centuries ago, but no longer flesh so much as sea foam or soft crystal, shot through with a greenish inner light.

She walked between the sailors and soldiers, looking for her as-signment. When possible, she kept to shadows and took on their darkness. Tonight she was not here to sup, but merely to identify and confirm, as instructed by Calybo, the Afrique, eldest and greatest of the Eaters' island clan. Calybo in turn followed the orders of one of the island's Vanir, those just beneath the sky: Guldreth. Valdis's par-ents had long ago told stories about Aesir and Vanir and their wars, but none of that seemed to matter here, and she had never heard of

Aesir on this isle. Whose orders Guldreth followed was never made clear by any who had met her, so Valdis suspected that at the top of the island's command was Hel. Nobody she knew had ever seen Hel, no matter how old they were or claimed to be.

While ten of the island's clan wandered the beach, glittering figures of fairy glass and foam, supping of the gross, dark Spanish, young and old, the men in armor and boys in rags writhed and groaned as if suffering from bad dreams, as no doubt they were. Having one's life stolen was never pleasant.

Then Valdis found the one she was assigned to. The boy lay on a small patch of disturbed sand, filthy, his hands grasping as if trying to catch hold of ropes, but not caught entire in the spell laid on the camp. As she leaned over him, he looked up through heavy-lidded eyes and seemed almost to see her. Those eyes rolled in fear.

So young!

Gliding closer, then kneeling to peer into his face, she felt such a surge of confusion and hope that her entire body seemed caught in a flash of lightning. He was scrawny and not particularly handsome and smelled of sweat and horses and salt water. He must have come from far out at sea, far beyond the gyre. Normally, such would be prime fare for Eaters. But not this one. He had reddish hair. She had been told by Calybo to look for it.

The sense of smell given to Valdis and her kind was extraordinary. They could smell backwards and forwards, and connect what they smelled to what others over centuries had smelled. This boy smelled alive, of course, growing out before him rich lengths of time like a plant making sap. He had a very long and busy life ahead of him, and she would not take that away, nor even borrow of it.

As for the life behind him ...

Nothing! He had memories, but no time, and this caused her more wonder and confusion. She pulled back from the boy, not at all sure of her power to keep him still.

A few yards away, Calybo ministered to an old man, making strange noises. Valdis recognized the old man despite his wizened face and shriveled form. He was Widsith, a lover to Guldreth; husband to villager Maeve; and friend to Maggie, healer and leader of the blunters who managed the drakes along the shore. He had been gone for over forty years and had aged accordingly, so Calybo was doing what centuries past he had agreed to do for this one man: replenish the returned Pilgrim with what he needed to remain useful to Travelers and Crafters — health, denser bones and teeth, younger flesh, and time enough to report and inform the island, and prepare to go out again.

It was ever Widsith's task to explore the outer world and make his own estimation of how the plots and plans of the Crafters had changed things. For it was important to all on the island, including the Eaters, to know just what the Crafters were doing, as much as anyone could.

Without yet taking even a small taste of this boy's history, it was obvious he was different from any other human on the island, and for that she was glad. Looking at his face, Valdis remembered some of what she had lost by being saved by the Eaters. She imagined herself and this boy sitting in a cabin on the side of a mountain and talking while snow swirled outside. He would tend a fire and smile at her. She would draw forth a blanket and welcome him to her warmth.

Except that she was no longer warm.

And this vision would never come true.

She leaned in, touched her lips to his forehead, then kissed him lightly on his own lips and neck. All she could manage with such brief contact was to grab a second or two, an impression from whence he came — but even that little was difficult. Calybo had said, recruiting Valdis in the Ravine, that if she found the right boy, his memories would be jagged and incomplete, his emotions electric — perhaps dangerous to an Eater.

Calybo was the oldest Eater on the island, full of time and great-powered. He could usually recharge a servant at small cost. But Widsith . . .

Long Calybo lingered over the old man, hand on his heart, and then, with a look of resolve, sank his head to the Pilgrim's chest and sang an awful song of exchange. When Eaters consumed time, they were silent, stealthy, not to arouse or disturb. When Eaters gave, it was a sickening, noisy process, half scream, half chant, as if the memories that accompanied those years were being voiced against their will and shared with the listening air . . .

It took many minutes for the old African to finish. He stood, straightened his night-dark garments, and looked her way with a frightful, hungry face — a face of utter exhaustion. He would be days rearranging his store of time to feel well again.

Along with the boy, Widsith had also brought the Spanish to this isle. This aroused Valdis's curiosity, dulled by long centuries in the Ravine and the mix of memories absorbed with her quotient of time. What purpose might the Spanish have here? What tales of the finished lands could the Pilgrim tell? And would he tell those tales only to Travelers, among the few authorized to convey them to Crafters — or just to Guldreth?

The Eaters were done for this evening. They would keep to the woods or, sated, return through Zodiako to retrieve their horses.

Valdis never questioned anything about Guldreth, though deep in her dozing memory, in the Ravine, later, she would wonder about Guldreth's relationship to the Pilgrim . . . How important this old man was to a near-god.

And Guldreth shared her bed and energy with other human lovers. Mysterious how those relations were maintained!

And of course there was this red-haired boy, another mystery, who aroused something even more untoward within the youngest Eater in the Ravine. Something that could never be, for in her brief sampling, Valdis saw that this boy had been touched by a being even more mysterious than Guldreth or Calybo, perhaps more mysterious than the Crafters or Hel herself.

A man with a white shadow.

Cardoza Rising

MANUEL NUDGED HIM with a sandaled foot. "It is done, for now," the old man said.

Reynard rolled to see pale yellow light brushing the far tops of the tallest trees, divided by distant shadows — hills behind the forest. The sky lightened in the east, over the far promontory, and dawn spread a slow golden glow along the bellies of the clouds, which parted and seemed to rise and dissipate, as if swept by a gigantic hand. A great dome of pale blue cast beach and forest in cool, tempered light.

Manuel toed him again. "Wake whilst there is still food. The soldiers strip the ship and eat their fill." He reached into his mouth again and wriggled a tooth between two dirty fingers. "Scurvy," he said. "We arrive none too soon."

Reynard examined him closely. Manuel had always seemed ancient-old, but now he looked younger, straighter, with thicker shoulders, and even — could it be? — happier.

A sailor descended the ramp closest to the galleon's bow and spoke to the boys. Reynard recognized this burly man from his first hours on the ship. He had been the one who locked the cage. Now he seemed grayer, less burly, and stooped. The cabin boys, only children the night before, were taller but skeletal, as if they had grown overnight without benefit of food.

"He watched last night from the rail and saw folk with glassy white hair and shiny skin move amongst us," Manuel said in a low voice. "So he telleth them, 'We have been visited by glass people.' He saith they touched *thee*, boy. But thou hast not changed."

"You are th'one who's changed!" Reynard said in accusation.

"It is obvious already." Manuel squinted, wiggled his tooth again, then pulled it out and threw it aside. "The scurvy still taketh its toll. For me, boy, another night comes not soon enough."

"Who *are* you?" Reynard asked, fascinated but frightened.

"Who are *we*, boy?" Manuel responded. "Thou'st know what the glass people speak?"

Reynard glared, then shook his head.

The cabin boys lay down as a group on the shingle, like beached fish, so still and pale, no longer boys but adolescents, and not looking at all well.

Cardoza removed his mare from under the tent, then mounted her, taking command despite her skittish protests. *El capitán* told *el maestro* and the soldiers that now it was light, he would do reconnaissance, but the horse spun and sprayed sand and gravel. Two soldiers managed to grab her halter, and Cardoza descended stiffly, as if he ached all over. True enough, his beard was streaked with gray and his brown hands were wrinkled and marked with ropy rivers of veins. What was happening here? Had time fled in the deep night for all but Manuel?

For all but Manuel — and possibly himself?

Angry, *el capitán* gathered up five soldiers, those who still seemed strong enough to follow his orders, and took a crossbow from one. He vowed he would hunt for game and find a refuge from this haunted beach, not to stay here another evening. *El capitán's* small band followed him into the forest.

That left *el maestro*, most of the soldiers, and the sailors to fend for themselves. Many returned to the galleon.

Manuel got up to fetch the last of the moldy rice. "Hunting is dangerous here. But no matter. We have blacksmithing to do. Eat what the sailors leave us. Eat what thou canst."

A few hours later, as the day warmed and the sun overtopped the promontory, Cardoza returned with a half-satisfied look and a limp deer — a kind of buck with a broad nose and mossy antlers.

Manuel stopped Reynard from hammering out more shoes. "In Iceland, they call that *hreindyr*," he said. "Here, 'tis not eaten without permission."

"Permission from who?" Reynard asked. "How is it you know so much?"

Manuel squinted again.

The cook was already cleaning and skinning the animal, and several boys, ravenous, huddled around the butchering. One ran up to the forge clutching a bloody chunk of heart, to steal embers for another fire. Manuel did not stop him.

Cardoza mounted the head on a stick, as a kind of trophy.

Soon a bit of meat was given to each of the sailors and soldiers, and walking between them, chewing on a thick, dripping slice of roast, *el capitán* seemed more at ease, more in control — more pleased with himself and his prospects. But still with an air of quiet fear.

Within the hour, the animal had been consumed, even its bones cracked and sucked. None of it was given to Manuel and Reynard. The soldiers did not trust them, and Reynard was half convinced he knew why. Manuel's appearance was scaring even him.

"We must return to sea as soon as possible," *el maestro* said, studying the sky through eyes wrapped in thick flesh. His lids seemed always ready for sleep, but Reynard saw the large man was no fool, and no lackey for *el capitán*, whatever his terms of service. He instructed Manuel and Reynard to pause on the horseshoes and start making brackets for a patch to the galleon's hull.

El capitán did not disagree. But he ordered another group of soldiers to prepare to move inland. Cardoza and *el maestro* walked off to discuss these matters, the very large man moving slowly, reluctantly. An argument followed. *El capitán* refused to delay his departure. Soon he ventured off again with a larger group of soldiers — perhaps sixty, Reynard guessed — leading the skittish horses by their reins. The beach was left to the sailors, *el maestro*, and around thirty soldiers.

One of these, equipped with a loaded harquebus and a little tinder ready in an iron box, approached their small forge. Another with a saber approached from the opposite side, as if they wished to outflank Manuel and Reynard. The pair stopped their work on the brackets and closely studied the unhappy men.

"*El maestro quiere hablar contigo con ustedas,*" said the soldier with the saber.

Manuel led Reynard to the beach.

El maestro sat on a barrel near the bow, in the shadow of the galleon, as sailors came and went on the ramps. The biggest man on the ship, he had lost a notable amount of his bulk in the night, but his hair showed just a shade grayer. He pointed to Manuel. "The English boy told us he knew this place."

"It was to make himself useful," Manuel said. "He did not wish to be thrown overboard."

El maestro shrugged. "I know thee, Manuel. Thou art a sailor with much experience, not an easy man to deceive, and my little ears have heard thou speak'st to this boy as if ye wouldst share secrets."

Reynard did not want to learn too soon that they were about to be executed, and his mind wandered in a kind of self-defense to other matters—to an observation that there were no mosquitoes here, and no biting flies. And all the fleas and lice had died! Perhaps it was the wrong season. But it was summer, no? So where were the insects? Drake and other travelers had observed that the seasons reversed only as one moved south beyond the equator. Was there another equator as one sailed farther north?

And what did the ship-crawling lobsters prey upon when they could not climb up on galleons? Were there other predators in the woods, natural predators, and not just spirits? Predators that resented hunters taking down their *hreindyr* . . .

"What was it that visited us in the night?" *el maestro* asked Manuel. "These *gente de vidrio*."

"I do not know their names," Manuel said.

"Vampires, of a kind? I have read Lucius, *Culo de Oro*. I know of spirits who drink blood, but never of a land where they still live—except perhaps the Indies."

Reynard listened closely, trying to understand.

"*El capitán* tells me this boy is *Gitano*, like thee. Is that true?"

"I am not clear on his ancestry, or mine own, for that matter—but there are many such in Spain, and who can know?"

"Hath this place an ancient Gypsy name, old man?"

"Not that I am aware of."

"How about the boy? Would he know?"

"Nor him," Manuel said.

"He nameth it 'the land where the wind sleeps.' Doth he still believe?"

"That was my translation, *señor*. Clumsy at best."

Reynard said nothing.

"Deceit and ignorance. How like *Gitanos!*" *el maestro* said. "I would soonest get back to sea. But *el capitán* doth wish to stay and find towns and people he can pillage. Since he never reached London and hath no victories to his name, he thinketh this could be his

Mexico or Peru ... But many died in those far lands, and I prefer to support his conquests from beyond ... away from *los vampiros* and out from under those eagles — if they are birds at all. My ship hath had enough of large ambitions."

Manuel listened with a humble frown.

El maestro spat in disgust. "Finish the hardware for the patch. Soon we will have felled enough of these damned trees to free my ship at high tide, or when the land doth breathe again. Thy choice will be stay with *el capitán* or go with my ship. But for now, thine only choice is to work."

Blunters

A SHOUTING ROSE at the tree line.

Reynard and Manuel covered the fire and moved through a tight-ening crowd of unhappy sailors and cabin boys. In the middle of the gathering, ten or twelve paces off, they saw two middle-aged men with dark brown hair flanking a lone woman with a broad face, wide green eyes, and black hair, slightly younger — and all wearing leather jackets and pants. The three appeared healthy and strong and car-ried thick leather satchels.

Soldiers surrounded this trio with half-pikes presented, but de-spite the ominous greeting, the newcomers surveyed the galleon's complement with an alert equanimity, as if expecting anything, but assured they would prevail. The sailors and soldiers were exhausted and near panic, but *el maestro* urged all to maintain their wits. Here were people who might have answers.

Manuel kept his eyes on the leather satchels.

El maestro approached the newcomers with hands open and empty, though his sword and three knives were slung on his waist. They exchanged words Reynard could not hear at that distance, soldiers relieved them of their satchels, and *el maestro* then called for Manuel to come forward.

The woman eyed the spiked head of the deer with apparent disgust, then spoke first — to Manuel. The old man glared a sharp warning at Reynard to stay silent, and shook his own head in response. The woman took a breath and tried again. This came out, Reynard thought, as Dutch or German, which Manuel knew well enough.

"She says we should not be here," Manuel translated. "And we should not have killed the deer. It belongs to important people and is forbidden."

"How sad," the cook said, sure of *el capitán's* favor.

The woman spoke some more. Reynard heard and half understood only "*Als wij nog een nacht willen leven.*"

"If we want to live another night," Manuel translated for all, "we should return to our ship and go home."

El maestro said in passable Dutch that the ship had a great hole in one side, but they would soon have it patched.

The woman now focused on Reynard, her brows knit, and called out, in English, with an Irish lilt, "Thou art not of them?"

Reynard shook his head.

"Thou hast come on a ship filled with weapons. Thy weapons?" She looked with a frown at the few soldiers in their armor and helmets, the sailors in homespun and canvas — all thin and wan. Desperate and afraid.

"Not mine," Reynard said.

"What we learn is that there hath been a battle — a war," the woman said. "Other ships packed with soldiers arrived in recent months. Maybe thy leader will find them out there, maybe not. Because of the Eaters, I think few remain. Fix thy ship. Get ye home whilst ye can."

"*Chronophagos*," Manuel whispered to Reynard. "Eaters of time. For me, useful."

"Why art ye here?" *el maestro* asked them. "Why come to this beach? To spy?"

"We blunt dragons," the woman said, lifting her satchel. At a flick of *el maestro's* finger, two soldiers took charge of the bag and emptied it, showing a mallet and a kind of chisel.

El maestro raised a bushy brow.

"This is the season their nymphs rise from the waves and hang in trees. We must find them and blunt them, spike the *exitus*, the *ostrium* of their sacks, or when they split and emerge, they will fly free and kill and eat whom they will."

The soldiers returned the bag and the implements.

"We saw them!" *el maestro* said. "Under the sea, following our ship — was it one also, hanging from a tree on the little island?"

The woman nodded. "We have no time to waste."

El maestro took Manuel aside, and they spoke more.

Manuel said, "*El maestro* tells me that one of these creatures visited us last night and grabbed up a dog."

The two men, keeping close to the woman, maintained a watchful silence.

"He would also know about the Eaters of whom you speak. What is their food?" Manuel did not seem to be asking a question to which he, personally, required an answer.

"They eat lives," she said.

"Are they vampires?" *el maestro* asked.

"They care nothing for blood. It is thy time on Earth for which they hunger. From those protected by pact, they take only seconds or hours, from the sick conclusion or the strong middle of our days, as exchange for their protection, or as part of ritual. From such as thee" — and she looked sharp points at *el maestro* — "without protection, thou wilt lose young months and even years, night after night. They come again and again until thou fad'st to dust or leave."

The sailor who had watched from the boat told *el maestro* that the white forms had approached Manuel and the boy, the *Gitanos*, and touched them both, but they were either younger or no different. The sailors and soldiers regarded them with renewed fear and suspicion.

"I, too, see no aging," *el maestro* said. "Is it because they are *Gitanos?*"

"No," the woman said, and regarded Reynard with a strange sharpness, as if she feared him as well. She then looked off to the water. "We need to finish our work, and soon."

"Keep these three here," *el maestro* said. "Do not let them leave. *El capitán* may need guides for his ventures inland."

Manuel suggested that was not wise. *El maestro* ignored him, and soldiers bound the trio and made them kneel on the beach. *El maestro* ordered them to bring two cages off the galleon, and the woman and men were roughly thrust into one. The burly sailor grinned as he locked them in. His gums were bleeding, and he had lost considerable hair and many teeth.

"And these two, hold them in th'other," *el maestro* said.

Manuel and Reynard were locked in the second cage, some yards away. The burly sailor handled them roughly, his breath a stinking fume, and the other sailors and skinny boys murmured approval, while the soldiers studied the trees and the sky with apprehension.

"It is not going well," Manuel observed. "I doubt anyone here understands what is about to happen . . . Dost thou?"

Reynard shook his head. He could feel odd and frightening tugs in his thoughts, even vague memories, but without shape, like forgotten dreams — and yet not *his* dreams, and not in the least connected to his short life. Perhaps he was still hearing, at a distance, the words his father and uncle, his mother and grandmother, had spoken, their stories, their legends. But he did not think so. The glassy-skinned woman had stared at him so strangely.

Something new was being awakened, something he had never expected and most surely did not want, any more than he wanted to be lost at sea and stranded with Spaniards on a strange shore.

An Advancing Front

*E*L MAESTRO hath made plans to push the galleon from shore and return through the gyre," Manuel said, his lips close to Reynard's ear.

The boy had again been dozing, if only to pass the time, and this woke him quickly. The light said it was late afternoon. He sat up blinking, and saw Manuel squatting beside him. They watched four sailors fasten the patch to the galleon's side with bolts and nails and then caulk it with tar. Ten more sailors, accompanied by a ponderous, grumbling *el maestro*, surveyed the upper beach, poking sticks between the shingle and into the sand, perhaps to measure the tide from the night before.

"Will the ship stay afloat?" Reynard asked.

Manuel shook his head dubiously. "The wood here is unfaithful," he said. "They will as like sink out beyond the breakers and become food for the big lobsters."

"Methinks they are not lobsters," Reynard said.

"Agreed," Manuel said with a wink. "Dark doth sweep us soon. *El capitán* maketh preparation to move inland, away from the beach and the dog-eating dragons — and find places to hide from the glassy skins. The soldiers might kill me and thee before they go. Or they might think death awaiteth us here anyway, and why bother?"

"They want to conquer? But they know nothing about the island . . . do they?"

Manuel said, "Philip commandeth dominance — that, and the spread of the Inquisition. It is what they are trained to do. *El capitán* believeth he will never reach England, or even return to Spain, yet still feareth what Philip might think of him . . . as if the Spanish king learneth his exploits from a crystal ball."

"Doth he so study?"

Manuel smiled. "Philip never so observed the islands named after him. I was there with Salcedo, in Manila, where the *nao de la China* load and take their name — Manila galleons. Philip did not learn the foolishness of his generals, and the valiant efforts of many priests, until he heard it from human lips — his own spies and officers. And so . . . no crystal ball."

Were the priests monsters, or saviors? Manuel seemed capable of holding both opinions at once. "Dark soon cometh, and the glassy skins will be back," he said. "I doubt any army, no matter how strong, can twice survive such visitors."

The First Death

Reynard again passed through numbing fear to a murky darkness where memories and fancies rose like a shoal of fish beneath rain-spattered waves. Was he back on the hoy? He whimpered and drew up his legs until his knees met his chin. He spent empty hours going back through early memories, as if to make sure they were still there — but why? Then he came upon the night his grandmother had died. Her name was Ringbrae, an ancient name, she had told him, from the great grassy meadows east of the rainy marshes but south and east again of Russia. He knew little of any of those places, so he pictured them as his grandmother had described them, filled with great white stone fortresses, and wagon and horse trails across endless seas of grass populated by her people, stone people, who built more when they were stopped, and so were never allowed to stop, but rolled on and on in their great caravans, pulled by small, strong horses with brushy manes and patient eyes.

Ringbrae was in her nineties when she died, tended by her widowed daughter, and took a long while doing it. As her dying dragged on, she received guests from around Southwold, compatriots of many shades of olive and brown, as well as pale villagers and fishermen who had come to her for words and charms. She had given them all the satisfactions they requested, and so now they honored her as few of her people had ever been honored, and she received their company with a sad, patient smile, remembering the troubles they had given to her husbands — for she had had three, two of whom had fled in fear, fear of her some said, and one of whom, the longest of her marriages, had died in his blacksmithing shop in the unexpected, fiery breath of a forge, leaving her three years in a place of dark visions.

Reynard's father had taken over the smithy, and had taught the young Reynard skills between forays with his uncle on the hoy, fishing and carrying goods up and down the coast.

Reynard remembered her deathbed. Hay and moss under sacks was constantly turned and refreshed, and so the old woman had smelled sweet, like timothy, but also like old buttermilk, and he had wondered why she did not get up and continue her stories. The dark folks and the pale folks came from around Britain to pay their respects. Ringbrae had finally tired of receiving them, and asked seven-year-old Reynard if he had seen her dead husband, and when Reynard said shyly that he had not, she had turned away with that same sad smile and said, "I have told the far, good folk about thee, boy. Eftsoons I will be real, and thou as well."

He frowned at this nonsense, as if she were insulting his intelligence, but she smiled assurance. Then she had coughed, vomited blood, and died.

Wide-eyed, he had seen those last moments, and his mother's frantic endeavors to keep Ringbrae with them. But those efforts had been bootless.

Maggie Strong

THE STREETS of Zodiako were in an uproar. Even while planning proceeded for two weddings and the funerals of three elderly townsfolk, with all the necessary rituals and precautions that both entailed, people skulked from their houses and now, as night drew near, took refuge inside the old stone parliament or in the long halls of the temple, hiding from moon and stars like mice between bins of grain.

Maggie made her grim walk through the gray dusk, past the graveyard and three fresh-dug pits decked with ribbons, hoping to encourage those recent and doubtless surprised spirits to depart quick and clean from their isle. She took a stone path north toward the stables, on a most unexpected and unwelcome mission. As the town's only physician with experience in Eater magic, she had to hurry and tend to a victim of the kick of a horse . . .

An Eater's mount.

A clan of Eaters from the Ravine two miles inland had been through Zodiako the night before, and though they were not rogue, and had not broken their ancient pact, and showed no signs of doing so, their presence, even in passing, was not welcome. Children did not sleep when Eaters were near — nor for that matter did their parents. But children had the most to lose.

Furthermore, the Eaters had left four of their horses in the care of the local stable. Eater horses were in themselves unsettling, with their restless ways and strange eyes that seemed to have witnessed paths and trails unknown to humans — and probably had, since Eaters were known to venture near the island's heart to, so it was said, commune with gods and beasts that no longer existed anywhere else.

The kick from such a horse could embed a wound with strange dirt indeed, dirt that sparkled and burned and left the wretch — a stable boy of tender years — writhing in agony. At least he would not die of an infection. Such wounds, in her experience, always cleansed themselves. But left untended, they could also cleanse the world of the boy so afflicted.

Still, the true rub of the matter was that Eaters on foot, without their mounts, were going about deadly serious business down at the shore, and did not trust even their horses while so engaged. And that meant there might be new arrivals from the outer world — people not subject to the pact, and thus attractive to all Eaters, and more so the outliers of their kind.

For Maggie Strong, that was both an alarming possibility — that unaware peoples might find their lives cut short! — and a welcome, even exciting one. She had lived her entire life here, but had often, since childhood, felt a rude, undisciplined need for words from the outside, words on history and how the human races had changed, and what the world's, and the island's, fate might be, as Crafters molded their stories, their plots — their long plans.

She entered the stable slowly, cautiously, not to make any loud sound. The stable master, an old friend named Kule, nodded toward the rear stalls where the Eater mounts were being kept for the time being.

"They just appeared," he said. "Januk came on them by surprise. The stall gates were barred by a silver rope, and he was curious — had never seen such before."

"So he pulled on it," Maggie said.

"That he did. The animal reared and struck him."

"Where is he?"

"In the tack room."

She went with Kule to a long extension from the middle of the stable, with haylofts above and stone grain bins below, and the tack arrayed on one wall of the closest bin.

The boy, Januk, was familiar to her, though she did not go to the stable often. She did not ride willingly, having been thrown from a supposedly tame and child-friendly horse at the age of six, giving her the limp she still demonstrated when weather was gray — which was much of the time in Zodiako.

The boy lay on his back, grimacing at the rafters and hayloft, one thigh bare, bruised, and clearly marked by the down-striking hoof. She bent beside him, with a wince, then knelt and said, "I am Maggie. Thou art Januk, son of Senilil and Mark, in truth?"

The boy's face was a mask of pain, which he was trying his best to conceal, and failing. "I am," he said through gritted teeth. "Why doth it burn?"

"Thou hast strange land in thy leg, boy. It will help the wound stay clean, but give thee odd dreams tonight. We will clean out the dirt and give it back in a small bottle, to light thy way in the dark."

The boy was in too much pain to find this appealing, but she knew it would make his reputation with the other youngsters. She asked Kule to bring her a clean wrap. The wound's blood clumped black and clotted, as if cauterized, but a couple of inches of flesh lay loose and exposed silverskin and a beefy nubbin of muscle, and there along the rip it was — a sparkle like embedded stars. The Eater horses had been to the chafing waste not long ago.

Kule handed her a half-clean rag, the best to be had out here. She asked him for some of his famous *uisquebaugh*, which he kept hidden in the back of the tack room for purposes other than treating wounds, and, grumbling, he went to fetch a jug.

"This will hurt thee worse than the kick," she said to the boy, and took a curled edge of the cloth to rub away the glitter she could see. The boy shrieked, and Kule returned just in time to help her hold him down. He sat on the boy's midsection, light enough and gentle.

She had removed all of the glitter by the time the boy passed out, and now she spread the rag and scraped the shining dirt into a small glass jar. The boy's dreams had already begun, she saw, for his eyes weaved fast under their lids and he moaned not in pain, but at what his dream-self was seeing. Maggie wondered what those visions might be.

Some claimed Maggie's outward-facing curiosity was caused by her drinking of the wildness of her drake charges, the fluids tapped when nymphs were blunted. She opened the baked clay jug and poured out a good glassful of whiskey over the wound, then took a line of gut and a needle and began sewing it up.

"Will it suppurate?" Kule asked, eyes bright and proud that he knew that word. He had seen or himself endured often enough that necessary stage of healing—redness, puffiness, and the copious discharge of yellow pus—that signified flesh knitting and returning health. Or, just as often, creeping red lines, stinking blood, and death.

"I think not," she said. "If we have got all the dirt out, the wound will heal slow but complete. He'll have a good scar, but he is young, and maybe that, too, will fade."

"When will the glassy skins return for their horses?" Kule asked. "I want to be gone when they do."

"The boy's parents have been told, have they not?"

"The father's on grave detail, and his mother is out cleaning the

King of Troy's hut. I am sure they will miss him soon. They know he works here."

"Then help me carry him to their house," she said. "Where is thy daughter?"

Kule shrugged.

"Canst thou fetch her from the still in the forest, and ask her to watch till they return?"

Kule nodded reluctantly.

"Thou canst leave soon as his parents take him home," she said. "Th'other horses seem quiet."

"Frightened," Kule said with a tweak of his nose. "They wol not make a sound until these be gone."

"The Eaters will return in a few hours, I suspect. But if they come again, and they will, I advise thee to tend their mounts personally, and not assign them to an ignorant lad whilst thou dost hide and mewl."

Kule gave her a resentful glare, but he knew Maggie too well to sass. "Keep the jug," he said, as if offering up a valuable gift.

And she did. She knew a scout who might enjoy it.

Maggie helped Kule return the boy to his family's cabin, where the father waited, weary and stained with dirt. Then she made her way down a lane between the temple and the parliament, the last hundred yards covered by a long slate-shingle roof. Beneath the slates, the overhead beams, every twenty feet or so, were painted on both sides with scenes from history and story. Nobody she knew had painted the beams, and nobody confessed that they knew anyone who had painted the beams, but they were painted, and the paintings were changed every few moons, while nobody was watching. She had learned to ignore their enigmatic and sometimes disturbing depictions, but now, heading at a brisk walk for a meeting with her chief scout, she glanced up and saw a fiery red eruption spread destruction across the beam right overhead. She closed her eyes to avoid its details, then looked down at the bricks and stones of the walkway and hunched her shoulders. The unknown, perhaps incorporeal, artist was unhappy, and so was she. Too many things were happening at once, and what worried her at this point was not that things could go wrong for the town, but that people would panic, like horses in a paddock beset by the scent of tigers. If the town lost its cohesion and discipline, she had always thought that was just as like to hasten their end as any twist or twitch of the Crafters in their far kraters.

Besides, she had never seen a Crafter, much less met one. And she *had* met with Eaters. Maggie remembered when her mother and father had taken her, as a child, to meet a clan of Eaters, to receive their protection ... A story and a ritual experienced by most along the western shore. But she had little memory of that time. She had been three years old.

Hel had given birth to so many offspring, most of them more monsters than people. Maggie had been told by her mother that Eaters had once been highest among these, almost Vanir — strong among the island's elusive dark elves and dwarves and trolls, now serving mostly in the chafing waste, some said ... But Hel and her Crafters had taken it upon themselves, for some slight or other, to temper Eater immortality with dark need, followed by a warning — a severe and unwanted pact tying them forever to humans. Maggie had often wondered if the malleability and proliferation of humans had brought Hel's curse upon Eaters. Who could know? Crafters did not always observe Hel's ways, even less after Hel had hidden herself away in long sleep. They may have in their own contrary plan decided it was more dramatic, more satisfying, that humans on any of these seven isles should not remember a time before they devoted a portion of their lives to the Eaters, or the truth of how that relationship was forged.

Upon her mother's death, Maggie had been put in charge of the town's blunters. She had kept that position for twenty years. Just two days before, three of them had headed southwest through the lively woods, and had not yet returned nor sent message to explain their delay. What now worried Maggie was that what had led the Eaters to the shore had prevented the blunters from finishing their work, and wild drakes might even now be loose over the beaches and headlands, where the lively woods approached the sea. There had not been a drake attack near Zodiako for years, because her blunters were so skilled, so well trained —

And knew better than to stay out after dark, for nobody liked to tempt Eaters, even with the pacts, so it was said, still strong.

So much upheaval, and so many signs.

Maggie opened her leather satchel wide and shoved in Kule's jug of whiskey. What could her chief scout tell her about all this? More, perhaps, with incentive.

Faithful Wings

THE THREE leather-clad figures in the far cage had not said a word, but as dusk settled and clouds covered the sky, bringing on a strange, smoky gloom, the woman put fingers to the corners of her mouth and whistled high and shrill, piercing Reynard's ears. He looked at Manuel, but the old man simply maintained his patient stoop — keeping his attention on *el capitán* and the assembled troops. Cardoza had formed the soldiers into two columns, men with short swords, halberds, and half-pikes foremost, preparing to carve their way through the forest, toward the volcanic ridge that lowered over the north end of this beach and might lead them inland.

"He leaveth just before dark. The man's an idiot," Manuel said.

No thought to bringing along any of the three prisoners and their satchels. *El capitán* had never made it ashore on England, and that might mean he had never fought a real battle, never dealt with the necessity of planning . . . Or guides.

So Reynard guessed, but he was young and foolish, his uncle had informed him often enough — so how could he know? He did know that he would rather stay in this cage than accompany the soldiers.

Soon both the sailors and the soldiers might quite literally run out of time, one group at sea, the other . . .

At the questing fingers of the glassy skins.

Reynard thought of the female face that had leaned over him in the dark, cheeks and forehead aglow like some beautiful, frightful dream. Somehow, they had seemed to share a sympathy. He caught Manuel looking at him, scowled, and shook his head. What was the old man to him? Were they also somehow connected, protected together? Not now, certainly. Except that they did share a cage.

Reynard's legs were cramping. Manuel's legs no doubt were cramping as well, and worse, but he did not show the pain or complain.

Twilight here lasted far longer than it did even in England. His uncle had told him that the line between night and day in the tropics was like the cut of a knife, but the farther north one traveled, the longer twilight lingered. His uncle had been south of the equator with John Hawkins, taking slaves to the Caribbean, and had vowed he would never do that again. But he had seen the tropical sun and knew how fast daylight faded. Here, the dusk seemed to last forever. Reynard had spent many evenings trying to understand the why of that, but never having been in the tropics himself, and never having asked his uncle pointed questions about the ways of the natural world seen during those slave voyages, which had so affected his uncle and of which any mention made him morose, he had never reached any conclusions.

He shifted to make room for Manuel to stretch out his legs. Manuel's age seemed to be creeping back. His skin was like old leather, his eyes were turning yellow again, and Reynard caught him pulling out another tooth and throwing it with a curse through the bars.

"Night cannot fall soon enough," the old man said.

The two lines of Cardoza's soldiers vanished into the forest like snakes crawling under a bush. For a few minutes more, those left on the beach heard chopping, swearing — calls and commands — but soon all that faded.

Meanwhile, the tide nearly full, sailors pushed and pried with logs and branches to dislodge the galleon and shove it off the beach. It remained stuck fast. Digging quickly and inserting the trunks of several trees, ten men hung from the trees first on one side, then the other, and began to rock the great ship while the tide was swifting in. Others at the bow shoved, calling in unison, as the ship's boats rowed out through the surf, hauling thick ropes from the stern. It took over an hour, well into the long, smoky twilight, but a last grumble of the hull was followed by sailors shouting with joy, waving their lanterns to get the boats to pick up those left in the shallows.

The black outline of the galleon was soon dozens of yards from the beach. The sailors and *el maestro* were strongly motivated by what they had suffered the night before ... But could there be any kind of escape?

Manuel grumbled, "The most junior glassy skins do not enjoy tides or rivers. *El maestro* and the sailors are safe out there from low Eaters ... but that meaneth not they are safe."

"How long did you live here?" Reynard asked.

Manuel gave him a thin smile, not to show his teeth. "I appeared thirty when last I left, maybe forty years ago. The expedition before that, I left when I was your age, and returned older than I am now. I have lived on this isle, off and on, in total, for maybe twenty years. And off the island — maybe five hundred."

Reynard instinctively pulled back from the old man. "Are you human?"

"Yes, boy. Very human. Perhaps more human than thou!"

Not that he believed any of this, or that it mattered in the least. Reynard was pretty sure death would be upon them all before any long, slow sunrise. The woods might reject the soldiers, forcing them to take out their frustration on the prisoners in the cages. The ship might anchor offshore, send back boats, and finish the work of dispatching them.

But then a brisk, whirling breeze came up, raising clouds of sand and gravel. Something flew over the cages with great, gritty swooshes — something that could see in the gathering dark.

"Drake," Manuel said. "Not the one that took the dog. Bigger. I pray it is paired!"

Reynard wanted desperately to know what that meant. "How paired? In a team?"

"They drink the tap after a blunting. That maketh the young drake theirs to rule."

And Reynard was no better informed than before! "Can you speak it plain?"

Manuel shrugged. "Thou wilt see soon enough."

Darkness was complete, but a sliver of moon emerged and a woman's face came gray and quick outside the bars of their cage. She was of middle years, weathered but lithe and strong, and wore leather like those in the far cage. She moved soundlessly, and in her quick survey, paid particular, frowning attention to Manuel.

"Thou hast returned!"

Manuel met her study with downcast silence.

With a knowing wink at Reynard, she moved to the other cage. A brief conversation followed, and the visitor returned to the darkness.

"That would be Anutha, I think," Manuel said. "Last time we met, she was but a girl. She acteth now like a scout."

"You know all these people?" Reynard asked.

Manuel shook his head sadly. "Some have been born since I left."

The three in the far cage arranged themselves as if preparing for a tumble, and the woman whistled loudly, summoning a second gritty wind. Something big landed on their cage and lifted it from the sand, then dropped and split it open.

Reynard raised his head to see.

"Keep down!" Manuel shouted. The clouded moon brightened to show wide, transparent wings descend over their own cage, and in similar fashion, it was careened and plucked open by darting, shining black arms — thorny, jointed arms with strong, scissoring claws. Manuel rolled free of the bars and across the shingle. A broken bar gouged Reynard's calf and then he, too, was free, but under another broad shadow, another pass of the sparking claws, he flattened again and his face fell into a lick of wave.

Something very big and black folded broad cathedral-window wings along a long, slender body as it settled on the shore a dozen yards off. The head was extraordinary — a cubit or more across, with two long, wide eyes like doubled melons covered with jewels, and a pinching, cleaving mouth that opened and closed in three parts. Reynard was sure the creature was watching them. It leaned over to suck at the water, then spread and flapped its wings, hopping then rising and blowing sand until Reynard covered his face with his hands.

Only then was he grabbed and lifted by his underarms — with hands, not claws. "No fuss, boy," said the one Manuel called Anutha. Scraps of wood lay all over the beach. The three from the other cage surrounded them, and with Anutha's help, Reynard got to his feet, limping, half blind, and saw four more people approaching from down the beach, not Spanish — dressed in leather like the others, and also carrying satchels. The window-winged beasts had flown off and could not even be heard.

"Dana, have you all you need?" Anutha asked the woman in command of the first three, who had summoned these beasts with her whistle. Manuel looked upon the woman called Dana with profound respect, then held up two fingers. "Two!" he whispered. "She is paired with two drakes!"

"They took our tools and put them in a chest," Dana said. Her male companions quickly found the chest some distance up the beach, broke the lock with a twisted horseshoe from around the cold forge bricks, opened the lid, and in brighter moonlight, held up three satchels.

"All here!"

Anutha nodded approval. "Now we go."

Helping Reynard and Manuel, the group quickly pushed into the woods on the southwestern verge, opposite where the soldiers and *el capitán* had gone. The branches rubbed and rustled around them, and a breeze, following the tide, moaned through their leaves. The trees seemed to have their own opinions about these intruders, limbs reaching out to touch and welcome the ones that wore leather and carried satchels, other limbs whipping at Reynard and Manuel with disdain, raising welts.

"Halt!" Anutha called. Between the grit in his eyes, the whipping of the trees, and the final darkness, Reynard could barely see her. He felt something cold and wet and looked down at his feet. Ocean poured into the woods, rising to his ankles, then to his knees. Far behind, through the forest and into the hollows and crevices of the mountains beyond, came a kind of deep sigh, as if the land itself was breathing, and on the exhale, dropping the shore deeper into water. That breathing tide was already high enough that the galleon might actually make it past the breakers! Somehow, as much as he hated Spaniards and feared the warriors who had threatened his Queen, that possible escape seemed a grand thing, a triumph of their kind against the strange land they had found . . .

And it meant his own escape might be possible, as well.

Then, from where the ship had been tugged out to sea, they all heard distant, frantic voices. They looked out through the branches with mixed awe and fearful sympathy. The calls began as shouts of warning, then rose in terror, followed by screams of agony. Some of the voices seemed to come from high over the water, as if men were being lifted hundreds of feet into the night — and dismembered, their cries ending abruptly.

"Sailors on the galleon," Dana said, clinging to Anutha. She pulled from her satchel a softly glowing knob on a stick, which brightened as she spun it in her palms. "They kept us from our duty, and now they suffer." She tapped Reynard's shoulder, then Manuel's, and they all moved up a wooded rise and away from the lapping waters.

"The town's in danger," the beardless boy said. He was younger by a couple of years than Reynard, his round brown face topped like a watch cap by thick, coal-black hair. As he rummaged through his satchel, his eyes took a wily slant, and when they moved on, he handled himself with almost strutting confidence.

Manuel warned, "I know these soldiers. They will strike soon."

Anutha surveyed the combined parties: two from Dana's captured group, older and experienced, and four newly arrived, two of late youth and full of confidence, two more quite young and perhaps untried. And of course Manuel and Reynard, capabilities unknown. "There are not enough of us to make a difference," she said.

Dana made her decision. "No time to walk to town and back and drop these two off. They will come." She pointed out the narrow path through the trees, leading down to another portion of the beach.

"Big year for drakes!" the beardless boy said, smiling excitedly at Reynard as they exchanged places in the line. Reynard studied the restless trees, touched his wounded leg, and made quick appraisal of his chances of fleeing — and living. Slim at best. Besides, he was fascinated by the group's task.

"The town hath a dozen defenders," said a pale-skinned man with hardly any nose and long, knotted flaxen hair.

"Paired to drakes," the beardless boy explained to Reynard with a sly nod. "Just right for nasty visitors. I'll be paired as well."

"How do you speak with them?" Reynard asked.

"We will show you," the beardless boy said. "Stay close."

Dana said, "The woods are in turmoil and will resist. That will slow us." She took the lead, followed by her two older partners. Anutha took a step back and let them pass. Reynard tried to clearly observe this hierarchy through the throbbing pain in his leg.

Anutha rejoined the line behind Manuel. "I think thou must be th'one called Pilgrim."

"I was given that name, long ago," Manuel said.

"Dost thou know a woman called Maggie?" she asked.

"I do," Manuel said.

"And dost thou know me?"

"I believe I do."

"I had seven or eight years when thou last went to sea. Now I work with Maggie and Maeve. Dana is Maggie's daughter. And of course thou know'st Maeve . . ."

"Maggie's older sister," Manuel said. "She must be in her sixties, and Maeve, in her eighties. I hope she is well and alive."

"Maeve is eighty-four," Anutha said with a wry twist of her lips. "Still alive, but feeble. Thou hast kept thy wife waiting a long, long time, Pilgrim."

Dana called over her shoulder, "There be nymphs and drakes in our future, more important than far-wandering husbands or the Spaniards they guide. Boy, canst thou travel with that leg?" she asked Reynard.

Reynard tried to stand straight. He noted that the men in the team now looked on Manuel with no small distrust. Their distrust included him, he realized, with an added twinge. "I can walk," he said.

"I can travel, as well," Manuel said. "But I will stay on the beach and distract the Eaters."

Dana looked back, expression barely changed, but Manuel seemed to be confirming something for her. "That would not be in our best interests," she said, brows pinched.

Anutha said, "I know not thy connection, but before we hand ye to the Eaters, I await Maeve's judgment."

This irritated Manuel. "I bring her what she needs, that which I promised long ago," he said.

Anutha sniffed and looked away. Dana said, "That is for Maggie and Maeve to judge. For now, we move together."

Reynard had to agree. Even if the wild, window-winged drakes did not find them, the glassy people — those all seemed to call Eaters — would return, and Reynard felt it was hardly likely they could be lucky again. So why was Manuel willing or even eager to stay behind? And then Reynard knew, as if he had understood those strange scenes on the beach for the first time. Manuel needed those visitors. They had something for him.

They brought him youth.

The procession worked through thickly twisting branches, then, reaching a stubborn impasse, split their line in two and left the difficult, narrow path to find other ways. Dana faced the boy as he limped past. "Thou think'st we let the drakes hatch to fend off Spaniards?"

Reynard was embarrassed by the direct question, though not surprised by her inflection. As a young man of no particular prominence or high birth, everyone older addressed him so. And when he spoke to horses, he gave them highborn respect, as one should, for all horses are noble. "I wis not what you keep them for. They scare me."

"As they should. It hath been a hard year for tracking nymphs," Dana said. "They come ashore, hang in trees or off rocks, and we boat out to find and blunt before they rise. If we blunt them, we can pair them with defenders — but split wild, they be a danger to all."

"We saw them from the galleon," Reynard said. "Out in the bay."

"Maybe with thy guidance we can find them again. After the feast the *ddraig môr* found on that damned galleon, the wild ones already out there will fight and mate and spread their eggs in the deep waters . . . and next year will be far worse." Dana used Welsh-sounding words with an old flavor, like *drake mar* — sea dragons. Reynard's grandmother had often dropped into Welsh when she was angry.

The blunter's face was calm but hardly placid. As they trooped and stumbled through a low, thorny brake, she seemed to judge him more kindly. He sensed a deep intelligence, and her strong, taut features reminded him of his grandmother so much he wished he could remember more Welsh and use it to reassure her he meant no ill. But the words were not there. Not yet.

None of the blunters hacked at the branches, however much they annoyed, as if they respected the trees and bushes that made their journey difficult, even devious — for twice Anutha had to reverse course, swearing under her breath, vowing that the trees were playing tricks again. But she seemed to feel an almost perverse affection for them, and touched a few as she passed, as if she knew them.

When the dark finally fell, Dana let the knob dim. "Stay close," advised a small, big-chested fellow, and Reynard and Manuel found themselves bumping shoulders in the center of a circle.

"They were not touched the first time," Dana said to Anutha.

"Why?" the beardless boy asked. "If Eaters are thieves, will they not take from anyone?"

Neither answered.

"I hope they be not thieves," the boy finished in a lower tone.

"Doth not matter if we sleep," Anutha said. "They are not ghosts. Eldest outside, youngest in."

Manuel seemed expectant, almost happy. Reynard doubted he would himself sleep.

And then . . . he did.

And sometime in his fitful repose —

Was it a dream?

Again he saw the glowing face of his glassy-skinned visitor on the beach, so beautiful and strange — and she stroked him along the nape of his neck, and he did not care.

A Hidden Boat, and Islands in the Mist

MANUEL GRIPPED his shoulder, and Reynard came awake with a start. The morning was well upon them. Nobody appeared frightened or hurt — or older.

"They seem to favor me, no?" Manuel whispered to the boy.

Reynard looked at him with wonder and concern. "I did not hear a thing."

"We do not, most often," Manuel said. His beard was darker, the skin on his hands smoother, less wrinkled, less spotted with age — and he had more hair. Reynard pushed away and rose with the others in the small clearing. They all seemed subdued, like cattle before slaughter — but also relieved.

"They were not here to take," said a swarthy man with wide, nervous eyes.

"We work for them as well," Dana said. "Thou'rt looking well, Pilgrim," she said to Manuel. He stared off into the bushes.

Dana and the young men made a fire of castaway twigs. The trees did not seem to object. Dana heated water from a small stream and brewed a brothy tea. Reynard found it salty but restorative.

Anutha came through the woods and told them she could see three nymphs on rocky islands near the shore. Dana said, "The boat is hidden south. Let us hope it is still there."

The party pulled leaf-wrapped breakfasts, bread, and a small loaf of soft cheese from their satchels and ate as they moved after Anutha. Dana offered Reynard a share of hers, and Anutha shared with Manuel. Both took it with gratitude. They had not eaten since being put in the cage.

Minutes later, they emerged in a clearing on a headland overlooking the ocean and gazed out across a rosy-gray mist that hid the horizon. The ocean in the harbor was calm, with long, low swells sliding gently up a narrow beach of pebbles, black sand, and fallen dark brown boulders. They saw no sign of the Spanish soldiers.

Dana curled aside a gate woven from dried fishweed, a kind of carnivorous seaweed, toothy edges still visible on the leaves, and led them down a roughly sculpted stairway to the beach below. As they approached the water, they saw two bodies — mangled, partly eaten. Sailors. They did not pause to bury them. But Anutha took resolve. She had to return to the village. "There are a great many Spaniards and not so many drakes or Eaters," she said. "You know well these beaches and islands. I have to track and tell the town where the Spanish are."

And so she left.

"We have little time," Dana told the rest. "Our work is just as important."

"We know," said the shortest and stockiest of the group. "But I would like to get home and defend."

"And summon our drakes!" said the beardless boy.

"If we move fast, perhaps we shall," Dana said.

Manuel's movements had smoothed and quickened, and Reynard watched him with more respect and perhaps more fear — as did the others. But Manuel clearly enjoyed the change, and some-times would pause and just look at his hands, feel his face, and murmur something Reynard could not hear — a word, a name, a prayer.

In the shadow of the headland, they came upon the mouth of a deep black cave, its upper lip hung with dry moss, like a green and gray mustache. Two of the team cleared another woven gate, and four more entered and soon dragged out a wooden boat, flat-bottomed, smaller than those that had flocked around the Span-ish and English ships — about twenty feet from stem to stern, with three pairs of oars neatly tied along four thwarts, not much different from the dories Reynard had fished from as a young boy. The carvings along the gunwales were much fancier, however, like those on peasant boats in Flanders, and still carried color, showing stumpy, stylized versions of the winged creatures he had seen the night before — the creatures this crew was meant to manage. With some awe, Reynard studied the carvings. He had once examined a dead bat and had concluded its wings were little different from his own hands, the skin stretched between longer, skinnier, more frag-ile fingers, and a flap extending from the little finger to the feet. But based on the carvings here, and what he had managed to see in the near dark, sea dragons — drakes — had at least four wings, one larger pair before the smaller, each wing made of translucent membrane stretched along three long, slender struts, with panes ar-ranged inside the struts, like pieces in a stained-glass window. The carvings showed four spiked black legs tipped with crab-like claws, and emerging from the body behind the neck, two gripping arms, also with claws, but smaller. The long slender tails behind the wings were patterned in a mosaic of brown and silvery blue. The heads featured four jeweled eyes, two on each side of a black bump of a nose. Below the nose opened jaws like the mandibles of a crab — or the mouth of a dragonfly. He wondered why he had not seen it sooner — perhaps because, unlike darting dragonflies back home, harmless and common, these creatures had scared him so badly from the first. Still, what was carved on the gunwale seemed most similar to those buzzing insects that populated English marshes and rivers ... though of course much larger. He wondered at the connection.

The beardless boy observed Reynard's interest. "'Ware that nose," he advised, pointing a callused middle finger at one carving. "Cook you through, it will — if the drake dothn't know you, or dothn't like you!"

"What is your name?" Reynard asked.

"Nem," the boy said. "Short for Nehemiah. Yours?"

Reynard told him.

"Fox. That is rich!"

The others introduced themselves while Dana finished her inspection. She pronounced the boat sound and big enough to carry them all. "We can only hope we aren't interrupted," she said. "Where be t'others' clothes?"

Sondheim, tall, quiet, flat-nosed, with shaggy flaxen hair, and MacClain, the swarthy one, with nervous hazel eyes and muddy brown hair, delved deep into the cave and brought out two dirt-stained, leaf-speckled sacks. Dana reached in and withdrew two buckskin shirts, tied at the front, and two pairs of canvas pants, wrinkled and dank but wearable. "Put these on. The water's colder out there."

"Whose are they?" Manuel asked. Reynard was not sure he wanted to know.

"Spares," Sondheim said, with an accent that reminded Reynard of Norwegians or Swedes.

"Given to the poor by ill luck," Gareth said. He was a small, bushy-haired man with outsized chest and shoulders that seemed to be wearing through his shirt, revealing pale skin through holes and loosened patches.

"Their previous owners no longer need them." Dana finished the topic with a scowl, as though both lightness of tone, and concealing their coming peril, were equally improper.

Manuel put on the breeches and shirt handed to him. Long, pale scars from years of cat lashings spread across his back and buttocks. Apparently the restoration of his years could not erase such markings. Reynard stripped off his rags more shyly and dressed quickly, but his foot caught in a pants leg. He was not used to skins as clothing, and his toenails were still ragged from salt and shingle. Dressed, he and Manuel looked less like sailors and more like hunters — which they now were, apparently.

They carried the flat-bottomed boat to the water, where it bobbed at leisure in the slow swells. Then all waded out around the boat and hoisted themselves aboard. Three teams took turns rowing steadily out to sea — out to where the galleon had gone, Reynard thought. Where the galleon had vanished and all aboard had perished, most likely.

Sitting between the two current oarsmen, Gareth and Nem, Reynard studied the bluing mist as the headland and beach fell behind. This weather was not so different from Southwold's the past few springs and winters.

Manuel kept watching the sky.

"'Ware of fishweed," Gareth said. "Lies just beneath the surface, doth put out nets and eat more than fish. There!"

He pointed to a wide tangle of brown and green kelp, or what looked at first like kelp, rising and topping between the crests of the waves. Broad brown leaves seemed to stick up like hands pointing to the boat. Then a stalk with several bulbs on its length churned and twisted, clearly moving toward them. Gareth prepared an oar and gave the stalk a good strike, which made it thrash and curl back.

"Nymphs eat the weed, or the fish the weed doth snare. We do not bother. Awful stuff," Gareth said.

"See the teeth?" MacClain asked. The edges of the upright brown leaves were lined on both sides with small, bluish teeth, like the teeth of a small shark. "Got bit once. Never again."

Reynard swallowed a groan and wondered if the wreck of the hoy had ever passed through such a loose and wandering forest.

The dory entered the wall of mist. From the shore, the sound of waves faded, and they were enveloped by a knotted, twisted arras of more gloom, as if the fog itself questioned their wisdom in being here. Against the swish of the oars and the grunts of the oarsmen, he heard muffled sounds from something larger, deeper, under the water — and from the far, subdued shore. A change in the very air around them made the fog churn and swirl in strange ways.

"Is that the weed?" Reynard asked.

"Nay," Gareth said. "Weed is silent, mostly."

"You have heard the breathing, no? The island is alive," Manuel said to him in a low voice.

"How alive?" Reynard asked, in an equally low voice.

Manuel lifted a hand and waggled it slowly, with a press of his lips and a side glance to the water beyond the breakers. "Quaking land, volcanoes, the greatest named Agni Most Foul, seldom seen or visited — and farther inland, beyond mountain ridges, and through many passes, a pale waste, the chafing waste, so-called, surrounded by a ring of great shallow bowls called hereabouts kraters — and into these kraters few dare go. Not even Eaters."

"Oh," Reynard said.

So far, he and Manuel had not been asked to row, although Reynard would have been perfectly willing, just to feel useful, to *be* useful to these people on whom likely his life depended.

A wide grayness rose in the mist ahead, and Gareth, who seemed to have the sharpest eyes, pointed it out to Dana, who instructed the oarsmen to move in that direction. The cause of the shadow was slowly unveiled — the half-submerged hulk of the galleon. Water sloshed through the hole open once more in its side — patch missing — and there was much new damage besides. Decks had been ripped to splinters, as if clawed up by hungry cats in search of mice, and half-eaten bodies draped the side rails, limbs loose in the waves. Soon the once-great ship would sink and never again be a danger to England.

Reynard wondered what had happened to *el maestro*.

"The soldiers are now alone, with no means of escape," Manuel said. "And mayhaps lost in the wily forest."

Dana looked over the wreck with something like sorrow. "Anutha'll track them and report to the town," she said. "None of that is our concern, not yet."

The rowers resumed their course.

"Just two drakes can do that," Sondheim said to Reynard, assuming Manuel already understood. "Twenty could make of this coast a dead waste. Queen Hel once set them to keep men under control . . . but then thought better, and gave us means."

Gareth held up ten fingers, signifying the paired sea drakes available on this coast. "Great power, but not enough," he said.

"What can you do about the wild ones?" Reynard asked.

"Nothing," Dana said. "Some just beneath the sky, Vanir, can hunt them, but not the children of men. We can only hope any wild drakes we miss will fight and kill each other. To find a new crop of nymphs near this shore, we have to visit islands they have favored in times before. There are two here. Likely you passed one such as you came up on the first beach, but we will take that one last, because it is a difficult landing, and we will need do the most we can before we put ourselves, and our work, in danger."

The boat creaked in the swell. Reynard asked, "Do we get weapons?"

"No blunter hath more than a knife, but for our chisel," Nem said. Reynard glumly surveyed their prospects at that news — heading south to find monsters that had just wrecked a great Spanish ship, or at least finished the job begun by the English, perhaps by Drake himself — named after a drake!

The *human* Drake, Reynard added in his thoughts, would have carried a sword along with a pistol . . . And doubtless a fearful cohort of harquebuses.

"If you cannot hurt them, and cannot kill them, what do you do if they attack?" he asked.

"Our best," Sondheim replied. "'Tis all we have ever done."

"And if you be paired, do your drakes defend from other drakes — from wild ones?"

Dana said, "They will not kill. But drakes fight all the time, for females, for territory."

"We have seen drakes eat another, when it be weak and silly," Gareth said.

"That we have," Dana said. "We can be paired, yet never know their hearts."

"If they have hearts!" Nem said.

"Oh, of a kind," Dana said. Strange to think that she was in charge of so many men; his uncle might have thought it stranger still. But then perhaps he could have been reminded of Reynard's grandmother, if that uncle, and that grandmother, were still alive. On a few occasions, the young Reynard had seen his father stand hat in hand before his mother-in-law, head bowed. Strong man, stronger mother.

Thoughts of those already lost reminded Reynard that he likely wore the clothes of a man who had died on just such a mission as theirs. Not that Reynard was unused to dead men's clothing. Poverty spread such gifts from dead to living, and especially to the young, often enough.

They looked up at a thrumming and a musical trill that quickly filled the air, like big drums under shrill fifes. A shadow passed over, and they all flinched.

"Drake?" Reynard asked Nem, who nodded.

"Maybe two," the boy said, and forced a smile. "But they do not swoop! Not hungry, I guess. Filled with sailors!"

Manuel said, "They are yours, paired, no?"

"Maybe," Dana said. "But they still have independence. Anyway, think nought of that," she warned. "Tough enow to find and blunt nymphs with our keenest wits."

She seemed to know her way in the gloom, and soon, in the middle distance, they saw two dark gray pillars with a forested ridge like a causeway between, raising more sounds of splashing waves. The ridged and rocky island was taller and wider than the lone pillar the galleon had passed on their uncontrolled approach to the beach.

The blunters rowed in slowly, backing water as the waves hissed against more black sand. Reynard's experience of sand was limited, but sailors he had met in Southwold told him black sand was likely old lava. *I saw it many times on the shores of old Atlantis,* one grizzled fisherman had said, as they spread their nets and built fires to smoke the afternoon's catch. *In the Mediterranean. Finest sea in the world.*

Irish Sea is the finest, another had said, holding up a cudgel.

Manuel poked Reynard out of his memories. "Keep thine eyes open," he said.

They rowed around the island, looking for a landing. And they found it, though it was already occupied. They pulled onto the deeper beach beside a round vessel, very like a currach, an Irish skin boat, but about ten feet across, with a silvery membrane stretched around the oval wooden frame rather than tarred hide.

Dana was unhappy to see it there. She bent to touch the shimmering skin. "Not one of ours," she said.

"Made by men," said Gareth.

"But none just above the mud would use drake wing," MacClain added.

A man's voice came out of the woods overhanging the beach, and a large fellow with thick-muscled arms, stripped to the waist, deep brown skin heavily tattooed, leaned out on a red-barked tree limb, smiling like a freebooter. "Plenty of work here for blunters," he said, then swung down and walked across the beach. The man's face had been ritually scarred, then patterned in swirls and stars with red and black dyes. He appeared no more than thirty years old, but his eyes were deep, the color of firelit shadow, and his hair was a stiff brush, like close-packed hog bristles.

Dana said, "That boat's worth more than your life, if it was sold in Zodiako or inland."

"I never sold such," the man said. "And that is not my boat." He held out his hand, not to her, but to Manuel, and then to Reynard, with a half smile. "I am guessing one of you is new, and one just returned. I am Kaiholo."

"Soundeth like an island name," Manuel said. "But I do not know it."

"Your lands have not found mine," the tattooed man said. "It was my father's name, and the name of his grandfather."

Manuel shook the extended hand. Reynard followed. The others refused. The hand was rough-callused — a seaman's hand.

"I have dishonored none of them," Kaiholo added, with a moue at their fellows, "and I say again, the boat and its skin are not mine. Though I do on occasion ride it . . ." He shook his head as if at a difficult memory. "Whenever possible, I swim."

"Whose boat is it, then?" Dana asked, a pale cast to her face.

"*Hers,*" Kaiholo said.

Manuel turned away and looked down at the black sand, but Reynard caught a glimpse of both old shame and hunger.

"What presence commands thine attendance?" Dana asked. "An Eater?"

"Not an Eater. One just beneath the sky. Last night, before we went to work, she told me two important individuals had arrived and deserved high attention, though not *hers*, not yet. She also told me that a young female Eater and the Afrique protected them — and that under the old rules, the Afrique restored to an old man some of his lost years. Be you that man?" He directed his question to Manuel.

"I was given time by the Afrique," Manuel said.

Kaiholo scowled. "I do not like the air when Calybo is near."

Manuel asked, "Your mistress sought no protection for the others from the galleon?"

Kaiholo looked away. "None," he said, "but for you and the boy. Is that how you know Guldreth?"

"I will speak of that in town, when I am there," Manuel said.

The blunters drew back from Manuel and Reynard.

Kaiholo said, "Like you, I am just above the mud. My mistress told me to keep lookout — but she confideth little." He turned to Dana and her blunters. "As for ye, she hath already downed one of the wild ones, her limit for this season, whoever doth measure. She let two tame ones pass, and they did damage to the great ship out there. Was it ye did direct them?"

"Not as such," Dana said. "But they caught the scent of our enemies."

"Do you object to Guldreth taking a wild one?"

"As she is just below the sky," Dana said, "it is not for me to object. Her harvest leaveth one fewer wild drake to worry us this season."

Kaiholo rested a leather-shod foot on the frame of the skin boat and explained, for Reynard's benefit, as if he had already judged their levels of knowledge and thought he had the most to learn, "Nymphs refuse to attack a boat stretched with drake's wing. For the high ancients under Hel's skies, there are elder advantages, elder protections — including defense against drakes. But my mistress is at her limit. So be wary out there." Again to Reynard he added, or more like confided, "Hel made the drakes to keep watch on the children of men, and protect these shores from invaders."

"But the invaders are here anyway," Dana observed.

"We shall see how they fare."

Did this strange tattooed man — more woodcarving than human — work for someone like the glassy-skinned visitor Reynard had seen during their first night on the beach? He had thought she might be a dream, until, after the second night, he had witnessed Manuel's rejuvenation.

And what was this talk of Hell?

"Not all of the Spaniards were killed," Dana said. "Soldiers still move inland."

"Give them a few days," Kaiholo said. "Eaters rarely miss a chance to add to their years. All children of men are here on their sufferance."

"And on the sufferance of Travelers and Crafters," Manuel said, in a chiding tone.

"Them, too," Kaiholo said. "When Hel returneth, she may or may not decide to keep us, whether we interest the Crafters or no." He studied Reynard more closely. "Where from, lad? Eastern Albion?"

Manuel moved between them and held up his hand. "Enough. These have work. When they are done, I would return to speak to thy mistress."

Kaiholo shrugged this off. "Full of questions, I wis. I cannot guarantee she will be here, but may I make compense for her unpredictable nature, and guide ye to a prime location?"

"We know where to go," Dana said. "And what to do when we get there."

Kaiholo seemed much given to shrugging. "By dark, I have to be strong and alert. There is at least one wild drake out there ... By tonight, there could be four or five. If I were you, I would get your blunting done before dark."

More than ever, Reynard wanted to wake up, to get away from the war at sea, the wreck of the hoy, his dead uncle and the other fishermen . . . the galleon, *el maestro*, *el capitán*, and this unknown island.

"Where doth your mistress sleep?" Nem asked nervously.

"I do not know that she sleepeth, as we sleep, or where she is — other than that she is up *there*." Kaiholo gestured at the topknots of woods that crested the island's two headlands, with a lightly timbered causeway between. He looked to Dana. "Under a drake wing tent."

"How do we keep safe and away from her?" Nem asked, but Dana hushed him.

Kaiholo turned his attention again to Manuel. "Can you, *would* you, tell me why Calybo treateth you so well?"

Manuel did not meet his eyes.

"Or how many years he hath banked and delivered to you?"

Dana intervened. "Thou and thy mistress — whatever clan or status, she tradeth years for her favor, true? How old art thou, really?"

Kaiholo drew his brows together. To Manuel, he said, "If my mistress asketh — and you have a name known to Calybo — even below the stars —"

"Not thine to know," Dana said. "Not until he reporteth to Maggie and Maeve."

Kaiholo was not easily assuaged. "I feel my mistress's time clean and sweet, like silver. What is in this old sailor's added years, I wonder? What borrowed or traded memories? Some of mine own, mayhap?"

Manuel stared him down but did not answer. Did the tattooed man pose a danger?

Kaiholo smiled slyly, turned, and walked toward the eastern headland. He threw his arm out to point up into the trees along the ridge. "Dead drake that way. Mistress harvested the wings. Beyond, on the northern headland, hang four sacks. Now sleep I must. Fare ye well."

"How doth she share?" Nem asked his back. "Doth she kiss . . . or more?"

Dana reached out and cuffed him. He did not take it amiss. But the tattooed man looked back and grinned in pure jovial menace.

"Maybe thou wilt ask her thyself. She would like thee."

Nem shook his head, crown of black hair swishing. "No, sir!"

Reynard could not agree more. He was as far from Southwold as he had ever been, physically, emotionally, and spiritually . . .

And apparently these people showed respect to, if they did not outright worship, a queen who came from Hell.

Blunting, and Things Thereof

As THEY PUSHED through the brush and trees below the ridge, Dana muttered that she had long suspected there was a high one wandering around the southwestern shore.

"What sort of devil is that?" Reynard asked.

"Not far from angel," Manuel said. "Vanir, just beneath the sky."

"How do you know this?" Reynard asked. "Are there books or teachers for such things?"

"No books," said Dana.

Said Sondheim, who until now had stayed quiet, with a glance at Manuel, "Let us find the nymphs. We blunt them, mark them, and after that, they are of no use to Queen Hel." He was a thin, rope-muscled fellow with skin roughened by years of wind and waves, and almost certainly a sailor. But then, to get here, how many of these must be sailors? How many had been here a long time, and how many were still due to arrive?

"Hel is dead and gone," said Gareth.

"Hel can never die," Sondheim said.

"I keep no company with those who worship Hell and its demons," Reynard said between clenched teeth.

"Not *that* Hell, mooncalf!" Sondheim said, scoffing. "*Queen* Hel."

"Hell hath no queen!" Reynard said indignantly.

The others chuckled, or simply smiled. "You will catch on, if you live," Sondheim said.

"Then tell me, what is the difference?" Reynard asked. "What doth your queen rule?"

"She is not *our* queen," MacClain said, and Gareth agreed.

"She be far older than your Satan or your Hell, and deadly beautiful," said Sondheim. "Queen Hel birthed all peoples, and most monsters."

"Not me," Gareth said. "I am no heathen."

"Nor I," MacClain added. They were near the crest of the suspected headland, Dana foremost in the climbing line.

"She made this island," Sondheim added, warming to the subject. "Made the Eaters, raised up the drakes ... Made the entire world, some say."

"And so I say, not *me*," MacClain insisted.

"And yet here you are, consorting with those who serve the high ones and blunting drakes!" Sondheim said. "Hel made all in which we believe."

Angry, MacClain reached out as if to strike him, but Dana blocked his fist.

"Hel did not make me, neither," Nem said under his breath. "And she is not coming back."

"Shut it below, now," Dana said, and leaned over between branches to pull up MacClain, who did the same for Gareth. Sondheim was rough with Nem, yanking him after by one arm.

"Leave the boy be!" Dana said. "He is no pagan, and he knoweth his craft, which is more than I can say for some of ye." To Manuel and Reynard, she added, "Without parents, he is not responsible."

"At least I know who my parents were!" Nem said.

"I'll treat him right when he hath a drake at his beck," Sondheim grumbled.

"One sip!" Nem said. "I am ready."

One by one, they clambered onto the headland, just beyond the natural causeway.

"You are exceeding quiet," Gareth said to Manuel, as if blaming him for their disagreements.

Manuel showed his stronger, more numerous teeth in what passed for an ingratiating smile. More teeth — but not a complete set by any means. Getting younger might improve that aspect, but only a little more than it erased lashing-stripes — too many years of long, hard voyages, bad captains, bad food, and scurvy. Reynard's uncle's teeth had not been much better; he had blamed that rough voyage with Hawkins to Africa and then to Jamaica, and had never gone to sea again with Hawkins or his ilk. Instead, he had settled in Southwold, married, and fished with his brother, Reynard's father.

Tears came to Reynard's eyes.

"There will be a meeting. Maggie and Maeve will decide," Dana said. "If these two pass, they rise just above the mud and get village names — if they want them. If they are not eager to leave!"

"Nobody leaves once they are in the pact," Sondheim said darkly.

Manuel balanced on a line of broken lava, thick with ropy creepers and what looked like overlarge ivy. They were at the western end of the ridge, rock topped with soil and thick with trees that had withstood years of wind and high waves, trees of paper-flake bark with blood-red wood beneath, but not lively; quiet, stolid, with nought but treelike opinions.

Reynard took hold of a branch and tugged to make sure he could rely on it, and one by one, they swung out to stand under a hanging sack very like the ones seen by the watchmen on the galleon a few days before. It was a strange and beautiful growth, to be sure, over five yards long, and hung motionless from the thickest branch of the reddish trunk, over the pounding waves. Reynard thought he saw through a greenish, hard-looking section, near the thick, twisted cord from which the sack hung, an inner quiver of something soon to break out, soon to fly free.

"Is that a drake?" he asked.

"Soon," Nem said. "And a fine big one, too. Colored like turquoise and opals, I think."

Gareth reached out to brush the sack. It did not move.

They arranged themselves beneath the shrouded nymph in a U, the open part of their U facing the ocean, and Nem began a high, sweet chant, which they all took up in order, according to rank — a noisy chorus, Reynard thought, but strangely beautiful.

Manuel contributed a few words, then shook his head, as if he could not presently recall more. Dana seemed to think that this confirmed all her suspicions — and Reynard wondered, had Manuel done this before? It seemed he had! Reynard felt a tug of meaning as well, and he did not like that, for he could have no connection to these people . . .

To any who would sing lullabies to unborn monsters!

Dana gathered up her satchel, opened the flap, and drew out what looked like a chisel, bright as moonlight, with an ebony handle. She expertly climbed the tree's red trunk, slung herself along the sturdy branch, and there hung by legs alone, like a squirrel, and lowered her torso, chisel gleaming in one hand. Reynard was afraid she would fall, but no one else seemed worried and they continued to sing.

The sack swayed as she drew one hand along the cord, and within, the nymph shivered violently, as if to toss her free. Grim-faced, Dana brought the chisel down on a part of the upper casing that Reynard could not see, and the chisel's tip steadied, seeming to find a groove. From her hanging satchel, she drew out a small crystal container, its neck wrapped in a loop of rope. Pushing the satchel aside to view the top of the sack, she wrapped the vial's rope around her other hand, near the chisel, then let the loop expand and fall around the upper-most bump. The vial now hung a few inches below the bump. With the container thus positioned, she reached back to her belt for the hammer, raised it, and tapped twice the chisel's ebony handle.

The chisel sank deep.

The sack flexed violently, as if in pain, and Reynard tried to stand aside, but could not break free of the grip of the others. The violent swaying and shivering continued for long minutes, and Dana, steady despite the struggle, smoothed the bump with her hands, as if reassuring the casing's occupant. A brownish liquor flowed from around the chisel, and she filled the vial, capped, and withdrew it. She then backed off along the swaying branch to straddle the trunk and waited. The sack's contortions subsided into shivers, and it hung still.

"Fresh, it is brown," Nem said reverently. "In time, it becomes clear."

Dana crawled backwards along the trunk, joined the rest of her blunters, and held up the bottle, murmuring an oath that echoed their song. Then she slipped the vial into her satchel.

"For town and ally," she said. "This drake will not attack, and serveth humans now, if they drink or dab her liquor. Three remain on this isle, and maybe three on the other rocks. If we row quickly, there may yet be time."

"What of the sleeping high one?" MacClain asked.

"If she be merely a high one, and not Vanir!" Sondheim said.

"Not our concern, I hope," Dana said, looking at Manuel. "Stay close. I might use thee to bargain. And the boy, too."

Gareth had been surveying the beach below the ridge, and said they should get on with their work. "This be a longer day, for so the island moveth beneath the sun," he said. "Not long enough, maybe."

"What season?" Reynard asked as the group clambered across the ridge, grappling from tree to tree to the opposite headland.

"Small matter," MacClain said. "Time here is what it wants."

"But how do you know when to fish or farm?" Reynard asked.

Manuel touched his finger to his lips.

The next pair of nymphs had climbed up from the waves together, as if friends, though Dana assured Reynard that nymphs in the sea rarely did other than fight and try to eat each other. Still, these nymphs had capsuled and hung themselves from two thick limbs on a single red-bark tree. The headlands were thick with these quiet trees, and Dana hoped their final drake of this day — if the tattooed man had spoken truly — would hang from one on the last pillar-like island, the island too dangerous to risk earlier.

MacClain and Sondheim forgot their prior disagreements and blunted these two, then handed their vials to Dana.

"No more nymphs here," Gareth confirmed, after returning from a prickly saunter. "And none on th'other side. Sun's a-lowering."

"Did you see her?" Sondheim asked, with a catch in his voice.

"No!" Gareth said, and chuckled like a young raven.

Very strange, gloomy, difficult to absorb . . . And yet here Reynard was, leaping from the boat through the rough waters, tugging a rope to make it easier for Dana to transfer, for she was clearly exhausted.

Miguel and Reynard were told to climb out on the wave-splashed, boulder-strewn base of the final rock to wait. The lone nymph they had seen days before from the galleon had not yet split. MacClain and Gareth, clinging to the pillar high above Manuel, kept watch for swimming nymphs, for not all came up in one season, and not all came from the same batches of eggs at the same time — and of course, the same time could be different in this strange clime for every year, even every month!

It was Nem's turn for the last nymph. He climbed out on the tree and performed the blunting quickly, drawing and capping another vial of brown fluid before they all returned to the boat and launched through darkening waters.

Reynard had fallen into a deep gloom, but he rowed beside Manuel, whose strength was a match for the others. If they were favored by the Eaters, as Dana and Kaiholo seemed to share the opinion they were, then Manuel was the superior in favor, for unless Reynard was more naïve than he thought he was, and less observant, there had seemed to be some resentment by Kaiholo of Manuel, some feeling that one of the high ones — a powerful and very old one, perhaps equal to this Afrique, Calybo — had shared her time with the old man, as well as himself.

Had that been the one named Guldreth? A high one, just beneath the sky — could such a one be a Vanir, whatever they were?

The waves were more intense now, and the boat moved off from the sharp rocks. The sun burned somber orange above the far mists, and then descended, and twilight took hold of the last of their day.

An hour later, Dana ordered the boat back in, and they began the journey back to the coast. Dana's satchel was full. She seemed satisfied, but Manuel still had questions.

"How do ye know all nymphs are found?" Manuel asked. "Kaiholo saith there could be five or more."

Gareth scoffed. "Eaters often tell us in their visits."

"How? When they come and take their due?"

Gareth looked aside.

"It was not an Eater that told ye, but a man," Manuel reminded them.

"And was he wrong?" Dana asked. Her head lolled as if she were half asleep.

"And what happened to the first people who arrived, when they found the drakes?" Reynard asked. "How did you all learn —"

"Enough," Dana murmured.

Sondheim looked toward the distant sound of breakers on the beach. They did not see the galleon again; it had probably sunk, and with it, all hope Reynard had of building another boat to get away from the island. Unless he could purloin one of those currachs, or a boat like this one . . .

"Be not sad," Nem said with a youthful brightness Reynard could neither understand nor share. "Life is good here. Challenging, but good. And never boring!"

Reynard could make out the glowing of the waves on the beach, and the others pulled the oars with great, grunting strokes, as if the island might try to resist, to slough them off, unless they used their full effort.

Just before the boat's prow pushed up on sand and shingle, something out in the sea, between the islands, gave a tremendous groan, peaking in an awful shriek, as if a monster had been savaged and left to die.

Reynard cried out. The others leaped over the sides and dragged the boat with Reynard still on a thwart, too terrified to move. Gareth reached around his torso and pulled him out with a single burly arm, then planted him several steps up the beach.

Nem grinned. "Always alive, always a challenge!" the boy said, face flushed. "There are more things here than drakes and Eaters, newcomer," he said to Reynard. "Many more!"

The Scout's Tale

A_S EVENING FELL, Maggie carried her lantern under the covered walkway, ignoring the painted beams every twenty feet, as she always did. Still, scalp tingling, she glanced up and saw several with sailing ships, and two illustrating drakes and their offshore breeding rocks. One showed glistening shadows fighting with armored men.

Maggie picked up her pace.

The world outside their isle had been in obvious turmoil for over a thousand years, with pilgrims, refugees, sailors, and wanderers seeking new lands and the hope of new lives, as well as new histories. Zodiako had once been half its present size, with a quarter the population. In the last century, as measured so imperfectly here, many hundreds had arrived on the southwestern shore and found their way into Maggie's town, and not just fishermen but freebooters — some English, some Portuguese, a few Dutch. Earlier there had been Norse and Danish voyagers — her people — and earlier still, brown, sun-kissed folk from the far Pacific and Asia, who had soon built great canoes and fled to other islands in the ring of Tir Na Nog, islands more friendly to their needs.

But most of those visitors had arrived before Maggie's time, and according to those who knew and had lived here even then, the migrations had not been nearly so large and frequent. Now, apparently, hundreds of explorers, unsure of whether their motivation was discovery or wealth, were finding ways around the unmapped regions of the greater world, and arriving more and more often on their isle's shores by the dozens of vessels every year.

The Eaters disposed of most of them, and since these new arrivals were not protected, and were not explicitly part of Hel's pact, there was nothing the townspeople could do.

At the end of the covered walkway, the parliament building, made of shaped and cut lava, rose ten yards above a green quadrangle dotted with trees brought from other lands. Trees native to this isle were not much suited to servitude or town life, or any sort of domestication. While trees from the lively woods might not just walk away, as some thought, when early builders had tried to make use of them, before they were cut down, they often died of themselves and took on unpleasant forms, as if they had once been people — and who knew? A thousand years or more before, some of the townspeople might have become trees, and that could happen again, anytime . . . Who could judge? Crafters could imagine anything.

Stepping up to a side entrance, a thick oaken gate mounted in the stone wall, she took a steel key out of the satchel. She inserted it into a great black lock and opened the gate to a hall that ended on steps that led up to the nave of the temple and another locked door that went left to her room in a far basement corner, where drakish matters were discussed. Her chief scout, Anutha, gone for days now, had her own key and had entered a short time earlier — no doubt after rounds at the smallest of the town's three taverns. Maggie could hear her singing in rugged sweet tones, words she did not quite understand, perhaps in Shelta or Zigrany, languages she knew Anutha was familiar with from her contacts with Travelers.

She opened the door and swung it wide. Anutha sat on a bench behind Maggie's hewn desk. The scout was thin, in her middle years, but very strong and fit, with short-cut gray hair. Her regular garb was a jerkin and pants of black and brown leather, with shiny gray nymph-shell greaves. She looked up as the door opened, eyes both bleary and weary.

"Good life, Anutha," Maggie greeted.

"Back to you, doubled," the scout said.

"What report?" Even three paces away, Maggie could smell the mead on the scout's breath, like a beehive souring in the rain. Now was not the best time to hand her Kule's jug. She needed a coherent report. Maggie knew this rugged, dedicated woman had the best eyes of any, but she always looked tired, as if the world's sights had long since worn down her enthusiasm.

"You have brought something for me, no? Or am I too drunk already? Give it here . . . please."

Maggie reluctantly opened her bag and handed her Kule's jug. Anutha popped the cork, and took a long swig, followed by a shrug and a grimace. She let her chin drop, belched, and raised a hand. "Sorry."

Maggie pulled up another bench and sat across from her. "Visitors?"

Anutha nodded. "Dangerously many, and well armed, but they have already attracted Hel's defenses."

"Eaters?"

"Both from the Ravine and the wastes south of Agni Most Foul. Not the most prosperous nor honest clan, but not servants to the Ostmen, either."

The Ostmen was an old name for those who now followed the Sister Queens on the far eastern shore.

"The Ravine dwellers passed through town late last night," Maggie said. "They stabled their horses here. Some had recently been to the wastes. A young boy was injured."

"I noticed folks were nervous," Anutha said, and belched again. "Or guilty. Why were Eaters visiting the wastes? Perhaps they were actually going to the Crafter cities. I wonder what business would call them there?"

Maggie shook her head. "What drew them to the beach?" she asked.

"Spaniards in a ship of war, a big one, badly mauled. Some sort of great sea battle, and recent, too."

"Sailors?"

"And soldiers. They seemed to have been long at sea before being caught in the gyre. Smelled shitty, tired, many wounded but still full of fight. Two leaders with cruel bearing — ambitious. One a highborn son of privilege, th'other a fat seagoer used to running ships."

"A general of war and an admiral," Maggie said.

Anutha took another pull from the jug and looked at her with heavy-lidded eyes. "Also an old man and a half-grown English boy. They are with your blunters. No sign they have finished their work on the drakes, I am afraid."

"Then wild drakes might make an appearance soon."

Anutha raised the bottle and took another swallow.

"How many paired defenders have we on watch?" Maggie asked.

"Seven for the town. Among the blunters, only two have met their drakes."

Maggie clapped her hand on her knee. "The Crafters' plan spins on. I have heard that in the southern waters, a virgin island queen fights a southern king — her brother-in-law, if rumors lead to truth." This Maggie had heard from an English sailor five years ago. That sailor had not followed town's ritual, had refused the town's hospitality, had tried to build a boat — and had been adopted by an unpacted Eater. The sailor had faded over a few days, losing all his time; nothing she could do against such foolish will. But he had wanted to get home. And now he was in that windowless house where all that are human will dwell soon enough.

"You have sources beyond the island," Anutha said, after another ripe belch. "Why do you need me?"

"Sailors arrive with tales. Some survive, for a time," Maggie said. "But you are more dependable. Usually."

The scout looked woozily around the small room. "They should all just get married and make babies. Stories end happier that way."

"It would seem Elizabeth, a virgin queen, is unsuited to making babies," Maggie said. "Besides, her half sister married the southern king. No babies, and it did not end well."

"As we have heard," Anutha said. "Until I saw an opening, I kept to the lively woods, away from the Spanish."

"And the Eaters?"

"The ones from the Ravine arrived the first night, right after a wild drake snatched up a dog."

Maggie closed her eyes.

"Those from the Ravine gathered quite a few years, I think. But some on the beach were protected. An Eater wench of only a few centuries approached the young boy. Upon Calybo's orders, she seemed to study and claim him." Anutha looked hard at Maggie. "Calybo was there. He favored the old man."

"You recognized the old man?"

Anutha nodded. "I say, that first night, he could have been a faded, wizened copy of Widsith."

Maggie's interest rose. Calybo was rarely seen along these shores, but had always attended to Widsith when the Pilgrim returned . . .

"That interests you," Anutha said.

Maggie did not answer, but her face betrayed her.

Anutha leaned back and lifted Kule's jug. "If it is Widsith . . . Hath he betrayed the island? Was it he guided the Spanish to the gyre?"

"Did he seem favored by the general or the master?"

"No. He was kept in a cage, along with the boy. Dana and the blunters were clapped in another cage. Shall we tell Maeve?"

Soon they would have to bring the old man and the boy to Maeve for confirmation. And if the Pilgrim had returned, he would very likely find favor from Calybo and Guldreth, and the Travelers would carry his reports to the Crafters. What was the boy to him? To anybody on the island? Maggie tried to puzzle out all the implications. "Not until we are certain."

"Am I to go out there again?"

"Of course," Maggie said.

"To fetch the blunters."

"To help them break free. Wild drakes will be a danger until they are all back at their labors."

Anutha lifted her short sword, a Roman sword, she proudly claimed. The scout's eyes glittered. "May I kill Spaniards, with town's blessing?" Anutha's mother and father had been Jews, persecuted by a Spanish queen, how long ago, Maggie was not sure — time not running the same outside the island. But many decades. "Long have they hated such as I. I would do it with pleasure."

Maggie crossed herself. It was said the Crafters could not see you for minutes after you paid homage to the Lord. Whether she believed that or not, she did not want to be seen allowing or commanding murder. "Kill only in defense," she instructed. "And raise no alarms. We are still vulnerable."

"War's coming soon whatever we do," Anutha said. "I am sure the Sister Queens will find use for men of cruel bearing, if the Spanish survive the Eaters — and if they are allowed to move east."

"Who can predict the unwinding of Crafter tales?" In all her years, Maggie had never clearly anticipated when Crafters might feel the need to unleash strife and violence, but it was said that several of the most powerful paid particular attention to murder and war. It brought out their coldness and fury in a way all in Zodiako might

soon feel. The Sister Queens' long war in the east against King Annwyn, and his defeat, now putting their conquests at a pause, was
rich with story and incident, it being the amusement of both Queens
and Crafters to complicate island lives with violence and change.

"Well, it is certain that the Travelers have been uneasy," Anutha
said. "Many trods wither and fade. And year after year, less word
from the Crafter cities."

The Sister Queens held sway over regions that lay a thousand
miles from Zodiako, if one followed the coast — the only way a sane
human would go, unless they were guided by Travelers. Travelers
on any of the islands that made up the polar ring of Tir Na Nog
could draw their own roads, straight or devious, using the talents
and permissions bestowed on them by the Crafters in payment for
their words and songlines.

Anutha was right. They both could feel it. A simple life was a
sweet life. Life in Zodiako had been sweet, she surmised, for far too
long. Or something else was happening. That tingling in her scalp,
while she was passing under the painted beams . . .

Maggie, with failing legs, a dead husband, and three foolish children, dreaded such prospects — but looked forward to tales of the
outer world, perhaps to new books. She longed to fill her life with
books! Only four had come her way in the last ten seasons.

So perhaps she wished for the same things.

Anutha handed back the jug and rose awkwardly from the chair.
"No time for rest," she said.

"Never again," Maggie said under her breath as the scout departed, with a slight weave in her step. Maggie knew she would be
sober by the edge of the village. She closed the door, then, at the
sounds of shouting, swung it wide. Making her way outside the great
stone building, she watched men and women running, and stopped a
young man with a scythe to ask why.

"Men with swords!" he cried. "Swords and guns!"

The Siege

✺

Wisps of orange-lit gray smoke drifted through the woods as the returning blunters and their two charges climbed a bluff above the beach. Smelling smoke, hearing distant shouting and the echoes of musket fire and explosions, they ran quickly along the winding path to Zodiako. All around them, the trees whipped in their own breeze, branches rubbing and leaves whispering distress.

"God grant we are not too late!" Dana cried as they leaped over a low stone fence and ran past an outlying barn.

Reynard's first view of the town was against an arras of smoke, backlit and confused by silhouettes of people running, screaming, shadows flash-projected by the sparking orange of guns.

The blunters stepped over the newly dead. Some wore armor — most did not.

Reynard had never seen a village attacked and set ablaze. He joined Manuel as the blunters paused in the town's arched gate, and then entered a narrow lane between low, stone-walled houses. Flaming thatch already filled the night with a sickening stench. Within these outer dwellings, they came upon wavering lines and broken squares of Spaniards, confused, pale, and stricken, like ghosts out of Hell, so gaunt and weary they were, but cursing steadily and flailing swords, half-pikes, and knives. Muskets and harquebuses had already been fired and were not yet reloaded.

Twenty or more Spaniards fought at another, higher palisade with townsfolk young and old, men and women, who harried them with pitchforks and scythes, taking heavy casualties but driving the invaders into a fenced meadow streaked white and gray with running, bleating sheep, butting and upending some of the warriors in their panic. Other Spaniards had battered down a gate through the palisade and fought their way into the town's main square. The blunters followed groups of villagers and managed to get through as well.

Inside, five of the town's paired defenders, three men and two women, backed up against the side of the temple and stood their ground, raising wooden shields and even heavy gates and doors against slashing half-pikes, then flung aside their protections and simultaneously put fingers to lips and whistled, sounds rising and swirling like banshee wails. Dana, MacClain, Gareth, and Sondheim joined them and whistled as well.

Shaking his head and wearing a sick grin of fear and envy, Nem stayed close to Widsith and Reynard.

Below the hall's low hill, more Spaniards carried torches from house to house, setting fire to everything that would burn. What little Reynard could see revealed that the warriors were nearly all old men, weakened by the Eaters, out of their element and terrified. They were still clad in heavy armor, which glinted and gleamed in the firelight but seemed to drag them down as they tried to find military order. Some were prickly with arrows or lay on the dirt and grass, dazed and moaning.

A dozen villagers straddled high rock walls or ran up the roofs of low barns and used these vantages to loose more arrows into the invaders, with devastating effect. Others were flinging spears or throwing knives, which mostly rang off the helms and cuirasses. Wisely, many of the villagers were trying to avoid close engagement, but some, more than he could count — literally, since they were moving so fast between firelight and shadow — had rushed in with long knives and a few ancient swords, getting too close for Spanish half-pikes to be effective and bowling over the soldiers, kicking away their torches. Reynard knew little about war or tactics, but he could see that these bolder men and women were sacrificing themselves to deplete Cardoza's troops before they burned and ransacked the entire town. How many Spanish were so engaged? He estimated sixty or seventy, about half the soldiers from the galleon. And how many defenders? No more than thirty across this side of the town. But they were bringing down more and more of the Spanish, and that made the soldiers weep and scream with frustration and fury — finally giving them enough resolve and energy to remember some sort of discipline, re-form their lines, and make feints against two ragged groups of defenders.

The Spanish pushed six youths back and around other buildings, chasing them between the small, dense-packed houses, catch-as-catch-can — stupidly, it turned out, for the youths were leading them into tight corners and ambuscades, as more townsfolk gathered their rude weapons and ganged up, four against one or two, then breaking and fleeing as the soldiers formed tighter squares, only to come around from behind as well as in front, thrusting into these wandering knots of Spaniards with pitchforks and sticks and whatever else they had at hand.

Reynard lost track of Manuel, then saw him hefting a pitchfork and moving on two soldiers, thrusting the sharp wood tines into one, then swinging him around with real strength into the other, tumbling them both into a wall of flaming straw on a rack, which set their own inner clothing on fire and drove them into burning, shrieking flight.

Two more Spaniards focused on the old sailor. One raised a scim-itar and swiped at Manuel's fork. The second maneuvered behind with a long knife in each hand.

"Here!" Gareth handed Reynard a scythe. He took it, still unsure whether he could kill, but swung it at the closest of Manuel's attack-ers, distracting him as a gray-haired woman in leather ran in with a wooden shield and bowled the man over. Manuel then made quick work with his fork, and together, the gray-haired woman, Manuel, and Reynard focused on four soldiers trying to make a space for two of their comrades to reload harquebuses. One succeeded, and waved his companions aside to aim. A thunderous roar and flame spouted from the mouth of the gun, taking down a stout young woman and whirling an older man, leaving his head a ruin. Without thought or plan, Reynard's choler peaked, as his uncle had once said happened in battle, and he jumped in, raised his scythe, and swung like a reaper with all the strength of a fisherboy casting nets and arranging tackle, or a smith swinging hammers and bending steel. The long curved blade dug deep into the Spaniard's arm and knocked the gun from his hands. But then Reynard had difficulty pulling the blade free, and a tall old Spaniard in armor lurched in, an arrow in one leg, but still wielding a great sword — only to have Manuel spring from shadow and push his pitchfork up under the man's helm, then whirl him around and into that same wall of burning straw. Manuel re-leased the pitchfork, not to get burned himself. Immediately, two more soldiers set upon them, wildly swinging muskets.

Shadows overhead! The air filled with a buzzing roar. A great black drake, the largest Reynard had yet seen, dropped from the sky and thrummed over one of the invaders, bit off his head, and tossed it across the lane, where it bowled through the door of another house. That done, the drake hopped onto an attacker madly swing-ing a long knife, having flung aside his musket. This Spaniard swung himself off balance and staggered, too worn to make any sound

but a rough, husking grunt. The drake shook out its wings and ap-
praised him, as if looking over a puzzle, then rotated its wide, glittering head, pinched the man's waist in its mandibles, and bit through.
The drake's rear arms pivoted forward to seize the pieces and, still
clutching them on both sides of its thick body, the wings beat briskly,
and it rose and carried the halves out of the village.

Reynard found himself flat on his back, coughing at the enveloping smoke, his vision narrowed to foggy circles. Manuel was obscured or missing. Dana and Sondheim lifted him, and they all
stood in another narrow alley between broken rows of houses. He
slumped and leaned against a wall, unable to lift his scythe, shook his
head, and rubbed his eyes.

Dana whistled, and another drake swooped over the town's tree
line, fanning the flames of a thatched roof, then, lifting and landing, hopped and grabbed a lone Spaniard trying to flee. The beast
flew this poor old Spaniard high into the air, then dropped him
onto another burning roof, where he crashed through to the floor
beneath.

Reynard closed his eyes and covered his face with an arm, wondering if the drakes would mistake him for an enemy. This new concern, mixed with the horror of the battle, was both paralyzing and
intoxicating, somehow very different from the terror of the galleons
at Gravelines, yet necessary and even sensible — between the har-
rying drakes and more village defenders with and without weapons, men and women and several youngsters, Nem among them, his
face pinked with heat and anger, plunging a pitchfork over and over
again, making sure the fallen Spanish were dead, if on the ground,
and if alive, poking and herding them into the meadow for more
drakes to take their pick — at least six drakes now busy on that hunt.
At long last, the Spaniards, already depleted by Eaters, were meeting their match, their betters, and facing unexpected weapons —
monsters beyond their understanding.

And then . . .

It was over. The cries of the combatants subsided and were covered by the crackle of flames, billows of choking smoke, and then — wailing grief. Manuel tied a kerchief around a red-dripping slash on his arm, his eyes distant and sad.

Villagers by the hundreds came from other parts of the town and formed lines, passing water in buckets from several wells and a stream, working with scant success to douse the fires.

"Where is Cardoza?" Manuel asked. "We must save a few. We must learn their plans!"

The moonless night was dark and deep and long.

The fires dying down or extinguished, grim-faced villagers led teams of horses and wagons and began to load and carry Spanish dead to a meadow just outside the town, where they left them unburied for now. The village dead were covered with blankets and sheets and, when those ran out, with cloaks and capes and coats, before they were taken to the temple, which looked to Reynard like an English church, with a steeple.

Manuel had returned from looking at as many of the Spanish corpses as he could, as many as he could find. "He is not here," the old sailor said.

"There are fifty or more gone and as many hurt bad," Dana told Sondheim and Gareth.

"We saw Maggie and Anutha. They are still alive."

"I know. But we lost three blunters. And there is a drake out on the meadow, badly wounded. Likely will die."

"Whose?" Nem asked.

"Asquith's, I think."

"Asquith's among the dead," Sondheim said.

Dana called forward Gareth and Nem and asked them to take

Reynard to a place where he could get food and drink, and sleep for the rest of the night.

"The houses are in bad shape here, folks are being sent to other homes, and many of the barns have burned," Gareth said, flexing his broad shoulders and sharing the exhausted Reynard's weight with Nem.

"There is a sheepfold out on South Road, near the stables. The old shepherd's place. Take him there. It is beyond this mayhem, and will serve until morning."

Dana and the blunters, led by Anutha, were met by a candlelit procession of ten men and boys and four women, in deep twilight at the edge of the destruction. This procession was guided by the older, gray-haired woman who, Reynard now saw, bore a resemblance to Dana, perhaps mother to daughter. He wondered if this was Maggie.

In the middle of the grieving and preparations for funerals, news of their success with the nymphs on this part of the coast was met with the gray-haired woman's sad approval, as if they had done all that could be expected — and perhaps all that was necessary.

The paired defenders were brought forward and treated with respect, but no congratulations, and the whereabouts of their drakes were inquired after, but few knew much. Drakes that had killed and likely fed on humans were not responsive for days, Nem told Reynard in hushed tones. "And they did eat, I saw them!" he added.

"How many more Spanish still out there?" Maggie asked Manuel.

"Maybe fifty," Manuel said. "Dependeth on how many died in the forest."

"We stabled Eater horses the last three nights," Maggie said. "Let us hope the Spanish have had enough."

Manuel and Reynard were now studied without being touched or questioned. Nem spoke to the other youngsters, some also injured and bandaged, in a language Reynard could not understand — not the Basque that Manuel had used, that he had heard from other fishermen, nor the Tinker's Cant of his grandmother, but something else mellifluously round and complicated.

The assembly split in three, and Nem, Gareth, Manuel, Maggie, and Dana continued on, Manuel a few steps to one side. Reynard wobbled along between Gareth and Nem, barely able to keep his feet under him as they took him to the edge of a tree-ringed clearing, between several magnificent, spreading oaks, onto a trail covered with ancient cut stones and bordered by woven fences made, Reynard thought, of willow or perhaps hawthorn. The candles provided little light, and the group seemed to want to keep them at least partly ignorant.

Dana and Maggie were conversing in quiet tones.

Manuel murmured to Reynard, "They talk about me. And about thee."

"Will they kill us?"

Manuel made a face. "Not likely," he said "We have fought beside them, and we have both been touched and recognized."

"By Eaters?"

"By Travelers. Those who connect," Manuel said.

"I do not remember them," Reynard said.

"They will be more obvious, in time," Manuel said.

"Who are these from the town?"

"The older woman is Maggie," he confirmed. "She is in charge of the blunters who work this coast. She reporteth to Maeve. Both rely on Anutha."

"Quiet," Gareth warned.

They passed these lanes and continued on in a tight group, lit by shaded lanterns. After a walk of a mile or more, they saw candle-lit windows in the distance and came upon a wide, cleared common, with another sheep-dotted meadow behind split-rail fences, and more people emerging from rounded stone houses with smoking chimneys, men and women and a few children commenting in several tongues about the fight, as they had heard it from this side of town, and of the return of the lost blunters, and how many more could now be placed on the rolls of paired defenders. They seemed more interested in those facts than in the facts of the battle.

Reynard flinched as a black shadow passed over the woods. Three children leaped the enclosures and began to push and whistle the sheep into low stone mangers along the fence lines.

"They eat sheep? The drakes?" Reynard asked. Nem scowled as if this was a stupid question.

The first light of morning turned the bottoms of the clouds a fiery pink. Smoke still tainted the air. Reynard was led by Nem and Gareth to a stone barn with a wooden shed projecting from one side. They half carried him to a cot near a line of narrow stalls and laid him down on a rough blanket, where he rolled over and closed his eyes, but could not stop his tumbling thoughts.

Maggie took Manuel to the farthest stall. Reynard pretended to be asleep, but listened to their quiet converse. "I presume thou wilt stay nearby?" Maggie asked Manuel.

"Of course."

"May we call you Widsith, the Pilgrim, once more?"

"It is been too long since I heard that name."

"How long gone this time, and where to?" Maggie asked.

"Thou wert a beautiful young girl."

"How long?"

"In the years I felt, maybe forty. Long enough to visit China and live by their ways. They are ruled by Mongols now, the same who oft rise out of the grass like hornets and plague the west."

"Crafters too clever by half," Maggie said doubtfully.

"Methinks the world groweth now by itself," Manuel — *Widsith*

— said. Which name would Reynard call him? Were any of those names privileged and private?

Maggie asked, "Didst thou marry?"

They had moved almost out of Reynard's hearing. His body ached all over. He could barely turn his head.

"I married for a time," Widsith said, "there, and later, once in the Philippines, islands named after a king of mixed abilities at best."

"Thou didst vow to return to Maeve," Maggie said.

"And I have."

"She is very old."

"I did not mean to be away so long."

"Dost still love her?"

"Of course," Widsith said.

"Even whilst thou wert here, I remember thou wast not faithful."

"My time with Maeve was all I wanted. I did not volunteer — the town volunteered me! Can I see Maeve now?"

"She hath ruled from seclusion the last few years. She wanteth not, of all men, that thou shouldst see her so old."

"Her age meaneth little to me."

"And thou wouldst make her young again? How?"

"I will persuade."

"Maeve doth treasure the time she was given, and is stubborn she needeth no more."

"That is not her decision!" Widsith insisted.

"Did Calybo fill thine own cask of years?"

"He did. It is my due."

"So thou couldst leave at any moment, spend yet another forty years beyond the island, and abandon Maeve, leave her alone yet again all that time!"

"I shall stay a while. A long while."

Maggie huffed. "Thou dost believe that, in truth? Once thou hast done delivering thy tales, thou wilt not flee on another long voyage?"

"Who tendeth thine allotment, Maggie?"

"None beyond the pacted years. Sad, is it not? I will never leave, and so never see the finished lands."

"Wouldst thou like that?"

"No," Maggie said. "Despite all, I am a widow, but I am happy here."

"Was he a good man?"

"The best."

"Wilt thou marry again?"

"None I have met. Hath the boy you brought here, at such cost, greater value than our town?"

"Certes he is a mystery I would love to solve." Widsith spoke now in a low, soft tone, barely audible from Reynard's position. "Hast thou wondered what it would be like to meet the Crafters in person, have they persons — to submit this boy like a proper writ?"

Listening to the distant converse, Reynard shivered, but knew not what he could do, nor where he could flee. In the morning, he would explore and try to find out.

"No," Maggie said. "I am dubious thou hast so much courage thyself."

"I have seen many strange lands, the results of much Crafter plotting. I might summon courage, to answer questions I have long held."

"Most likely thou'lt hand this boy to the Travelers, to carry bundled and helpless to the cities around the waste. And then thou shalt leave, renewed of years, to gather more evidence of Crafter plots. And for that, for a ready ship, maybe thou'lt again seek out the Spanish and offer thy services!"

"They are done with me. Anutha did inform thee I was caged with the boy?"

"She did."

"Comb I favor from Cardoza like sparks from a cat's fur?"

"No," she admitted.

"And Maeve?"

"I am sure she is already asleep. We all need sleep. Go take thine own rest. I must play captain to the sentries."

And that was the last Reynard heard before ache and sleep overwhelmed him.

Of Childers and Bone-wives

Reynard felt something nuzzle his bare foot and opened his eyes. He had slept soundly, the sleep of fear and pain giving way to healing, as if, all else aside, his simply being on this island soothed him like a balm.

Again, Reynard's foot was nuzzled. He looked down the length of the cot and saw, in a ray of sunshine falling through a narrow crack in the roof of the fold, the familiar, silly face of a goat, rolling and sliding its lower jaw back and forth, chewing cud.

He had slept through the day and into the next. He looked around for Manuel, but the old man — he would have to stop thinking of him that way! — was nowhere to be seen. Doubtless the Pilgrim had wandered off to attend to other business — perhaps this Maeve, his wife. Or to arrange to trade Reynard for Traveler favors.

But this morning, Reynard was anything but afraid. He rose and discovered that his body had a kind of liquid vibrancy, as if it liked being here, liked waking — despite his fears. But he was thirsty and very hungry. And then he spotted, in one corner of the stall, a small table supplied with a loaf of bread and a pewter flagon. He sniffed the flagon: mead, sweet and pale. He sipped, then took a bite of bread, hearty and dense. In a few minutes, the small breakfast was gone and he was not so very hungry. The goat remained, watching him and chewing philosophically.

But the goat was not alone.

Something moved up into the light beside the goat and stared at Reynard. It was a child, naked ... but small, little more than knee-high, all its limbs proportioned to that size, appearing perhaps five or six years of age, with scrubby brown hair and black eyes ... neither a boy nor a girl. Just too small.

The goat turned its head, poked at the child with some irritation, and the child vanished.

But there were others in the manger. They walked, moved, flitted like moths — four, five, six. He stopped counting. One paused nearby, held up a hand, and smiled.

"Greetings," Reynard said. The child danced around him, still smiling, and then popped like a bubble. A tiny musical note followed, and the goat bleated, then moved away into the shadows — bored.

Strangeness everywhere, Reynard decided, and looked around. Beside the table he found an iron chest, opened to reveal worn leather shoes and patched clothes folded neatly. He stripped down, then knocked out the shoes and shook the breeches and shirt and vest. His uncle had taught him that on faraway isles, one had to be careful about creatures dwelling in clothes and footwear. Would the spirit children hide there as well?

He tried the new garments and the shoes. The shoes had holes in their toes, through which his own toes poked, but the breeches and shirt fit reasonably well. The vest was too tight and so he left it off. He then put into the chest the garments that had presumably belonged to a now-dead blunter. Waste not, want not.

A few minutes later, he pushed through the wicker gate of the fold and emerged in watery sunlight. The fold was a few dozen yards from an intact manor house with stone walls and a slate roof. Apparently the fight had not reached this far. Both house and the fold were surrounded by tall trees, all rustling naturally enough in a light breeze. Above the trees the sky was still hazy with smoke, but the sun shone through warmly, and he felt encouraged that he had been left so long to sleep and recover from another awful night.

"Fine morn for childers," spoke a gravelly voice behind him. He spun around and saw a bald, elderly man with a long, brown-stained beard, sitting on a milking stool beside the gate. "They seem to like thee."

Coming out, Reynard had not noticed this figure, but now the man surveyed him from a hunched angle, holding a long, flute-like reed with a bowl at one end, from which unwound a steady curl of thin white smoke. Reynard knew of tobacco; it was smoked often by sailors and, he heard, Raleigh and the Queen's folk, but never among fisherfolk in Southwold. His uncle had shunned it because of the example of Hawkins, whom he had hated with a dark passion.

"Children?" Reynard asked, feeling a moment of such strangeness that his fingers prickled and neck hair stood on end.

"*Childers!*" the man with the smoking flute almost shouted. "Little ones, come and go — fine weather for 'em around thee, lad."

"Are they fey — are they fairies?" Reynard asked.

The man drew with a hiss on his reed. "They come, they go. They harm no one."

"What are they, then?"

"Childers. Get used to them." He pointed the reed's bowl around the corner of the manor, away from the fold. "Thou art free to go where thou pleasest — but perhaps not the town for a while. The townsfolk think the Spaniards were led to the island. They might blame Widsith, or thee, but Dana and Maggie work to calm them, and testify thou art no danger and fought hard for Zodiako." Another long, sucking draw and smoke expelled from mouth and nostrils. "There be no more breakfast here, 'less thou be'st a goat or a sheep."

Reynard's discomfort had grown to a peak. "I have eaten and thank you. What know you about the old Spaniard?"

"I am *old*, lad. Widsith is no Spaniard, and hath not that luxury in which I wallow — to grow *old*." He waved his smoking flute. "Widsith hath said I should send thee on his trail. But I saith back, thou art free. Git. Whither thou goest, no matter to me. Thou art a chain, boy, and I am the anchor. Cut loose." He fluttered one hand and drew on the tobacco again with the other. The smoke that filled the air was at once sweet and acrid.

"Which way?"

Reynard wondered if he should simply avoid Widsith and find his way to the beach. But his inner pleasure was strangely compelling, and gave him courage despite the words he had heard two nights before.

He wanted to explore but not to flee.

The elderly man shrugged, then consented to point along a path through the margin of trees. Reynard started to walk, and then to run, away from the fold and the manor house, his shoes making soft scraping sounds along a well-trodden path rutted by wagon wheels and dotted profusely with evidence of sheep, horses, and kine.

Very familiar. Just shite, some fresh.

After a while, deep in leafy shadow, he stopped to catch his breath. The holed toes of his borrowed shoes provided little protection against roots and stones. He removed them and stuffed in thick leaves and grass. Then, for a few long moments, he sat under a white-flowering tree, taking stock. He had made a kind of pact, a strange sort of friendship, with a man who changed his age as he changed his name. He had seen many things in the last few days: sea monsters and at least one tattooed islander or freebooter. And of course, he had seen vampires who dealt in time, years taken or given ... And beyond that, perhaps most formidable and frightening of all, drakes that killed at the behest of those who drank their birth liquor. He had just seen as well the strange, airy souls of lost children, perhaps waiting to be born. He neither needed nor wanted any more marvels. He had to find his way to a place that was not wrapped in dream, or nightmare, or perhaps the gloom that comes after death. Should he continue along this path or strike out?

"Surely I am not the greatest mystery here," he murmured. "And not so valuable as a town!"

Perhaps not even worth his food and shelter. And as for food ...

His earlier sense of balm and health was seeming illusory, the more he considered. He wondered about his meager breakfast. Could he eat in this land without partaking of something unholy? Was there food to be found on this island that would not threaten his very soul?

Thou art wiser than that, lad. Thou pray'st the prayers of others. Find thine own strength, and thine own way.

Reynard turned to see whoever had spoken, fearing it might be the dark man with the white shadow, but the words, the strong and stern advice, came from inside his head. Still, he thought the voice sounded familiar — raspy, smoky, deep and deeply female, like his grandmother. Did the dead come here to haunt ... perhaps to become child-ghosts and be reborn in the east, where, he had heard, such things were believed?

He looked down, closed his eyes, wished for a sign. Nothing. And so he looked up. The high branches obscured most of that twisted sky, but daylight still filtered down, as if through a stamped pane of window glass. That light said, however soon he might face doom, for the moment there would be warmth, familiar trees, solid ground beneath his worn shoes.

Ahead, he heard high laughter and female voices. Were they

women, humans from local farms — or the Eaters he had seen on the beach? He hid behind thick brush and listened. Several, perhaps four, were walking lightly and quickly along the path he had just abandoned. He pushed aside a branch and saw the first of them, dressed in long, filmy robes, her shoulders draped with a dark leather jerkin. Over the jerkin, swirling waves of brown hair fell to her waist — and then came into his sight three others, similar in appearance, like sisters. One had reddish hair, two brown, and one black. They were speaking a kind of ancient English, mixed with something that could have been Icelandic. Old, accented oddly, some words half familiar . . . but definitely neither Spanish nor Dutch.

And then, he thought, *Greek.*

The four paused just yards away on the pathway and turned slowly, like weathervanes, until they faced where he was hiding.

"What is this?" one of the brown-haired women asked.

"Widsith!" the black-haired woman exclaimed, and laughed. "He speaketh o' a new boy who hideth thoughts and memories — a poor and pure son o' the sea. This is his lad!"

"Come out, English boy. We mean no harm. We are gentlefolk thou shouldst ken."

Reynard stepped from behind the bushes. The ladies — for clearly they were used to a kind of deference, looking at him, addressing him as if he were a wayward hunting dog — surrounded him and stroked his hair, his face, his clothes, intent, until they drew breath and sighed as one.

"Not ours to ply," the first brown-haired woman said, and asked her companions, "Do we fetch him back?"

Another, with locks longer and hair darker brown and straight, falling like a third garment almost to her calves, said, "Knowing his blood, he'll find a way."

They all sighed again, like a soft breeze in the woods, then continued forward on the path, away from the town, speaking to each other with sharply sibilant words that seemed to penetrate his ears, like the flash of bird wings fleeing a snake — and yet, words he almost knew, had once heard spoken, but had never bothered to memorize. Words of travel, questions buried in each — questions he could not answer!

"I do not belong here!" he cried out, tears coming to his eyes.

The black-haired woman suddenly stood before him. He had not seen her move! "Why hast thou no memory of place and line? Here, on this blessed isle, no memory for a boy maketh him like a knight without armor. Remember, or another will find and use thee — less gentle than we who are conjured by the King of Troy."

They each touched three fingers to their rosy lips and laughed again. "Or not. Is Widsith young and favored once more?"

"Such fickle charms!"

"Follow us, then," the last lady said, smiling over her shoulder. "Our time is short, our candles dim, and we *are* going."

And so he followed. The way through this wide, shadowy glade seemed to wind back past trees he had already seen, and yet the women, in a loose grouping, laughing and singing alternately, waving their hands as if in pure enjoyment, seemed always to be walking straight ahead, always away from the village, the town —

But here was the bush he had hidden behind when the women first passed — he remembered the broken branches from his emergence and saw an impression of his foot.

It was on the fourth loop of this game that he saw the four women walking through a wedge of sunlight. The sun, angling under the clouds, was late and golden, almost orange, and as Reynard struggled to keep up, he realized that the slanting light passed *through* the women, as if they were made of gauzy silk. Their clothes, their hair, and a kind of stick outline of their bodies shadowed within.

He stopped and bit his lip —

And from the corner of his glance saw Manuel, Widsith, perched on a rock beside the path, whittling a stick with a small knife. The formerly old man smiled in sympathy. He looked thirty, at most forty years of age. He still had a bandage on his arm, but he moved the arm freely, and it appeared strong.

Reynard squatted before him, elbows on his knees and chin in his hands, and studied the man's clothes, his demeanor.

"Now dost thou learn," Widsith said, highly amused.

"Learn what?" Reynard asked.

"Not to follow the toys of the King of Troy."

"And who might he be? A true king?"

"No king, 'struth," Widsith said. "An old mage, powers weakened by time and foolishness. Still, he hath a certain skill."

"He maketh women to walk in the woods?"

"A favorite subject, I think. They last the length of a candle, and then fade to the sticks and old bones he keepeth in piles near his hut. He deviseth clever names for his illusions. These he calleth bone-wives."

"How long doth the candle last?" Reynard asked, surprised by his calm.

"A few hours, no more than a day," Widsith said. "The King of Troy is benign, mostly — and so some in Zodiako, used to wandering magicians and childers, and sometimes hallows, like to think they tolerate his toys, even ask him to provide entertainment for village parties — though he can be unpredictable. Oft his hallows look saintly, but approach too close — and they bite! But now thou'rt here, and all on thine own instinct, while the town maketh grieving and mending, let us visit the old mountebank." His look was at once crafty and guilty, and Reynard dug deep to find any trust. Yet Widsith had yet to do him wrong, and had shown courage throughout, whatever his deal with the island might be.

Reynard got to his feet. "Why go to this king who is no king?"

"I want his judgment o' thee, to confirm or deny mine own. Other than that, he can inform us of where we need to go."

"He is human?" Reynard asked.

"He may not know anymore."

"And *you* are human?"

"Aye, as I have told thee already," Widsith said. "By the grace of history, and the will of this island, I am still human. Ready?"

Reynard allowed he was still more hungry than ready to go witness illusions. "I have eaten, but not enough!"

"On occasions, Troy feedeth his visitors, though the hunger is assuaged only for the length of a candle — like his bone-wives. But our visit will not take long, methinks. And we must return to Zodiako soon."

The King of Troy

THE WOODS east of Zodiako seemed ancient and mostly undisturbed, unlike the forests in England, so often cleared to make ships or charcoal. These were not lively woods, Widsith pointed out — those tended to hug the shore, like prickly thorns, to protect the island. "Not that they are all that effective," he said. "They mostly display a stubborn individuality, not a communal defense."

Here, many of the trees were overarching wonders, bigger than any oaks Reynard had seen, rising to the mist-filtered sun, as if it were their proud duty to push through the canopy and cast all else in dappled shade. The lower decks of shorter, broader trees — Reynard guessed they were related to walnut — sometimes spread out like thick-rooted spiders through the litter and blankets of leaves, roots crisscrossing and humping the trail so that no wagon, and not many horses, could pass.

Widsith picked carefully along the half-obscured and winding path, stepping or climbing up and over the greater roots, making little bird whistles or muttering some or other incomprehensible name, as if he recognized some of the trees and was wary of them. Reynard saw deer, or something like deer, three or four of them, peering through a far veil of branches, unafraid. Suddenly they disappeared — and just as they did so, seemed to become people — small, lithe people. Were these the *hreindyr* Dana and her blunters had tried to warn the Spaniards about? Perhaps they were just ordinary English fallow deer, their shadows playing tricks. They did not make themselves obvious, whatever their breed.

The Pilgrim observed that the island's day was showing signs of being short. The glade was already slipping into murky shadow, which Reynard did not much like, however benign the King of Troy might be.

"His toys deceive," he said as he followed Widsith, nearly tumbling over a big root. He recovered and observed, "They speak riddles and nonsense."

Widsith looked back and smiled. He was definitely getting younger — only a few gaps remained in his teeth. "Troy's powers rise from etymon, and he knoweth many ancient tongues."

Pay heed.

Reynard stiffened at the voice in his head. "Etymon — what are those?"

"First words that give birth to later words. The roots of all language — and much sorcery. Hel, I am told, saw that something was lacking in her creation, a blankness that must be filled. So she swept across the endless grasslands she had already made, and found the first Travelers trying to live there. She had forgotten making people, but thought these might be useful. So she walked among them, first as a gazelle, then as a lion, and finally as a woman, and in this form, the Travelers were willing to listen to her. And so, at her command, they spread out from their herds and horses. They listened to birds and insects, and took from their sounds and music many words.

"Still, this was not enough — the birds and insects had their own flesh and need. So she ordered the Travelers to look inward and draw up, as if from a well, their own human etymon. She told them to listen and remember the words they found in their own flesh and blood. In time — which she spun out as a lark, a fancy, very little like the time we know today, at least beyond these islands — the first Travelers carried these words over the new lands and seas, across their known world — those parts that had been finished — and offered them to other tribes, other humans. So began human languages other than grunting and whistling. Then they reported back to Hel, who used these new people to finally fill the blanks in her creation — though not all."

Reynard was surprised by this long and doubtless blasphemous tale. Widsith chuckled. "I have long held my peace on such affairs," he said. "The Spanish would have gutted and hanged me."

Reynard could hardly believe any of it, so much did it differ from what he had heard in church. Still — his grandmother had spoken of such things, and his mother had not denied them, nor his father in the time before his death. *The first word is the first mother.* Reynard felt his own pulse quicken.

He asked, "The world is not finished?"

"No more than this island. Many more words remain to be found and fill in more blanks. So listen inside and out to Troy's nonsense. What doth he hide in riddles? Where will deception cross over to instruction — at least, to hints?"

"But you called the King of Troy a mountebank!"

"Oh, he is that. His powers amuse and even cause alarm. But he is a kind of scholar as well."

"He is an old friend, is he?"

"And an old teacher," Widsith said. "Some think he hath met Hel, and learned much from her own lips — but I am not sure of that."

"He is that old?"

"Without Eaters, he is sustained across the centuries. Someone favoreth him, but I know not who — or what. Perhaps he brought with him his old Greek gods." Widsith seemed to lose himself in memories. "Be alert and listen close. To hear an etymon, a first word, is to feel one's heart quake and bones shiver."

"What words did the Travelers bring?" Reynard asked. "What were the first languages heard here?"

"I do not know," Widsith said. "I have not lived that long! Quite a few arrived from England and Ireland when Norse raiders cut misery along those coasts. Others of Danish and Norse stock arrived from Greenland when the seals failed them and the trade in walrus tusks moved south, to Africa, where elephant tusks now have greater worth. I have heard from Sea Travelers like the tattooed man that much older folks, furtive and cautious, took their carved gods and sailed north to settle other islands around the circle. I know not if they are still there. The Norse and Danes and Swedes fought with the English at first, but both lost and learned, and now they abide mostly in peace. Those early times were rich for the King of Troy."

"He deceived them all?"

Widsith nodded. "Deceived, guided, and protected. A gentle enough old soul, he did not wish destruction on any. And he did not wish them to destroy each other. So . . . What think'st thou he showed those who fought, till they recovered their senses?"

Reynard tried to imagine gentler battles on the beach, magic wars back and forth. "He could have sent forth bone-soldiers, till the living broke their blades and tired."

"In sooth, that was the way of it," Widsith said, tilting his head in admiration.

"But the Eaters are not kind! In the village, and in the woods, how many Spaniards did they drain?" Reynard asked, with a frown, as if the question itself tested his borders.

"Eaters share purpose with all the islanders," Widsith said. "It is their pact with Hel. Though not all Eaters obey. Some say that is because it has been so long since Hel walked these shores."

"And what about Crafters? Did Hel make them for her own purposes?"

"Thou dost not know even what a Crafter is."

"Do you?"

"Fair enough. I have yet to meet one." Widsith looked at him with a peculiar wrinkle of his lips, as if remembering his own youth and envying Reynard. "Who asketh . . . in thy head, boy?"

Reynard considered for a moment. "There is my uncle's wit and my gram's knowing. They would ask."

"They seem wise as voices go." A last tinkle of laughter echoed from up the narrow lane between trees and bushes. Widsith frowned. "Best be with friends when night falleth, no?"

"Yes, but what do we fear?"

"We stray from town, and not all Eaters observe the pact, but others just beneath the sky, more powerful than those who stray, have interest in thee, and would keep thee safe to speak, boy."

"What have I to tell?"

"Gossip!" Widsith says. "Not just Guldreth, but Maeve, and possibly even Maggie and Dana, are eager to hear news of the King of Spain and the Queen of England, and their war, and how English and Spanish women bear up under all that, and how valiant strong and handsome men fight and die for Queen and country. Even better, thou canst tell them what dress be favored by women in the court."

"Oh." Reynard looked unhappy. "I do not know that! This King of Troy, was he really ever the King of Troy?"

"Was he ever Priam?" Widsith laughed. "No, boy. Likely that was his stage name in Makedonia before he arriv'd here."

Reynard had never heard of some of the places Widsith talked about, and he frowned again.

"Makedonia," Widsith repeated. "Home of Alexander, called the

Great. Ask the King of Troy about *him* sometime. Get him drunk, and he'll claim he knew Alexander . . . in the Biblical sense."

Reynard flushed, though he was hardly innocent. He had heard the Spanish were more forgiving in such matters, but suspected that was war talk, to make English sailors hate them more — not actual truth. So his uncle would have judged. "Is it all queens and no kings here?"

"A king was defeated. To the west, and across the blasted waste at the center, a mountainous, icy desert now belongs to powerful Sister Queens, who do not believe in Queen Hel, or the island's history as most often told here. But they are far away, at least . . . they were when I last departed." He looked uneasy. "Most around here serve the Travelers, who serve the Crafters, of course."

"Have you ever been summoned by the Crafters?"

"No," Widsith said.

"But how do you report to them?"

"I deliver my story to those who serve them — the Travelers."

"Who commandeth the village and on this coast?"

"You have met Dana and Maggie. They serve Maeve, and in truth, all are the humblest and sweetest," Widsith said, with another wry face. "But in the Ravine . . . who can know?" He frowned at a strange glow from the far side of the forest. "This is not normal night. Something is casting a deep shadow — and it is not Troy!"

Around a bend in the path, a man stumbled between the trees, then fell to his knees and pitched onto his face. The *hiss-crack-POP* of a harquebus resounded, followed by shouts and what sounded like cannon or powder blasts.

Widsith grabbed Reynard and hid him in a thicket of alders, keeping close while the battle seemed to move off, or diminish. Then he walked from the thicket and bent over the fallen man. "He hath semblance to a *grumete* of Cardoza . . . but that boy was younger than thee, and this —"

Out of the gloom, half visible in the best of lights, came a glassy figure, dressed mostly in black furs, like the Russian sables Reynard had heard of.

Widsith got to his feet and faced him.

"Pilgrim," the figure said. "That one is mine. Back away and let me finish."

Widsith wiped his hands on his pants, bowing slightly in his retreat.

The Eater seemed to slip between one shadow and another, and suddenly stood beside the fallen *grumete*. He knelt and bent over the man's torso, then rolled him over and laid his ear on the man's sternum, as if checking for a heartbeat. Deep-pitted eyes watching Widsith and Reynard, the Eater's face became a fog, a swirl, and then merged with the fallen man, who now simply folded inward, like one of the collapsed houses in the village.

Leaving a pile of drifting ash.

"His time is done," the Eater said. He rose slowly and touched his face with both hands. The face reacquired a sort of definition. "Didst thou know this man?"

"He was but a boy," Widsith said, not looking directly at the Eater, but not backing off any farther.

"He is still here," the Eater said, and tapped his chest, then peeled back a fur and showed pale ribs beneath the flesh. "He hath bright memories. I will savor him. It is mine only amusement." He looked between Reynard and Widsith. "Thou art both protected," he said. "I used to be pacted to Calybo. In those times, when thou wast a young sailor, I served thee at his behest," the Eater said. "Dost thou remember?"

"I know nought of that," Widsith said.

"Sometimes I hide and listen! Now I have no tribe and live nowhere, and sleep everywhere. I know mine hours fade. I take what I must where I can. It is not to my glory thus to be seen."

The Eater turned and vanished back into the forest.

"We should move on before more arrive," Widsith said.

"How far to Troy's camp?"

"Near." The Pilgrim studied the gloom. "There likely will be tests and barriers. We may have to cross a trod."

"Like a fairy trod?"

"A road for Travelers," Widsith said. "I hope they remember me!"

They walked on, avoiding tree roots and the deepest shadows.

King of All Tricks

Now they heard music — flutes and tambourines, as if there were a troupe of players ahead.

"We are close," Widsith said. "He never sleepeth in the same hut for more than a few days. He hath been for years moving around this clearing like a dog finding his rest — so I suppose we just . . . Wait! There are Travelers."

Reynard looked deep into the woods, then down, and realized they were not far from an actual trail — which he had not seen before. The trail crossed their rude path perpendicularly, and they heard horses and people a few yards off, hidden by brush and leaves, but closing slowly.

"The King's tricks?" Reynard asked Widsith.

The Pilgrim shook his head. "These make their own roads. Queen Hel empowered them long ago . . . and they have served her ways ever since."

Three sleek horses came into view, well-curried and fed, and on their backs rode two men and one woman, men dressed in wide-lapeled leather greatcoats over jerkins, with silver-buckled leather belts and wide, sun-shading hats. The woman wore a red cape, somewhat faded but still grand. Seeing they were being observed, the first riders doffed their hats and murmured to each other in a language that tugged at Reynard's memory. Tinker's Cant, or Rom, he was sure of it!

"They are Roma!" he exclaimed. Widsith hushed him, but the women looked their way with disapproving frowns.

More horses and riders followed, then a great, wide wagon, almost the size of his uncle's hoy, on wheels as tall as a man, and pulled by a train of six great draft horses, twenty or more hands high, as proud as any horses the Spaniards had landed and much larger and stronger. Children peered from windows in the wagon. The trees that had closed around them were now politely spaced to each side of the road, bowing as if in deference.

A train of almost twenty riders followed the great wagon, all caparisoned like festival players, smiling and laughing and chatting, and Reynard could hardly believe they were not in the presence of the King of Troy's magic.

When the procession had passed and could not be seen, and only faintly heard, the road closed again, the trees moaned and leaned and obscured, and all was as it had been before.

Widsith relaxed a little, then urged Reynard on.

"Do we see them by permission, or by accident?" the boy asked.

Widsith squinted at the boy. "I wonder whether they came to get a look at thee, young fisherboy."

"What am I they would care?"

"Indeed, what art thou?"

They walked on another hundred yards, over difficult, thick roots and overgrown paths, when Widsith paused again and looked up and beyond Reynard's shoulder, eyes growing wider. Reynard started to turn, but Widsith stopped him, hand on arm, and said, "Be still."

That was almost impossible.

"More Rom?"

Widsith grabbed his arm and dug in his fingers. Reynard felt his flesh creep, but pulled free, then swiveled to look at whatever was behind him — and saw a woman, a very tall woman, rising through the branches of one of the great spider trees. He looked up into her face, but she was not looking at him. With her intense blue eyes, like the eyes of twilight itself, she was focused on Widsith.

"Thou art not Hel, old man!" Widsith said to the air around them, if not to the immense spectral woman, now leaning as if about to topple. "We are friends. Thou hast no need to frighten."

And then . . .

The tall woman was gone. A rain of leaves and sticks fell from the air she had filled, along with a few thin bones, and Reynard smelled a burned, brothy odor, as of soup boiling too long in a kettle.

A gray and red man, striped like a tiger, emerged from behind the tree where the woman had risen. He was naked but covered in fine, silky hair, the longest hanging from his crown and covering his face like a veil. Reynard was fascinated by the precise trim of the veil — red where it covered the mouth, which could not be seen.

The edge of the veil puffed.

"Who might this be?" the striped man asked. "The perilous boy himself?"

Widsith watched the striped man closely, as if unsure what additional wonders he might perform or traps spring.

"Once more, is he the *dangerous* boy?" the striped man asked. "That one who bringeth Spaniards and Travelers into my woods, and doth so afflict my dreams?"

"He may be," Widsith said. "But so have I, and thou dost know me."

"Truth! These woods are full of new dangers, and they follow *thee*, Pilgrim," the striped man said. "Why hast thou brought them?"

"I return to report to the Travelers, when they are ready, and found this boy along the way. I come for thine opinion on him, and to ask what thou hast done on this coast whilst I was gone."

"A cordiality, I suppose," the striped man said. "And if this be the *awkward* boy, the one some say is of interest to Crafters, I would be introduced."

"By your proper name?"

"My player name will suffice," the striped man said, walking slowly before them, bare feet padding in the litter and kicking aside a couple of what might have been rib bones from a previous dinner.

"Reynard, make the acquaintance — I believe, lest this be another of his illusions — of the King of Troy, fabled in song and legend."

"No need for flattery," the striped man said. "I am beyond good reviews, unless they come from mine illusions, who know the art well. Greetings to thee, Sir Fox. And where is Ysengrim now, young beast — awaiteth he inland to join in more japery?"

Reynard was not familiar with Ysengrim.

"That is the wolf thou dost oppose in legend, young trickster," the striped man explained, with a veiled glance at Widsith. "An unpleasant character."

"I am no trickster!" Reynard said, gritting his teeth. "I am a fisherman, and wonder why you, sir, though famous, have no audience."

"A joust of tongues, is it?" the striped man asked after a moment's pause. He sounded more than a little drunk. "It hath been many a year since any so challenged me. In honor of the occasion, I appear, for a time, as I am. Though the aches and chills of an aged frame are tiresome."

The striped man vanished, and a frail, elderly man in a long brown coat stood before them, hands out, palms up and wavering, as if beseeching coins. "'Tis a strange fisherboy who doth not admire wonders and signs. A *dangerous* boy to be sure."

"He is but a fraud," Reynard said to Widsith, speaking more in anger than conviction. He had no idea how they had been fooled and was ashamed at being frightened.

Widsith stepped lightly on Reynard's left foot. "The King is neither fraud nor harmless," he warned. "And I bring thee to appear before him, to acquaint and ask, witness and judge — not anger or insult."

The King of Troy, stooped and quaking like an aspen in a breeze, waved his ancient hand for them to follow, and said, "I venture that thou, Widsith, hadst a worse look till Guldreth sent her minister. Didst thou know this Pilgrim then, Young Fox?"

"He was very old," Reynard said as they fell in behind the magician and he led them on a straight path between the trees, though no path had been visible minutes before.

"And now he is not," the King said. "My wonders, gentlemen, do not involve Eaters. Eaters are not enchanted by my works, nor by me — though they borrow of my time, of course. They borrow time from most on this shore. But from me, they take little, as I am so old and my time is stretched so thin, like wine puddled in rain! Compared to Widsith, I am a lamb, and he is a wolf, fed by those who keep and value him." He grinned, entirely un-lamb-like, at both of them. "Is that thy plan, too, young Fox?"

Widsith raised his hand and swept the air around Reynard. "Is the boy followed?" he asked.

The King of Troy paused on the path and held out his own hand to stop Widsith's sweeps. "Do not so disturb his airs," he said, perturbed. "Mine own thoughts are more fog than substance, nowadays."

"I asked, is the boy followed?"

"No, his line is clean," the King said, but then looked up at Widsith. "Wait. There is something . . . Something I do not credit!"

"And what would that be?" Widsith asked him.

"Hath this boy ever consorted with a Crafter, or something very close to a Crafter?"

Widsith shook his head. "No, of course that would be impossible for a mortal. He hath been touched by an Eater, that is all. And I doubt the Eaters have contact with such, either."

"Well, there is a trace . . . Hast thou in mind odd presences? Visitations?"

Widsith looked to Reynard.

"No," Reynard lied, not yet trusting either the Pilgrim or the King of Troy.

Troy's Camp

In the dark of the woods, stray beams dropped pools of silvery light on what appeared to be nine or ten kitchen middens or, charitably, caches of firewood larded with the bones of cattle and horses and pigs — all but skulls — and draped rags, ornamented around the base with rusty iron pots, the slop and scrap of many a meal. Reynard remembered the spectral ladies that had taunted him in the wood, and how these dames had, in fade of sun, revealed inner workings of bone and stick, like marionettes wrapped in dream and strung with flesh and hair.

"Is this your trick yard?" Reynard asked.

"So some claim," the King of Troy answered, and pointed them toward a lean-to within the ring of six wide-rooted and towering oaks. "Thou bring'st the boy for my denial, or my confirmation?"

"I was not myself sure," Widsith said. "It has been so very long since we have seen the like."

"By which thou mean'st, one who attracts the special attentions of Eaters? And like thee, mayhaps hath value to the Crafters? And this from a man who has never had an audience with one!"

"No," Widsith admitted.

"Well, I will think on't. Thine instincts may be good. What I must ask is, why have the Travelers not yet gathered this boy into their wagons and ferried him to the kraters? If he is their duty and treasure, more than you, they have always moved quick to take advantage. Or is there something I know not, that you do?"

He stared accusingly at Widsith, then Reynard, and Reynard flushed at the suspicion that the magician knew he had lied.

"My question for thee is, would he be of so much use to the Travelers that they would imperil this island by bringing him here, along with Spaniards — along with me?" Widsith asked.

"Not the Travelers as such, but others, those just beneath the sky, who also serve Crafters. I can see a little into thy thoughts," Troy said to the boy. "Thou hadst a woman who taught thee the languages of Ogmios?"

Reynard nodded. *Stone people.*

"But your line is clean," the magician said. "Thou dost remember, but I cannot see. Well, whatever these truths add to, I would take the boy to those better able to appraise him, and I would do it soon. I am busy enough here, Pilgrim, and will venture no further opinion."

"I see thy labors, magician," Widsith said. "Too many balls to juggle, doubtless, what with distracting the Spanish, or the Spanish arriving here at all, and now, with the village."

"I am perplex'd by this, and likely many others around thee," the King said. "Was Cardoza aware of this island? If so, who told *him*, and who told *that one*? Thou seemest most immediate, Pilgrim. Didst thou?"

Widsith made a bitter face. "Cardoza would not have been my choice for a leader of troops. No, I did not tell him."

"And yet he is here." The King of Troy stared around at the trees, the leaf-covered ground, and blew out between pressed lips, a blatting appropriate for neither him nor the circumstance. "There are many layers on this island," he said. "I see some, not all. If thou, fisherboy, fox-boy, canst see deeper, down to the base, that would indeed make thee a treasure. Thou couldst control immense magicks, not look-see-wonders. What dost thou perceive beneath this seeming wood?" He waved his arms and performed a faltering, clumsy pirouette, then peered goggle-eyed at an astonished Reynard. "Well?"

Widsith looked between them.

"I know nothing of layers," Reynard said. "God made the world and put us in it."

"Ah," the King said. "Be that what thy grandmother taught thee?"

"No," Reynard said. "She did not speak of Bible matters."

"Didst thou know that by grace of the Crafters, and Hel, insects once ruled, that our world was an insect world?"

Reynard, aghast, was too stunned to answer or play their game.

The King waved his hand again around the woods. "And of course spiders and crabs and the like. What a fine mystery that is! We like it not that Hel might have for a time resembled a crab, or a grass-hopper, and shared their thoughts and hungers. But she shared not our prejudices in any way. I would imagine that crabs, spiders, and insects were experts at ogham! So many pointed legs to align on a branch or trunk. And they were far smarter than we can now imag-ine, and larger as well. The drakes are but a remnant of that world. And beneath those insect masters, in the earliest layer —"

A deep, loud voice grated from the trees beyond the lean-to. "Are we not engaged, old Troy?" the voice roughed and gargled. "Who are these that distract thee?"

The King tried to usher them away from that copse. "Pilgrim, 'tis awkward for thee here. And more awkward for this boy, at the mo-ment. I wish thy company and witness, but God's truth, best ye be off to Maeve and serve her needs."

Widsith peered with an intense frown into the shadows behind the King's rude shelter. "Why the toppling sweven, Troy, and why the red-and-white trim and fringe?" he asked.

"Send them to the Inferno!" the voice called, followed by a cough-ing howl like a jungle cat. "Do it, and show me next the way!"

Troy seemed bemused. "A stray spirit of Dante," he said, "who once visited me when his poetry lagged and sputtered."

Widsith shifted between the King and Reynard, as if to protect the boy, but clearly he did not know what was out there, or why the King was warning them back.

"As I say, a mere wisp of the past!" the old man said. "I have seen behind and around this boy, and confirmed him for thee, and thus performed my work for Zodiako," the King insisted, eyes doing their bleary yellow best to carry his irritation. "Time now to serve other patrons, fulfill other contracts and duties."

"It is you behind the voice," Reynard said, peering with a squint into the gloom beyond the lean-to. "I have seen it in country fairs. It hath a silly name, like a wind among cards."

"Mean you *ventriloquist!*" The King looked upon him with a sud-den glowing smile, the growling voice forgotten. "A new word, soon minted. Thou know'st of fairs and those who work them? Tell me, what new tricks and plays? Have new mountebanks better puppets than I strutted before thee?"

"No evagation," Widsith cautioned. "It is I who wander in person, not our minds. To the task —"

"The devil with ye!" the cat-growler said, then shrieked to a har-py's pitch. Reynard ducked as something feathery swooped and puffed close to his scalp — something like an owl with the head of a lynx.

The King leaned his head to one side, and again twisted his grin. "I teased the Spanish. They thought to do harm, and, whilst some insist mine arts are best applied to lost lovers and stray children, they have other uses, that thou know'st well."

"Thou it was didst lure the soldiers to where Eaters and drakes found them!" Widsith said.

"Not me, entirely," the King insisted, hands flagging like old leaves. "Spanish hopes for murder and treasure guided them to their own doom. I filled mine old pans and laid trails of nuggets and coin, defended them with affrighting hags and tottering castles, into open fields and rocky heights, and the brutes followed their own vicious nature."

Reynard had to be impressed by such a ruse, but then shivered at the calm he felt, exposed to all this strangeness. He was not afraid of Widsith, a most changeable man — and he was not afraid of the King, who seemed decrepit . . . but he *had* been afraid of the toppling hag and the striped red and white man. And so . . .

He had fallen for the King of Troy's tricks, just like the Spaniards. Illusions worked for both the King and for Zodiako, it seemed. Did the tricks, the visions, work on or against the glassy-skinned Eaters? He thought not. Perhaps the Eaters were themselves illusions raised by greater sorcerers than the King. This Queen of Hell, for example, mistress of crabs and spiders, queen of devils, who had not yet been explained one way or another.

"Go!" the King insisted, hands working like autumn flags to warn them back.

"But I fear for thee, old friend," Widsith said, with a hint of cruel jest, "and miss the tales we promise each time I leave and return!"

"Soon enough," the King said. "But for now, in the company thou keep'st, all is unsettled, and some will visit thee I do not wish to meet."

"When? Of what strain?" Widsith asked. "I have no fear of Eaters high or low —"

"Nor doubtless will this boy," the King said. "But others wander from the waste not seen here for many centuries. Giants and bogles and smaller, stranger wights, and ghosts in shrouds, and those who shape signs in the dark — some visible, some not."

"Attracted to the boy? Protecting him?" Widsith asked.

"Doth he want protection?"

"I saved and protected him," Widsith said.

"Perhaps he is their goal, their guide, and not thee and thy tales, Pilgrim. I'll do my best to make them pass us by, but ye should go now!"

Out of the Woods

"I⟶T IS STRANGE how I remember these woods and these trees," Widsith said as they looked for the path back to Zodiako — a narrower and more winding version, Reynard guessed, of the road traveled by the wagon and its entourage. "Think'st Cardoza is still lost around here someplace, or hath he been found and put to better use? Is he even now spilling poison into the porches of the ears of eastern queens?"

Reynard shook his head. "Maybe he is dead."

"Oh, no," Widsith said. "He hath not the mark, and the Eaters did not finish him — merely dined. Someone about the waste, in the krater cities that serve Crafters, wished him preserved for other uses."

"What be these kraters?"

"They surround the chafing waste at the island's heart," Widsith said. "A wide circle of great cups or depressions, served by cities and staffs of special Travelers. These Travelers go there to carry my tales, and not just mine — but the tales of any who arrive. I have never seen them. I have not been invited."

Reynard looked through the trees. Left on his own he could never have found his way through the tangles of trunks and branches and roots. What presented a path to Widsith seemed but a puzzle to Reynard.

"What about the Spanish horses?" the boy asked. "Other than Cardoza's. Did the drakes kill them as well?"

"I doubt it," Widsith said. "The drakes know better, are guided better, if they were blunted by Dana's people."

"What about the Eater who looked at me?" Reynard asked. "The glassy girl."

Widsith made a face. "No longer a girl," he said. "Five or more centuries old."

"Like the Eater who gave you years? He sounded awful, doing that to you."

"Calybo. It did not feel pleasant to me, either. But necessary."

"Is he an Eater?"

"Yes. A high Eater. The Afrique hath been here for much longer than I have been alive."

"Who giveth him orders?"

"Guldreth," Widsith said, looking askance.

"She it was we almost met on the island?"

This irritated Widsith. "Enough!" he said. "It is Maeve I report to when I return. But Maeve avoids me, thus far." He lifted his brows and sighed. "None of the island's women will have me, it seems."

"You call Guldreth a woman?"

Another sharp look, very like his uncle's displeasure at a question too clever by half. "Not in simple parlance, lad. Nor is the glassy one who studied you a woman now. No sane man expects favor from such, beyond the pact."

"And what about other high ones, the Vanir? Are they truly in command of this island?"

"Not alone. It is Crafters who mold and command all around us . . . and inside, methinks."

Reynard thought of the dark figure with the white shadow, and wondered whether Crafters controlled him, as well. Or the man with the feathered cap. Or the Queen of Hell, whoever she might be. He resumed his silence until they passed the field of dead Spanish, now almost empty, cleared by some group or some force, leaving only scattered items of clothing and a few rusty weapons no one thought worth collecting.

"I am truly to blame for this," Widsith said quietly. "Always before, I returned alone, or with simple fisherfolk. Now the outside world makes that impossible. Our land is under siege. I should be among these dead. I should be a ghost!"

Reynard considered this and found it somewhat insincere. "God's truth?"

Widsith gritted his teeth and gave Reynard a stern glance. "I have lived centuries by this strange grace. I do not wish it to end now, truly. Nor do I wish to lose Maeve and my reason for returning."

"So long as the powers you know supply you with more years," Reynard said.

"Foolishness doth make thee no more pleasant," Widsith said.

"What did you witness, out there during the great sea battle with my people? What was that battle like for you? Did *you* feel protected?"

"I was in as much danger as any Spaniard—any Englishman. Many died around me."

"And after, what made you lift me from the sea? Why would these people value me, or thank you for my life?"

Again, Widsith looked aside, as if thinking of matters still best left unsaid. "I thought I saw something in thee that could bring me favor, when the Spanish would not. Here, those of us just above the mud always seek advantage and favor from those just below the stars."

"And have I brought you favor?"

"Thou dost promise great change. The Spanish promise change,

but also destruction. Since I could not arrive here alone, by bringing thee I hoped for a balance. The King of Troy seemeth to agree."

"But I have no signs. I have no power, and nothing to tell!"

"I confess to possibly making a bad decision." The Pilgrim
stretched out his arms. "One of many. We shall see."

Reynard flushed at this. "I would flee now and take my chances
with the ocean!"

Widsith shrugged this off as well. "What chances do either of us
have, or this town, or any humans on this island? Cardoza hath suffered a defeat, but it is apparent someone here favoreth his presence,
even without most of his soldiers, and not just for his few horses."
He stopped and rubbed his chin. "And what about me, boy? Dost
thou sense great currents aswirl?"

"The Eaters favor you," Reynard said. "I have nought else to say
of your measure."

"Eaters favor me because of the ancient pact."

"With Guldreth?"

"With the Travelers and the Crafters, I presume, but I have never
had it explained. If the Travelers show no interest in thee, on behalf
of the Crafters, I fear the island will be finished with all this coast
and Zodiako ... Except for Cardoza. And that I do not comprehend."

They had found their way back to the outskirts of Zodiako, where
quiet and shadows ruled as dusk fell, and arrays of candles gleamed
on posts and rails at the crossings.

"Who hath command o' the ghosts?" Reynard asked.

"Spanish ghosts seem of no interest to those just beneath the sky
—and so they are free to leave, if they can find their way. I mislike
such thoughts. I equally mislike condolement. Let us see if Maeve
will have me now."

◆ ◆ ◆

Dana and Maggie invited them into the blunters' sanctuary, which, while intact, still smelled of smoke. Of burned flesh.

"Maeve is in the temple," Maggie said. "We will ask questions, then takest thee to her."

The two women walked around Reynard. Maggie touched his hair. Reynard jerked back, not liking to be treated like a child. "The fold-keeper, the old man outside the barn, keeper of goats and sheep, gave us his judgment after meeting thee. He seeth things clear."

"He doth burn tobacco and breathe it," Reynard said with a pinched face.

"A foul habit," Dana said. "He proclaimeth thou art followed by a gray wisedom, an old woman with ancient ways. Who might she be, boy?"

"Troy saith not," Widsith told them. "His line is clean."

The women ignored this and waited for the boy's answer.

"Perhaps my grandmother," Reynard muttered. "If she be here, she will prove a comfort." He hoped her spirit would not find a trap.

"The fold-keeper told me thou sleep'st in peace," Maggie said. Dana stepped back and let her mother take charge. "Around the fold, seest childers?"

"The spirit babes? Aye."

"Aloof, or friendly?"

"They smiled and played and vanished."

"Friendly, then," Maggie said.

"What are they?" Reynard asked.

"Nobody knoweth, boy," Maggie said. "But they do like to flit in the dusk and play, if their larks be play. Thou'lt know if they be not friendly. We put thee in the fold for the judgment of the old man, but also the childers. Doubtless Widsith relied upon that old faker." She pulled up a cane chair and sat between Reynard and Widsith, then leaned forward, face in hands. "We lost thirty-seven townsfolk, five blunters, and one drake," she said.

Sad silence.

"Maeve taketh it hard," Maggie said. "We are all like sons and daughters to her." She stood from the chair and walked toward the door. "Creatures and tenebria are disturbed. Visitors we have not seen in a thousand years come from the center of the island, and the Travelers seem not to know what to do with them! And now Widsith's return bringeth thee." She studied them critically. "What news could charge the krater lands, and our lives, after so long calm breath and gentle winds?"

Reynard wondered if he should tell them of the man with the white shadow, or the man with the tall feather. He decided he would hold such in reserve for when he felt more trusted, more a part of this group — if that could ever happen.

"We are done here," Maggie said, grim expression showing her dissatisfaction with this conversation. "Do what thou must."

"Maeve hath condoled with mourners at the temple," Dana said. "She tells us to send thee there."

Maeve

THROUGH DRIFTING SMOKE, on the way to the temple, they passed under the walkway's painted boards, each displaying a scene from the town's long history. Reynard wished there was more time to study them.

The next to last board was freshly painted with a vivid landscape of lava and burning forest.

"No doubt Travelers will again seek thee out, in their own time," Widsith said. "As for Maeve — appear of some use, for my sake."

They paused at the end of the walkway. The last board, beyond the flames and lava, was sanded to a blankness. Widsith reached up and touched it. "The Crafters' tale rolls on. Watch and learn, young fisherboy."

To Reynard, however, the blank board seemed to point to something less conclusive.

Across a flagstone path, the nave and transept of the temple were embraced by more than twenty enormous, twisted oaks.

"Canst thou feel it?" Widsith asked softly. "I have been gone too long. I know not what more I can do for her." He pushed open the central doors. Inside, the transept to either side seemed dark and empty. Down the aisle that defined the nave, floored with packed dirt and stomped-down rushes, the pews were also empty. At the far end, near the altar, a single candle outlined a lone dark figure kneeling on a pillow. Even from here, Reynard could tell the figure was spectrally thin, and Widsith seemed both saddened and frightened by what they were approaching.

Reynard counted sixty pews, and looking up, estimated that the arched roof was a hundred feet above them. Even in England this would have been an impressive structure. But there were no stained-glass windows, no sculptures, very little ornamentation.

The end of each pew supported a stand on which a single book was placed. All the books looked as if they might have been Bibles and were very old. Some stands closer to the altar carried not books but scrolls, brown and fragile and even older.

They came to the end of the pews and the space before the altar.

"I am here," Widsith said.

The spectral figure got up from her knees. A dry, whispery voice said, "And welcome, to be sure."

The figure turned and Reynard saw a woman so old the fat of her face and neck had melted away and parchment flesh stretched tight on her cheeks and chisel nose. A thin aura of white hair stuck up from her age-spotted crown. She might have been a corpse in a reliquary, not that he had ever visited such. Her eyes were bright enough, but looked more like tiny stones than human eyes. She held up a skeletal hand heavy with five great gold rings, and crooked her pointing finger to invite them forward. Her knuckles made soft little snaps, as old knuckles do.

Reynard held back, but Widsith did as she bid, and embraced her with extraordinary delicacy.

"Who be this . . . young creature?" Maeve asked.

"He is called Fox," Widsith said.

"Reynard," the boy corrected.

"Greetings, Fox—Reynard. Sorry to meet thee in such sad times." She stepped away from the pillow where she had knelt and walked around Reynard with a fluid grace he would have thought impossible. "Hast shown him to Guldreth?" she asked, her voice like leaves blowing along a road.

"She was asleep," Widsith said. "Her man did not seem interested in waking her."

"Ah, would that be Kaiholo, the one with tattoos all over?"

"Aye. I will take the boy to the Travelers soon, whether she seeth him or no." This seemed to contradict what Widsith had said earlier, and the fact that a band of Travelers had already passed them by, but Reynard merely glanced at him, then focused his attention on Maeve.

"Wilt thou?" she asked, with some amusement. She gave Reynard a sad, knowing look. "Fox, didst thou recently see Travelers, or didst they come to see thee?"

"I do not know who they wished to see," Reynard said. "I *did* see *them.*"

"Be not disappointed. They may have been distracted by unexpected visitors from the krater lands — outmoded beasts, likely fugitives from failed histories . . . But I would not know."

"Such creatures have come here?" Widsith asked.

"None in Zodiako have seen their like. They keep to the Ravine and the ridges, but some were seen by our scouts. True giants, I am told. Cyclops and men who run on four legs like wolves, with human heads and hands. To those who travel regular outside Zodiako, like Anutha, and Kaiholo, the island seems upturned and all the beasts riled and poked." Maeve looked at Widsith with an unreadable expression, so bony and wrinkled. "Thou wert away too long," she said.

"There were so many wars and journeys, islands and lands . . ."

"And wives? I trust curiosity led thee on."

This stung the Pilgrim. "And duty! No need for thee to forget me and join the others in age. Thou didst know I would return."

"I did not forget thee. Nor did I think thou wouldst lead the Spanish to our town!"

Widsith fumed. "I volunteered for their ships, to return here, and had no control of the circumstance."

"Thou couldst have diverted them," Maeve said softly.

"I would have died. I had to return . . . to thee. To make my report. And I found the boy."

"But who asked thee to bring him here? Was it Guldreth? And what did this one so lovely, and so near to the sky, say before thou last departed our isle, that thou wouldst guess this boy was needed, or special . . . or mayhaps a sign?"

"Before I left—"

"Forty years ago!" Maeve said, her parchment skin pinking with what might have been anger. Delicate veins showed through her pale flesh.

The Pilgrim seemed to collapse a little. A tear fell from his left eye. "Thou hast always seen deep. Yes. Guldreth told me that I should look for a special sort of *Gitano* out there, young and unlearned, except in secret signs."

Reynard looked between these two like a chicken wondering who would wring him and pluck him first.

"He would have black hair, she said, but the sea would turn it red, and thereafter it would become black again—in the company of those who knew his quality."

Maeve lifted a lock of the boy's reddish hair. Again, Reynard drew back and raised his arm as if in defense.

"Is he innocent?"

"On the edge of manhood."

"A dangerous time for a boy, prodigy or no. Hath he had love from woman or man?"

"I know not." Again, a strangeness to his tone.

"That is an important bit of knowledge. Perhaps thou shouldst ask him before meeting with Guldreth."

Widsith agreed with a sidewise nod. "Most strange, why did the Spanish get through the gyre?"

"Obvious, because they carried thee and the boy," Maeve said.

"And why hath she allowed thee to grow old? She knoweth I favor thee."

"'Twas my decision. It hath been hard watching this island grow in perversity greater even than its mystery. The Travelers, the chafing waste . . . all ring with unwanted change."

"When I deliver the boy, I will command Guldreth to bring thee more time!"

"Command her? Thou findest such high favor in one just beneath the sky?"

Widsith looked aside once more.

"I am become mortal again and see now, in thy long absence, that mine is the right choice. Besides, as thy wife, knowing what I now know, I would never ask for her help," Maeve said. "My bottle is sealed. I will soon give the Eaters the last of my time, but can no longer receive."

"I must correct thy thoughts!" Widsith said, in agony now.

"Never. We had a good year, right in the middle of some of this island's best years, when queens and kings reasoned together and Travelers moved freely and unafraid, and Crafters seemed content. The Eater who tended to me honored my request to take months from mine end, when there seemed little hope thou wouldst spend another such time with me. Hadst thee more timely returned." She smiled with such sweet longing as she stroked Widsith's face with thin fingers, that Reynard thought he could see the girl beneath the parchment flesh, the youth beneath the age. "I had hoped thou mightst be gone no more than a decade, or less, and that thou wouldst get Guldreth to instruct Calybo to make thee near mine age, no younger, and we could both love as mature man and woman and enjoy a fine twilight. But when that decade passed, I knew we could never match, and I gave thee up to the island, and prayed Calybo would only make thee younger, as always, but not for me — only to send thee on thy way again to serve. My life seemed not so important."

"I will go to the Ravine now and beg," Widsith said. "Guldreth is indebted to me! The Travelers as well! I spent two thirds of a long life out there!"

"And I spent that same time here, I did not marry again. Didst thou?" She stood her ground, but her face softened. "Stay, and tell me some of what thou sawest — before thou tellest Guldreth or the Travelers, and before they tell the Crafters. That will be reward enough! Long have I desired to hear about the finished lands, and thou hast seen them! I am ready to hear, and then to die. Mine end will be swift. The Eaters have always borrowed from these last times, and left behind such glorious memories of others mine own age, or older, who have gone before. Some of the eldest of our islanders fill my dreams. The Eaters have been generous beyond their nature."

Widsith's voice cracked, and he wiped his eyes. "I shall not accept this! I still have need, and influence, especially now . . ." He looked to Reynard. "We will go to the Ravine and persuade the Eaters they must make Maeve young again, if nothing else, as reward to me! That we can share many summers again."

Reynard was fascinated by the fragility underlying Maeve's apparent graceful strength. Was this what aging was like when Eaters borrowed from your later years? And how did that affect them?

"Persuade which? Calybo?" Maeve asked. "He is assigned only to thee and cares nought for me. Valdis, then? She seemed a young one in their ranks."

"I did not see her, only Calybo."

A young-seeming female Eater? Was that the one who had visited Reynard on the beach?

"Well, she came that first night I returned to mortality," Maeve said. "She held me so briefly, as if in sorrow, as if I might be a kind of friend or mother to her, and shared with me memories of northern islands and long ships, and of strong men and women she had not seen since she was a child, badly hurt in a storm. A yard and sail fell on her and broke her back. Her parents brought her here through the gyre, and donated her to the Eaters, that she might live. From me, that night, she sipped mere seconds. But she sealed in my time. I will no longer take."

"I will convince Calybo she needs to return and reverse that course."

"Impossible," Maeve said. "Once sealed, I approach a point that ends a line." Her smile was that of a woman already dead, Reynard thought — teeth prominent behind thin, pale lips. She seemed almost as translucent as an Eater herself. "Anutha hath told me more than thou, husband! That when the Spanish ship arrived, and the Eater Ravine was made aware, Calybo called upon Valdis and gave her a separate mission. She was instructed to take no time from this boy, but to pass along some memories — and not to belabor the Spanish, so that the other Eaters could take their due. What could be Valdis's purpose, her mission? Did Calybo order it, or Guldreth?"

Widsith shook his head.

"Once, I was informed of these things," Maeve said, "if only to support the stock of lives from which Eaters drew. Now, as I near mine end, other than Valdis, few of our marvels reveal to me anything important. This maketh me innocent again, giveth a new sort of youth. And so having capped my years, I am eternally reborn."

Widsith paled at that thought. "Thou hast lived a good and decent life here — I choose not to believe it will end soon."

"Then why was I left behind? I wished to go with thee, this last time, suspecting by thy words, thy demeanor, thou wouldst be gone for many, many years."

"I wanted to take thee, but thou wouldst have died long since. Times are hard on the sea and out there, in the far isles."

"Thou couldst not have left me as a serving maid with the Virgin Queen, or in the court of Philip's daughter?"

This amused and moved both of them. Widsith softly stroked the back of her hand. "Thou know'st what would have happened."

"I do! I would have left the side of the Queen or the girl, chased thy departing sloop or galleon, and gone with thee. When we reached those distant shores, I would have seen thee laugh and dally with brown maids, and I would have lost my purest love in anger at thy brutal needs. And then I would have stolen a great ship to return to our isle."

Widsith nodded. "Thou wouldst have done all that."

"My life is here," Maeve said. "I understand this island, but little of the greater world thou hast visited, that one they say Crafters do shape and refine."

Maeve stepped forward, but this time with little certainty, and Widsith supported her by the arm. They walked slowly back down the aisle to the door, and Reynard followed. On the steps, Widsith lifted her — she seemed light as straw — and carried her through the great oaks to her home, a small cabin on the edge of the village, its fences burned and walls scorched. Maggie and Anutha were waiting, and as he lowered her to her feet, Maggie grasped Maeve's outstretched hand. Anutha took the Pilgrim aside and whispered to him. Reynard heard little but the name Valdis. Anutha and Maggie then escorted Maeve into her home and closed the door, with a stern parting look from Anutha.

The Ravine

WIDSITH AND REYNARD stood on the porch while the trees rustled and leaves and sticks rolled and skittered by. The old woman, to Reynard, still seemed to be speaking — but the voice was not hers. It belonged to the wind in the forest.

"Let us take two horses from the stable," Widsith said. "We must be swift."

The time it took to walk to the stable was short, but the twilight was already dense. Reynard looked upon the place where he had seen the childers, but they were not present, nor was the keeper.

As they led two horses from their stalls, Reynard asked, "Is Guldreth an Eater?"

"She hath not their habits. But she is almost as old as Queen Hel, if Hel were still alive."

"And we are just above the mud?"

"We are."

"And you loved her? How is that done?"

Widsith crossed himself just like a Spaniard, then excused the gesture with a swift pass of one flattened hand. "Mount," he said. The horses received them with flicks of their withers, and they nudged them into a run. They were going to the beach where the blunters stored their boat, Reynard thought, but Widsith took a turn in the deep and twisted woods, and instead they pushed along a well-traveled trail for a couple of hours in darkness and dappled moonlight, the horses seeming to magically feel their way to where Reynard smelled ice . . . a strange, sour kind of ice.

And then they came upon the southern end of a great cleft cut or split in the land, sunk by several dozen yards below the trees and the broken tops of stone walls. Chill air poured from the cleft, air that seemed to nip and tug at Reynard's hair and skin. He felt something strange and dangerous in the cold that lapped and surged before them.

"This is the Ravine," Widsith said. "Pacted Eaters dwell here much of their time, near enough to partake of Zodiako and the surrounding towns and farms. It is their due."

Reynard stared into the Ravine, his face crooked by a curious sensation — that he knew this place, that he had been here before. The Ravine curled like a serpent between two crenellated ridges, once carved by an old river and now edged by clumps and ribbons of forest and filled with a long, strange, broken glacier. "Are you here to beseech Eaters, to demand that they save your wife?" he asked.

Widsith shook his head sadly. "After what she hath asked of Valdis, the sealing of all her years, such a request is bootless. They have not the power now."

"But the Eaters have been tasked to serve us, if what you say be true. How can she seal herself from them?"

"That, too, is part of the pact. None can force beyond a point the will of a woman, or any human."

"I thought Eaters were all-powerful!"

"Powerful, but they serve. They did not make the pact. 'Twas made for them."

"By the Queen of Hell?"

Widsith grinned sadly at him. "I think thou hast not yet got the right of that."

The horses did not like the air from the Ravine any more than Reynard did. Widsith did not urge them on. "We await here," he said. "Our appointments arrive on no human schedule."

Reynard peered into the shadows. "I see nobody."

"Nobody is here, at the moment. What is it that thou dost see?"

They dismounted. "A scarp covered with sharp stones."

"Aye, and what else?"

The horses anticipated no profit in chewing the rank grass and bushes that grew around the Ravine, so they scuffed their hooves and hung their heads.

"Ice in strange forms," Reynard said. "Perhaps last year's snows."

"This ice cometh not from snow. It is shaped by the peculiar talents of the Eaters within. What else?"

Reynard suddenly clutched his chest, as if his heart pained him. "I know the ice cometh not from snow. I know about the talents of Eaters. I *do know this place!*" His tongue numbed with the stupid audacity he felt. "How is that possible?"

"Thou'rt sharing something, methinks." Widsith said. "Likely thy muse hath supplied thee with impressions — a thing many of us have felt at times, if it suits the Eaters." His own face took on a crooked look. "Canst thou journey through the memories?"

Reynard closed his eyes and stretched out his arms, as if to avoid bumping into obstacles. "I see it deep," he said.

"Tell me what thou seest."

Reynard tried to explain, but his words tripped him up.

"Just remember," Widsith said. "Words will arrive."

"I am walking, but not walking."

"Of course. Thy mind moveth, not thy body."

Reynard kept swinging his arms like a loose-limbed puppet, but did not move his feet. Sights and narratives arrived in broken continuity, but assembled and formed histories, rides, walks, whose details were more than elusive. Not finding the right words, he seemed to stumble onto other words — Nordic-sounding words. "Is this from the girl, the young Eater?" he asked. "From Valdis?"

"Likely," Widsith said. "Though neither young nor much like a girl anymore. Hath she taken a fancy to thee, young fisherboy?" He smirked like the old sailor he had just been.

"I do see it . . ."

His mind journeyed deeper into the Ravine.

"There is much at the northern end," he added. "Have you been there?"

"I have, but not directly, and not on a horse," Widsith said.

Reynard closed his eyes tight to see the high cliffs, and between them, heaves of pale, broken ice surrounding a winding path, connected by great arches draped with icicles the size of trees, in some places holding up scaly roofs. At least seven ancient castles clustered at the northern end, all in serious disrepair, remnants of past wars between opponents he could neither see, remember, nor understand. Most of those castles had been empty for a very long time — perhaps a thousand years, if that meant anything here. No Eater seemed compelled to do the work necessary to restore or repair them — since none wished to live there.

And none of their original inhabitants were still alive.

Along the entire Ravine stretched many arches, bridges to nowhere, carrying no traffic but hiding, under their parapets, little cubbies, small caves, compartments and apartments — some still filled, others having stood empty for long centuries. And some holes were filled by things neither living nor properly dead!

"The monsters Maeve talked about," he said. "Have they come here?"

"Likely," Widsith said.

"Many?"

The Pilgrim shrugged.

"This is an awful place," Reynard said, eyes tight shut.

"Continue," Widsith urged.

"I sleep! I dream!"

"But thou wilt go on."

Valdis, young by the standards of other Eaters, had watched this place for centuries, but many mysteries remained. Some things had never been clearly explained to her.

"Eaters share!" Reynard said, dismayed. "They convene and spread their own lives!"

"Ofttimes Guldreth hath hinted at such, but seldom let me see. Thou art truly favored!"

"I see not how this be favor. How can such a being favor a mortal?" Reynard shook his head and stopped speaking. The pictures and stories came too fast. He squatted before the Pilgrim like a lost child, tears streaming down his cheeks.

The horses watched both with glazed eyes, as if about to fall asleep.

"That is a mystery I have no answer to," Widsith said.

"You should not have brought me here!" Reynard moaned. "My soul is fretted! I have no protection, no purpose!"

Widsith sat beside him with a sigh of both impatience and sympathy. "I have faith thy thoughts and worries shall resolve."

Reynard looked left, eyes still closed, and saw a corridor of memories, all dark, as if shrouded in night and despair. There was a permeating sense of loss all around the Ravine. So many still figures here and there, covered in ice or leaves, hiding in cubbies, frozen in sadness! They frightened him. Eaters, though in a way immortal, could sometimes simply lose interest in their necessary routines. And if they did that, within a few months or years, their sea-foam bodies, called by some *meerschaum*, along with their glassy skins, crumpled and fell in like old mummies. For an Eater, this was only a partial sort of death. A disembodied wisp remained for another few years and, sometimes, would pause people on the island's roads and ask difficult, puzzling questions, frightening without means or intent — for such wisps were no threat, and in time, paradoxes and puzzles unsolved, themselves faded to night air and moonlight.

He shivered at the thought of meeting such a wisp. Widsith gripped his shoulder to stop the shivers from becoming convulsions.

In a way less marvelous than their lives and purpose, though no less explicable, Eaters did with water what insects do with silk. Over thousands of years, they had filled the Ravine with their homes, like sculptures in an age of ice, showing sometimes creativity, sometimes necessity, depending on their origins and natures.

"Are we invited in?" Widsith asked, caution foremost. "'Twould not do to trespass."

Reynard opened his eyes. "I do not know," he said. "But I feel her presence."

Widsith patted Reynard's shoulder. "This is but a small part of thy purpose. Lead on," the Pilgrim said.

"I am here — and I am there!" Reynard whispered. He paid no attention to noises behind them. Widsith looked away from the Ravine, into the rocks and woods, away from the ice and cold, and saw men and women of their own kind gathering. Many had come from Zodiako, some wounded and on crutches, and others had come from farms deeper in the forests and meadows, all part of the trade that allowed humans to survive on this coast — to survive and support the Eaters.

"Eaters must eat as well," the Pilgrim said, then quietly explained to Reynard the process. Mortal farmers and hunters traditionally approached the Ravine, during daylight, once each month, moving silently to refill the troughs and heap plates with the sorts of foods Eaters could tolerate, even desire — organ meats, wild animals that ate nuts and grass, dense black breads, cow's or woman's milk mixed with deer's or pig's blood. And on occasion, human blood itself—drained from someone recently dead. There was none such on this occasion. Those who died of violence were abhorrent to Eaters.

Widsith nodded to an old farmer and a hunter, bow slung over his shoulder and arrows in his quiver. Reynard viewed with some intensity small mountain animals, marmots and squirrels and rabbits, carried on a sled. The villagers sang a somber prayer of summoning. The farmers and townsfolk barely glanced at them, so intent were they on laying out their offerings.

"So few, this time," Widsith said.

Exodus

VALDIS ROUSED from a numb dullness. Sleep for an Eater was never simple or easy. Her rest was hardly rest at all, in fact, and sleep very nearly impossible, fired as both were with vivid flashes from the lives of others — key moments of love and violence, disappointment and revenge, betrayal and injury, but also discovery and knowledge — a strange and broken sampling of humanity's best and worst.

How long Valdis had been on the isle, she did not know, did not remember — so crowded was her memory with the lives and times of others. But there had once been awful tides and mountainous waves, and a battered longship had been caught in the island's gyre, and she could still recall, in a dim and childish way, the soaked and agonized faces of a man and a woman. They must have been her mother and father. Their ten-year-old daughter had been injured by a storm-loosed sail and would soon die, and they had convinced a carl to take them north, at risk of being caught in the legendary tides, in hopes of finding this misty shore and leaving her here to die, if need be ... Or not to die, but to be found. Given freely to be raised by those of the island, for it was said there were people here who never sickened, never died, but benefited from the charms of witches and magicians and devils — or were themselves witches, magicians, and devils.

And so those Norse voyagers had left their daughter on a misted shore, and she had not died. She had been found. A one-time mother had somehow recovered from centuries past enough kindness to lift up the limp girl, whose time had run dreadfully low, down to minutes or less — and had named her Valdis, which some said meant Dead Girl, and others said, meant Saved from Valiant Death.

The one-time mother had summoned another, much older than she, who had vast stores of life, to donate time and something resembling health to the girl, in exchange for her fealty.

Her dwelling was no sort of home for a living woman, made as it was of sticks and leaves pressed into banks of crusted ice. But for an Eater, it was enough. Her skin did not require softness nor any sort of luxury. Her hair kept itself clean without attention, as did her clothes, which were woven of threads secreted by the large, jointed, and heavily armored creatures that dined on the trees above the Ravine. She required no warmth, and could in fact wander through snow and ice without freezing her bare feet or blanching arms and fingers that were already pale. Hel had designed Eaters to be free of such concerns, that they might focus on all they saw around them — generally at night, for they seldom went out by day.

But now she felt a connection. One was near who could all by himself make her travel by day. The feeling caused a diamond light to grow in her deepest thoughts that had until now known only shadow. On the southwestern shore beyond Zodiako she had ministered to him, connected with him ...

And now it seemed arrangements were being made for them to meet again. Great change was vibrating up and down the Ravine.

She pushed up from the litter, slowly and deliberately brushed herself, emerged from her cubby, and climbed steps hand and foot up the rugged icy slope. The walls of the Ravine were lined with doors cut from stone, or shaped from ice and frozen mud . . . and out of these doors crept many Eaters, little more than shadows.

The shortest paths out of the Ravine lay along the slowly flowing river at its bottom. Often in the night Valdis had watched Eaters glide the length of that river, trailing ribbons of dim green light, dipping hands and kicking feet to raise frozen walls for their dwellings or sculpt strange shapes for amusement.

Some of the more ancient and ornate creations rose like bird wings to direct a northerly wind along the bottom, tuning its steady sigh into a ghostly dirge. These wind-song blades, on close inspection, revealed veins of blood and even, in their fogged depths, frozen bodies from Eater wars fought ages ago. Now Eaters rarely fought each other, as the Travelers and high ones they served mediated their darker and more violent tendencies. Valdis liked neither the bird-wing shapes nor their history. There was not much about being an Eater that she did like.

She had conveyed some of these truths to the boy while she ministered to him on the beach. Guldreth and Calybo had told her she could, that she *should*, so minister — but only to the boy. Would the boy understand, or would he be repulsed? She had touched such life in him, such warmth! And such a complexity, not quite the reverse of her own inner echoes, but more direct, more *useful*.

And still . . .

He had no time in him.

The Eaters that had left their houses formed processions that moved both south and north, along paths carved in rock and ice, up and down the Ravine. The last of the daylight was of no concern to them, apparently.

A number of beings seldom seen, leftovers from Crafter dreams only vaguely unleashed, were moving out ahead of the Eaters. The worm-like servants, however, had been left behind and peeked from many doors, dark eyes glinting like bubbles on a pond, crickling in alarm and waving their feelers. Those winged creatures who flew messages and warnings from the caverns beneath the northern fortresses made their escape just below the arched trees, buzzing and whirring, then wheeling north like an uncertain cloud of bats in the silvery light of the gathering evening.

She could feel the unity that radiated from all, and though none had struck a tocsin or conveyed instruction, she knew she must leave as well. If the Eaters departed, the Ravine would go back to its natural state, and the water locked up in the walls, the houses and sculptures, the historic wing-song graveyards, would melt. That flood would carry both the corpses of servants who could not fly, of those who would not leave, and the old sourness of Eater persuasion — a nasty vitriol.

Her appointed companions — Widsith and the young man, Reynard — were at the south end of the Ravine. She knew this much and little more.

She followed the trail that flanked the left side of the river and as she walked tried to utter a prayer to Odin, but the words would not form and her lips seemed to freeze. She had no such freedoms here.

On the boat, he could not pray, either.

He had no time.

Now her mouth felt dusty-dry.

She had not felt fear in hundreds of years. But now arrived the one thing that could even in her situation inspire fear.

Hope.

Valdis's eyes were clear jade green, and by evenlight, it was difficult to know where her lids ended and eyes began. She turned those eyes on a large, dark figure that rose up behind her — then she stopped on the path and stood aside.

"Pardon, milady," spoke a deep voice.

And a giant passed her by. It was Kern, who along with Kaiholo, and at times the Pilgrim himself, served Guldreth.

She followed his massive shadow.

The Melt

❂

NIGHT WAS EARLY but also slow in its arrival. Reynard held
up his hands and saw his skin was bluing, with little white spots.

Widsith murmured, "If there is no meeting before stars twinkle,
we will leave."

"Do you mean a meeting with Valdis? Why should she care?"

"Because of thee. I venture to guess, no more," Widsith said. "I do
not now cross oceans, but navigate a land of fable." He worked his
horse back and forth a few yards, then swung it around. The farmers
and villagers had departed, leaving behind open baskets of offerings.
"We seem to be here for nought," he said. "But let us tarry for a moment of confession."

Reynard stared in surprise at the Pilgrim. "What need I confess?"

"All who come to any of the seven isles, and hope to survive, must
bring a gift, a bribe — a treasure. I bring stories of the outer world.
Valdis, I assume, brought her young life, and forsook that to become
an Eater. Even Cardoza, I suppose, based on what we have been told,
brought some ability of use to the Sister Queens. But . . . boy, what
bring'st thou?"

"Nothing of value," Reynard answered. "I arrived, like you, in rags."

"Nothing hidden, no sigil of stone or metal to charm the Sister Queens beyond the waste?"

"Nothing."

Widsith turned away. "In a place like this, origin of all tales tall and wooly, and all lives small and pitiful ... One too often expects treasure. Perhaps it is my time with the Spanish."

Reynard had heard versions of that same question before, from his uncle or other fishermen chiding him about his value, his place in their world — and though they meant it to train and discipline, he himself still wondered. Feeling his face grow warm, and wishing to put some yards between him and Widsith, Reynard led his mount away and approached the trays and boxes, but knew better than to touch them.

Then he felt his neck prickle. The voice he now heard echoed from some deep cavern in his heart.

The first mother is the first word.

Bring'st thou the first word?

Followed immediately by the sound of rocks being disturbed.

He opened his eyes wide and stared beyond Widsith into the chasm, into the shadow of the broken trees, and saw someone quite large taking slow, steady steps up the scree.

He shivered, his fingers moving in an old story his grandmother had told about stone people and Picts.

Widsith held his horse as still as he could. Both horses were more than uneasy.

"Who is that?" Reynard asked, hand stroking his horse's neck.

"That is Kern," Widsith said. "He is formidable, but no danger to us."

The shadow came up the scree until the creature, or the man, crested the rim of the Ravine. He was easily six cubits tall.

"Thou hast survived another round of Crafter muggery," Kern called to Widsith in a voice deep and wide. "Welcome, Pilgrim. I hear thou'lt make a request. Calybo told me thou'rt unhappy about something, though he refilled thy years at great discomfort."

"Yes, sire. I have a request. Though I have told this boy 'tis unlikely granted."

"Is it about Maeve?"

"Aye."

"A very popular lady. Thou hast often taken wives. Why dost thou feel so strongly for this one? Surely she is not the most beautiful, although, I hear, likely the most faithful."

"Before I left, we had not a single wedded year, and now she is in her last hours."

Kern's chuckle was like a distant storm. "Thy situation, thine and hers, would be very romantic, would it not? The sort of tale Crafters enjoy spinning. And in the end, we on this isle live and work, like the rest of this unfinished land, for Crafters. To whom dost thou carry the request?"

Widsith bowed his head. "As thou say'st. I bring news from the finished lands. That is mine only coin. Travelers are meeting us soon, and once I deliver this boy to them, and tell my stories, I can leave and resume my journeys, as is meet."

"The boy? His opinion?"

Reynard said, "I have no home, here or anywhere. I have a mother in England, but no father, and no power, no money, nothing but . . ."

He was about to say *a word*, an etymon, but that was not exactly true, either.

"And would your mother miss you?" Kern asked.

"She would." But Reynard could not remember her face! Somehow, recovering memories from Valdis had erased other things, things so familiar, but now gone. Had they ever been there at all?

Was there even a Southwold he could return to?

Kern said, "I have had no mother for many years, and my father . . ." The giant stood for a moment like a rough-hewn statue, then turned and said, "Bring the boy. Calybo, as it happens, is here to lead away his chosen Eaters. And so is Guldreth, albeit she will also soon make ready to leave."

"Where are they now?" Widsith asked.

"Kaiholo knows. Should it please Guldreth, he will likely meet us before the old bird cavern." Kern looked back at Reynard. "Knowest thou my breed?"

"Anakim, I trow," Reynard said without thinking.

Kern did not take it amiss. "Some called us that. People of the lower North called us Hiisi, and those became devils. Others called us Cyclopes. But I have two eyes." He winked at Reynard. "I have not seen mine ancestors since I was a babe. My mother was Anakim but loved a mighty man, I hear, but mine aunts killed him before I was born. Guldreth took us in, she so enjoyed my mother's tales." The giant looked back down the Ravine and said, "Other than my mother, I never knew an Anakim could stand humans. Pilgrim, thine affection for Maeve is the least of Guldreth's worries this season. Crafters themselves are in peril. Mayhaps they are dying. I know not which, but they grow weaker and less in control."

"No!" Widsith cried out, as if this defied all reason.

"I understand thy distress. They are the reason we have gathered here, all of us. But the Travelers tell me those who still live take great pains to bury their departed fellows. And I can attest that there is a plain of open jars that few of the Travelers dare approach . . . Shaitan's ovens, some call them, baking infernal loaves!"

"You have been there?" Reynard asked, squinting.

"I have, on Guldreth's missions. And so has Kaiholo. The island's interior is at a rolling boil. Other than Eaters, many flee who once served both Guldreth and the Crafters, claiming to be in danger. On the other side of the isle, the Sister Queens have summoned outside help with the coming war. It is said thou hast supplied some of that, Pilgrim."

Widsith shook his head and patted his horse's neck. "That was not mine intention. It is all upturned and rooted wrong."

"Indeed. For the nonce, the stock of humans at Zodiako is too small to matter — but their drakes may be of use. Some of the larger ones, at least. Come," the giant urged, and descended the scree. "If I do not cause a fall, 'twill hold for ye."

"And our horses?"

"Leave them," the giant said. "Traveler and Eater horses are the only ones that will travel in the krater lands."

They dismounted and sent their horses back to Zodiako with firm pats on their withers. Widsith seemed most unhappy with this change of plans. "Follow close," he told Reynard. "Move not from me whatever thy temptation or wonder. I sense Eaters and others will flee this way, and all along our path."

"That be true," Kern said over his shoulder. "And we shall not even see most of them."

They followed the giant and gingerly descended the scree into the depths of the Ravine. The chill penetrated Reynard's clothes and skin down to his very bones, where it either tingled or burned, he could not tell which. Not all things that work and move on their own, he thought, live by warmth and the sun. Down here, the Eaters and others seemed to thrive in the night and cold. The ice that climbed in sheets on both sides looked like frozen moonlight. He wondered how long he and Widsith could last in such a clime.

The clouds above the arch of trees parted now. Moonlight cast the broken rocks of the scree in stark black and gray. Reynard looked up, but briefly, fearful of stumbling and falling, for the rocks had shifted again and the path was no longer smooth. Despite his size, Kern seemed to drift over the roughness like a hovering spirit, but Widsith had no such grace.

The heaves of hoarfrost now clumped into knife-edged sheets of foggy ice, growing more and more transparent as they wound down along the rocky trail — and embedded in them were contorted figures, bodies, dozens and dozens in the hundred yards they traversed. Neither Kern nor Widsith commented on them, and Reynard had no urge to look into their faces, when they were visible.

They passed beyond the ice sheets. Two trails rose on either side of a slow, narrow river. Widsith said in wonder, "I have never been this far." He stared at the giant's broad, receding back. "I am told we should seek out Valdis."

"I passed her on my way to find you," Kern said. The giant was making faster progress than they, and neither Widsith nor Reynard wanted to be left behind, so they took more chances and stumbled and fell more often, gaining cuts on their elbows and hands, and once, Reynard tumbled headlong, until he felt as if sharp rocks had scalped him. Widsith examined him quickly, said he was fine, but blood dripped down his forehead and into his eyes, and he could barely see what little there was to see.

As Widsith helped him along and used his sleeve to wipe back the blood, Reynard resolved yet again he would do everything he could to flee this awful, evil island, even had he no home to return to.

"No leaving now, Fox," Kern called back, as if he could hear Reynard's thoughts, feel his anger. "You would lose the path. This Ravine is no longer the home of the Eaters — it is now but a deep scar in the island, clogged with old ice and dead castles — a fracture shared by desperate spirits."

"What will they do?" Reynard asked, his voice shaking.

"Go into exile," Kern said, answering his last question. "Lost races dwindled to a few ... Tenebria, some call them. Bad omens. Bad dreams."

Widsith watched Reynard closely, to judge whether his courage might fail him. They were walking along a narrow trail, carved partly from ice, partly from stone, above the river and the upraised frozen blades that seemed to interrupt and shape the constant breeze

from the north. The river seemed to be moaning. Reynard thought
he saw shadows and shapes, and sometimes felt a kind of breath on
his cheeks, but the others did not react, so he tried to ignore them.

"And what do you hope to do here?" Reynard asked.

"Pass through quickly, find Valdis, find Kaiholo, speak one last
time with Guldreth before she leaveth — at her request, to see you,
boy — and take Eater mounts from the caverns below the fortress,"
Kern said, looking warily side to side. "Then ride to find the trod and
the Travelers we need."

The high doors in the walls were growing fewer, the walls wider,
and the river had lost its upraised blades. The arched trees overhead
were thicker, but had fallen in several places.

"We are in the lair of creatures that bring food and water for
Eaters — more than humans can supply, and more suited to Eater
tastes. Servants of a sort," Kern said. "I wonder they have not already departed, with their masters!"

"Are they dangerous?" Reynard asked.

"No," Kern said, "but they do not like disturbance."

What little Reynard could see of their surroundings through
blood-dimmed eyes was a half-circle of ice-rimed pillars, and draped
between them, what looked like inverted tents or cocoons. For a moment, Reynard wondered if this was a rookery for drake nymphs,
but out of the pendant hammocks peered pale, dusty faces with
tightly slitted eyes and open beaks, like recent fledglings. Each was
the size of a small dog, and a few poked gray, knobby wing-shins
above their beds.

Reynard looked with suspicion on the draped sacks and their inhabitants. "What sort of birds are these?" he asked.

"Not birds," Kern said.

Widsith said with a lip-curl of distaste, "Nor are they bats."

"Do they bite?"

"No," Widsith said.

"Yes," Kern said.

Reynard's scalp was still dripping blood. Kern raised his hand, then ventured off a ways and returned clutching a handful of moss, which he applied to Reynard's wound. "Hold that, young human," the giant instructed. "We need to clean you before your audience."

They heard a squeaking cry. A small, squat, bird-faced gray figure, having flapped down from its sling, stumped on folded wings toward them, gripping between shoulder and head a leather bucket sloshing with water, which it offered to Kern with a gnarly whistle. Then the creature swept up a three-fingered foot and demonstrated what the giant was to do with the bucket. Kern took it and before Reynard could react, upended it over him. The water stung like lye soap, and he feared it would put out his eyes, but instead it sluiced his scalp and cleared his vision, and between the moss and the liquid, his bleeding finally stopped.

Widsith took him by one elbow, and they walked on, passing between the pillars into a wide space flanked by ragged glacial walls. The mottled, marbly whiteness rose hundreds of feet on either side to dark stony scarps fringed with dense-packed lines of forest, many of the trees having toppled. Reynard lifted the moss from his scalp and looked up.

"Kaiholo!" he cried.

The tattooed man emerged from deep shadow and tipped a salute. "The high one demands our presence," he said. "Well, some of us. After this day, I'll be of no use to her. As for the Pilgrim — I cannot speak for his welcome. Follow me." He led them on and around the fallen trees.

"Are Crafters gods or humans?" Reynard asked, curiosity pushing through propriety, considering where they were. "Of this world, or makers of tools?"

"I was told by a drunken Traveler, in a tavern long ago," Kaiholo said, "that they be human neither in shape nor demeanor, but possess some powers found in gods. Before his fellows gathered him, he explained that long ago, at the invitation of Queen Hel, Crafters traveled from afar ... But from whence, he did not know. Nor did the others."

"Not gods, and not the Queen of Hell's children!" Reynard exclaimed, angry at the possibility he was being teased.

"He is deluded on Hel and conflates," Widsith said to Kern.

"Make no such mistake when you meet the Travelers," Kern said. "They know the truth. Crafters assume their own mantles, and press the krater cities around the waste to serve their eccentric needs, and for these circumstances, and these failings, we on this and six other islands, I think, all live."

The tattooed man now focused his attention on Reynard. "Boy, some claim thou herald'st great change."

"I do not feel it," Reynard said.

"Guldreth so informed me — just an hour past," Kaiholo said. "She hath abandoned drake hunting and the southern shore, and makes her way to a chamber in the high maze of the old fortress. Now all is muddle in the krater lands, and she prepareth to join her kind and escape."

"Escape where?" Widsith asked.

Kaiholo shrugged. "She confideth not."

Kern looked back along the declivity, toward the hollow in the fall of ice. "Let us move on. Best be swift."

The northern third of the Ravine had been overgrown centuries past by mats of vines like no growth Reynard had ever seen — strong enough to hold trees that had toppled from the steep sides. The trail they followed twisted among great columns of stone spaced like struts in broken wagon wheels. These held back crushing and groaning walls of melting ice that released pools and swirls of their own fog. They saw their way only by cold, scattered stars peeking through the mats. Kern, Reynard, and Widsith hewed close to Kaiholo. But they moved too swiftly in the darkness for the boy, and he stumbled often over roots and stones.

By the time they reached the end of the path, the roof of vines had been ripped open by the fall of several of the largest trees, and now, eyes adapted to the starlit dark, they saw a high, wide wall of close-hewed and fitted stone — a wall that must have once been interrupted by hundreds of windows that were now, along the lower reaches, chocked by flat, ugly bricks, as if, for those inside this wall — this advanced face of an unlikely fortress — the gloom of the Ravine was still too bright. Narrow steps had been thrust into the wall, crumbling and cracking the stones. Anyone who dared to climb was protected only by a winding, crumbling balustrade of woven wicker, following the steps in their jagged, back-and-forth ascent like some prodigious basket-snake.

Reynard kept close to Widsith, who followed as Kaiholo and then Kern began their climb. He paused and reached for what he thought were flowers growing around the wicker.

"Do not touch," Kern cautioned. "Many biting things here." He opened one hand to show scars on a palm.

Reynard withdrew his fingers. Small and brilliant red even in the shadow, the flowers resembled little sprouts of flame rising from circlets of blue petals. At the nearness of his fingers, they withdrew like anemones on a tidal beach and chirped like crickets, taunting him.

"She collects Crafter refuse," Kaiholo said, and showed scars on his own palm — unmarked by tattoos. "Fascinated by all things Crafter!"

"Plans for creations never approved," Kern added. "Undeveloped or forgotten schemes. Ephemera. Things that know not any way home, nor whether home awaiteth. She arrangeth them like a gardener, even here. As for those devilish, nipping flowers — they came here as seeds carried by strange clouds from the krater lands, falling in muddy rain." Kaiholo looked up at the narrow holes in the thick canopy of vines. "Best avoid such rain, or you will be crusted like a reef."

After they had all passed, the flowers slowly reemerged and shivered.

The first flights of steps took them, slowly and cautiously enough, to a wide indented cleft. From here, more steps forked like lightning ascended to a few open porticoes, which passed through roofless walls and led to more staircases halfway up this next prodigious, sealed-off facing.

Even this high above the blocks of melting ice, the air burned and clogged Reynard's nose with the pervasive odor of an unholy, devilish chill.

Beyond the masonry walls, more steps now became apparent, climbing to a wide parapet just beneath a half-dome inset with a frieze of mosaics whose subjects Reynard could not discern from this vantage.

"That is her door," Kaiholo said, and lifted a snake-patterned brow at Widsith. "Hast thou been here?"

"No," Widsith answered.

"Privileged as thou art," the tattooed man murmured.

Reynard wondered at the patience of these suitors, and how they felt about each other — or the high object of their devotion.

"Still too dark," Kern said, and wandered off to explore this level, his silhouette fading until he was no longer visible. Then he emerged from the far side and announced, "Someone hath provided." In one hand, like an eagle clutching a bundle of twigs, he displayed four sticks with glassy knobs. Kaiholo and the others gratefully took one apiece. Kern then spun his stick in both hands until the knob gave off a dim gray glow. The others, and then Reynard, did likewise.

In the powdery pools of illumination these sticks provided, little

creatures scuttled away. Weirder still was an aura, no more than a
hint, seen only when looking away, of a kind of dim firelight beyond
the glow of the sticks, ascending high along this wall, with passing
suggestions of huge shadows . . . All of which vanished as soon as he
looked at them directly. He did not ask about these. He was not sure
he wanted to know.

They passed the wingless corpse of a drake, and their gray lights
and presence caused commotion among hundreds of little feast-
ing creatures. Reynard had never seen such as these. Some seemed
formed of rare gems, and others resembled rodents made of plates
of metal that took the shapes of muscles and fur and ears, with eyes
like illuminated rubies. These flowed back to resume their consump-
tion of the drake, though with irritated awareness of these new men.

"After she harvested the wings, she had some large metal beast
drag it here for her pets," Kaiholo said. "Such treats do not last long.
To complete her great cloak, she will need to gather permissions
from whichever faction is victorious in the krater lands."

"Then it is a war," Widsith said.

"Will she take thee with her?" Kern asked Kaiholo, glancing at
Widsith.

"She doth not reveal our fate," Kaiholo said. "Or dost thou mean
the Pilgrim?"

"Either," Kern said. Reynard was still thinking over the phrase
"great cloak," presumably made of drake wings. A cloak for whom?

"When dealing with a power just beneath the sky," Kaiholo said,
"I assume nothing, and advise ye likewise. What I do not give cre-
dence to is the tale that thou, Pilgrim, wast once taken by her as
a lover!"

Kern grumbled that he shared that disbelief.

"Even so. She did not bring me here," Widsith said.

"Kept secrets?" Kaiholo asked.

"As one of her station should," Widsith said.

The steps were solid enough, but also infested with more tiny crawling things, which managed to mostly escape their feet. Reynard felt an edgy investigation of the cut on his head and brushed something away with a moan of disgust.

"Patience," Kaiholo said. "We will soon be there."

"She maketh a cloak for herself?" Reynard asked, unable to hold back curiosity any longer.

"Queen Hel, I presume," Kaiholo said. "Only she could wear it. Ah, we are here."

They had reached the top of the steps and a broad portico that followed the curve of the upper wall. The passing shadows and hints of firelight were left behind, to his relief. Sunlight blocked by leafy boughs outshone their glowing sticks. At Kaiholo's example, they left the sticks propped against a wall. Smells of cooking meat and perfume issued from the far reaches of the portico, which was lovely in a shaded way, like a residence in a castle built of dreams. Here the small scavengers had given way to knee-high, furry creatures shaped like jesters' hats, with a pair of stalked eyes on their peaks, and four or more scurrying feet to support them.

"These be not so threatening," Kaiholo said, "but watch the hidden corners. This high lady hath peculiar things in her garden."

Nobody came to greet them. Kaiholo proceeded first. Kern had to stoop as the ceiling had dropped a couple of feet. Columns like the insides of broken shells, spiraled and pearly-pink, became more frequent. The far walls were covered by a mural more pattern than picture, as he had heard from his uncle were found in Moorish palaces, but in motion, steadily progressing through shades of gray and green. His uncle had also told him, one long night at sea, about those regular shapes, which he said held clues to navigating seas and crossing land — but that did not seem to be their purpose here.

They paused cautiously between two columns. Beyond the columns, a cold fire flickered.

Kaiholo looked over his shoulder. "Caution is wise when meeting those just beneath the sky," he said. "Adore, worship — but do not fear. Even for those who have known favor, time passeth and moods change. Truth, Pilgrim?"

"Truth," Widsith replied. "What hearest thou about her mood toward me?"

"Nothing. I find her hapless drakes. I am not her procurer."

"I have been in the Ravine off and on for years and seldom seen her," Kern said.

"Thou art a monster, and so thou art allowed to stay?" Widsith asked. Kern asked in turn, with a wicked grin, what monstrous trait gave the Pilgrim access.

Reynard reached out to touch a spiral's rose-pink smoothness, very like broken seashells on the beaches of Southwold.

"This place is cold," Kern said. "But I see no ice. Ice everywhere but here!"

Reynard looked up at a small scuffing sound. The others alerted as well.

"She is here," Kaiholo said. Now it was Widsith's turn to suck in his breath. Reynard wondered why he was afraid. Had they not been lovers? Had he not pleased her?

Was it possible to please such a being?

He tried to clear his thoughts.

Like sap streaming through ghostly vines, light slowly grew around them in vegetal tangles, weaving through a space beyond the first ring of columns. The cautious visitors observed, transfixed by both wonder and concern, while the veins of light filled in the spaces around them. Now they saw that they stood on one side of a low, wide chamber filled with rank after rank of disks, bigger than most shields, arranged upright like plates in a cupboard. The disks appeared to have thin edges almost as sharp as knives. All gleamed with their own inner light, and each was different from the other.

"Hast thou seen these before?" Kern asked Kaiholo.

"Only heard of them," Kaiholo answered. "And thou, Pilgrim?"

Widsith shook his head. "They are new to me."

"Shaded moons stolen from the darkest nights!" Kern said.

"Quaint," Kaiholo said, picking at his teeth with a patterned finger.

They approached the first row of disks. Reynard tapped one. Each disk was hard and translucent, as wide as Reynard was tall. He touched the nearest disk's rim. It did not cut, but made a bowed ringing sound at the roughness of his finger.

"Do that the right way, it might bid thee enter!" Kern suggested.

Reynard stooped to peer into the center of the first disk, and found shapes beneath the shining surface: shoals of fish swimming through dark curling weeds, all caught in a moment of stillness, and graced with more artistry than he had ever seen. Bolder than the others — so far — he stepped up to the next disk and bent to peer again. In this one he saw layer upon layer of strange, great trees, falling back in a thick blue fog, as if in some ancient morning, perhaps the morning of the world. Other shapes rose between the trees, and he realized that lizards the size of houses lurked in that fog, as well as bird-like creatures that perched on stone pillars and spread their wings like cormorants. But these were neither birds nor drakes, and each grinned with a mouth full of teeth no seabird had ever possessed.

Reynard could not help himself. He turned and studied the disks in the next row. These revealed ebony depths filled with clouds of diamond-bright stars, like a clear, dry night sky. Behind that disk rose another, revealing islands floating in a void — not islands on a sea, but scattered in empty air and topped by great castles dotted with lights . . . impossible realms of impossible people!

He frowned in frustration. These disks seemed important, more than just a collection — but a history, a library! There was not time enough to walk down the rows and do justice to them, to tally row after row, each disk as delicate and astounding as the first.

He turned back to the disk that contained a forest. One of the lizards had moved! He was sure of it — moved closer, head angled as if to study him!

"They are sorcerer's mirrors!" Kern said. "Why doth she allow us to bear witness to such Crafter work?"

Widsith seemed lost in reverie, gathering enough courage to stroke one disk, then stare in wonder at his fingers. "Finer than anything I saw in the east. 'Tis as if Pu himself had embedded Crafter thoughts in fine white clay, then fired it to wondrous porcelain."

A female voice spoke. "I am leaving soon. Come forward and say farewell before all here is gone."

A Drake Wing Cloak

WIDSITH STEPPED to one side and looked between the columns. Kern tried to see over the moon-disks, but bumped his head against the low roof.

Beyond the ranks and rows, on the far side of the chamber, stood a female figure of middle size, dressed in a cloak patterned in thin silver, like the shining skeleton of a decayed leaf — or the framework of a drake's wings.

"She doth wear her wings!" Kaiholo said. "All is indeed tumbled and new."

At her gesture and invitation, they walked between the columns toward a dais on which were set several stools and a basic wooden throne. Reynard saw that this figure's skin was like tarnished silver, and she looked upon them with the large, golden-brown eyes of a roe, flecked with gold like nuggets in a stream.

She removed her cloak and set it aside on nothing visible, where it took on a limp but cared-for drape. She wore a long dress like the bell of a flower, also made of drake's wings, and a vest that tightened at her waist but loosely wrapped her shoulders.

She spoke again, in soft tones, using words Reynard did not understand. Kaiholo drew himself tall and full of dignity. He motioned Reynard forward. "She asketh for thee first," he said. Widsith seemed to question this decision, this request, but when he tried to stand in front of Reynard, Kern stopped him and shook his head in warning.

"Come, young Fox," Guldreth now said. "I would have advice from thee, if thou art th'one who can deliver it to me. I believe thou hast met curious beings — yes?"

The companions who had accompanied Reynard into this strange place seemed to fade both in memory and vision. The tarnished silver woman glided, her long bell-shaped gown rustling, leading him down the ranks of disks, hundreds of disks or more ... the rows dividing like tree branches farther and farther back into her apartments, which seemed many, with doors and arches opening to yet longer hallways leading deeper and deeper into darkness, seeming to shrink until he was afraid he was already lost and would never find his way back.

And wherever she went, there were the disks, each bearing an image of some impossible place, or creatures that did not exist, or faces of beings not entirely human, until he felt dizzy and filled with their dreams, their delusions.

"I would myself speak to these figures!" Reynard said. "I would ask who you are, and why you have need of me." Reynard's eyes grew heavy-lidded, his look desperate.

"The dead or the great answer through the living and the lesser, but only when they desire. You say you were taught by your grandmother. How long since her passage?"

"I was a child," Reynard said.

"Then she doth not roam in shadows to seek her favorites, and none can summon her shade without knowing many secrets, many languages not bestowed on the living — even those just beneath the sky."

"She is here?" Until now, he had thought Guldreth was asking about his two visitors, the man with the white shadow — the man with the feathered hat.

"A grand Traveler. I believe she hath protected thee for some time. Dost thou feel her, Fox?"

"I do not feel or see her."

"No surprise," Guldreth said. "And yet, thou'rt here, and this is the first time a grand Traveler of her stature hath visited this fortress, dead or alive. I wonder if the dead can still convey a Traveler's boon?"

Reynard shook his head, ashamed at his ignorance, and of the fear that now froze him to his bones. Actually being in the presence of the dead was true necromancy, sure to condemn one to Hell — or the infernal regions, rather. "What boon is that?"

"Words, Fox. Words new and words old, words that have shaped lands and peoples, and given power to formless ones who had none before. I would almost wish to be a Traveler, just to know such power!" She waved her silvery hand at the disks in this side hall, in the back chambers, all glowing faintly like moons behind clouds. "All these sketches the Crafters have made began with such words, words given to them by your kind — by Travelers. Travelers gave them purpose and power, and out of all that . . . we arise and struggle. Our lives begin, we work and do battle, and our lives end. The power of words!"

Guldreth's voice seemed regretful. He reacted to that instinctively, as if he were some sort of strange gentleman hoping to provide comfort or solace.

"A phrase echoes in my thoughts," Reynard said. "The words are not strange, but their meaning is."

"May I hear them?"

"'The first mother is the first word,'" he said.

"Ah! You *do* know the secret of Hel's islands," Guldreth said. Her dark silvery smile was extraordinary, her lips like the petals of a blue rose, had he ever seen such — he had not — and the teeth behind them were small and perfect, their color between ivory and polished silver coin.

"I know nothing! I have heard those words before, and now I believe, I think, I might hear my grandmother's voice speaking them to me . . . yet she is silent!"

"Powers such as your grandmother have ways of leaving messages. Since arriving, thou hast received the memories of an Eater, true?"

"Yes. Some of them."

"Valdis?"

"Yes."

"She obeys, then. She was appointed by me, through the Afrique, to tend to thee as well as he doth attend the Pilgrim — or better. Not to give more time, but key memories — or a key to memories! — to shape thy purpose. Remember now, when did thy grandmother teach thee?"

Reynard stumbled back through his earliest memories and came across feelings of warmth and calm, of deep reddish light and pushing and kicking against a yielding barrier . . . living in warm darkness, hearing his grandmother's voice in comfort and ease, but distant, as if from far away, along with a softly beating drum and pulsing pressure.

He looked up and around at the residence and the room behind Guldreth, at the rows of disks, as if they contained those very memories — but then his eyes were drawn back to the silvery face.

Reynard had caught only a glimpse, through eyes not yet opened, of where he had been when his grandmother had told her tales.

"I was in my mother's womb," he said.

"Ah!" Guldreth said with a flush of delight, as if seeing a marvel fulfilled. Reynard could not imagine her polished skin could take on such an inner glow. "And so it is still thine. I see her appear on thy face, like a fine mask!"

"Now that I hear those tales again, how do I find them in an infant's memory, all grown over by later life?"

"Are they, now? Thou hast done well enough so far," Guldreth said. "Thou art here."

"Not by my own doing," Reynard said.

"All will be found, if being found is what thy grandmother's messages need and want. So tell me. Did she foresee that thou wouldst meet a man with a white shadow? A man who doth make roads hither and yon through widths and lengths we neither see nor feel?"

Again, a shock. She saw through his skin, down to his every moment! "I do not remember any such warning, though I do remember such a man."

"Ah, 'tis hard to ask a babe to carry gems to his future self! But if thou knowest such a man, then he must have tasked thee even beyond thy grandmother's whispers. And that is treasure I would spend elsewhere, were I you.

"Soon I depart and will not return. I carry mine one work with me — the great old Queen's cloak, of which what I wear is merely a test, a pattern — and will instruct my servants to shatter these toys and baubles, which Crafters have discarded and which no longer move me, and if humans found them, would vex them to madness. But I am still strangely sad to do so. What thinkest thou of these ancient dreams? Go thou back and walk among them. See more. Some are quite beautiful — and some not even I can comprehend. But thy fellows wait to lead thee on."

She glided off and led him back between disks from which he averted his eyes, already overfull with creations that had never been born or finished, through halls and doors and arches to the low-ceilinged courtyard. Her gown draped and flowing behind her like the plumes of a peacock. At her commanding gesture, he followed a step behind, avoiding the gown, afraid it might shift like a ghost and catch up his feet, so silvery and elusive it seemed.

Guldreth paused before a disk that had been pushed aside from a row. She said, "This one is a puzzle and favorite." The pale plate was covered in blue flowers, of no sort he recognized. Some of the flowers had captured insects in a kind of cage of their petals, and as he looked closer, he saw that the insects were playing a game very like chess, while waiting, he assumed, for their inevitable doom.

"Noble patience and courage!" Guldreth said, turning around to another disk. "And now, this one . . . I have studied this one over and over, and wonder what thou thinkest?"

This plate, like many of the others, was twilight dark and showed gaunt men and women walking in endless lines around a fortress that spread over many hills, with walls that rose to touch a gossamer curtain in the sky. In the upper part of the disk, the curtain had parted to show something indistinct peering through, not a face, nothing he could understand, but watching, and not through eyes, of which it possessed none.

"I have never seen a Crafter," Guldreth said. "That may be the most they have revealed of themselves to any between earth and sky."

"Be they more powerful than you, milady?" Reynard asked.

"No. More creative, however. None hath seen their like since Hel lured them here. If she did lure them here. Few of my kind are in agreement on that."

Reynard removed himself from between the rows and stood near her, vexed enough himself by floating lands and lizards the size of houses — and faceless ones the very demigods could not decide upon.

Guldreth returned to her dais and gathered her train around it. "Valdis will take ye to meet the Travelers. I am told by Calybo that they will escort ye to the krater lands, and beyond — to the eastern shores, if needs be. To the extent that Travelers are warriors, they will protect . . . but I would rely on your fellows first."

"Must I meet Crafters?"

Guldreth laughed a bell-like laugh. "I would not wish it on any-one, Fox. But for thee, it must be. The young Eater Valdis — and believe me, boy, she hath still a sort of youth — will guide all of ye through the troubles, and not just Kaiholo, handsome as he is, nor Widsith with all his wiles and secrets."

She held up her hands and seemed to shield her face against the glow of the disks.

"I see thee, Pilgrim, back there in the shadows! My heart doth leap to know of thy return. I hope thou hast made peace with thy wife, and regret that thou shalt fail in finding her more years. To-gether, Fox, all these fine human creatures and the half-human Ana-kim — blessings upon the woman who gave him birth! — will escort thee to where thy message, thy grandmother's words, will be even more welcome. Even more important. But there is no going back to Zodiako, young man. Tell them that path is no longer open, that the Ravine is dangerous, and thou shouldst leave by the caves beneath this fortress. Valdis can bring ye horses." She looked up as if listen-ing to music. "Is it not lovely? But here, for all those just beneath the sky, our time comes to an end."

Embarrassed, Reynard looked away from Guldreth's gold-flecked eyes and gleaming face, away from her robe of drake's wings, afraid of what he had heard, of all he had forgotten and must remember again to be of any use to this extraordinary being. Widsith and Kern stood back beyond the disks, between two of the shell pillars, and Kaiholo between them. Kern was so stooped over he might as well have been on his knees. Their faces showed dismay, and Reynard wondered why . . .

But then he turned back.

Guldreth was gone.

Lost to knowing what to do next, Reynard crossed the open space under the lowering roof to rejoin them.

"How could one love a creature like that?" Kern asked.

Widsith sighed. "Practice and patience and a quiet tongue."

"And how could Maeve put up with such a rival?"

"The same," Widsith said. "And we had not long together to find the challenge in it. We did not hear all she said to thee, Fox. Canst thou recall and tell us now?"

"I carry a message from my grandmother," Reynard said. "And Guldreth saith the Ravine is no longer open to us. It is too dangerous."

Kaiholo nodded. "The northern caves will lead us out to where we can meet Travelers."

"Did Guldreth hear thy message or find it in thine eyes?" Kern asked.

"I do not know all of it myself," Reynard said. "She said you — I mean, Valdis — must deliver me to Travelers who will escort us to the Crafters in the krater lands. She told me to trust the young Eater."

Widsith said, "Hardly young to thee, boy!"

Reynard set his face in a stubborn mask. "Yes. That one."

"Thou sound'st most eager to see her again, Fox," Kaiholo said.

"She shared memories."

"But is she still here?" Widsith asked. "Be there any Eaters left in the Ravine?"

"I passed her as I came to meet ye," Kern said.

"Did she speak?" Widsith asked.

Kern shook his head. "The rest of the Eaters have departed. I searched."

Kaiholo confirmed this.

"Calybo may lead them off the island," Widsith said. "We will learn soon enough. Come, boy." He put his arm around Reynard's shoulders and urged him away from the court where Guldreth had kept her collections.

As they descended the steps under that great half dome, Kern first and Kaiholo last, with Reynard and Widsith between, the giant asked the Pilgrim, "On thy long voyages out in the finished lands, didst thou ever find God?"

Widsith chuckled. "I would think a giant would know God the better for rising closer to His house."

"I have never reached just beneath the sky," Kern said. "Too much of the human in me. Didst thou?"

"I met many who knew Him well," Widsith said. "Spanish sailors. Wives in Manchu land and in the Philippines and the islands called Malayo. I spake with those who knew God as Allah, and as pagan golden idols such as Jagrenat, which is carried on a great wagon of wood and iron, pulled by a hundred men on many wheels that crush and deliver his worshippers like beetles direct to a pagan heaven. Those who call God Allah lust after the gems and wealth given to Jagrenat, but have so far failed to secure them. I knew those who look much as you, Kaiholo, and sail great canoes across the wide Pacific. They worship severe, frowning wooden statues raised in forests of their kind, like markers in a graveyard. And I know this well — that all the Gods they worship have been shaped and planted by Crafters, to make the world more interesting."

"I believe that can be said of us as well," Kern said. "Doth that make their Gods any less real?"

Widsith chuckled again. "No, nor any weaker," he said.

"What of the Christian God?" Reynard asked, feeling more and more lost and discouraged.

"Which Christian God?" Widsith asked. "The God of Philip and the Pope, or the God of Elizabeth and Henry? Mother of God, Mary, or Son of Mary and God Himself, Jesus?"

Reynard had tears in his eyes from all he had experienced, afraid of what he might believe himself in a few more days.

Then he felt his heart grow cold, as if the Eaters' snow had filled his chest.

The first word is the first mother.

That is your God now.

From the chamber above came a cacophony of crashing and shattering. Reynard looked up, startled.

Widsith shook his head sadly.

Kaiholo said, "Were I brave enough, I would have studied them longer."

Under and Out

They walked along the base of the fortress, looking for an entrance to the caverns beneath. "The air smells sick," the tattooed man said, and spat.

Through sun scattered by high vines and trees, looking into what passed for morning here, the Ravine's shaped ice walls were growing spiky. A sheet broke away from the far reaches of the fortress and collapsed with ponderous grace, grinding and crashing. The echoes ran south along the Ravine, and then returned in a rough staccato chorus.

Kaiholo said, "Soon the Ravine will flood, and that flood will carry the rotting bodies of creatures too afraid to leave. Let us not be among them."

They came upon a high, dark entrance, half hidden by old masonry. Kaiholo entered the cavern. Kern and the rest followed — all but Reynard.

"Thou hast a stubborn face," Widsith said in passing.

"I would understand what my use is to them, to any of you!" Reynard said.

"The boy doth grow a beard," Kaiholo said cheerfully, as if none of what they had seen, or were experiencing, mattered. "Let us train up like mules — arm to shoulder, the giant at the rear!"

"Boy, go or stay," Widsith said, exasperated. "Thou wilt learn more if thou goest, and if thou stayest, likely die."

Reynard returned his piercing look, then took up behind Kern, until the giant stepped aside and let him and Widsith join the line as Kaiholo had suggested. Guided by the tattooed man, who spun his orb but seemed to already know these caverns well, they walked along in gray-lit murk for hundreds of yards, then saw a faint gleam ahead.

"More ice," Kern said, pointing to the right-hand side of the cave. "It is still thick here."

"And still alive with Eater power," Widsith said.

"There is a brighter block ahead," Kaiholo said.

The block was a pure, clear sheet of smoothed ice, veined in both snowy white and ethereal blue. Through a particularly thin and transparent spot, they made out a moving shadow — face rippling but clear enough. The face frowned and vanished.

The strangely beautiful shade who had leaned over Reynard suddenly reshaped in front of them. Though dressed in a shimmering, diamond-marked fabric, she did not seem to wear it with conviction.

"Guldreth hath loaned her a shift," Kaiholo whispered to them.

"Drake wing?" Reynard asked.

"No," Kaiholo said. "She is not that far above the mud."

Valdis spoke in a voice soft as a passing breeze. "Guldreth doth command me. I am to deliver this human child to the proper Travelers, who will take him to the krater lands. We will meet them at the join of two great trods. She telleth me they expect him."

Reynard could not keep his gaze off the Eater's pale features, her sea-foam flesh and deep-set green eyes that flickered like lanterns in a huge black room. He could not decide whether she was terrifying or beautiful, but one thing he felt, beyond any doubt, was that she was neither young nor old.

"The cross-trod nearest to the northern end of the Ravine is already halfway to the krater lands," Kern said.

"Thou hast been there?" Widsith asked.

"I have so ventured."

Valdis's whispery voice took on a deeper timbre. "The Ravine is draining. Our path will be crowded with spirits and frightened beasts. We must move quickly. Eater horses are fast, and do not always kill the humans they carry. The stables are just north of here."

They walked in deep gloom for a time, Valdis leading the way. She did not need a spinning lamp.

The roof of the cavern rose to an echoing emptiness. Ancient stone pillars, dark purple lava bricks, and what looked like intricately figured ivory or bone, emerged from the gloom and defined a stable, a dim line of stalls in which Eater horses stood very still, eyes closed as if asleep. Valdis opened the gate and led them through. "I will choose a horse for each of you," she said, and looked to Kern. "Even you. Once assigned, do not try to put a rope on your mount, or look it directly in the eye."

Reynard counted all the animals he could see. The stable housed at least ten, sleek and fine of form, their coats like wet velvet, black or gray. Valdis spoke, and the animals opened their eyes and raised their heads. She then led them one by one out of their stalls. Not themselves Eaters, they nevertheless reacted to the humans with a proud disregard that persuaded Valdis to take each aside and whisper in its ear. At her words, they uttered high, piercing cries, not so much whinnies as like the sounds made by swifting owls and other hidden night creatures.

She matched the giant with a great draft horse, a mare, the largest Reynard had ever seen, bigger even than the ones that had drawn the great Traveler wagon back in the woods near Zodiako — but black as pitch and with amber eyes. "This is yours," she said to Kern. "I hope you can control her."

"I will try, O mistress," Kern said, and stood by the mare's flank.

"Move over there," she instructed, and the giant guided the horse to just outside the gate.

Valdis now brought forward a horse with ornately marked haunches — a combination of branded scars and shaved hair. "This is for you," she said to Reynard. Lacking stirrups, he could only haul himself up by holding on to a hank of mane and swinging his legs over, as he had done in his uncle's shop, positioning horses to be shod. He sat up straight on the mare's back, legs gripping her cold ribs, and wondered who had marked her — and when. Was she meant to survive magic, curses?

Valdis led a third horse to Kaiholo, a slender mare with a strong but nervous gait. She now pointed to Widsith, and he stepped up to the pale gray gelding she had chosen for him, the shade of an early dawn, with eyes the color of a sunrise cloud. "This was one of Guldreth's prizes. She hath no need of it now."

"Did these animals ever cross the chafing waste?" Widsith asked.

"They have," Valdis answered.

"A boy in the village was kicked by one," Widsith said in an undertone to Reynard. "He hath a bottle containing the dust, which doth sparkle and give visions."

"Are we to go there?" Reynard asked.

"Mayhaps," Widsith answered.

With all but her mounted, Valdis walked back into the stable to bring forth her animal, a stallion black as the walls of the cave. His eyes were black as well. He was difficult to see at all. Valdis mounted him as if taking flight. She then issued a thin whistle, high and sharp as a needle, and the remaining horses kicked and reared, and then ran out of the stable and toward the northern exit.

"They run as if —" Kaiholo began, but cut himself short when they heard a great rushing sound and hundreds of bat-like animals flew over them on stubby wings, brushing the cavern's roof — ignoring the riders below, but making great haste to leave.

Kaiholo grimaced. "Little time. Let us move! Unlikely we ever return." Valdis now whistled softly, and all the horses paced north with fluid grace.

Reynard looked back at Valdis, but turned away when she seemed to notice. Despite his fear, he felt a strong curiosity about what she knew of him, and he of her, and how she — if she was a female, still — would travel in daylight, beside humans. And he was curious about her story, if she had one, if she remembered — and perhaps it was best that she did not.

The glow that Reynard had thought might be daylight was deceptive. They passed into a narrower cavern hung with many creatures that themselves supplied the light. The running horses had long since passed, leaving prints in the sandy floor.

"Someone hath added decorations," Kaiholo said doubtfully, and batted aside a hanging, curling shape like a small blue monkey, but with wide, glowing eyes and a grim, gaping mouth.

Reynard was alarmed. "What are those? More servants? Why do they not flee as well?"

Hundreds dangled from long threads attached high in the gloom, twisting slowly and illuminating with their pale beams the sandy road, uninterested in the visitors below — or anything else.

"Monkey lights," Kern said. "They have been here for as long as I. Someone doubtless strung them to light a better path, as it is dark in these caverns even for Eaters. They fear nothing and do not eat."

"Fine servants!" Kaiholo said. "Would any object if we take a few with us?" He bravely grasped one of the small creatures and perched it on his shoulder. It did not bite or protest, and its eyes pointed ahead. He tugged on the strand that attached it to the ceiling, saw it was dry and dead — more like a rope — and reached up with a knife to cut it. The creature remained quiet, so he took another and placed it on his other shoulder, then cut its cable as well. "I will light the way!" the tattooed man said. "Anybody else want to host?" The others declined. He patted the head of his left-hand monkey. It briefly closed its wide bright eyes.

Soon they were beyond the hanging menagerie. Kaiholo's pair provided all the light they needed as they moved forward. They rode now on a gray sandy floor, as if a river had once flowed through the Ravine, debouching at the cavern's exit. To the echoing, sandy scuff of the horses' hooves, they rode on for some hundred more yards, all the time accompanied by a musical dripping and a suffocating awareness of the great massif of stone above.

For a few dozen yards they passed what might have been the bones and spine of a great monster — until Reynard pointed out that this was the wrecked hull of a ship. "How did it get here?" he asked. "How old is it?" Nobody knew. Kern said this was the first time he had seen it. Reynard leaned to run his hand along one of the ribs. The Eater horse looked back at him. As instructed, Reynard looked away. "Very old," he said. "Not so much wood as marble."

"I do not doubt the abilities of Crafters to put things where they wish, and take them from whenever they wish — even the beginning of time," Kaiholo said.

"The end of the cavern is not far," Kern observed. "I can see it, like a single lantern."

This time the light was true. They emerged under bright sun and a cloudless sky. Kaiholo gently lowered his monkeys to the sandy ground. They blinked, then crawled back into the cavern. "Obedient," he observed.

Valdis watched them without expression.

"We are out of it," Widsith said. "Thanks to whatever God you please."

With bored grace, their Eater mounts climbed the rough lava slope that led up from the cavern. Ahead spread another wall of forest, or perhaps jungle. Reynard did not recognize any of the trees.

Valdis pointed that way. "A cross-trod lieth beyond that forest," she said.

"I have never gone so far," Kaiholo said.

"I have," Kern said. "But I saw no signs of humans or others. Certainly no Eaters."

"You would not see them when they pass," Valdis said.

"Do you see them?" Reynard asked her.

"Yes," she said.

"Came they this way?"

"Both ways," she said. "They are all gone now."

"Even Calybo?" Widsith asked.

"Even him."

Kern hmmed softly. He studied Reynard riding beside Valdis, stiff in his saddle, as if escorting a maiden — a strange sight indeed, given that Valdis looked even more like a ghost in light of day and hardly seemed to burden the horse.

But Reynard saw that she cast a dark shadow.

Old Ice and Two Trods

ON THE EDGE of the forest, a dense wall of dark green, Valdis pulled back on her horse, wheeled it halfway around, and said calmly, "Flood is here."

The men looked at each other, hearing nothing, but the horses, without guidance, broke into a run, then stopped abruptly and spun to face the cavern. Reynard held on as best he could with neither saddle nor stirrups. The rumble grew to a roar, and a frothy tide of sour grayness, higher than the horses' withers, rushed around them. Reynard clung to the short mane with both his hands and all his strength, and felt his horse flinch in pain as chunks of ice and pieces of branch and smaller rocks struck legs and belly, and then, as all their horses shrieked, larger stones and even boulders.

The horses did not resist the flow, but stampeded to keep up with it, and right alongside them flew or swam creatures he had never seen before — nightmare creatures, furred snakes with great fangs and huge red eyes, winding around or climbing over spinning chunks of melting ice, hissing and screeching, gripping the horses' legs or biting at them to hold on, as the flood bounced riders and horses from trees and rocks hidden in creepers.

Reynard thought he saw, over the neck of his animal, a gargoyle or something like it — a hippogriff, perhaps, though he had seen such only once, spouting rain off the roof of an Aldeburgh church. The creature, trying to stay above water on its spread wings, already half drowned, stretched its head up, gave him a beseeching gape of its beak, and went under.

They had no choice but to go with the flood into the trees.

Reynard heard Widsith call his name just as something wrenched him about. He let go of the mane and tumbled into the water.

Separation

He is here!"

"Where is the Pilgrim?"

"I do not see the Eater!"

These voices sprang up around him, muffled by water in his ears. He tried to open his eyes, but the lids were stuck together by mud. Someone helped him roll onto his back, and he coughed up sour water and what few things he had eaten in the last twelve hours. When he tried to sit up, Kern was there to help him, calling out to Kaiholo. More water splashed on his face, but this felt different, fresh and cool, unlike the melted ice from the Ravine. Soon he had wiped his eyes and pried them open. The day was blurry and overcast but still bright.

"Where are the horses?" Reynard asked, and managed to get to his feet. Surprisingly, he was not terribly bruised, though he had bumps on his cheek and brow. He was covered in sticky mud, as were the tattooed man and the giant.

"Two are over there," Kaiholo said, pointing to a gap between two large boulders. "Maybe they were lifted and dropped by the flood."

"I see not Widsith nor Valdis nor th'other horses," Kern said. He was worse off than Reynard, face covered in dirty blood and both eyes nearly swollen shut. But he walked bravely and called out for Widsith and for Valdis.

"Is the Ravine empty?" Kaiholo asked him.

He nodded. "It must be. It sloped this way, down to the caverns. Everything flowed to this end."

Reynard walked toward the gap between the boulders, to see how wide it was, but Kern stopped him. "The horses are afraid," he said. "They will not let me get near them."

"Are they injured?"

"Likely."

He thought of the furred snakes biting and hanging on. "We have to see to their wounds! Horses are delicate, tossed like that, and where are we if they die?"

Kern agreed. "But do not go near them. Let them come to us!"

Reynard picked his way around the boulders and through the debris, pausing only once to examine a dead thing he found wrapped up in a deadfall of logs and broken branches — a thing with a bony crescent for a head, a long gray body, and many, many legs. He made a disgusted, frightened sound and pulled back to take a different path.

Up a brushy slope, away from the tangles of sticks and dead things, Reynard looked for another way between the boulders and found a roundabout path over a clump of solidly nested rocks of all shapes, some of them curious indeed — as if the exit from the Ravine had hosted tribes of sculptors or Medusas. He worked to the crest of the conglomeration and peered into a gap in which the two Eater horses were stamping and making their strange night sounds, though subdued and weary. He clucked and called to them. They alerted but did not stop pacing. They seemed stuck and unable to find their way out of the hollow, which worried him. Had they been lifted and deposited, as Kern guessed? If so, they might be badly hurt and beyond his means to save. But still, he slowly descended the suggestive rocks and finally stood on one edge of the gap, arms at his side, keeping still and quiet. He glanced over his shoulder. The closest space between the big boulders took a lock-and-key curve, which made it difficult to see any exit. It was just wide enough to squeeze a horse through — but no horse would willingly make that journey without guidance, he thought.

Finally, one of the horses — it was Kaiholo's mount, and the other was his own, with its curious patterns — sidled up to within a few paces, shivering and desperately unhappy. Reynard had nothing to offer and kept his hands by his sides, head bowed, the picture of quiet calm and he hoped familiarity, though they had not been together long.

Kern perched near the top of the pile, also quiet.

"Can they get through?" Kaiholo called from the other side. Kern hushed him.

"That must have been frightening," Reynard said to the pair. "It scared me, but I am a lot smaller."

The horses watched him, cross-wove in their pacing, and showed the whites of their eyes — more a golden yellow, actually — as if they were considering stamping him.

He wished Valdis were here to advise him — or warn him not to try!

"We can get ye out of here, but it will take some squeezing," he told them, and walked slowly around them, then stepped into the gap as the horses watched, without ever meeting their eyes — as Valdis had advised. "See? I can do it. I think thou canst get through as well, and there is more room on the other side — and maybe food."

Kern squatted atop the rocks, still silent.

"We all need to eat," Reynard said. "And I would like to see to thine injuries. Thou hast blood on thy hock. And thou hast a gash on thy withers. Pretty deep, I think. Come here and let me look, and then let us go through."

His calm speech and steady demeanor seemed to be wearing down their resistance. His own horse came up within a stride and lowered its muzzle, then shoved it into his cupped hand.

"Good," Reynard said, and turned to the other animal. "And what about thee? Kaiholo, come down and join us."

"There is another horse out here!" Kaiholo called. "I think it is Valdis's."

"Your friend doth await thee," Reynard murmured, stroking the muzzle and underjaw.

Kaiholo entered the gap and stood aside when his horse stamped and snapped, not yet ready. "They seem to favor thee, Fox," he said ruefully. In time, paired with their riders, the horses calmed and finally seemed almost placid as Reynard pulled and cajoled them through the gap, one at a time. The fit was tight for Kaiholo's animal, but he seemed ready to leave, and made it through quickly, maneuvering the double bend as if it were a common thing, then stood shivering, nostrils flaring at all the strange smells — and at more debris and strange bodies caught in the lower scrub trees beyond. Now Kern brought up Valdis's mount. The horses greeted each other with whickers and tail flicks and laying their heads close, like all horses Reynard had ever known. They had been Eater horses for all their lives, Reynard guessed, and might be used to strange sights, but seldom anything like this. Reynard himself couldn't even put a name to most of the dead creatures.

Kern left the group and walked to the left into the shady woods, then returned. "There is a notch or break over that way. Let us see what is on the other side. The horses will warn us if it is not to their liking."

"What if it is not to our liking?" Kaiholo asked. "What if it is dead wood all the way?"

"It is not," Kern said.

"You have been here?"

"And beyond. I told you, giants have privileges. I need to find my horse."

"And we need to find Valdis and Widsith," Reynard said. They guided the three horses toward the notch, then led them right through a thinning patch. The darkness beyond was slowly revealing a slope, and perhaps fifty yards up the slope, above the flood, dead trees that had not been painted with mud.

But before that point, the crest of the flood had delivered a sad sight — Kern's mount, the huge draft horse, lay dead in a patch of debris, head almost doubled back and limbs twisted.

Kern spent a few minutes with the corpse, which Reynard found touching. The giant then rose.

"Let us find the others," he said.

"I wish we could have gone around the coast," Kaiholo said. "The sea is much friendlier to my people, even with its hungry beasts."

Reynard looked at the two and saw they were near the end of their wits, beyond exhaustion and demoralized. He remembered his mother and father and their ways of dealing with travail in themselves and others. They would always speak of family, and origins — of the things people were most proud of. "I am told of Land Travelers and Sea Travelers," Reynard said. "They draw great ropes of words across land and sea. But who travels the sky?"

"Ah — those be the birds!" Kaiholo said, perking up at least a little. "The feathered ones take their songs to both land and sea and carry many secrets, if thou couldst only listen."

"I'll listen," he promised, but there were no bird sounds in the trees — and none of the larger trees were in the least like those he had seen in England. The branches took spirals and spread great leaves and small, or bundles of reddish needles, or bluish thorns.

They climbed the slope above the Ravine's wash and stood atop a low hill, in the shadow of a ridge that stretched from the inner ring of mountains to the shore.

"The horses must eat. There be no grass or herbs or suitable leaves here," Kaiholo said, and then raised his head, alerting at a noise. Kern heard it as well.

"Is that Widsith?" Reynard asked.

Kern warned, "We should take deeper cover." The horses recognized their alarm and kept quiet as they all sought to hide in a thick brake below the crest of the hill.

Kaiholo silently made his way through the brake to examine a hollow in the ridge beyond.

"Someone's looking for us," Kern guessed, dropping to a squat. "Not anyone we wish to meet, I trow."

Kaiholo returned a few minutes later. "There are bodies," he said. "Men. Not Spaniards. Nine or ten at least. I did not tarry to count. Judging by their kit, I think they are folk from the eastern shore. I do not know why they have come all the way here. But they did not find what they wanted. They are dead."

"What killed them?"

"I would say a great Eater. They have been sucked down to the last instant."

Tying the horses, Reynard and Kern took the path Kaiholo had found and came to a shadowed silver waterfall and a trickle of stream from a shelf along the higher ridge. Here, lying half in, half out of the stream, like soft and slumbering stones, lay nine men . . . or what had once been men. One was having the hair on his careless skull parted by the fall. The others were nothing but bones draped in pallid wet skin.

Kaiholo stepped into the stream and knelt beside the closest. "Scouts or pickets. Too many, I would say. Could point to a greater march. Mayhaps they were deceived and drawn here."

Reynard thought of the way the King of Troy had deceived the Spanish.

Kaiholo fingered the corpse's jerkin, cut and stitched from a finely tanned skin — not unlike those worn by the blunters. The rest of their kit consisted of thick trousers and sturdy leather boots, and each still carried a pair of good swords, one short and one long. One — the poor wight enjoying a perpetual shower — had a musket slung on his shoulder. None showed wounds. They had simply been drained of time.

Reynard moved closer to examine the swords of the nearest. "No thievery!" he remarked, but there was more than a touch of fear in him as he sensed a swirl of breeze, here in this hollow that likely shielded them from moving airs. If one was drained of all time, could that possibly leave a ghost? "I thought most of the Eaters had departed," he said, his tongue almost as dry as it had been on the wreck of the hoy.

"Valdis?" Kaiholo asked Kern.

"I have never so measured her abilities."

"Then Calybo!"

"Possible. If he hath stayed behind, it is to protect something of great value to those just beneath the sky."

They pondered this for a moment.

"Maybe they seek the boy," Kern said. "Maybe they found Widsith and questioned him."

"He would not speak of me!" Reynard insisted.

"Thou dost not know the ways of Annwyn," Kaiholo said. "Kings and heroes will all talk under the ministrations of the doctors of the Sister Queens." He held up his hand at the boy's further objections.

"We lose ourselves in questions we cannot answer. If these be scouts, and they surely have that look, there are many more soldiers and retainers out there. Perhaps an army, or at least a great war party. Let us keep away from the broader and easier paths this new group will likely follow."

They moved up the ridge to a shelf that did not look as if it had been traveled recently. Here the forest's strange corkscrew trees produced thin foliage and thinner branches, the wind making them dry-rustle.

"The trods cross about twelve miles beyond the next wrinkle in the island," Kern said. "There are great wrinkles and small, and still finer ones. They come and go at the behest of the Travelers."

"They can do that?" Reynard had seen a trod being laid out back near Zodiako, but still could hardly credit his own eyes.

"Like making a bed," Kern said, and spread his hand along an imaginary counterpane. With pinching fingers, he appeared to pick and flick a tuft from the unseen blanket.

"Then they know magic?" Reynard asked, lost in a boyish hope for wonder, which suddenly, as he realized how that sounded, drew out a blush.

"They know wrinkles," Kern said. "Ask the Sea Traveler how he flattens waves."

Kaiholo blew out his nose, offering neither answer nor argument, and pointed the way. Kern touched Reynard's shoulder and pointed to the tattooed man's horse. They were not riding, they were leading, but all three horses were now energized by the presence of something they were first to sense.

"Likely the other horses," Kern said. "And maybe their riders."

Old Things Have Their Day

THE LEDGE that abutted the ridge was ancient indeed, as was the ridge itself — one of the great vertebrae of the island that formed five spines, all of which were known to the geographers of the Travelers, so Kaiholo asserted — though he knew little about them himself. "I know the oceans and the way the island shapes weather out to sea," he said primly. "Less the land. Kern must know the land."

"I have been to the cross-trod, but not much around. These spines are ancient, however, and I have heard they are covered with trails. Those change year to year, as Crafter plans spill out and over."

"Then what goes truly back to the beginning?" Reynard asked.

Kaiholo studied a muddy stretch. He rose and pointed to the distinct mark of a hoof. "Someone's been by here, or at least a horse," he said.

Reynard took a look. "It has been shod recently," he said. "I think Widsith's mark is on it. It is a Spanish horse."

"Doing what, and doing what here?" Kaiholo asked. "Are the Spanish all over this island now?"

"Most are dead," Reynard said. "There may be forty or fifty left."

"Are the Travelers seeking them, too?" Kern asked.

"They could have Valdis and Widsith," Kaiholo said. "It seems word hath spread about their value . . . And thine, fox-boy."

Reynard looked uneasily along the ledge. "This taketh us inland, doth it not?"

"Once it did. Toward the crossing of the trods," Kern said.

"And toward a Quarry of Souls," Kaiholo said. The others looked at him. "Guldreth spake of it, and so hath Calybo."

"I have never been there," Kern said.

"What is that?" Reynard asked.

"It is where faces and manners are seen in old rocks by experienced Travelers," Kern said. "They are quarried and made available to imprint childers, and those cast in Crafters' designs."

"If we move along this ledge, is that our next destination?" Reynard asked.

"Likely," Kaiholo said.

"Would those of Annwyn want to go there?"

"Not to the Quarry," Kaiholo said. "It is been dormant for centuries, played out, some say. And Travelers do not favor those who work for the Sister Queens, their servants or their allies. A contentious bone in a great skeleton of resentments."

"Who would be willing to bargain for us?" Reynard asked, a dark thought forming. Could he trust Kaiholo, could he trust Kern? So far, all they had done was guide him to where those he knew sought his protection had vanished.

"Dost thou mean to ask, who would pay?" Kern said.

"Who would pay?"

"Opposition to the wishes of the Travelers doth demand a rare currency. Strategy and weapons, mayhaps."

"Are the Sister Queens fighting the Crafters?" Reynard asked.

Kern and Kaiholo looked at each other. "Perhaps that is the way of it now," Kaiholo said, "but I fear the results! We have long served those just beneath the sky, and the Sister Queens do not."

They walked along, but found no more hoof prints or other spoor. The corkscrew trees and shrubs here were thin but grew fast, like weeds, as if they feared all might soon end.

"I asked what things stretch back to the beginning," Reynard reminded them. "Or is it all remade and forgotten by the Crafters?"

"Well, Eaters, for one," Kaiholo said. "They were not called that in the beginning times. They were simply part of all those just beneath the sky, children of Hel, most agree, and that means she was here in the beginning as well — probably before the beginning."

"What about this isle?"

"Oh, aye, all the Tir Na Nog were here in those times, and likely Earth and most of what we see of the sky."

"Crafters do not reshape the heavens?"

"Not that I have heard," Kern said.

"But it is said people now study the sky with better tools," Kaiholo said. "I would use those tools myself, and learn better the roads of the sea."

Reynard had seen some of those tools in Aldeburgh, in shop windows, made of brass and iron and with crystal and glass parts. Their quality and glitter had fascinated him. "And us? Are we reshaped? I mean humans, and giants."

"Nobody knoweth that," Kaiholo said.

"But the Travelers were always here?"

Kaiholo hmmed again. "We found our place on the islands after the Crafters arrived, but likely we served our own kind before then. Spinning language and tales across land and sea. What would humans be without words?"

"Dumb," Kern said.

"You are half human!" Reynard reminded him.

"True, and all my days I have struggled to favor my greater half, and keep my head straight." He smiled at the boy. "Anakim and other sorts from old were as liable as humans to do stupid things. Which doth make their tales all the more interesting."

A Quarry of Souls

THE LEDGE got wider and the growths on it even thinner until the weeds and tendrils of creeper vanished entirely and left clumped dirt and bare rock, scraped and revealed as if by a giant harrow.

The horses were still interested in something ahead, and eager to move on, but Reynard could not hear or see anything that encouraged him.

"We are on the edge of the quarry," Kaiholo said. Kern nodded agreement. "Could be nothing more."

"What sort of stone?" Reynard asked.

"Old," the giant said, "even for the Tir Na Nog," and they let the horses walk faster.

In an hour they found the greater ridge had curved and cupped a long valley, within which churned thick white mists like steam in a cauldron. The ledge had offered up a strangely clear and smooth road into this valley.

"This must have once been an important trod," Kern said. Kaiholo kept his silence as the ledge road led them deeper into the cauldron and through the mists. Soon they saw rockfaces with clear signs of having been worked — flat faces edged around by chisel marks

from where great sheets had been split away. Shards of stone littered
the base of each face. The grayish depressions where soaked wooden
wedges had swollen and split the blocks and sheets were obvious
even to Reynard, who had once visited a limestone quarry with his
uncle. He had been twelve when his uncle had been called to repair
sledges and replace oxen traces.

Kaiholo and Kern seemed too quiet.

"It is just stone," Reynard said.

Kern looked away. "Mayhap we were all of us found here," he murmured. "On that, I seek no final answer."

Kaiholo pulled up beside Reynard. "There is a slab ahead that
showeth polish. It might have been worked but spoiled before deliv-
ery." They rode along the road until the slab rose above them, a span
of golden-brown granite shot through with strange, sky-colored
crystals — the top of the slab towering thirty feet above the road, its
width at least fifty feet.

"Who would have carried this?" Reynard asked. "No wagon, and
no team of oxen!"

Kern said, "I have heard that some of my people used to work
these quarries. Given giants, they would need no oxen."

"Could they carry a monster block like this?" Reynard asked. Kaiholo also seemed curious about Kern's answer.

"Perhaps," the giant said.

"How could any human woman have survived such a romance?"
Kaiholo asked dubiously.

Kern grinned and shrugged, and they moved on.

Near the southern end of the quarry, they found stacks of finely
cut sheets, some raised up on wooden pallets and shelves. The edges
of the slabs and sheets had worn to pebbles and sand in most cases,
but Reynard walked before the smooth surface, strangely drawn to
the patterns in the stone — to the whorls and brown and gold ribbons that drew out the rock's long-solid currents.

"Once this lay on the bed of a great sea," Kaiholo said. "Or so we were told by high ones many years ago."

Kern countered, "The story I heard was that one of Queen Hel's servants spent idle hours drawing in a river of rich golden mud, and then tossed flame over the river, boiled it away, and baked the stone hard."

Kaiholo laughed. "I wonder which story is most marvelous?"

Reynard touched the stone and ran the tip of his finger around a whorl. "It is so like a fine lady's eye," he said. "I see an eye here, a face there . . . and a strange creature over there!"

"Any creatures we know?" Kaiholo asked, and again blew out his nose. "Let us leave this place. I do not enjoy ignorance in troubled times."

"Is this a krater?" Reynard asked as he climbed back up behind Kern.

"Not as such," Kaiholo said. "But I have never seen a real krater."

"Do only Land Travelers cross the island entire?"

"So many questions!" Kaiholo said in pique.

"And so few answers!" Reynard responded in equal irritation.

"Get this boy to his destination before he doth gut us with curiosity," Kern said.

"But we have to find Valdis and Widsith!" Reynard said.

"Perhaps they will meet us at the trod." Kaiholo did not sound convinced.

"If the trods still be there," Kern said.

This prospect made Reynard miserable, as if he was losing yet another family. And that in turn showed him how lost he had become, that he would regard any of these beings as familiar and worthy of trust — even Widsith!

They took the smooth path out of the quarry and found rugged, boulder-strewn grassland beyond. The lands here seemed to share little nature with England or the other places Reynard had seen or heard of. Features were scattered like sketches on an old artist's table. He had seen one such artist working on designs for a small parish church in Aldeburgh, his table messy with charcoal, chalk, and sheets of buffed skin from old psalters — what he had called palimpsests. "I use them over and over again," he had said, "for the parish cannot afford any more!" He had lifted his gnarled and bony hands to Reynard's clear-eyed gaze and chuckled toothlessly. "Soon I'll join those old skins and be myself scrubbed clean! I await a better artist to sketch me anew."

Reynard pulled himself out of his reverie to see a large candle burning in the middle of their path. Such a sight by itself meant nothing to him — any strange sight might point only to a nicety of Crafter story. But this candle he knew, by its steady golden glow, belonged to the King of Troy. Neither Kaiholo nor Kern noticed it, and he decided against alerting them, for reasons he could not explain even to himself.

The Eater horses glanced at it in passing, and then turned their heads to look at him with their black and amber eyes, as if accusing.

They all walked on.

The Delay of an End

A̶t dusk, Kaiholo found them cover under a decaying, mildewy canopy of branches and leaves. Green moss draped like old lace between three wide trunks — two dead oaks and a kind of maple showing only a few broad green leaves.

For some time now, Reynard had observed the growth overlying the leaf litter like a great carpet — a dark red fuzziness unlike any he had seen in England. He pushed his foot into the softness, finding it more alive and springy than he had expected, given the sad aspect of the trees. Furthermore, when the dusk light was right, he could see wide whorls and other patterns in the moss, and now these were outlined by a slanting shaft of sun and sparkling rubies of rain.

He wondered how long it would be until evidence arrived of the King of Troy's activities ... Bones and sticks wrapped in ghostly illusion. Strangely, he was looking forward to something changing — something that might bring back Widsith and Valdis. He wondered if the King of Troy knew where they were, and perhaps had helped them after the flood from the Ravine.

Kern towered over him. On the other side, leaning against a moldy gray trunk, the Sea Traveler sighed. He patted the trunk. "These trees look to make a station on the ancient trod. They have sheltered Land Travelers for thousands of years. The ones we are waiting for could sense and find us here."

Kern squinted up and out at the dead branches. "Live ones, I hope," he grumbled.

Reynard now paid attention to another aspect of the woods they had seen since leaving the quarry, and in fact since they had survived the flood from the Ravine — silence. No animals called, nothing flew or buzzed. Other than a dry rustling, nothing here seemed interested in making itself known.

He could feel a pressure, what seemed like a breeze blowing, but between the wide trunks of the trees, likely it was no movement of air but a draft that passed through flesh and bone like water through a net and caught only thoughts, spirits — soul. That strange waft made him feel like he was dying. He had felt that way on the hoy for days before being rescued.

The path spread ahead of them, winding dirt and leaves, wide enough for two horses and no more.

"Is this still a trod, then?" Reynard asked.

"Not to my knowing," Kaiholo said. "But it may be all we will be allowed to see, until our whole company arrives."

Then horns blew. The horns seemed to carry their sound on the same breezes that tugged at Reynard's spirits, and made him feel like he was about to throw up.

"Land Travelers," Kern said.

"No!" Kaiholo said. "Much more. Hide!"

They did their best to obscure their presence, and even the horses stepped back into the shadows of the three trees. From the southwest came another chill breeze. They saw three figures walking along the ancient trod. First came the scout Anutha, shuffling along as if half asleep, her leather garments torn, and face bruised and swollen. She clutched an arm to her chest in a leather sling. Behind her fol-

lowed Widsith, and Reynard stifled an urge to cry out for him ...
and then came Valdis, at which his heart seemed to freeze in his
chest.

For she was followed by a figure Reynard had seen only once
before —

Not much larger than any man, and dark upon dark, with the
same mirror-glints in his eyes as Valdis, but an invisible aura of tremendous power and time, and a manner of weary boredom ...

The Afrique, Calybo. The high Eater who had restored Widsith
on the beach walked close behind the Pilgrim, looking not just bored
but wary, as if this entire situation threatened all he valued, not that
he had a soul to value anything but his duty, and perhaps not even
that, now.

Kern rose. "I will greet them," the giant said. "Nobody else break
cover."

He walked through the gathering shadows of dusk to the edge of
the trod and waited there until the four had come close enough to
hail.

At his call, Calybo moved to the front of their line, saying nothing
but inspecting the giant as if he might be a tiger. Then the Afrique
bowed his head and allowed Anutha to step closer. She looked up
and widened her eyes, as if waking from a bad dream.

"Art thou alone?" she asked, her voice hoarse.

Kern did not answer this, but said, "Where have ye all been?"

The high Eater looked directly at the sheltering triplet of trees as
if they covered nothing and concealed no one and said, "Valdis, be
these the ones Guldreth assigned to thy care?"

Valdis, herself little more than another shadow in the dusk, answered, "All are here. The others fear you."

"Well they should," Calybo said. "For I am angry. I have been
called back from the coast and have lost any hope of escape."

Widsith said, "Fox-boy! Come forward."

Kern waved his arm, calling on Reynard to break cover like a fawn and join the group. Anutha's face was a mess of clotted blood, bruises, one eye swollen half shut. Though her step was uneven and her color poor, she still had a presence that belied any evidence of defeat; she still fought, this time against the pain of her injuries.

"Who treated ye so?" Kaiholo asked. "We saw scourers ... All dead."

Anutha touched her bleeding cheek as if to close it up again and said, "The same roving bands that killed most of our scouts and many blunters. Calybo caught and reduced them before they could kill us. He found us in what was left of the village and took us around the Ravine, over the high ledge, and through the dying woods. Long have I feared meeting him ... but now he hath saved so many!"

"What happened in Zodiako?" Reynard asked, again feeling that winter wind in his chest.

"The Spaniard," Anutha said. "He found another army, or it found him. The army of Annwyn and the Sister Queens. All left in the town fought, and I saw many die. The rest have been gathered up by scourers and taken on great rafts out to sea, possibly to the eastern shore."

"There is no shame in facing disaster and living," Kaiholo said.

"We fled Zodiako," Anutha continued, "over the ridge, along the ledge, and past what was left of the Ravine."

"What about the drakes?" Reynard asked.

"Many dead, the rest ... I know not. Dana seems to have escaped and taken her blunters with her." She held up her pack and removed a heavy, clinking sack. "Maggie gave me these before we last saw each other. She said they were from the last of this year's nymphs." She reached into the sack and removed a small glass vial, stoppered and waxed. Reaching in again, she withdrew a second. "She did not believe any in the village would be left to fight, and I had the best chance of escape." Anutha made a face that betrayed her sorrow and self-recrimination. "The King of Troy came out of his woods and joined the fray with all his powers, dozens of his tricks that deluded, chivvied, and fought well ... but they could do little to defeat the armies of the Sister Queens. I did not see what became of him."

"There was a candle on the trail," Reynard said.

Kaiholo and Kern looked at him doubtfully. "We saw nothing," Kaiholo said. Kern agreed.

"Troy might have left a message for the boy alone," Widsith said. "Or ... it was a wish, a fancy. There was nothing more?"

Reynard shook his head.

"Troy out here is far from his piles of bones and wood," Widsith mused. "We are a sad lot if we rely on his help alone."

"I did not see Dana and her blunters after we parted ways," Anutha said. "But as we fled, hiding all the way, we passed thousands of troops from Annwyn arriving from three directions — south around the coast in ships, west along the radiant ridge on th'other side of the Ravine, and from the north around the great icy plain."

"Who can survive there?" Kern asked.

Anutha shook her head. "Still, hundreds made that journey. Zodiako's defenses, already weak, were routed. Our town is done, for now."

"Why target the town?" Kern asked.

"Anger. Ambition," Anutha said. "The Queens have both in abundance. Long have they felt abandoned on the other side of this isle whilst we are favored by the Travelers and protected by them and, we thought, by the Crafters who value our Pilgrims and their stories."

"The Queens do not send out explorers or fishermen?" Reynard asked.

"Not ever, to my knowledge," Kaiholo said.

"Whence came their new army?" Kern asked.

"The Sister Queens made treaty with the Spaniard," Anutha said. "Cardoza leads many of their troops now." She lifted a vial and clinked the sack and said, through gritted teeth, "We will dispense these vials to those who can use them best. In a few days, there will be plenty of new drakes to avenge our town. As well, the mountains and forests are now haunted. Forces flee the krater lands. I doubt the Sister Queens will succeed pushing through the island's center."

"What sort of forces?" Kern asked.

"The southwest coast could not have held them all," Calybo said. Valdis, in the shadows, made a small sound.

"Primal," Anutha said, "I could not see them, merely feel their passage through me. The Forces that shape nature and the beasts of the field. The Forces that make the weather and winds and roil the seas."

"The fingers and muscles of the Crafters," Kern said. "I have felt them on occasion as well. If they desert the Tir Na Nog, then the Crafters truly are finished."

"Annwyn and the Queens can frighten such powers?" Reynard asked.

"Something hath frightened them," Anutha said. "That is all I can speak to."

"All within the krater lands appears upended," Widsith said.

"And yet that is where we are going!" Kaiholo said.

Valdis drew up her cloak. "Travelers are close," she said, looking upward.

"Watch," Widsith told Reynard, and pointed. The path ahead grew like an uncoiling snake and pushed aside bushes and trees as if they were stitches on a cloth.

"From the coast?" Reynard asked.

Both men shook their heads. Anutha said, "I think they serve their kind in the krater lands."

"Are they the ones who collect your tales?" Kern asked Widsith, and the Pilgrim nodded. "I know some of them," the giant said. "There is one called Nikolias, and a woman called Yuchil —"

"Shhh," the tattooed man warned. "Trods are temperamental." Kaiholo lowered his chin as if staring into the bright sun, then raised his arm, and a line of tall men dressed in dark brown and purple appeared at the far end of the road, leading and surrounding the great wagon Reynard and Widsith had seen earlier.

The wagon and its company slowly closed the distance, a mile or more through the divided woods. The party they could see consisted of three men on horseback, wearing voluminous black pants and high leather boots, purple or red shirts, and wide, sun-shielding hats. One small girl broke into a dance, her long red hair swirling like a banner. Strange arcs of light seemed to intersect them all.

The procession stopped, and a tall, thin man in a checkered robe, with a reddish-purple Scythian hat draped on his long head, climbed down from the wagon. A silver-haired woman with young features peered through a rug-like cover behind the driver's bench.

"I am Nikolias," the tall Traveler said. He was almost a match for Kern — half a head shorter and no less. "We are here to escort you to the krater lands. She who rules the wagons is Yuchil." The silver-haired woman nodded and looked off to the far end of their road. "These she treats as her grandchildren." The girl growled like a cat and swished a claw-hand. "But for Calafi," he added with a wry smile, "who admits to no parentage." This seemed a sort of joke among the Travelers. Nikolias waved a staff. From no clear distance behind arrived two additional wagons, each magnificent. Reynard could not see that they had either drivers or occupants.

The trod rippled along its distance, and the trees rustled in no wind whatsoever — but two more wagons rolled up behind the last.

"I hear a familiar voice," Nikolias said.

Widsith rode forward and touched his forehead. The young armed men stood glowering between him and Yuchil. They all cast uncertain glances at Valdis and especially at Calybo.

"How often have we conveyed thy tales to the servants in the krater lands?" the tall man asked, smiling.

"Beyond count," Widsith said.

"The time before may have been our last," Nikolias said. "All the Islands of the Blessed are in turmoil. But we can only try to perform our duty."

"I am grateful for thy company," Widsith said.

Nikolias's troop gathered around him. He introduced the young warriors. "This is Andalo, with two swords and three knives. He believeth in being prepared!"

Andalo gave them the merest nod, then positioned his horse between Calybo and the wagons.

"In training are Sany and Bela. They protect our trods."

"You brought many soldiers to Zodiako," Sany said.

"Indeed. You did not arrive alone," Bela said.

"There were Spanish soldiers on the ship," Widsith agreed. "Many died on the beach, in the lively woods, and in Zodiako. I know not where the survivors have fled, though we hear that they have gone over to the Sister Queens."

"We hear that also," Nikolias said. "Causing much trouble, though not the only cause."

"But this lad . . . I found him and brought him as well."

"And his name is?"

"Fox," Widsith said.

"Reynard!" the boy corrected.

"Reynard it is. Welcome to all of you."

Calafi kept her eyes on Reynard, no longer smiling.

"Rest now, and food," Yuchil proclaimed. "We shall all need our strength." Anutha came forward, supported by Kaiholo. "Your scout needs our attention as well."

"I can travel," Anutha insisted.

"Mayhaps, but let me look at thee in the wagon."

Kaiholo helped Anutha climb up into the back of the first wagon, and Bela guided her behind a curtain.

"We begin in the morning," Nikolias said. "Calybo, Valdis, ye art welcome to travel with us."

"That we will," the high Eater said. "For as long as we can."

First Night on the Cross-Trod

THE TRAVELERS brought out loaves of black bread and cut them with their sharp knives, then handed them around to all. Jugs of water were handed down from the third wagon, and all drank their fill. Reynard wondered how many Travelers the wagons held. Not all seemed willing to appear — or, he thought, maybe they were not all present yet.

Yuchil climbed down from the first wagon and laid out sturdy brown woolen blankets for those who had none.

"The scout is in a bad way," she told Widsith. "She hath taken poorly in one of her wounds." Yuchil pointed to Valdis, who kept away from them all, staying off the trod. "This young Eater hath been told certain things, and given certain instructions . . . That may be why the scout is not offered succor. She is very ill, well past what we can do for her." Yuchil climbed back into the first wagon.

Reynard finished his bread and water and laid himself out on the blanket under the thin branches and the scattered stars of a clouded night sky, and slept as best he could.

Widsith woke him just before dawn. "You were moaning," he said. "Nikolias insists you come with him."

No word on the Pilgrim's emotions at joining up again with his fellows. The last few days had somehow added to his years and depleted his returned youth.

From the shadows to either side came Valdis and Calybo, and then Kaiholo. No others appeared, and Reynard felt strangely alone, as if still lost in sleep.

The small group did not ride and did not walk far. Reynard wondered at the circumstance of the Eaters on the path, but felt only the weight of his own ignorance.

"Take off thy shoes," Nikolias instructed Reynard.

"Why are we out here?" Reynard asked.

"Thou shalt walk decalced on the trod," Nikolias said.

Reynard did not know that word.

"Barefoot," Widsith explained.

Reynard still did not understand, but he pushed off his slippers with his toes and handed them to Widsith, then studied the others for some clue as to what they expected.

"The trod will judge," Nikolias said.

"Judge what?" Reynard asked.

"Thou shalt not feel the same to the trod," Nikolias replied.

"The same as who?"

"Stop asking questions," Kaiholo advised, his tone soft. The morning was getting brighter, and a few dozen yards back they could hear the Travelers preparing for the day's journey.

Kaiholo, Valdis, Calybo, and Nikolias walked down the path about fifty feet and turned to beckon Reynard join them. "Now walk," Nikolias said. Reynard kept his eyes on Valdis, what he could see of her, for once again the Eaters resembled smoke or fog shaped into human forms. Her eyes glinted. Calybo seemed to have no eyes, only dark caves in his face.

"Walk," Nikolias said again.

Reynard stepped out between the groups. Kaiholo waved him forward. The trod felt hard underfoot, but there were no sharp stones or thorns.

"Do your feet tingle?" Nikolias asked.

Reynard shook his head. "No."

Kaiholo reached out to him. He almost touched the boy's fingers . . . and then he felt the ground differently.

"The boy is not the usual sort of Traveler," Nikolias said.

Yuchil had walked up silently to join the group. "His heritage is clear in his face and in his blood," she said. "What he doth remember, and what his grandmother hath taught him!" The silver-haired woman seemed puzzled and disappointed. Reynard for his part did not remember telling her anything about his lineage.

"The trod knoweth Travelers, but the boy is not truly one of our clan," Nikolias insisted.

"What is he, then? A master magician like Troy?"

"Hush!" said Yuchil. She knelt and touched the trod with outstretched fingers. Then she raised her hand to her nose and sniffed the fingertips. With a quizzical frown, she beckoned Nikolias to do likewise. He did, and they put their fingers together and rose.

Valdis and Calybo watched. With the least gesture of her hand, Valdis might have signaled to Reynard . . . but no one else saw it. Then he saw Calafi on the path, walking slowly toward them . . . surrounded by childers!

Nikolias doffed his hat and crouched before her on the path. She whispered to him, and the childers vanished one by one, as they had in the stable, like soap bubbles.

The silver-haired woman came to Reynard. "Calafi senses something different, and once again, she is our guide. The boy is a new kind of carrier, and a new kind of messenger," Yuchil proclaimed. "The words he doth carry are new. This boy must go to the krater lands, and soon!"

Gifts Good and Bad

◉

"I AM CONFUSED," Reynard said as he and Widsith carried jugs to bring water back from a stream for Yuchil's cooking. Kaiholo and the towering Kern trailed behind through the dense dry woods, and then caught up with them at the narrow run of water. Kaiholo squinted out over the flow with a yearning disappointment, as if he missed the sea. The four stood on the banks while Reynard filled one of Yuchil's jugs and then did the same with theirs.

"Why confused?" Widsith asked over the water's steady bubbling, sliding sound.

"Why must the trod judge me? And how doth it judge, and speak its opinion?"

"Nikolias knows more than any of us," Widsith said.

"It hath judged," Kaiholo said, "but the judgment is mixed and puzzling."

"Childers are never easy to explain," Kern said.

Kaiholo added, "Nikolias and Yuchil do not know what the trod is saying—and perhaps the trod doth not know, either! But Yuchil wants you to proceed, even so. That is a kind of faith."

"Or she is simply rolling the die," Widsith said.

"That sweepeth not my confusion," Reynard said.

"Many are the languages Travelers have shared," Kaiholo said. "The words Travelers brought the Crafters became flesh and growing green things and the fish and ropes and slimes of the sea. Words raised mountains and islands, roused storms, and lay over them calms. Words were brought that passed into age and never again made their play. Ancient words we still carry in our blood, and new words we speak through our blood and with our tongues. Our very shapes and dreams are strung out with words. So many words the Crafters have wielded since Queen Hel allowed them, some say chose them. Or did she?" He focused a sharp look on Reynard, shook his head, and walked off with his jug. Kern joined him, with a backward glance.

"What did I do?" Reynard asked, following the giant's form up the bank and over to the trod.

"'Tis not thee, fox-boy," Widsith said. "What fates the Crafters decree have been especially hard on those who ply the deeps."

Kaiholo acknowledged this.

"May I speak, knowing also the sea, and having sailed often with those far islanders?" Widsith asked.

"Of course," Kaiholo said.

"They knew the stars early on. They have gained and lost islands, in fire and storm, and along with them entire peoples, some they were, some they served. They know the sea as a spiteful wife. Did thine uncle share that opinion?"

"We knew many who died," Reynard said.

Widsith cocked his head. "Languages divide and give us new reasons to hate — like the tower of Babel. Knowest thou that tale?"

"Of course!"

"That tower might as well have been built by Travelers, and they have carried a strange curse ever since — a curse that maketh them strong, until, some say, the day they are not, and then they will be harried and persecuted across the Earth. Perhaps that will be because they gave the Crafters power."

"But I still do not understand! What be Crafters, and how can they do this?"

"I know some from Guldreth, and some from Troy," Widsith said. "When Crafters first came down from the sky, invited, some say, by Hel, and until they had words, their minds were like the dark between the stars — shapeless. They brought to Earth, to the Tir Na Nog, and some say to the moon, the power to shift fates and change time and space — but they knew not how to record their tales or make others act out their plays — until Hel invited the Travelers to meet them."

"How did they live, seeing such?" Reynard asked.

"That I do not know. Lacking language, the Crafters could do nothing and know nothing. Now they shape all of our history — and perhaps fill in the dark between the stars as well."

"Guldreth collected the early drafts of many histories," Kaiholo said. "You saw them. It was her passion."

Kern returned through the woods and sat beside them, watching this discourse with quick eyes — especially focused on Reynard as the boy absorbed the tale wrapping round all tales.

Reynard squatted by the river, picked up a pebble, and threw it into the flow. "How can words give such power? We tell stories, but we cannot make such things," he said.

"We are not Crafters," Widsith said. He smiled ruefully and filled his own jug. "When they came here, Guldreth told me they fled from some force or malignity worse than themselves — but now, with the Travelers' foolish gift, they fear no such malignity."

"A lover's bed is ripe for secrets," Kaiholo said.

Reynard studied the Pilgrim's changing expressions — amusement, disdain, and back to a defensive kind of amusement. "Crafters have neither human shape nor sympathy. They exercise their powers to make history without regard for how we feel, and so we are in their thrall. But they have no far-seeing eyes, no crystal ball, and so they send such as I out to discover and report — that they may celebrate their achievement! They wonder about what they have done ... How doth it make the world different?" The Pilgrim poured his water back into the river. Then he bent and scooped again. "And why should not this island remain contented, and at the center of creation? I would it were so."

"Because the Eaters supply you with time," Kaiholo said. "The Sister Queens believe that what the Eaters and Travelers did was evil and all should be punished. The result is, this island is now broken."

"Are the Queens correct?" Reynard asked.

"To bed," Widsith advised, "before we speak more heresy."

As he lay in his blanket, Reynard had a strange sensation of being back in England, falling slowly and lazily asleep in the tumbledown, net-festooned shack of his uncle — and thought that he had ever wished for knowledge and marvel, but would now exchange all he had learned, all he had seen, for this simple bed and a life of black-smithing and fishing, a life where he might meet a young woman and bring up a family, subject to all the weaknesses and failures of his father, but nevertheless human.

But the voice spread smoke over this dream and memory.

You are the first word.

You are here.

No rest until it is done.

The Road Before the Pass

The next morning, with wagons underway, escorted by their retinue, Calybo rode alongside Reynard for a few miles. The Travelers did not like riding with Eaters, and kept away from both Valdis and Calybo. The boy furtively watched the high Eater's nightlike features and saw behind his face an even older shade — the ashen light of ancient lands and ancient times under a bright and baking sun.

And now, some of what Valdis had infused in him rose up, and he knew some things he could not possibly know.

There, Calybo wandered through the streets of Timbuktu and served kings and caliphs, and knew the men and women who made books. He carried words and memories between them, and shared time between many, and from them rose empires.

And now he is here.

What can he share with you, young Fox?

For how long, and to what ultimate purpose?

In turn, Calybo met one of his glances and openly studied Reynard. His eyes were as distant as stars reflected in a lake. "What didst thou think on the wide ocean waves, when death looked upon thee?" the high Eater asked.

Reynard was surprised by the high Eater's tone. "I grieved for my uncle," he said. "And for my shipmates. I thought I would never see their like again."

"And hast thou seen their like since?"

Reynard was about to say no but felt a double-edged guilt, and looked around at Widsith and the giant, at the Sea Traveler, and then back to Valdis. "I have found new friends, but not new family," Reynard said.

"I have long had no family but Eaters," Calybo said. "We are full of histories we share like water in the breast feathers of desert birds. But the pasts we carry are rarely our own. Hel's pact made most Eaters — including me — into slaves of those we are ordered to serve."

"You mean, the pact you sealed with the Queen of Hell?" Reynard asked.

"He hath not yet the right of that," Widsith said from behind them.

Calybo leaned his head forward, as if infinitely weary. "She doth not rule the netherworld, if that is what thou mean'st. But she created much we see around us, and some say invited the Crafters to our isles, and she even now commandeth from afar, though I have not seen her for ages."

"We are all slaves to some order," Reynard said. "Our priest in Southwold spake on it. We are slaves to the freedom of God's duty."

Calybo raised his head slowly. "My duty hath been to protect the island, and in that course, I have diminished the time of many and carry their lives within me. I would be free of all of that, and all of them! What if we were free of our histories, free of those who demand we serve their will, when we have contrary wills of our own?"

Reynard's cheeks heated at the mere thought of such defiance.

"Surely you, like our defenders in England, guard us against worse fates," he said, thinking of the English sea captains and Elizabeth — and Walsyngham. "You have held back the Spanish!"

"It is all of a rope. Five centuries ago, reckoning by time beyond the gyre, a Danish family carried their dying daughter to this far northern isle. They had heard of a way of saving her from awful injuries, and being pagans, had no fear of the dark designs into which they were going to weave her. Anything was preferable to endless death, which was all they could imagine for her, for a young girl had no entry to Valhalla. Their guilt at having put her on their boat, at watching the mast fall and cut her almost in half — that haunted their nights and days until they arrived here and were met by the blunters of Zodiako. The blunters saw the girl, listened to her father, and summoned me from the Ravine."

Reynard watched the high Eater closely, as if he might sprout wings and fly, so unlikely was this act of confession.

"I met them and explained it would be better for her to die among her people. The girl had but ten seasons and was barely aware of things about her — but her father said, 'We give her to thee, that she may find new tales, new stories, and new fates, for I have delivered her only to Death, and there is no love there.'"

Calybo rode quietly for a time. "Dost feel her fate when thou look'st upon her — the fate she might have had, had she not been injured so long ago and put in my care?"

Reynard could only nod and be embarrassed by the paralysis of his tongue, for he had indeed felt something like that — and had no idea what it meant.

He startled himself by saying, "Do you think of her as a daughter?"

Calybo said, "In all the time she hath been with our people, I have sensed her quality and mourned her circumstance."

"An Eater can mourn?"

Calybo's look now was like a thunderous cloud at midnight. Reynard held the horse against a strange pressure that affected them both. "Her father was not a royal king, but a master of storms and following seas, of voyages that drew songlines between many an isle and across several continents. She hath that quality as well, young Fox. She is a deep well of many words. First words, some call them. She inherited the songlines, and they bind her to a different fate."

"Her parents were Sea Travelers?" Reynard asked.

"They were," Calybo said. "Of the highest order."

"Like Kaiholo?"

"Even higher."

"But those in the wagons avoid you both!"

"All have prejudices, even here."

Reynard drew his brows together.

Calybo said, "Thou art as different in thine own away as Valdis. And I say this as someone who hath measured and traded time with tens of thousands, man, woman, and child. Thinkst not thou art grand or irreplaceable — that hath yet to be seen. But interesting to such as I, to such as Guldreth — and to a Pilgrim like Widsith. And apparently to the trods and those who smooth them, though they do not understand thee or thy purpose."

Another long silence. Then Calybo asked, "I believe, in England, thou didst encounter a man with a white shadow?"

Reynard flinched, and wondered if he should confirm this meeting — but more to the point, how he could lie to this being? "Did Valdis inform you?"

Calybo said she had.

"That question is why you speak to me at all," he reasoned, brow furrowed. "Do you know him?"

Calybo shook his head. "Neither human nor just beneath the sky, rare to being singular, in mine experience. Once he visited the Tir Na Nog and spent a season on the seven isles preaching a new language, a language where words equal measures, or numbers, or symbols that can be all. He doth not serve any man, nor any power," he said."He is *new*. I wonder he is not some new sort of Crafter! But he hath human form — he simply cannot cast a true shadow. For such as I, he foretells either an awakening, or an end."

And with this, the high Eater reined his horse aside and resumed his place to the rear of the line, behind the giant, who did not seem to have noticed any change.

The Company of Drakes

THE SNAKING gray clouds turned black, and a thin silvery rain fell that smelled of a great storm but delivered little moisture. The line of quiet wagons stood in this evening gloom, colors muted, interiors silent. The forest around them looked sick, almost dead.

Reynard wrapped his sleeping blanket around him, tucking it under his arms, enduring the damp to keep away the cold. When sleep was clearly useless, and as dawn turned the tops of the trees rusty brown, he got out of his wrap and walked over to the nearest wagon, then climbed up on the step to peer inside and down its length. The bunks that lined both sides, to a boxy enclosure with a black pipe thrusting through the roof — what might have been a kitchen — were empty, the curtains open as if someone had just climbed out. The other wagons were the same. He seemed alone. There was no sign of Anutha, supposedly under Yuchil's care. Widsith was gone, as were Kern, Kaiholo, Calybo, and even Valdis — perhaps off taking care of ablutions, though he had his doubts that Eaters needed such. At first he thought no one was with him, but the dancing girl, Calafi, appeared out of nowhere and tugged on his sleeve, looking up at him like a curious cat.

"They have gone!" Reynard said.

"Be not afraid," the girl said. "They will return after the trod and the woods have been inspected. In this margin, trees have no sense. They are too close to the krater lands."

"Why do they look sick?"

"Too many changes," she said. "Around their dwellings, and even in death, Crafters twist rules and churn ways." She took a deep breath, spread her arms, then smiled. "The trees may not like it, but I do. The air is good here. I like the dreams. Dost thou?"

"I have had few I recall since I arrived," he said, ignoring his waking vision. He studied her. She studied him back, eyes clear and steady. The girl tugged his sleeve and brought him around again to the lead wagon. "My mistress and teacher have returned," she said.

"The wagons are empty!"

Calafi smiled and pointed, and he saw the lead wagon was gently creaking with occupants. Now he heard many voices inside, laughing and jesting, he thought, and the canvas sides were pushing out as if from the press of legs and elbows.

"Art thou hungry?" Calafi asked.

"What do you have for breakfast?" Reynard asked, and the girl laughed.

"Light fare," she said. "Broth and bread and a Traveler's prayer from long ago, when we began our journeys."

Yuchil emerged on the seat of the cab and smiled at them, just as Widsith and the others, along with Nikolias, Andalo, Bela, and Sany, returned from the sickly woods. At their rear, following Kern, came Calybo and Valdis, astride their black and shining horses. Even in the morning light, the Eaters seemed to attract shadows, and the Travelers still kept their distance.

"Thine own guardians are near," the dancing girl said, studying the Eaters with a severe frown.

Valdis descended from her horse and stood by her animal. From the first three wagons, front and rear, climbed down a procession of men and women, young and old, wearing black and purple.

Reynard watched as the silver-haired woman and Andalo and Bela set up a cauldron, and then Nikolias, the tall master of the Travelers, lent them a hand lighting a hot, smokeless fire beneath, using words wrapped in song that seemed to encourage heat. Another group set up a separate fire. Several of the younger men had been hunting and now brought forth small game animals — none familiar to Reynard. These they began to roast. Valdis and Calybo stood aside in tree shadows, not to upset the repast of all the Travelers.

"I hope we have food enough to sate a giant!" Yuchil said.

"I eat less than one would think," Kern said. She returned his shy smile.

Widsith and Kaiholo joined with Reynard, and helped Anutha, who moved slowly and seemed barely able to withstand her pain.

"What have you learned out there, scout?" Widsith asked her.

"The Travelers have shown me a wonder, and told me what they know. I have seen that the trod is alert," Anutha said. "And in trade, I have some wonders for you, and for them." She carried her jingling bag on her belt, and brought it forward with one hand.

Nikolias looked at the bag curiously and said, "The trods tell the tale. The entire island from forest to mountain to the chafing waste is a-twitch. The Sister Queens have lured the Spanish general to their service, and all that remains of his troops — and now they join those forces to claim the entire island for their country of Annwyn."

"Where is Annwyn?" Reynard asked.

"Far east and north, beyond the chafing waste — beyond the krater lands. Also, beyond the plain of jars whose graves carry dead Crafters."

Yuchil and two of the warriors helped Anutha to join the group.

She trembled all over, and her eyes were bleary yellow. He felt a sharp pang, as if he might be to blame — and perhaps he was.

"Time now to share drakes," Anutha whispered. "The last harvest of the southwestern shores. Who would be served best? Those who drink will find all their kin protected. The drakes will not attack them, but will defend unto their death."

Anutha took out a vial and handed it to the Pilgrim. "Thou hast defended Zodiako," she said, and insisted he take it. "Open, and drink it down."

Widsith looked aside, as if ashamed at his part in this. But he swallowed the contents of the vial.

"When will his drake arrive and be of use?" Kern asked.

She did not answer, but gave a vial to the giant next. He was astonished. "Take it! Swallow quickly. I do not know how it will react in Anakim flesh."

He used his outsized hands to remove the stopper, and slugged it back with a wry grimace. Then his eyes opened, and he said, "Not so bad. I like it! Anakim were made to partner with drakes."

Next she turned to Reynard. "Thou hast served the blunters as well as Zodiako," she said. He took the vial and held it up to inspect, hoping to delay the moment — but Anutha said, "Knowing from whence it comes doth not make it taste any worse!"

Reynard drank it swiftly. The flavor was intense — sharp and green and then warming, all the way down his throat. He wanted to cough, but clapped his hand over his mouth and did not, though his eyes grew wide.

Kern looked on with sympathy and amusement.

"What color of drake?" Kaiholo asked, as if Reynard or Kern or Widsith could already see their new defenders.

"They have not yet flown," Anutha said. "But soon! The last nymphs of the season were primed to leave their cocoons when we took these essences."

All this talk was in low tones and away from the wagons and those setting up the cauldron and fire, as well as away from Calafi — who had returned to the lead wagon.

Anutha said, "I know not which of the Travelers will find drakes of use," she said. "Other than you."

And she gave a vial to Kaiholo.

"To defeat the Sister Queens," he said, and swallowed the liquid.

Nikolias approached them, accompanied by Calafi.

To Reynard's surprise, more men emerged from the second two wagons, until almost forty gathered in clumps around the path. These spread out behind him, as if expecting trouble and providing a barricade to protect the wagons. They carried long knives with curving blades, and some wore dark metal plates on their chests and in front of their groins, connected by braided cord.

Anutha's sharply focused expression showed she was near the end of her stamina — but still seeking warriors to equip with drakes. Nikolias avoided her importuning look, but she stepped up to him and said, "Thou hast lineage and worth and have served many of my people," she said. "And this island."

Nikolias looked at the offered vial. "None of my Travelers have ever managed drakes," he said.

"I have one!" Kaiholo said.

"Still to be proven. Not me, however," Nikolias said.

"Then who is ready and strong enough?"

The lean man turned to speak in a hauntingly familiar tongue to those armed men and women now drawn up around him. Reynard listened closely, but while the tongue was vaguely like Rom, they also, he surmised, spoke in a code known only to themselves. Calafi kept close to him, curious more than protective.

"What should we do?" Reynard asked.

"They are choosing who among them should have drakes," she said.

"We are protected by trods," Nikolias said, "but two will accept your gifts." Nikolias chose Andalo, and Anutha gave him a vial. He examined it, then opened the stopper and swallowed, making a bitter face. Then Nikolias pointed to Calafi, who drew back her lips in a kind of surprised snarl.

"Why me?" she asked.

"Because thou'lt go with the boy, the Pilgrim, and the Eater into the krater lands, and may face Annwyn's armies."

Anutha pulled herself free from the men who supported her and walked unsteadily along the path to where Valdis and Calybo stood beside their horses.

"Take these," she said.

"Valdis should have protection. But not me," Calybo said. "Thou dost not have many left."

"Thou speak'st sad truth." Anutha shook the bag. It did not clink — it was empty. "The last vial goeth to an Eater. Maggie and Maeve said that was essential." She held up the last vial. Its contents swirled in her shaking hand.

The Travelers drew back a step as Valdis came forward. She took the vial and opened it.

"I am not human," she said.

"I would not harm thee," Anutha said. "An Eater can also be protected by a drake."

And so Valdis put the vial to her lips and drained its contents. Anutha smiled approval. Yuchil and the warriors helped the scout back to the wagon.

In the night, with a low breeze winding through the pass, Yuchil approached Widsith and Reynard.

"Thy scout asketh for thee," she said, and led them back to the wagon. Inside, the Traveler's vehicle had room for many people —

and a small nook in which Yuchil had laid out blankets and soft bolsters, on which the scout lay with eyes closed, barely breathing.

Widsith knelt beside Anutha and touched her wrist softly. She opened her eyes and sighed, then shuddered. "I trow some knife or arrow was dipped in venom," she said. "I wish the King of Troy was here. He might have a remedy. The Travelers, I fear, do not."

Yuchil met Widsith's look and shook her head. Reynard could not take his eyes from the scout's pale, heavily lined face.

"I have served Maeve and Dana for many years," Anutha said. "Along with Maggie, I have led the blunters to their charges along the southwestern shore, and found new grounds they had not known before, for nymphs often rise where none have ventured in years. I have heard many tales of thee, Pilgrim, and thy journeys, in our village, and even from those just beneath the sky, who valued thee as companion."

Widsith bowed. "I am honored," he said.

"I have heard from Maeve and from Guldreth herself that great change cometh, and the old ways must adapt. The boy is new. He knoweth not his beginning, and his end is not determined. But you will serve his destiny now more than your own. Guldreth said as much. We had many good talks over the years. Now, she is traveling . . . I know not where. Perhaps to fetch Hel." She clasped Widsith's hand and smiled at him, then closed her eyes.

Yuchil escorted them out of the wagon. Widsith was crying, and Reynard was dismayed until he thought, until he understood, that the difficult ways of Tir Na Nog, the devious rules and strange duties, had appealed to many here, to Widsith, to the Travelers — and to Anutha herself.

And now that was passing, and rapidly.

They returned to the fire and the night.

◆　◆　◆

Yuchil climbed down from the wagon hours later. "The scout is dead," she said. "The poison hath taken her. She was very strong, and carried out her duty. I wish her spirit to move swiftly and depart this island whilst it still can."

Two Journeys

THEY BURIED the scout in the deepest dirt they could find, and placed a spiked cross over the grave, with Calafi and Yuchil having carved farewell messages along the forward edges.

Andalo laid a dagger on Anutha's grave and with a forefinger, drew a line across his chest and down from his nose to his navel.

Nikolias convened all the Travelers around the wagons, and urged Widsith and Reynard to come forward. "You perhaps do not know our ways in the krater lands," Nikolias said.

Widsith said he did not, never having gone farther than this.

"Some Travelers never leave, serving always the Crafters, whilst others, like our clan, ride the trods and bring out news, such as we receive, and take in more news the krater land servants are curious to hear."

Reynard asked, "What will we find in the krater lands?"

Calafi nudged him. "Thou'lt see soon enough!" she chided.

"I want warning," Reynard said resentfully.

"Nothing can so prepare," Calafi said.

"The young man wanteth answer, such as we can give," Nikolias said. "The extent of our journeys taketh us to where Travelers who serve Crafters have built marvelous cities. Lately, the cities are sad, many in ruins, their inhabitants gone or dead. Those who have escaped tell of great discord. The results we see around us. Waves of Crafter change make the woods suffer and die. Even as far as Zodiako, Crafter plots are out of balance."

"What of the outside worlds, the finished lands?" Sany asked, focusing on Widsith. He finished his bowl and set it down. "Have they changed?"

"As always, there is cruelty," the Pilgrim said. "In all my travels, there hath rarely been peace. I am not convinced even in their best times Crafters know how to make a peaceable kingdom."

Nikolias said, face stern, "No report returned by such as thyself ever told of a paradise or realm where we would rather live than here."

Yuchil and Calafi brought more bread, cut it, and passed it around. The young warriors moved in to receive their shares. They looked curiously and slyly at Reynard, assessing his age and position. He returned their study with cautious composure, reluctantly aware that he was indeed under consideration for some sort of trade — perhaps sacrifice!

Nikolias instructed them all to prepare for the next part of the journey. "The trods must know us. Trods that have been stretched and smoothed hundreds of thousands of times are no longer just roads. They acquire pride — and sometimes judgment. They become highways of words."

Yuchil looked to Nikolias. "First words are first mothers," she said.

"Amen," Nikolias said.

Reynard stopped chewing his bread and looked between them, as if they might also sprout wings and fly.

From the last wagon climbed four children, all around ten or eleven years of age. Their raiment was black and loose, and they wore beautiful boots and belts embroidered in tarnished silver and trimmed with brownish red cord. Even in their youth, they looked on Widsith and Reynard with some disdain, and on Kaiholo and the giant with respect but no cheer. Calybo and Valdis they ignored, as if they could not see them. Two of the children walked ahead of the troop, looking left and right at the sides of the path, and down at their feet, stepping carefully.

To the other pair, Nikolias barked out orders. "Care for the horses and inspect the wagons! And prepare our guests."

These youths groaned at being so tasked. Andalo spoke short and sharp, and another held out ropes, with which the children ingeniously bound Kaiholo, Widsith, and Reynard to their saddles. Without a horse, Kern held out his hands and a young Traveler tied them together. Valdis and Calybo were left unbound.

"Never did like Eaters," said one boy, looking back at them with a curled lip. "Too much behind 'em, and nothing ahead I need."

Nikolias conferred with the other wagon drivers in low tones.

Widsith said to Reynard, "We expected to be met by Crafter servants. They are not here, and so we must make a decision. I think we are being taken through a cline, and not by choice."

"What is a cline?" Reynard asked.

Unhappily, Kaiholo said, "A nasty turn of weather, or a place where things can go very wrong."

Kern said, "They would keep you on your mount. And they fear I may thrash and injure."

Nikolias ordered all but the first of the wagons to turn about, and all but seven of the armed young men. Each of these tied a red ribbon to their sleeves. None of the children but for Calafi remained with the one wagon.

"He is sending them back," Widsith said. "Wish ye to return with them?"

Kern said no. Kaiholo seemed to seriously consider the prospect, but shook his head.

Nikolias conferred with Yuchil, and she made it clear she, also, wanted to venture on. They all watched as the troop split and all but one of the wagons were drawn back along the trod.

Calafi, Sany, Andalo, and Bela patted the horses and whispered to them. The Eater mounts seemed calm under their attention, and that impressed Reynard.

"Get thee beside me," said Andalo, pointing to Reynard. Calafi led his horse forward, and the others formed two lines ahead of the remaining wagon. Again, the road before them seemed to grow and widen. A breeze rustled the dry leaves of the treetops.

Reynard watched the road with sweating fear. "Where are we going?"

"Into the sun," Calafi said.

Nikolias said, "On this margin around the krater lands, our trods conflict with Crafter magic. We must beware and keep control."

The trees parted further, like ladies gathering up their skirts at a dance, and the road was now as wide as five horses or two of the big wagons. Reynard blinked at unexpected glare as the sun moved backwards above the overarching branches, the light falling and shifting like the tide between two seas, and his head spun as the wagon wheels rolled smoothly over a white, glittering path. He closed his eyes and wished for oblivion, any sort, even death. For they were moving in a way that wrenched his stomach and stiffened his spine until his shoulders wished to crack and split wide.

He slumped in the saddle, but the ropes held and kept him from falling. Calafi giggled and patted his calf. The rest watched Widsith, who was also experiencing difficulties, and while he leaned back, and his head rolled and his eyes closed, the armed young Travelers adjusted their hats and made small talk, the horses nickered and advanced, and the wagon rolled on.

• • •

"The worst part is over," Nikolias said as Reynard sat upright and focused his vision. "We are through the cline."

Reynard squirmed in the saddle. His legs and butt were sore, as if they had gone many miles, and now there were no trees to define the path, but only rocky terrain and low rolling hills covered with sere scrub. They might have come to a different country! Far to the south, a high jagged ridge rose in a wide blue-gray wall, floating, it seemed, on a sea of mist tinted golden-yellow by the low sun. Overhead, clouds coiled like a great flat skein of hair or wool, the center hovering and a wisp dropping like an incipient water spout or tornado below the far horizon.

The girl squinted up at him, then pointed across to Widsith, who was still leaning, snoring faintly, and she gave him a broad, toothy grin. "Thou dost win the game!" she said.

Widsith lifted his head, then coughed and sniffed. "Need to clear my nose," he said.

"Then blow!" Calafi said disdainfully.

"Calafi, be kind," Yuchil said. "Loose his hands and loan him a rag."

Calafi crossed to Widsith's horse and loosened the bindings, then drew out a thoroughly filthy rag from the folds of her robe, no doubt used to clean the noses of horses, and dangled it to him with delicate fingers. He took it, blew quick and sharp, and handed it back.

She wrinkled her nose and tossed the rag onto the rocks.

Reynard thought to look over his shoulder and see if Valdis was still with them. She was, behind Kern, and unchanged, though her horse seemed thinner. All the Eater mounts had been affected, worn and in need of a rest.

Calybo was not visible. He assumed the high Eater had left, as he had promised ... And felt a sense of loss. He would have asked many more questions! But that seemed an impertinence, perhaps another heresy.

"Five great mountains radiate the chafing waste southeast of Agni," Nikolias said, pointing to the distant ridge. "Know'st a cline, boy?"

"No, sire," Reynard said. He studied the trail they were riding and found it none too peculiar — just a well-beaten dirt track, cleared of the largest stones, he thought, but neither especially wide nor especially smooth.

"The trod hideth its quality," Yuchil said, passing to gather the ropes from those who had been bound.

"And well it should. A cline marks the irregular boundary near where the ridges join, and beyond which Crafters shape their weather. Soon we enter their lands and breathe their airs. We do not wish to argue, and so subdue our own magic."

Reynard nodded as if he understood, which he did not. "How far is their reach?" he asked. "Across the island, or beyond?"

Still dizzy, Widsith leaned his head forward. "Thou knowest the answer to that already. I go where their servants tell me, and bring back reports."

"Across the world, then," Reynard said.

"All for nought if they are fighting, or already dead," Kern said.

They moved on across the rocky expanse into dusk. A far line of low trees became obvious through the persistent layer of mist, burned and broken. Thick and cloying smoke rose from another ruined forest to their left, up to the sky, where it took hold of the sharp crescent of a new-risen moon and choked it in ghastly orange.

"What about the boy? Seek'st thou payment for him?" Nikolias seemed to enjoy provoking Widsith. "He seemeth more in demand than thee."

"He may be," Widsith said, implacable. "But his ignorance is thy safety."

Nikolias shook his head. "Methinks his ignorance is a curtain that soon will rise, and what say we then?" He spat into the dirt beside the path, looked around at the others, then at the colorful wagon, and finally at Valdis, shaded and still on her horse, paying no mind to anything, it seemed.

"What makes so much smoke?" Reynard asked. "There hath been a great fire!"

Yuchil said, "We have heard of such, seldom seen it. That is the burning of incomplete worlds. In this land, Crafters draw or write out drafts and enact them like plays, and not just plays for players but for nature as well. Thou know'st this, Pilgrim. It is why thou sail'st and return, to make report on those drafts that are set and finished and can be freed. No fault of ours or the Crafters, blessed be their ways, blessed be their successes . . . and no failures."

"How do drafts not set and fixed, how do those get burned?" Reynard asked.

"Like kindling rolled up and set alight," Nikolias said, "be they people or cities, animals or plants. This burned forest may be some draft or other, some fledgling of history unmade, burned through, and an ember, seeking to live, got loose — a burning man or woman or eagle or raven. Dost smell burned flesh?"

Reynard shook his head.

"Then perhaps it is merely a draft, a Crafter manuscript, and not people that today smoketh the sky," Nikolias said.

Reynard thought to ask for another cloth to cover his mouth and nose, but the others did not seem to need it, and soon the air cleared and they passed into a desert of brown sand, shaping wide dunes where nothing grew and nothing more could burn. The wagon seemed to have no problem crossing the sand — perhaps the trod was still active, through hidden. But after a mile of desert, they came upon a hardpan where the ground was marked by patterns, streets and buildings in outline, as if an entire city had been laid out by architects, and walls erected to form buildings, and people had lived in those buildings, and somehow had all been pressed down like flowers between weighted boards — pressed into the flatness, leaving only charcoal impressions shot through with silvery gray. The horses' hooves did not raise any dust.

Nikolias halted the wagon. The horses shivered, then drooped their heads to whuff at the flat gray and black ground. "Here, the trod ends and the krater lands begin. We use other landmarks to guide us," he said.

Calafi appeared as if by magic near Reynard's horse, looked up at him, and tossed her red hair. "I did so dream it. This flat land was once an entire long tale," she said, as the others walked or rode forward to listen. "Of a place, a people, a time. They grew and fed and loved and birthed, and their children were hearty, and they were on their way to being made real and fixed, but a high Crafter scuffed them down with pumice and black chalk."

"Was this thy land, Calafi?" Sany asked, smiling at the others. "Didst thou dream of a home and mother and father?"

Calafi frowned hard. Nikolias listened but did not chide or defend. Instead, he said, "A fine dream," then looked around with narrowed gaze and pointed an arm. "There be a few still in trace."

Calafi ran to where he pointed and stood on what might have been shadows — now part of the stony surface. "They fell flat!" she exclaimed. "What stamped them down? I know! A Crafter lost a contest with his fellows!"

"Crafters be neither male nor female," Bela said resentfully, touching his ribbon.

She ignored him. "Soon after, other Crafters burned that one in his krater, then set his ashes into a jar. This flat land be all that stays of it, methinks."

Nikolias said, "Whatever the truth of it, the lands here are uneasy, so be on guard."

"Against what?" Sany asked.

Calafi said, with another twirl, "Spirits and waves of lost creation!"

"No surprise," Widsith said. "What with Spaniards and war in the air, something hath decided to bring creation full circle, and might make Crafters front their own art."

Calafi now ran to Widsith with her fingers shaping claws, but Nikolias called for her to stop and she grimaced, then backed away. A fierce scowl darkened her features, and Reynard could not help thinking she was a creature possessed, for her voice was now that of a harridan or a harpy.

"Think'st ye not this land be devoted to human story," she churled. "Once all creatures were drawn and assigned here, and rose and fell according to the wizarding of the Crafters, who used them on fields of battle, and won or lost according to how they rose or how they fell. And outside this land, the mists rose and fell like great cloaks on the plays thus played, and humans came to think themselves supreme, and arrived to claim their privilege . . . and their gods were made here, and also rose and fell, but in the end, all were made low. And now there is a great field of pots. And who or what will rise again — be that known to any?" The girl, transformed, tried to twirl again, but her eyes vibrated, and she collapsed to one knee and lowered her head. Her breath came in quick, shallow drafts, and a pale dribble of foam appeared on her lips. Her limbs shivered, and she uttered little moans.

Reynard had seen this before — the falling sickness.

Nikolias descended from his horse and draped a crimson cape over the girl's shoulders. "Done now, are we?" he murmured into her ear. "Now get thee back to being a girl, and leave godly things to the dead gods."

As if by instinct, Reynard looked to Valdis, stiff on her mount, cold and steady — and saw a gleam in her eyes as of distant hunger or yearning, not for the girl, poor thing so grabbed and made to speak —

But for the force that had possessed her.

They rode on. After a few miles on the shadowy flats, they saw another burned forest ahead, backed by the ever-distant pale mountain ridge, and Widsith asked Reynard, "Any women in thy family like unto that one?"

Reynard had been lost in thought, but when Widsith spoke, he looked up and said, "A little like that." He startled himself by announcing this, and he had been thinking of his grandmother, not his mother.

"Would that woman have shared insight with this child?" Nikolias asked from his horse.

Reynard shook his head. He did not know. To his surprise, he did not remember ever knowing. This place was tricking both mind and memory!

Nikolias looked back and down at Calafi, who paced behind his horse, staring in alternation blankly at the sky, then at the flat, hard ground and the shadows that seemed to swim there. "Blessed be those with such connections, for they live long, and are never happy." The girl saw his attention and smiled shyly. He nodded in return and handed down a cake wrapped in paper.

Valdis noticed all this, but did not reveal her interest. Instead, she stared at the small of Reynard's back, which made his muscles curl until he had to reach back and scratch.

"Evening comes early today," Yuchil announced from the wagon. "We camp soon."

The girl eagerly ran ahead and again danced a pretty dance on the hardpan, then smiled on them all, sunshine and sweetness and joy at their company.

"She doth find relief," Yuchil said from the seat of the wagon. "Visions, like a storm, clear the air."

Plain of Jars

WITH THE TRAVELERS VIGILANT — all of them serving watch, including Calafi — and the wagon at the center of their camp, another peculiar dawn arrived, and Reynard was able to see the new terrain by what passed for daylight. He could make little sense of what he saw, but it still seemed gloomy enough to dry his tongue and make it cling to the breakfast of dried fish and porridge seasoned with red pepper powder. Widsith ate as if he had eaten such foods before, or even spicier fare. And likely he had. Reynard had not.

The girl brought a leather bag with water and they sipped from it, no more. Widsith pulled it down when Reynard tried to quench the heat of the breakfast.

"There is little water here," Nikolias explained, taking his quick turn at the bag and handing it to the young warriors. "And none more until we cross the pass."

Valdis did not drink from the bag, but squatted by her horse, eyes shut as if asleep — or lost in an Eater's strange reverie.

"This is the outskirts of the plain of jars," Nikolias said, "forbidden to all but Crafter servants, and still they do not arrive."

"Yet none doth challenge or forbid!" Widsith said.

"We must deliver," Yuchil said grimly.

Widsith gave Nikolias a look almost of resentment, but mostly of fear, and Reynard knew that none of them had ever been this far into the center of the island, or beyond. Silent, questions neither asked nor answered, they surveyed the prospects ahead.

"The horses are brave for us," Widsith said to Reynard as the wagon rolled on. Valdis passed them. Her form was like a wraith of smoke, but where the light struck her, she glinted, she gleamed. And her eyes in particular seemed to change color, more umber than jade.

Nikolias said, "We have to make way through this place before nightfall. Not even Travelers are free to pass here at all times."

A flat, arid paleness stretched many miles to the distant peaks and did indeed contain row after row of great black jars, many hundreds of them stretching off to the flank of the dark ridge of rock, one of the radiant mountain ranges that divided the island's center and embraced the waste. Each jar was surrounded by a rough wooden scaffold that rose to the rim and seemed to afford access to any who would dare climb. Reynard did not think he would be one such.

"Beyond lies the first of the krater cities," Nikolias said. "Right on the edge of the widest part of the chafing waste. Perhaps the servants will be there to greet us."

"I doubt it," Yuchil said, and climbed back into the wagon. Trailed by the warriors, flanked by Kern and Kaiholo, they rolled on toward the next great ridge of rock. Nobody spoke much, and Reynard remounted his horse and watched Valdis do likewise, but with a translucent lack of energy that made her seem more and more like a ghost.

Calafi approached Nikolias. "Valdis doth not like it here," she whispered.

"We were told to bring at least one Eater," Nikolias said. "I do not think any of us like it here!"

"Then how rude of them not to meet us!" Calafi said.

"Are Crafters truly buried out there?" Reynard asked Widsith, also whispering.

"So I have been told," Widsith said.

The road passed through the field of huge jars, on to the ridge beyond. Reynard looked to his right and then his left, trying and failing, mostly, to avert his eyes, not to stare directly at the ancient tombs. The tallest jar, he guessed, rose fifteen yards and spanned the same distance. What would need such a tomb, and why open to the sky? Did they miss the stars? How many were already filled, how many still empty?

They halted as the pass yawned before them, between two rugged walls of gray stone. Nikolias walked up to Widsith and stroked his horse's muzzle. "Still no one to greet us."

Yuchil leaned out from behind the curtain that covered the entrance to the wagon. "Are any of the innermost servants still alive?" she asked.

Nikolias made a gruff snort.

The wagon and party soon were lost on the other side of the dusk, right up against night. Reynard wondered how long they had before death or dawn, or worse than one, and never the other.

The Pass

WARRIORS, RIDERS, AND CALAFI followed the wagon down a
road paved with wide flat stones, grooved by the passage of other
wheels over long centuries, much like Roman roads in England.
These grooves, however, came in several gauges, or widths between,
showing that even larger wagons had passed many times before. The
Traveler wagon rumbled smoothly along in its accepted gauge. And
so they proceeded with very little water and no more food up a long
rise to the narrow pass, and as it swiftly turned dark, clouds driven
and chewed by high, cold winds flowed to wrap the peaks.

They paused again. Reynard's gaze climbed the walls on both
sides, and he saw odd little formations, irregular houses sporting
rough entrances, like eyries or extrusions for the benefit of climbers
— though not for humans.

Calafi also surveyed these high, empty dwellings. "Others come
here to rest, and prepare," she said, and her wrinkled nose told Reynard she was guessing.

Clearly unhappy, the warriors pulled their coat collars up to avoid
the chill wind that now seemed to want to drive them back.

Dark filled the gap.

"We are tired," Calafi said to Nikolias. "Can we make a fire?"

"I think a fire is needed, if this wind will let it burn," Nikolias said. And so they gathered shrubs and sticks from between the rocks, which here were banded red and black, while the girl came forward with a thin stone she had found that had markings on it.

"Can somebody read this?" she asked, then held it up. The markings were spirals and wedges, and all who gathered around the wagon and the fire shook their heads but Valdis, who crooked her finger for the girl to approach and bent over to take the stone from her. She held it up as if she could see straight through it. "A spell to bind dreams," the Eater said.

"What language?" Nikolias asked, but Valdis merely slipped down gracefully from her horse and replaced the stone in the dirt, where Calafi had found it, then walked up to the rocks, where she studied a crevice no one else had seen until now. With a long, studying glance at the others, she ventured into the side passage, leading the shadowy horse after her.

"I did not see that," Widsith said, standing beside Nikolias.

"None here did," Nikolias said, touching the rock face with outstretched hands. "And I neither see nor feel it now!"

Calafi made as if to follow Valdis, but also could not find any opening in the banded rock. She patted and danced a little, as if that would open the crevice again, but Yuchil spoke to her sharply and, dejected, she returned to the beginnings of the new camp.

For a time, nobody spoke, but all warmed themselves.

The wind was getting colder, whipping the flames.

"Perhaps she doth flee us, sensing our fate," Nikolias said.

"Pfaah!" Yuchil exclaimed, then brought up more flat rocks to shield the flames. "I have known many an Eater more honorable than most men."

"And women?" Nikolias asked, smiling, pitching in with Kaiholo to help.

Yuchil blew out her breath again. "If our way is blocked ahead —
and who can say it is not? — then perhaps she seeketh another way."

Kaiholo was skeptical. "No way out and no way in, I trow," he
muttered. Kern agreed.

"And we all were alert to such," said Andalo as he nervously fingered the hilt of one sword.

Reynard nodded to him, and he responded merely by staring,
then turned away. Bela and Sany seemed even more imperious. This
irritated Reynard.

"We should have looked into a pot," he said.

"Why so?" Widsith asked.

"To see a Crafter. If it is dead, what can it do to us?"

The warriors did not respond, but Nikolias blew his nose into a
clean rag. "Push not nightmares, and save thy sleeping soul."

"But have you ever looked?" Reynard asked.

"No, as I say, I have never been this far. But I heard once from a
man who *did* climb a scaffold. He was ever after laughing mad, and
could barely find his supper."

The First City

THE CLOUDS sliding along the heights of the pass were so dense they could not tell the difference between night and morning.

Reynard studied this low, coiled deck for a few minutes before rolling out of his covers and standing. He had slept in a quilted round rug from the wagon, stitched with Arabic words, he thought, but comfortable despite the presence of passages likely from the Moors' sacred and blasphemous book, and now he handed it back to a plump older girl with strong arms and henna-colored hair, one of Yuchil's assistants or perhaps her daughters, who, it seemed, rarely left the wagon but followed Yuchil's orders and found whatever was needed inside to supply their needs. She had not appeared before now. Who else was hiding in that wagon?

Widsith had slept in another rug and did not break a deep silence, as if still waking from a fraught dream, contemplating his doom, and that approaching right soon, in his opinion. Reynard, on the other hand, had reacquired, after the plain of jars, a kind of curiosity for what lay beyond the pass. He tried to get answers from Calafi, asking her what, if anything, she had heard from other Travelers — or had sensed on her own. But she only waggled her head, tossed her red frizzled hair, and danced to music he could not hear; and soon he felt a growing apprehension, that he might see all there was to be seen, and understand none of it! For no one, not even Nikolias, seemed inclined to prepare him in any way. Maybe they were simply as ignorant as he was himself. But surely when they had delivered stories before, they had interacted with those of their people assigned to receive them and carry them farther! Maybe they wished for him to innocently view what they themselves were so seldom allowed to see: whatever lay beyond the pass, down the smooth road. They would not even respond to his questions about how often they had been here before.

Bela and Sany and a warrior whose name he did not know talked as they doused the fire. Sany seemed to have Moorish roots. Bela, like many of the Travelers, hailed from the mountain countries in the eastern continent. Reynard stood a few yards away, listening to their mix of Rom and a pidgin of Tinker's Cant that seemed more eastern than Irish. They paid him no attention. "Papa is putting us all in danger, with the Eater here," said Bela, who sported only two knives and one short sword. Bela called Valdis a *Verdulak*.

Sany murmured, under his breath, "An *ifrit*, a *ghroul*."

Yuchil's strong-armed assistant, whom they called Sophia, shook her head. "She is no danger to us."

"Why say that?"

"Because she doth serve the paynim," Sophia said. "She taketh from them, and giveth to them as well. But she dothn't serve Travelers. We are not of the pact."

"'Tis not always true," Yuchil said. "I suspect some of our people have here made deals with Calybo, to live long enough to understand the Crafters."

The assistant did not disagree, but her expression was sour.

Andalo, cleaning and sheathing all his knives and two swords, said, "All is changing. No one is here to take our deliveries! Hel is no longer with us."

"Hel hath not been with us for most of time," Yuchil pointed out. "What matter to mortals?"

They saw Reynard's attention and turned away, walking around the wagon.

"Hath the Eater returned?" Nikolias asked.

"I watch," Calafi said. "She hath not."

Nikolias walked off with a shrug to urge the men to finish grooming and feeding the horses. Reynard walked over to where Widsith was shaking off the last of his deep sleep. The Pilgrim did his best to ignore all attentions and company, and did not even look his way.

Last Roundabout

THE LATER MORNING was only a little brighter than the night, but
they pushed on through the pass until they came to a wider spot between the walls. Here, the wagon-rutted path circled a single jagged
pillar. Widsith and Reynard and two of the warriors went around
the pillar and came upon a perfectly smooth causeway through the
last of the great rocks, paved evenly with hewn stone.

"Do we stop here and wait longer?" Kaiholo asked.

Yuchil and Nikolias again conferred. Nikolias shook his head ad-
amantly, but the woman seemed to win their debate, so he returned
to the others and said they had no choice. "We go where we have
never gone before," he explained. "Because we are not met, nor given
signs. Next will be the outermost cities of the krater lands, where
many Travelers are said to dwell and serve the Crafters. But all now
is uncertain."

The wagon wheels and the horse hooves were equally unsure on
this smoothness, and more than once the wagon slid sideways and
had to be corrected with careful management of reins and horses in
harness.

The other Travelers were gloomy, contemplating what they might find ahead, and disliking going where they might not be at all welcome.

Finally, a far misty landscape became visible — a wide valley into which the pass debouched. A few miles away, another ridge, central to the valley, as thin and sharp as a knife blade, interrupted the lowering cloud. Reynard could almost make out more shapes this side of the ridge, rounded and tall and huge, but obscured by thick mist.

Calafi ran ahead a few dozen yards and then returned with her widest gap-toothed grin. "A city in the form of a grand seed!" she called. "Flowers and stalks make caged seeds! This is like those, but great."

Yuchil clucked and got down from the wagon. Calafi danced forward, spinning, sashaying, and curtsying, as if introducing them all to unseen hosts. As well, she raised her hands into the air, fingers curling inward as if waiting to hold an apple.

On one side of the great blade of rock — also banded red and black — were what the girl had described as a great caged seed, and Reynard soon saw her description was apt. The structure hugged the near slope of the blade and rose almost as high as the ridge itself. It most resembled the late summer curled nest of a hedgerow wild carrot or cow parsley, with a protective outer basket of wood or stone, he could not tell which, though how stone could be worked so fine and delicate and yet remain strong, he had no notion. Within the up-curving frame of the basket, houses as big as manor estates were mounted on cross-works of beams, connected by stairs and ladders and held together in part by a thick tackle like the ropes of a great-masted ship. It all looked so absurdly fragile that a typical coastal winter storm might have toppled it and blown out its dwellings like thistledown.

Nikolias and Andalo guided the wagon across the last of the hewn road, onto another stretch of mud and broken cobbles, covered with puddles and now trackless. Reynard rode alongside Widsith.

Facing the mud, Calafi had stopped her skipping dance and now walked quietly beside the lead riders, making gestures with arm and fingers, as if trying to find a way to describe in a secret alphabet what they were seeing. She squinted up at Reynard.

Widsith rode with his eye on the valley, the blade-ridge, the curled structure emerging from the late morning shadow of the opposite side of the ridge.

In less than an hour, the wagon rolled into the shadow of the great basket, while the murky sun split its light along the ridge, falling on a stone and wood stockade that surrounded the city and the inmost fields.

"It is deserted," Nikolias said from behind.

"Or worse," Kaiholo added.

The fields were untended, overgrown, and the outer small hamlets of stone and mud-brick houses, within the stockade and spaced beyond it, were demolished and burned.

"No dead, no living," Kern said.

Widsith rode along a dry gravel pathway that seemed to point toward the distant rising cloud.

"These gardens were once magnificent," said Yuchil. "But now they are just sticks and dead soil."

Reynard could not take his eyes away from the great ribbed and vaulted edifice. The ribs could have been crafted of either wood or stone — or wood made stone! Raised on the flats of Southwold, having known only shingle-stone and driftwood buildings, separated by narrow lanes and fields crossed by mazes of hedgerows, the thought of life in such a topsy-turvy structure was inconceivable. For one thing, the stairways had no rails! Monkeys might ascend and descend, or leap from rope to road, or from strut to beam to strut — but anyone else, it seemed, must live in constant fear.

Andalo and his warriors could hardly conceive that Travelers who once lived here, and tended these fields, might have given up without a fight. "There must have been a great battle between the Sister Queens' armies and Travelers who served the Crafters, one side victorious, and th'other . . ."

"But why leave it empty?" Nikolias asked. "Those who were supposed to meet us claimed this was a rich land, full of rich peoples. How many remain? The Crafters who dwelt here are likely dead, and those who served them carried off in slavery."

"How can that be?" Andalo asked, like a little boy told that a favorite legend was not true and never had been. "Are Crafters not immortals, protected and ruled by Queen Hel?"

"Maybe, like us, they have their age, and pass away," Yuchil said. "If we could but see what the Pilgrim hath seen!"

"None of what I saw explaineth this," Widsith said.

Yuchil drew up her cloak to ward off the wind that still followed them. "It groweth cold and dank. We must leave now!" She rose and patted down her dress and overrobe. But the men did not move.

"Not until day," Nikolias insisted. "Who knows what mood ruleth spirits here?"

The others marked themselves and inclined their heads. Calafi climbed up onto the wagon, and Yuchil suddenly reached out and hugged her.

"How can Crafters die?" Yuchil cried. "They were our whole world!"

Reynard snuck away from the fires around the wagon, sticking to the shadows cast by broken trees and low rocks, as if he were himself an Eater.

Nikolias and his three warriors had joined Widsith and Kaiholo and Kern in passing around two great wicker-wrapped jugs of unwatered wine, hidden in the wagon along with everything else, and controlled by Yuchil . . . But the day had been so disheartening that Nikolias felt a little imbibing was in order, and Yuchil did not disagree.

They spoke very little.

But Reynard did not drink, and made his way quietly toward the outer fence.

The stockade had pillars of rounded boulders caulked with straw-mud and spaced with long lines of interwoven sticks and stalks not unlike the core of a field barricade in England, the sort meant to discourage bulls. The stockade had been broken through in several places, likely by soldiers. There were many marks of feet and hooves, but no sign of battle.

He stepped over a tangle of branches and through a gap and approached the rock foundation that rooted one great rib as it rose above the fields, above this part of the stony flats, to join with side arches that supported many floors, interconnected by thick rigging, ladders, and bridges, their lines and backstays hanging in sad tatters from curved masts, like a stricken ship rising out of a stony sea. He looked at the floor, paved with small pebbles, and saw a thick carpet of what might have once been leaves, now black with mold — as if the city had once been part of a great tree.

Reynard touched the base of the rib, and his hand found a long crack, then, around the circumference, another. The huge rib had been shivered several times along its lower length. How long would it hold? Had it always had such cracks, as sometimes showed in great masts?

He turned. The darkness was so deep it seemed bootless to venture farther. But then he caught a gleam behind him. The darkness was slowly being broken by what seemed at first to be fireflies, but which he soon made out as tiny flowers sprouting from vines that laced around the ropes and supports — flowers that glowed in the night. He approached one such vine and saw for a moment what he thought was a childer —

But it vanished.

The pale, dim light from the flowers showed him that just beyond a broken gate a narrow staircase lifted into the heights in a corkscrew, like an inside stair in a large ship. He could not see what waited at the top. Going higher might be invading the privacy of those Travelers who once served Crafters — and who survived being near them! What powers could those dead exert? What resentment, leading to what revenge? What magic had the Crafters passed to their servants? Not enough perhaps to keep them alive, or fend off the Sister Queens' armies.

Still, he wondered if it would be the better part of valor to just stop here and return to the wagon and the fires, the wine and the bread . . .

But then he saw a candle glowing about a third of the way up the steps, a tall candle that had not been there before and seemed to have been placed to guide him — even when no hand could have set it there.

He crossed the threshold of the broken gate and slowly, carefully climbed the steps to the candle, hand on the curved railing. He stood looking down at the flame, burning steady and putting out a tendril of smoke. Then a slight breeze flickered the flame and played with his hair.

"Are you here somewhere, magician?" Reynard whispered.

Came no answer.

But this would be a good place to gather sticks, if not beef and sheep bones. That is, should a magician wish to assemble swevens or topplers or other helpers.

Bone-wives.

He turned at a scuff.

Widsith came up behind him, followed by Calafi.

"She told me you had gone into the city." The Pilgrim did not seem angry. The tangle-haired girl favored Reynard with a guileless smile, then studied the flowers.

Now three more childers appeared and hovered around them — around the girl, actually. Their translucent faces smiled beatifically upon her. She held up her hands as if to caress them, but they all disappeared, again like soap bubbles.

"I saw a candle," Reynard said, pointing. "I see one now."

Both looked to where he pointed. "I see nothing," Widsith said, and Calafi shook her head. "I always thought the magician far too old to travel. He hath for centuries been a fire burning low, and Eaters cannot replenish him. Do you sense his presence?"

Reynard shook his head. "But I saw another candle, far back, and now this one. Why show candles to me alone?"

The candle burned low in its holder, and the flame flickered as if about to go out.

They looked to the Pilgrim as if he might have an answer, having known the magician for so many years. "As guide for you," Widsith said.

Calafi said, "Maybe he is dead."

"Then how could he place candles?" Reynard asked.

Widsith did not seem to find the notion incredible. "His bone-wives, mayhaps. After death, he could make puppets to carry out his final wishes. Each puppet would last the length of a candle. Before the candle went out, the puppet would need to make another like itself ... A jagged existence, but it hath a seeming of Troy. If he be dead."

"But why show only me?" Reynard asked.

"Let us climb higher," Calafi said. "The magician may have found something to show us all."

They resumed their climb up the stairs and entered a twisting shaft of rising columns wound through with vines and the tiny pale flowers. The overall silence in the city was broken by distant snaps and cracks, and a continuous rustling, as of branches in a wind-tossed tree.

For a time, Reynard wondered if the cracked ribs would all split and sag at once, and the entire city would fall in on itself . . .

Then they came to a round arched doorway accessing a curved corridor, leading to many other round doors on both sides. In the middle of the corridor, a single childer floated, softly imbued with its own light, its own distant existence, paying them no attention. Then it seemed to startle, turned, regarded them with translucent eyes — and floated swiftly into a doorway.

"Do we go there?" Reynard asked.

The girl nodded. "Only look," she said. "The city still doth contain many spirits. We do not touch or move anything!"

They passed into the next room, and saw it was wide and high-ceilinged but maintained the woven, rigged, and airy design of the rest of the city. The wicker floor was marred by signs of struggle — the marks of axes and sword blades, scraps of cloth, a robe tossed aside — but no blood, no bodies from any combatant or inhabitant.

Reynard was alarmed by this lack. "Where are they all, those who lived here?" he asked.

"Many have likely been taken as slaves," Widsith said. "But how none who fell remain . . . I do not know."

"Few fell, and many were taken," said a voice behind them, and Nikolias passed through the round door to join them. He carried a lantern and lifted it to reveal the room's deeper contents. "I have never been this far and seen so much. But I do know that the servants lived in their own kind of luxury, and perhaps valued life too much."

There were panels, like unto those that appeared in Zodiako over the corridor leading to the hall, but much larger, covered with arts and conceptions half sculpture, half paint, with much gilding to show sun and day.

Nikolias shined the lantern light along the closest panel and said, "Observe a plan, or a dream, or a fancy. All are the same to the servants of Crafters. Here was a Crafter design, being sketched and considered by masters of all arts and artifice ... But here, our own people provided the details." His expression showed both sorrow and pride.

The panel revealed a great palace sitting on a precipice overlooking extraordinary snow-covered mountains that seemed to march back, rank upon rank, to a radiant dawn. Another panel, half as large, showed another kind of palace, a great gray thing — and Reynard saw that it was not a palace, as such, but a ship floating on the water, buildings rising high from its hull, overseeing several ranks and levels of what might have been cannon, but arranged three to an emplacement, and far larger and longer than any cannon they knew ...

Calafi pointed to the sky over the palace. Very small, as if far away, a strange bird flew, its wings doubled, one above the other, supporting a long body tailed by a kind of box kite, not feathers. No feathers at all.

Most definitely not a drake, however.

A mechanical thing, flying.

"This was never delivered and executed," Nikolias said, wiping his eyes. "This pictured a time, a place, a history! And now it may never be. The Sister Queens have killed it!"

A sharp noise came from the winding hall beyond the door. Nikolias looked around them warily. "We must leave," he said. "We attract attention."

"From whom?" Widsith asked with a rasp of anger, sweeping out his arms at the emptiness.

The chief of the Travelers led them out of the room, but stopped, looking back — and gestured for Widsith to join him. They were facing a strange figure in carnival garb, backed by shadow, barely paying them heed, even when Nikolias spoke to it. It moved one arm, and a stick fell from the sleeve, along with other scraps.

Beside this figure, half-hidden in the entrance to another room, was a small pile of more sticks.

"Troy was here," Widsith said. "This was his work. Its time is coming to an end — the length of a candle."

The robe the figure wore faded and turned to tatters, and the rest of its body collapsed into coal and dust. When its dissolution was finished, Widsith — but none of the others — approached the remnants.

"This puppet is spent," he said. He nudged the small pile of sticks beside the crumbled mass, and picked up a bone, gray and dry. "But Troy may yet have a few tricks to play."

A Return

NEXT MORNING, a steady, hollow sound of hooves echoed from the pass behind the wagon, and Valdis reappeared on foot, leading her horse, head down and feet plodding. She walked by the warriors and the strong-armed Sophia to the wagon, where Yuchil poked out her head, as if expecting her, and handed her down a bundle of dark green branches tied with red ribbon.

Valdis laid the bundle before her horse, which acknowledged it with a shake of the head and a stamp of one foot, and then set to eating. Reynard could barely look into her face, she seemed so different now . . .

"What didst thou see?" Nikolias asked her, putting blanket and saddle on his own horse, as if they all must ride soon.

"The Eaters are convened at the next working quarry of souls," she replied. "Not for this krater, which is dead, but the next."

"All the Eaters? Pacted and unpacted?"

"All," Valdis affirmed.

"They have not departed?"

"No," Valdis said. "They tried, but it is now clear — we have no existence beyond the islands. Calybo says we have difficult duties before we retire to dust and shadows."

"Duties to whom?" Widsith asked.

"I know not. But the Sister Queens have combined to drive a great horde and move on the last of the krater cities. Travelers resist, but mostly, they die."

Nikolias stalked off and waved his arm for the wagon to prepare.

"Other news that is bad," Valdis said. "The Spanish general has instructed the armies of the Sister Queens how to construct snares that trap and kill drakes. Many have died. I do not know if any of them were yours to command."

This struck home. Reynard fingered the vial that Anutha had given to him, now empty.

Calafi had bent to observe the Eater horse's meal. "Snakebane!" she said. "Such would kill our animals."

"That is why I do not feed them snakebane," Yuchil said. "But one must accommodate guests and their needs."

"Even if they bring unwelcome tales," Andalo said.

"We will stay another night," Nikolias said, "and make sure none of our people are late in arriving."

"Foolish hope!" Yuchil said.

Bela came up to her, held out a sloshing skin bag, and told her the scouts had found a spring. "Then there will be tea," Yuchil said. She instructed him to pass it to the rear of the wagon and bring more, then sat back on the wagon seat and lit up a cobb pipe with a reed stem, not unlike the smoking flute Reynard had seen being sucked on by the unfortunate keeper of the fold. She puffed, blew smoke, passed it to Nikolias, and looked away, toward the great basket city and the fields and ruins below.

In its descent, the sun cut around the northern ridge, illuminating the land in a soft golden light that made it look even more desolate, yet strangely beautiful. A steady dusk wind blew grit from the fields. The upper reaches of the city, they all observed, were now crowding with birds — gulls, cormorants, puffins, and even a few hawks and sea eagles, who seemed to cause no stir amongst the others. All were silent.

"They have finally returned," Yuchil said, as she and Sophia handed the warriors and guests steaming bowls of gruel. "And no one to listen!"

Reynard looked to Widsith for an explanation.

"Humans are not the only ones who report the ways of this world," Widsith said, bowing his head over the gruel.

"This city always welcomed birds," Yuchil said. "Others, inland, took tales and histories from insects, and still others . . ." Her words trailed off, as if even she did not understand what else might carry reports to the Crafters.

"Was that why Troy came here?" Widsith mused.

Yuchil said, "He of all I know might understand the songs of birds."

Their bowls empty, Kaiholo scrubbed them with sand and carried them to the wagon. The young warriors and Sophia gathered wood and dried vines from the margins of the ruined village and made two bonfires to drive back the dark that would soon arrive. The Travelers gathered around the fires and stretched out their hands.

Yuchil said, "This be the same fire that warmed Hel when she arrived from the outer spheres and first thought of us. It attracted her to our world — the warmth and the light. And so she unveiled the stars, and then the sun, and life grew."

Nikolias said, "I have heard that Hel kindled these first fires to drive away the formless dream."

"I have heard that as well," Yuchil said. "The fire that burneth inside a woman, and warmeth a man."

The others laughed, and Nikolias afforded her a wry grin.

Calafi spun slowly before the flames and faced Reynard, eyes turned up to show their whites. All the Travelers sighed a deep sigh.

"Calafi hath snared a tenebrion," Sophia said.

"Is it a spirit of one of the dead around here?" Bela asked, and Yuchil hushed him.

"Ignore the girl. She will speak truth when it is time. Until then, she merely dreameth."

Calafi rotated two more times, and then stopped. She touched her arm with one spread hand, and shaped letters on her pale skin with splayed and folded fingers. Reynard tried to figure what words she might be signing. Then he saw that they were some of the age-old questions that gave poetic cues to tinkers and Rom who understood. His grandmother had once conversed with his mother in this way.

The girl's questions, he saw, were addressed to him, and she made that clear by looking straight into his face.

Who are we, you and I?
Are we larks that sweep the sky?
Seek we nests crisp and dry?
Are we doves that feather bed?
Who are we when we are dead?
Speak we words from those long fled
Whose spirits pace the land around
And dress for sleep on bloody ground?
Turn our signs into sound!
Who are you?
Who am I?

She settled beside him, knees drawn up, and used her stick to draw birds and snakes in the dirt. "I have died four times," she said. "Yet I am not an Eater. Who are they, and who am I?"

"A child," Reynard said, having no other answer.

"In this fire, I see Hel plain as day," she said. "She is not done with us, nor with thee."

"Good to know," Reynard said, and cringed as he bit the inside of a cheek. "Maybe that is my reason."

"Oh, no," Calafi said. "It be not so simple, methinks."

He tongued the brief flow of blood, then said, words a little mushy, "Is Hel another name for Mary, mother of God?" His stomach churned even to ask the question.

"Hel is Hel," the girl said. "When thou diest, thou wilt see. I hope to be there, to watch thy waking."

Reynard shook his head. "I'll be honored," he said sarcastically.

"Yes, that thou wilt."

He saw the boldness in the dancing girl, but also the fragility. "What visions have you now?" he asked.

"Oh, many. Some more dim than others. Clear enough, armies approach from the other side of the waste, the other kraters. The Queens are greedy. Very dim: they might kill us but save thee, I know not why. Then thou canst ask them who will replace the dead, and who will stare at the rocky walls, and find us in their designs."

"What doth that mean?" Reynard asked.

"These, mine own Travelers, value life," the girl said, ignoring his question. "We are brave enough to stay and defend, but none knoweth what is expected of us. Still, I am ready. I have died often enough."

"You see your past lives?" Reynard asked. His grandmother had spoken of such things, upsetting the churchgoers around her, in her weaving and threshing circles.

"Many, many," Calafi said. "The old ones in the quarries keep seeing me in their stone and sending me back. It is my eyes, I think." She blinked and brought parted fingers to her face, framing one eye.

Reynard shook his head, not understanding anything she said. "I, too, value life," he insisted.

"Oh, but being born is another way of dying. Thou didst die before thou camest here, didst thou not?"

He stared at her, irritated, even angry — but they were interrupted. Sophia brought the girl a blanket, wrapped her shoulders, and looked his way, but her expression told him nothing.

Reynard leaned over to Calafi and insisted, as if claiming some firm ground, "I have yet to die!"

"Oh, good!" the girl said, curling up to sleep. "Then it will be an adventure."

"Look," Kern said, standing on the other side of the second fire. "They leave!"

The birds had stopped wheeling and now rose high in the last of the sun, like sparks or bits of molten gold, and flew away from the city and the great blade of stone — south, as if fleeing a looming storm. The upper works of the basket city were again deserted and lifeless.

Yuchil called for tea to be made, and soon all but the girl drank of the warm liquid from flat steel kettles, and others arranged pots for boiling more gruel. The night seemed to surround them like a fog.

They ate and drank, and some wandered to the edge of the firelight to relieve themselves, women squatting and hiding their efforts with long skirts, men turning away as if this were the height of modesty, but none daring find cover in the fields in the dark.

Reynard took his turn, as did Widsith. "I piss less often now, and that is a blessing," the Pilgrim said to Reynard. "I would die another death before age creeps on me again."

An Echo in the Glooming

◎

IN THE NIGHT, the strange mud-gray night, Reynard opened his eyes and saw Calafi standing over him.

"The scout is hurt worse than any thought," the girl said. He felt he had known this already, but could not remember. "She is dead soon. The Eater can save her for a while longer, by sharing her time."

"As Calybo did with Widsith. Where is Widsith?"

Then he saw that Calafi had no real substance.

"But the Eater will not save her, *cannot* save her. Valdis needs must borrow from another, because her time is trothed and may not be shared." The girl wavered in the last light of the flickering fire, and then, behind her came Valdis to stand where Calafi had been, and his heart leaped. He could not see the redheaded girl anywhere, nor even much of the camp, and he wondered if he was still asleep.

"Will you save Anutha?" he asked Valdis. "She hath been brave! Take time from me if you cannot find Widsith or anyone else!"

"You have no time to share," Valdis said. "You are too near your beginning. No Eater can borrow from you, only give. And giving will spell the end for us all."

"I do not understand!" Reynard said.

"Hel has returned, and given her orders to th'one who made me what I am today."

Reynard rolled over in his blanket and found that he had not yet opened his eyes. And when he did, the night was still thick about them, and he saw Widsith lying not far away.

The Pilgrim was snoring.

With day, the fires were down, not even smoking, and the fields and ruins near which they had camped were cast half in deep shadow, the line of the shadow made murky by passing layers of cloud.

Reynard could not remember what he had seen in his deep sleep.

The Travelers brought them tepid gruel and chunks of a hard, mostly stale bread, like ship's biscuit. Lifting a spoon of the gruel, Widsith remarked how rice was far more common in the lands of his travels than in Europe, where wheat and rye and other grains supplied their usual needs.

Nikolias emerged from the wagon and cracked his joints with a rich variety of grimaces, then looked to Reynard and Widsith.

"Still no one," Yuchil said, peering from the back of the wagon. "We should be on our way."

"There is nowhere left to return to!" Widsith said, his voice breaking with both anger and sorrow.

"And no farther path here," Nikolias said. "Move we must, even so, to deliver the boy. Pack it away." The guards rolled up their sleeping blankets, kicked the fire marks around the dirt, and prepared horses and wagon to move on — though, as Widsith had said, there was no place for them to go.

"I would have saved Anutha," Reynard said to Widsith. He felt the muscles on his back and neck twitch and looked up at the sky and the rolling gray clouds, searching for shadows, for of course anything could happen here. They were near a dead city, on the out-skirts of a dead land.

"Listen to Valdis. Thou hast value, but no power, not yet," Wid-sith said. "And none here knoweth why. Anutha died from a poi-son in her blood. She died honorably, and she delivered the boon of drakes. As Maeve and Maggie would have wished." Widsith looked along the ridge, over the fallow fields. "Dost thou understand why the Eaters did not share?"

The Pilgrim's question cut deep. "What do you know about me?" Reynard asked sharply, as if his words might shake loose something hidden between them.

"In time, maybe."

Suddenly furious, Reynard turned away to hide the redness of his face. He had been told his visit had importance, but had never trusted such judgments, because he knew himself to be ignorant. The Spaniards, worst in his imagination, most skilled at war, had thrived neither in their sea battle nor on this island. And if this land had left its own people to rot under the shadows of a pair of unknown queens, after endless times under the rule of a Hellish goddess — what chance would *he* have?

The Next Silence

EAST ALONG the great blade of rock, evening mist was clearing from the caged seed city.

Andalo and Sany spoke with Nikolias away from the wagon.

Widsith had avoided Reynard through the night, but now stood beside him and listened to the guards. "Half of the Sister Queens' armies are most likely returning from their conquest of Zodiako and the southwestern shores, by sea and any available paths overland," the Pilgrim said. "The Travelers will assume that all their ways back will be watched by the Queens' pickets, ready to summon more troops than we can possibly defeat."

"The Travelers wish to keep going east?"

"Nikolias's only choice. Yuchil's as well, given how many soldiers may surround this half of the island. We know not how many Travelers remain in these lands, if they no longer serve the Crafters. But there might be some." Widsith studied the boy. "Nikolias may hope he can pass thee to the next group of servants, if they find any — and then, rewarded with food and water, turn about and head south or west."

"Is there an escape that way?"

"None that I know," Widsith said.

"The servants would trade me . . . to whom, for what advantage?"

Widsith shook his head.

Reynard drew himself up. "Calafi says it must be so."

"That girl . . . I have not seen her like. I would ask Yuchil where she was found, but I wonder if any of them could answer."

Nikolias approached and informed them they would try to roll their wagon a few miles along the blade of rock before nightfall. "Beyond, none knoweth what will be found."

Andalo and Bela came to them next. "We have seen many footprints," Andalo said. "Heading east — being herded by horsemen."

"The servants of this city?" Widsith asked.

"Future slaves for the Queens," Bela said darkly. "But they may not be able to feed or keep them all. We fear . . ."

He did not finish his fear. There was no need.

Calafi approached Reynard from behind, surprising him, and took his hand in hers. "I'll be with thee, whatever they decide," she whispered, looking up into his face.

Sophia brought the horses forward, and all mounted and followed the wagon. Calafi stayed close to Reynard and his horse. She never rode, always walked, but now she had ceased her dances and her spells, and her red tresses were knotted, for she refused the attentions of Yuchil and Sophia.

Seeing the mute swarms of birds had made the Travelers even more gloomy, as if the silent, wheeling flocks presaged their own doom, the end of their own worlds of language and meaning . . .

Their own silence.

Valdis, as always, seemed to find the comfort of shadow.

The garden lands, beyond the eastern end of the high, sharp ridge, became a jumble of uplifted plates of rock, punctuated by white hexagonal pillars, as if a great coat of varnish had been laid over the ground and broken by bones rising from below.

Yuchil raised her hand, and the wagon stopped. The guards dismounted and passed their horses' reins to Calafi, then opened doors in the side of the wagon and scooped out hay in great fist-clumps, while the Travelers on foot arranged their blankets and laid out cloth bags of provisions.

"They will feed the horses one fine meal," Widsith said. "What doth that wagon truly contain?"

"Whatever Yuchil needeth," Kaiholo said. "And that which her children require. For a while!"

Reynard had wondered if perhaps the wagon's stores were endless. How much magic did Travelers possess? If they commanded words, could they turn words into goods — into food and water?

The first word is the first mother. It is not her breast or larder. Words only guide and describe. They do not fulfill. Look to the silence of the birds! Their songs have never filled their stomachs.

Somehow, hearing that inner voice that still was not precisely his own, he felt ashamed of his hopes.

They moved higher up the rocky fields and into low clouds that made these places even more ghostly and unreal, not that any of it seemed real to Reynard.

"Where are the drakes?" Andalo asked Widsith. "I would have mine close!"

"That I do not know," the Pilgrim said.

"Can we sense their wills, their direction?"

"Not yet," Widsith said.

Kaiholo touched his jaw. "Perhaps they arrive only when we have true need."

Kern studied the gray skies with a broad scowl. "If the southwestern coast is conquered, many drakes are either dead or without masters. And a drake without a master is a dangerous enemy. Who hath killed its master, it must kill before its season is done."

Stars lit their way, but not many, and no moon, and still the wagon rolled on through the night, leaving the first krater city behind. And still they had not seen a krater, or crossed the boundary of the chafing whiteness.

But they could clearly see in the dirt and along the crusted rock the prints of many feet and hooves.

"I wonder they gave in without a fight," Andalo said.

"Maybe they had hope of rescue," Reynard said.

"From us?" Bela asked. "We were ever the lesser of Travelers. I wonder if perhaps they believed the island could not live on without them."

Reynard was reminded of those inland farmers and lords in England, who did not believe in oceans and far lands, or the peril they might bring.

They paused in the dark and stumbled about to water the horses. Widsith found an old sailor's rest. Sleep or rest of any sort seemed impossible to Reynard, who felt an inner pain he had never known before — a grief not just for lost family and friends, but for all those who might come after, for all who might arise in times of peace and prosperity — for he saw that such times might never come again, *would* never come again — and he was to blame!

He rolled over in his blanket, now dusty and itchy and miserable, and saw that Kaiholo and many of the Travelers were already up and about before the muted sunrise, off to brew tea and make thin soup. Reynard closed his eyes and squeezed them tight, as if to see into the greater darkness behind them — and when he looked again, there was Yuchil, holding out a cup of tea. Widsith had not yet stirred. Reynard sat up, took the cup, and sipped slowly, while she carried over a silken pillow and laid it beside him. She sat with a ladylike sigh.

"Thou still knowest not why thou art here," she said. "Whilst brave enough in battle, it be not thy calling to fight and kill."

"No," he said. "That my family hath never required of me."

"And yet thine uncle took thee out to sea," she said.

"To carry food to our ships. We are none of us warriors."

"Nor, except in extremes, are my people," Yuchil said. She shook her head. "Some carry swords, and will defend us, but they are not true warriors. They cannot be true warriors unless they are willing to begin wars, and they are not. But do not tell our young men I said that."

Reynard nodded. "I have been told I come from a long line of tinkers and wanderers," he said, hoping for better or at least clearer judgment than that from the King of Troy. "Can you tell if that is true?"

"Oh, there are many in England descended from the Rom and other Travelers. The Travelers have, after all, spread far and wide, and proven themselves as essential to kings and queens as any warriors. Not only do they bring the languages that tell the stories kings and queens love to hear, of themselves and others like them, greater still . . . But those languages convey power and strategy. Before the Travelers reached any of the lands we know, any of the lands that Crafters controlled and shaped, there was only base instinct and forgetting. Now . . . there is change and suffering and war. Which is better, think'st thou?"

He shook his head. "There must be good and various reasons to live, and they cannot all involve animal loss or animal gain."

Yuchil's smile was like a light in the early morning gloom. "Wisedom beyond thy years."

"Misery breedeth change in hearts and minds. Some call it wisedom."

"Thou hast remembered some things, Widsith doth tell me. Thou remember'st your grandmother speaking to thee in thy mother's womb . . . teaching thee some of her words?"

He nodded.

"If that was given to thee, then something else happened as well. Dost thou remember others who sought thee out and conveyed *their* words?"

Reynard looked into the silver-haired woman's youthful eyes, and noticed that Calafi had come closer and was listening. None of the others approached, however — they did not appear to notice them at all. "I remember a man with a white shadow, who spake to me whilst I hid in a hedgerow. And another man, who came whilst I was alone at sea. He had a feathered hat."

"Thy grandmother would have arranged another ceremony. A completion, as it were, of thy charge and task . . . a loading of the musket, a fletching of thine arrows."

Reynard frowned at her. "I do not remember any such ceremony," he said.

"She would have determined thy quality then, and armed thee with the languages she knew thou wouldst need. Inner languages. Inner qualities that stream now through thy flesh and along thy bones. Dost thou feel them, like cold fire . . . like the white shadow of the strange man, and the feather in the fancy hat of th'other?"

"I sometimes dream such," Reynard said. "But the dreams are deep in fog, and I do not remember them when I awaken . . . so perhaps, no."

"Time to awaken the dream and make it remember *thee*, young Fox."

"How can that happen?"

"It is like the beginning. May I speak to thee of that place, those people, that time?"

Reynard nodded, though he almost dreaded hearing such things, because of the responsibility they might bring.

"Once, people who would become like thee and me were deaf. They heard nothing, and only saw, and that not in colors, but merely in grays and blacks. The man with the white shadow is a presence from those times. He will not leave thee alone, ever.

"The people who would become human felt only the pounding of their feet deep in their bodies, as they walked a dark and silent realm, trying to find themselves and all who would come after. Many such passed into oblivion. They also felt the pump of their blood and the drumbeat of their hearts, and once, one looked up at a bird on a bare tree and thought she heard a thin, light sound. So she put her fingers to her lips and blew out her breath, and heard the whoosh — but also a high whistle — and others around her heard it as well, and so they were no longer deaf, and wondered what that would bring to them. It took a long time to hear the wind and the land around them, but it did happen in time, and the more they listened to the sounds they already knew, the more new sounds became apparent. Once, a woman screamed in pain as she was gnawed by some beast. They heard that, and made it into a word to warn and frighten.

"Another moaned in sickness, and that became another word, and with these new words came new fears and new ideas. It took thousands of years for these peoples to realize they lived on plains of rustling grass, and to know what grass was, and what ate the grass, and what ate the animals and insects that ate the grass, and the more they listened to these animals, and to the birds, the more words they acquired, and went to other groups of people, other tribes, and traded them words. The birds had song, and something like words, and the animals had their sounds, but only these people could grow and trade their languages."

"I have heard other versions of this before," Reynard said.

"As is proper, for all histories are personal. The first words became mothers to new tongues, and stories grew. This is when Queen Hel realized these peoples might be important, for they could teach *her* words, and she might move out of her own silence. And so she was grateful, and elevated them, and set them a long task: to carry languages around the world, but most especially, to build boats and cross the sea, and visit the Tir Na Nog, and provide instruction to the strange beings that had arrived on her creation, and that she herself feared and knew not. For they were shapeless beings, angry in their boredom, and had no tasks, and knew nothing of what they might be or become. And so their power would be a danger to her, she thought, unless she found them a place and things to do ... And she felt the first Travelers might help in that way.

"And so it was. Carrying their trade and their words on boats, and on wagons, and on horseback, and on foot, the first Travelers crossed the krater lands where these beings had arrived, and were still arriving, and in fear, met them ... trembled at the nightmares they seemed to be ... and spake to them.

"And the Crafters — for that was what they would be called — heard the human words, and saw how those who spoke moved and conveyed, their voices carrying meaning as well as story ...

"And it was here that they conceived of a string of stories that would move and compel, and help shape form as well as motion. Humans came to call this 'destiny,' but also 'history.'

"Queen Hel watched the Crafters as they took apart some of these visitors and stared deep into their flesh, and there found other languages that defined lives and shapes, and which history would then change. And they saw the potential in that flesh, in those bodies.

"For in the beginning was the word both of sound and flesh. And Hel was pleased, for she saw creation was underway at last, and change upon change would be our greatest story and worthy of many songs."

Calafi had listened to this with restless fidgets, but now she crawled over to Reynard and grasped his arm, the arm holding the cup, and sloshed it into the dirt. Then she ran her fingers along that arm, in bunches of two, then three, then one, then four.

"Ogmios speaks through those who taught you when you were a child," Yuchil said. "Calafi has felt the same fingers and many of the same messages."

The young girl looked upon him with wide and somber eyes. "Valdis felt them when she was mine age, I think," she said. "And that is why she is here, even though she is an Eater, and not a high one, either. In this she knows more than Calybo or Guldreth or any of those just beneath the sky."

Then she got up and ran away. Yuchil watched her sadly.

"I would wish both of ye child time," she said. "But I fear neither will ever know such."

Nikolias followed the girl to a mossy gray rock-thrust wall along one side of the rough road and spoke to her in low tones. She in turn rolled her eyes up into her head and began to tremble, and Nikolias held her shoulders to steady her. After she collapsed in his arms and appeared to sleep, he brought her back to the wagon and put her in the charge of Sany and Bela. "For a time, she must be apart from Yuchil and Sophia," he said, but did not explain.

Nikolias came to Widsith and nodded at him, then at Reynard. "A message sings in this krater air that our girl hears and interprets. We are at some disadvantage here, but not yet defeated. Before we cross this boundary, we must stay and adjust . . . as we did before."

Reynard could sense no difference in the air they were breathing and wondered why they had to linger so long—hours extending into two days.

After two nights, as he tried to sleep, he looked deep into his memories and thought he detected a kind of change in coloration, as if the tinting varnish of an old painting were being removed. Was

that the effect they desired, taking these airs? But when morning
came, all seemed much the same — as uncertain, strange, and of ill
prospect as before.

The young warriors entered the wagon with grim smiles and
brought forth what they needed: a clutch of fine swords and three
long yew bows very like those Reynard had seen in England, but also
a composite horn bow Widsith said was found more often on the
great plains of Asia. To Reynard's wonder and a smile from Kern,
they handed the giant a sword as long as he was tall.

These new weapons were all blessed by Yuchil and Nikolias, then
by Kaiholo — and Calafi ran through their ranks, making a sort of
inspection and drawing smiles, to which she responded with a serious glower. Reynard thought of Yuchil's judgment. Perhaps she was
wrong.

Kaiholo blew out his breath and settled into a far island prayer.

The First Krater

ANDALO AND SANY rode ahead and around an old wall of bone-colored blocks. When they returned, their eyes were wide and voices subdued. "We have a few miles before we must abandon the wagon," Andalo said. "And we need guidance."

"Why is that?" Nikolias asked.

"There is indeed a krater ahead," Andalo said, and Sany nodded.

"Ah," Nikolias said. "The Crafter the city served."

"But they kept it at a distance!" Sany said. "Do we proceed? Do we go to the edge and look in?"

"Is it like the jars of dead Crafters . . . bringing on madness?" Andalo asked.

Yuchil, Bela, Kaiholo, and Kern approached them, and Yuchil asked, "What did you hear, what did you see?"

"There was a cloud over the land, casting a long shadow . . . but we heard nothing. A few hundred yards from the krater, beyond the last of the road, there is a cleft in the earth and jumbles of gold-flecked granite."

"A quarry of souls, likely," Yuchil said.

"Now depleted and no longer mined," Kaiholo concluded.

"The houses of those who served the miners, those are empty and in ruins," Andalo said.

"And still no bodies," Sany said, looking askance. "But all along the way ... footprints."

Yuchil said. "Where there are no servants, likely there is no living Crafter."

"But even dead Crafters bring on madness!" Andalo said.

To which Sany ventured, "Mayhaps the Crafter is merely hiding! It could jump out at us ..."

"Crafters are not bogey spirits," Kaiholo said. "They likely had a hand in your history and lineage, and even your reason for being. Respect them."

"Then what do we do?"

"Observe that cloud," Nikolias said. "I have heard of such. The breath of Crafters makes its own weather, which can last for many seasons."

Yuchil withdrew to the wagon and joined Calafi.

Reynard looked to the path ahead. A tall candle burned in the middle of the rocky way. Widsith saw it as well, but none of the others.

Deep Granite

THEY PAUSED again to consider how to divide their group. Soon the wagon would have to go back, since it could not go on — go back to whatever fate. Bela brought scraps of wood, and Sophia and Yuchil lit a small fire and again made tea.

Valdis stood beside her black horse, away from the glow of the fire, silent as the land. Reynard could not see her face, she had found such deep shadow to cloak herself.

Nikolias gathered them around this last fire, before they doused it and scattered the ashes. "Do not look beyond the path we follow," he advised. "The servants of Crafters, when dead, persist. Their spirits cannot leave this island until all the Crafters are gone, and some say they are hungry for their freedom and might displace our own souls to get it — hiding in cover to fool Hel. But we have never experienced this. Even as Travelers, we know only what we have been told, meeting with those who serve — with never an explanation that satisfied."

Yuchil sniffed at this, as if it were possible she did not agree. But then, no doubt she would be riding the wagon back to wherever it must go, along with Sophia and the remaining children, all but Calafi seen so seldom. She afforded Reynard a sad glance, as if challenging his conscience on the importance so many seemed to bestow upon him.

"I would gladly give all to be back where trods watch out for us and none serve Crafters," Bela said.

Then, at Nikolias's instruction, Andalo and Sany and Sophia urged the horses to pull the wagon up a slight incline. From this last viable pathway, they could see the edge of the crusted, slicing lava that appeared to surround the krater.

Widsith said, "I see the cold rock that once spread hot from mountains of fire, but no mountains from which it would pour. Agni Most Foul is many hundreds of miles from here."

Nikolias said, "Long ago the sky rained fire, and the chafing waste was the center of a vast upheaval, neither hot nor cold. Each of the seven islands felt such throes."

Another desolate and scattered village confirmed what Sany and Bela had found — emptiness and more silence. Reynard and the Pilgrim briefly explored a shallow cleft in which gold-flecked stone had once been quarried and split into sheets — all broken now. Whatever souls had been described by the patterns in these sheets were now lost.

Widsith picked up a piece the size of his hand, and held it up for Reynard's inspection.

"I see an eye," Reynard said.

"Half an eye," Widsith said. "And no life in it."

They returned to the group and the wagon. Calafi resumed her place beside Reynard. Valdis also kept close, and her form seemed more defined, as if it was important for them all to know where she was and what she was doing. As if she was becoming more aware of a part she would soon play. She faced the direction the wagon was facing, perhaps studying their prospects.

Reynard looked at her for a time, as if he would attract her own gaze — not sure why he wanted to or should.

Calafi twirled her greasy hair in dirty fingers, and then grinned at him, looking remarkably like a young witch.

On the horizon rose a cold gray cloud, dropping silent flurries of snow on the land beneath.

"The krater," Yuchil said.

"This is the nearest of twelve that ring the chafing waste," Valdis said. "It is empty."

"We will make sure," Nikolias said. "Who will accompany me? Sany, Andalo — you stay here."

Widsith, Reynard, Kern, and Kaiholo gathered beside him. Sophia stepped down from the wagon and handed Calafi her leather apron. "I'll go with thee. For once, I would like to know what we have been doing here."

Yuchil reluctantly gave permission and handed her a short sword. Then she took the tethers of the horses and tied them, Eater and human mounts, to the back of the wagon. The wagon team stamped their hooves.

Widsith and Nikolias walked in silence between the broken stone walls and decaying huts. Reynard kept close to Kern and Kaiholo. Sophia followed them. The edge of the krater was about a mile and a half away, and the air became so cold its slow churn seemed to burn their faces.

Kaiholo and Kern simultaneously pointed to broken slabs of the same gold-flecked stone they had found fragments of in the first quarry.

"More faces and eyes for more worlds," Kern said. "Now forgotten. The master of this quarry shall never return."

Sophia was the first to spot, beyond the quarry, before they could peer into the krater's depression, a disk very like the disks they had seen in Guldreth's dwelling — the ones they had heard being destroyed. It lay wedged in the crust like a coin fallen from a purse.

Kaiholo and Kern walked around it, followed by Sophia.

"Is this one of their dreams?" she asked, holding out her sword as if the disk might be dangerous.

"Very like," Kaiholo said.

"You have seen many, have you not?" Sophia asked him. "You were the high one's consort."

"She had a number of consorts," Kern said. "None of us knew all."

Kaiholo stepped closer, knelt, and peered into its depths. Kern stooped over and bent awkwardly to peer from the other side. "This way, it is dark and blank," he said.

"Faded or never filled," Kaiholo said. "Is all here now dead and empty?"

Nobody spoke. The answer was sadly obvious.

They walked the last few dozen yards to the rim. The stony krater was about a thousand yards wide, and curved down, at its center, about a hundred feet. It seemed at first to have a smooth surface, but then Widsith pointed out shallow grooves or trackways drawn from its center and spreading in all directions, intersecting, fading and ending at the rim. At the outer extent of each track was a wide gray spot about the width of a disk. These spots, as if venting, pushed up ghostly pillars of cloud, flaking down snow — snow that did not stick, and never seemed to be there at all.

Nikolias said, shaking his head, "Our fellows told us that they tended to Crafter needs from afar — and never looked into their homes on Earth, as we do now."

"What sort of beast would take comfort here, under storm or sun, no shade, no protection?" Sophia asked.

Reynard followed the ghostly pillars rising up and up, until they spread out and seemed to form knots. Strange knots, tied in ways that drew his eyes in impossible directions. He covered his face with his hands, then slowly parted his fingers, like a child, and looked again, but saw only a final canopy of cloud and drifting shavings of something that might have been ash, or might still be snow ... he could not tell.

"No beast at all," Nikolias said. "But one that could make its own worlds and forge its own protections ... of which we see only marks."

"Where did it go?" Sophia asked.

Nikolias said, "It could not leave here and live."

"How did they move a dead Crafter?" Reynard asked.

Kern said, "I have heard of cloaking and many wagons, out to the plain of jars, a long journey for such a burden."

"Did your people have a hand in that?" Kaiholo asked.

Kern shook his head; he did not know all.

"How long hath it been dead?" Sophia asked, a better question, Reynard thought, though it guaranteed bad dreams later. All but Reynard and Widsith drew designs on their arms and across their chests, which Reynard had come to recognize as a three-barred cross — a symbol of Hel.

Kaiholo looked through the columns of vapor and across the krater. "Some are watching," he said.

Nikolias looked and shook his head. "Thine eyes are better than mine."

"Maybe four or five," Kaiholo said. "Now they are hiding, or gone."

The Dividing

A s yuchil and Calafi fed the horses, Nikolias and Andalo walked around the wagon, speaking in low tones. Nikolias approached Reynard and Widsith a few minutes later. "It is time for the wagon to leave. Soon dawn will light the way."

"Where will we go?" Sophia asked, with a sharp look at Reynard, to which he did not know how to respond. "There is no way back!" Yuchil came down from the wagon and joined Nikolias.

"For now, we divide," Nikolias said.

Reynard looked at his feet and his worn shoes. He could not think of a reason why he had not run off and left them, rather than explore the city. They could all return if he simply ceased to exist. His insides felt as knotted as the cloud that rose from the krater.

But now, he knew, there would be no fleeing. He could feel the tightening of his life, the reduction of his choices — the focus of his companions, those he had likened to his family in Southwold. When his uncle had called for him to board the hoy, he had not escaped. He could not flee now. All he could hope for was that soon he would know why he could never keep a family for long.

"Calafi and I will go on. The rest of our family will stay. The wagon will return to the fields around the first city," Nikolias said. "There should be water enough and wood to last until we rejoin. Yuchil has stores for a few days." With a look of sorrow and concern, Yuchil ran her fingers along his arm. He smiled assurance and returned the gesture. Calafi looked up at them, silent and serious. "Andalo will protect them with his drake — when it arrives. And we will leave our horses. This land will be rough on horses."

Yuchil and Nikolias kissed and made their farewells as everybody else went about their preparations. Calafi stood away from all, but watching, small, her shoulders low, eyes big, like a frightened rabbit.

Yuchil swung the wagon around. Sophia helped the team to maneuver and roll on. Bela and Sany took the reins of the riderless horses and urged them along with clicks of their tongues and light songs. The Eater horses screeched their night cries as they passed out of sight of Valdis.

With fewer supplies, and no access to Yuchil's magical stores, it was obvious their time was limited — that they must find, inside a day or two, those who might still exist to receive Reynard. They did not see the figures that Kaiholo had spotted earlier, nor anyone else — this land felt and sounded empty, and as they walked on, was plagued by drifts of salty dust that stung their eyes and made them sneeze.

"Salt is creation," Kaiholo said, folding a cloth over his mouth. His next words were muffled and accompanied by a sardonic squint. "All the seas are salt. We have salt in our blood. Why doth it have to creep into all our holes and sting?"

Widsith and the giant also covered their faces with a cloth. The Pilgrim dug into his pocket and extended a kerchief to Reynard. All regarded the boy with barely concealed resentment. Their loyalties were being put to the test, and he did not know any more than they!

Calafi danced around them, chanting her nonsense, looking more and more like a witch, and while small, not all that young. But she might have been distracting from their fear or anger.

The reduced group followed Nikolias down the rugged trail. "We will avoid the krater," he said.

"Dig deep, fox-boy," Widsith warned in a low tone, leaning close. "They need to be assured."

"I have nothing to give them!" Reynard cried. "Why did you find me, why did you save me?"

"I saved you to save myself," Widsith said, then fell back that the boy might simmer his anger alone.

But Kaiholo, looking ashamed, took his place and walked beside him for a few minutes. "I do not question thee," the Sea Traveler said. "I question this place, and all it asketh of us, and all it bringeth."

"Why did they not defend their city?" Reynard asked. "It was beautiful here!"

"Signs of the island's change might have overwhelmed." Kaiholo shook his head forlornly. "What was left to them? A dead Crafter? What work was left to them, and what were they willing to die to defend? Perhaps they were waiting for us. Or you."

"Myself, who knoweth not my use, my quality or strength? I fear I have none!"

"And yet, thou hast been judged by those who should know — Guldreth, for one."

Reynard gritted his teeth. There was nothing he could say — the Sea Traveler was trying to smooth the waves between them, but that magic was not natural for him.

"Others judged you. Maeve and Maggie — and Dana. Anutha even saved thee a drake. She said that thou hadst a fate, a place in the great map of this island . . . In its last days."

"Where did you hear this?" Reynard asked.

"From Yuchil, who tended her."

Calafi danced closer. "I have a fate as well," she said.

"Do you know what it is?" Reynard asked, his voice cracking.

Calafi turned to him with a sad glower. "No. But I know why thou art called fox-boy."

"Why?" Reynard asked.

"Perhaps thou wast once a fox! Thou barkest like one."

Then she laughed and ran off.

Something whirred in the air. Kaiholo and Kern hunched their shoulders and looked up. Calafi, close to Nikolias, cried out and fell to her hands and knees.

Nikolias crouched, and they all saw in the dawn light shadows flitting high west to east across the rugged land.

"They are here!" Kern shouted, his voice like a great horn.

Kaiholo said, "I do not feel them!"

"Nor I," Widsith said.

Neither did Reynard.

The eastern brightness above the waste, many miles off, was broken by dozens of wide, winged shapes, swooping and diving: more drakes than Reynard had ever seen, even during the first battle of Zodiako.

"They are not ours! They are death," Calafi wailed. "They bring *death!* My head hurts!" She wrapped her arms around her chest, and Nikolias clasped her and folded her in his cloak.

Valdis studied the sky in all directions. "They are not ours," she agreed. "They seek vengeance against those who killed their masters."

"That must mean the armies of the Sister Queens are near," Nikolias said. "Just beyond the waste, or nearer still."

"And being chivvied and reduced day by day," Kern said.

The Second Krater City

WITHOUT HORSES or the wagon, they crossed over the uneven and dusty boundary of the chafing waste. Kern and Kaiholo soon lost sight of the wheeling drakes, but knew how to maintain a course, and so they led the way, followed by Widsith and the rest, and trailed, as usual, by Valdis, who did not seem at all comfortable in the daylight glare.

"We cannot tarry," Nikolias said. "Nothing lives here long." He explained there was no water on the waste, neither wells nor rivulets, despite occasional bursts of rain. The strange and powdery soil sucked up all moisture and would leave them with only what they caught in their caps or sucked from their capes and clothes. "We must cross within a day," he concluded.

"There are prints everywhere," Kern said.

"The Queens' armies hoped to cross the waste with slaves?" Kaiholo asked.

"The Sister Queens never conversed with Travelers, except to kill them. They have never been here before, and know not the land," Nikolias said.

"And what do we know?"

"Almost as little."

Now they came upon many killed in the panic when the troops were attacked by drakes the day before. Bodies both of captors and captives appeared, first scattered, then in groups: elders, then women, amid signs of desperate struggle. Those soldiers, men of youth and strength, killed by the drakes, were obvious. But many more had died as well.

Widsith and Kern walked from corpse to corpse, joined by Kaiholo and then Valdis, who paused on the edge of a hecatomb of hundreds of dead, some still clutching the swords they had apparently wrested from their captors. Among them were soldiers in unfamiliar livery and armor, four or five of the city's occupants to each soldier — all dead.

"The army tried to kill their captives as they fled," Widsith said. "The servants stood their ground."

"They had no choice," Nikolias said.

Reynard felt a dreadful sadness. He thought again of England under Spanish threat, town streets filled with murder and fire.

From here on, they spoke very little, but within a few hours, as the dusk was falling again — the island's time being always uneven and unpredictable — Kern observed that they were only crossing part of the waste, a chord across the circle, as it were, and he predicted that meant they would soon come upon another krater — and likely another krater city.

Clearly discouraged by their surroundings and prospects, Widsith asked, "How do we know that city is not also empty, or that it hath anything from which we can learn?"

"The waste hath ever been a changing feature," Nikolias said. "Perhaps more so now. Its masters dead or injured, it trieth to delude any who cross."

Look as hard as they could, they saw nothing rising above the indistinct horizon.

The group, enveloped in starlit night, relied on Kaiholo's sense of direction and ignored the vague shapes of the many bodies, except for Widsith, who was searching for Spaniards. Reynard lost sight of Valdis but stumbled on regardless, following the Sea Traveler, and for some reason trusting him.

Within an hour, a new, sallow green light as faint as marsh glow appeared on the horizon, and as morning arrived, through a low silvery fog, another city came into view — a ring of towers, very different from the caged seed structure. The green glow came from within the ring.

Kern said, "Decay. Vast decay, and not of human bodies."

"An Eater hath died," Valdis said, taking shape beside them.

The glow grew brighter as they closed the distance, until they had crossed the chord and were once again in the vicinity of a great krater and the city that, at least in the past, had served its occupant.

"Every city had pride in its Crafter," Nikolias said, "and built itself unique."

The city now before them consisted of a circle of seven great erections, like cathedral towers, but where the towers in England rose straight, these faced inward and leaned toward an empty center, arching over the krater as if about to fall.

Between two of the towers, the group stood on the rim of a sere field covered with burned stubble. Kern stooped to feel the dry grass. The earth beneath the stubble felt warm. The air felt warm, with little sun to warm it. "Nothing hath been grown here in years," the giant said. He rose and walked over to a lone and crumpled man's body. "And yet there was reason to make war."

Cautiously, they advanced. On the rim of the krater — not very different from the first they had seen, and source of a twisted pillar of cloud — lay many more dead, Travelers of the krater city and soldiers from the armies of the Sister Queens. The latter had died both in pitched battle and under the claws and jaws of drakes — and four of the vengeful drakes remained as well, two stuck by bolts from crossbows, and two more dead but without apparent wounds.

Kaiholo knelt to study the closest, holding his nose against the smell. It was missing several of its limbs. Its carapace and head were wrinkled and yellow, and the edges of its wings were badly worn. Valdis joined him. "Their vengeance done, their season is over," she said, and lifted the wing's chipped edge.

"Not good for a cloak," Kaiholo said. The stench of death both human and insect was thick in the air.

"A day, maybe two, since the battle," Widsith said.

Valdis rose and turned to the south. A hundred yards off, five figures emerged from the gate of the nearest tower. The rippling heat of the land beneath the sere grass distorted and camouflaged them, but Reynard saw they were all dressed in dirty brown, carrying swords, bows, and pouches slung over their shoulders.

Widsith cried out in surprise as they came near enough to see faces. "You were the ones on the waste!"

"And we are not alone," said Maggie. Despite her years, and her limp, she seemed as strong as her yew bow, and wore the outfits they all wore — the leather of blunters. Nearly all the blunters from their first meeting on the beach of Zodiako were here. "My daughter is in that leaning tower." She pointed over her shoulder at the edifice from which they had emerged. "Dana hath questions that need to be answered. She will find us soon."

The youngest, Nem, short for Nehemiah, gaunt and careworn, stood beside Gareth, with his bushy red hair and outsized chest and shoulders. On the other side of Maggie, shifting on weary legs, was tall, flat-nosed Sondheim, his flaxen hair now tangled and greasy, and MacClain, hazel eyes still darting and sharp, hair still dark brown, but also dirty with travel and worse . . . and desperately unkempt.

Calafi kept close to Reynard, suspicious of these newcomers, until he introduced them and told her of their time blunting drakes. Then she smiled and stood up on her toes like a fine lady, holding out her hands and dancing around Maggie.

"We have been following Troy," Maggie said, also slowly turning, arms out, looking down on the girl. Gareth opened his slung pouch with a wry grin, revealing to Calafi and then the rest dozens of yellow tallow candles. "The magician is dead, but lives on in bonewives. They have guided us from the western shore to these cities. Have you seen them?"

"We have seen evidence he is not yet done with us," Widsith said, and gave Maggie a great hug, which she winced to receive, but then smiled and patted his arm.

"I have not the benefit of Calybo's ministrations," she said. "Travel is hard for me. There have been no Eaters in Zodiako since you left, and none just beneath the sky. Maeve is gone . . . That you have heard? She passed before the final assault."

Widsith's eyes grew misty, and he nodded.

Another figure came out of the gate and approached them at a run, and Dana stood with them, holding Reynard's hands in hers, and then Widsith's. Kern stood aside, as did Valdis, but Calafi hugged them all.

"You know Nikolias," the Pilgrim said. "He hath served Zodiako as guide and go-between many decades."

"I am better acquainted with Yuchil," Maggie said. "But it is a pleasure to meet the man who serveth her!"

Nikolias could not look away from the krater, or the thin mist that rose from its center and twined upward like a vine made of clouds.

"What happened here? Have the armies of the Sister Queens killed them all?"

"No," Maggie said. "There is worse news than that, we fear."

"Let us build a fire," Gareth said, "and cook the last of our food, even in this heat. Whatever our appetite, we have need of our strength, for we have cold tales to tell."

The End of the Tir Na Nog

GARETH SET a fire just big enough to heat their soup of dried fish and seaweed. He then took a candle out of his bag and carried the flame to its wick with a taper. Calafi squatted and stared steadily at the flame. It wavered as if breathed upon.

"Troy's bone-wives have fared wide," Maggie said, "and acted, like us, as scouts."

"How many could he raise?" Reynard asked.

"As a dead man, many more than when he was alive," Maggie said. "He had caches of bones and sticks across the island, around the chafing waste and near the krater cities. He sometimes sent his figures out to spy . . . and now those stores are all in motion."

Nikolias crossed himself. Reynard had seen enough Traveler magic to wonder at the old man's gesture, but decided that Troy's wonders might have origins earlier even than Travelers'.

"Still, I take comfort in his aid and presence," Widsith said.

"Oh, of a certes . . . he is *not present*," Maggie said. "He only worketh his way like a man winding his clocks."

"At any rate, we keep our promise to him," Gareth said. The candles made a small rumble in his bag.

Maggie turned to where Valdis had settled, under a dark cloak, caring nothing for the heat. "I have heard Eaters could not share time with Troy," she said. "Why not?"

"The magician made his vows with others," Valdis said. "And Eaters have another role to play."

"When will we see our drakes?" Calafi asked Dana sharply.

"Later," Dana said. "The company of drakes intent on vengeance doth disturb and unsettle those still partnered."

"How much later?" Calafi persisted. "I am a small thing, and need protection."

"And who gave you that benison?" Sondheim asked.

"Anutha chose around the wagon and gave them to both Travelers and to us, and also to Kern," Widsith said. "She seemed to know what she was doing."

"But at least one Eater hath the benison," Sondheim said darkly, "yet did not share time with her!"

Widsith intervened. "Ropes of destiny we cannot see rig this ship," he said.

The sun rose along the edge of a tower and hung there, halfway up, as if it enjoyed this vantage and would never leave, and they sweated, all but Valdis, with the heat from the sun and from the ground below.

Maggie unfolded and lay on her side. Her face showed relief; she seemed to find the heat rising through the soil soothing for her aches, like the warm waters in Bath, perhaps — which Reynard had heard of but never experienced.

She continued. "The hard news is that the Crafters are not being killed by the Sister Queens' armies. Rather, for many years now, they have been dying of their own kind of age. One by one, their time is ending, and all who serve them have been set free to find their own protection. And that makes the Sister Queens angry, for they hate the Crafters and their servants, but had hoped to kill monsters in their lair — and mostly they find only dead monsters, and weak and dismayed human beings."

"Have the Sister Queens sent their wise ones to look upon the dead Crafters?" Nikolias wondered.

Nobody knew.

"All that can be said this day," Dana said, "is that our time and purpose on this island must be coming to a close. And that seemeth to include the time of the Sister Queens."

All looked to Valdis. "And what about thy people?" Maggie asked, rolling over and rising on her elbow.

"Eaters have no place to go," she said. "Nothing lies beyond the islands. I seek mine end, whatever it may mean."

A Dead Crafter, and How to See It

As THE DAY seemed to wind down so slowly, they sought shade in the shadow of a tower, and decided to avoid travel in the ground's rising heat. Nikolias built Calafi a bed out of broken brush and dried leaves, above the warmth of the ground, and arranged his long coat as shade, and she lay on it, seeming to sleep at midday.

An end was coming, Reynard thought — he hoped.

In Aldeburgh and the small towns around Southwold, he had sought books and learning, had been spurned by the local, so-called teachers and wise men, but now could understand their disdain. Possibly it was not so much disdain as alarm, fear, as if a demon lad had knocked on their doors . . .

But he remembered the truth of all those encounters, even after he had met the man with the white shadow. And within him, there had been no fear, no wish to inspire fear. Were he dangerous, he had not yet been fused, nor the fuse lit.

Was the fuse burning now?

Was he living out the length of a candle?

The sun slowly descended beyond the clouds in the southwest, and the sky settled down as clear as he had ever seen it either in England, on the sea, or in Zodiako, free of both dust and cloud, blazing with stars and with something else he had heard of but rarely seen: great vague sheets of crackling light. Green and brown and pink ribbons rippled over the mountains and perhaps the entire north, illuminating the land around them bright as twilight, but coldly. Away and above this world, coldly, coldly.

Still, the heat in the ground remained, enough to raise a sweat, but Widsith and Nikolias and Kern approached and asked if Reynard still wished to see the krater. Suddenly, that seemed important to them all.

"I do," he answered.

Nikolias gathered them and asked Kern to fetch the blunters who seemed brave or foolhardy enough to do this.

A few minutes later, warily watching the sheets of light rippling like the curtains in God's window, Gareth and Dana and Maggie joined them on a path that led from the tower where they had done some exploration, down to the krater, which none had yet seen and Maggie said, shaking her head, that she did not wish to see.

"But I will not let my charges and companions do something and refuse it myself."

"There is someone else out there," Kaiholo said, staring out over the rise that defined the nearest rim of the krater. Reynard and the others saw nothing even in the brightness of the aurorae and dusting of stars.

"In the krater?" Maggie asked him, and looked to Gareth and Sondheim.

"Something just over the edge. A man, I think — an old man. He popped up and looked at us, then dropped and vanished. Perhaps he is one of Troy's."

"I'll go look," Widsith said, rising and walking toward the rim. Reynard noticed the Pilgrim was hunching his shoulders. He got up to follow, but Valdis took hold of his hand, her grip cold and peppery — as if sparking. He had not realized she was within reach of him.

"Let the Pilgrim explore," she said. "You will have other tasks."

"Do you fear the Crafters?" Reynard asked, angry at being restrained.

"I do not fear Crafters," she said, "but I do fear that no Crafters remain."

Kaiholo looked at them both, then went after Widsith.

Widsith quickly regretted his boldness, and regretted it none the less when Kaiholo moved up beside him. They walked in step through the ruined buildings and the strange gardens that surrounded the krater. The half-burned shrubs and patches of flowers rustled under the high, cold twilight of the sky.

"What knowest thou of these gardens?" Kaiholo asked.

"We saw garden ruins around the first city," Widsith said.

"And how do you know every city and every krater hath a garden?" Kaiholo asked.

"Guldreth so told me," Widsith said.

"Very well," Kaiholo said.

"She told you as well?"

The tattooed man afforded Widsith a single nod.

"In her intimacy?"

"Later," Kaiholo said. "She favored me even more than Kern."

"She favored Kern?"

"So Kern telleth the tale," Kaiholo said.

"Well, I was gone a long time," Widsith said, as if that explained anything.

"Not to her reckoning," Kaiholo said.

The rising twists of cloud caught and bent the starlight beyond, and aurorae played with them both in strange and even beautiful ways. Beneath it all, and around the two men walking, the remains of the gardens tried to struggle back to their glory, shoving forth flowers without color, without real life, but perhaps hoping to return to a scented and brilliant past, reflecting, Kaiholo said, the creation in the krater.

"What was it like to live in these cities?" Widsith asked. "Did the wind blow the waste's dust and salt all the time? How could they breathe?"

"Perhaps the gardens protected them," Kaiholo said.

"Art thou sure thou sawest a man?"

"Yes," Kaiholo said.

"What sort of man would survive the Sister Queens' armies? Could Troy still be alive?"

"If Maggie says not, I doubt it," Kaiholo said. "Perhaps this time, thou'lt report directly to a Crafter, Pilgrim."

Reynard stuck to the curving path between walls of fading shrubs, riddling what seemed to be a maze — but one that was ever-changing. The sky over the path was shaded by arching brambles covered with small, wilting gray flowers. He looked up through the brambles at the stars and aurorae, screwing up his face as if about to scream — when a shadow took shape beside him and a hand again touched his arm.

"You should protect yourself," Valdis said.

"I need to see what is in the krater. How can I be important if I am blind and ignorant?"

"Often enough here, ignorance is life," Valdis said.

The brambles rose taller still, the maze leading off right and left along more shaded paths, sprouting more flowers — which smelled sickly sweet.

"Why are these plants moving and changing?" Reynard asked.

"Because they still have something to protect."

"The giant and I speak of your time with the boy," Kaiholo said. "We have many things to puzzle. How came it you found him in the wide waters, in time to save him?"

"Luck and fate," Widsith said.

"And such an important lad," Kaiholo said. "You delivered someone to Maeve and Maggie that allowed Zodiako to die proud and certain of a place in this island's history. A great twist in any story, no?"

Widsith did not like this pitch. "His importance hath never been clear to me."

"Thou liest," Kaiholo said. "But look now to the krater. Will we find the man we seek, a dead monster — or a live monster?"

They slowly took those few steps and stood on the rim. Under the glowing curtains they could clearly make out the lines and serpentine patterns they had seen in the previous krater.

"Slugs leave trails across rocks," Kaiholo murmured. "What do gods leave?"

Widsith pointed to a dark and rumpled mound in the center of the krater, the cloud ascending from this like steam from a bowl.

At the same moment, far above the cap of the clouds, a great blue and red banner grew with a crackling sizzle that made Widsith's teeth hurt.

"The boy should be here, rather than us," Kaiholo said.

"Quiet," Widsith said. "Listen."

A voice whose words they could not understand came from behind the shape — a gruff and aged voice, hoarse and weak.

"Not Troy, and certainly not a bone-wife," Widsith murmured.

"Where be you from?" the voice called out.

"The southwest and Zodiako," Widsith called back. "Who art thou?"

"Once a fellow of some import," the voice replied. "Shall I show myself, or are you a danger and heavily armed?"

"Two swords," Widsith said. "Both sheathed."

A figure appeared from behind the rumpled mass, perhaps a hundred yards away, and walked unsteadily toward them. "Have you any food? Drink? Strong drink?"

Widsith held aloft his pouch, which contained some small pieces of stale bread. Kaiholo raised his water sack.

"That is all?" the man asked as he drew near.

"That is all," Widsith said.

"I know you!" the man said to the Pilgrim. "I have worked on your journeys. You are Manuel, no? Yet not so old!"

"Restored, but once Manuel," Widsith said. "Now I am called —"

"Widsith! Of course you would revive upon each return — that was the tale the Crafters launched generations ago. You are one who bringeth word of our labors!"

"Whose labors?" Kaiholo asked.

"Mine own, and many who once lived here! And the Crafters, of course. And be this the Sea Traveler Kaiholo, favored by those just beneath the sky? Where is the boy?" The old man halted four paces off. He wore shreds of what might have once been a grand gown, still belted by a golden cord and a great jeweled buckle. Across his shoulders rested two shining silver epaulets connected by more golden cord. His face was thin and bony, his cheeks wrinkled and sunken, and his neck seemed barely able to hold up his great bald head. His fingers, playing about the buckle but also rising to the epaulets, as if indicating his rank, were thin as bone themselves. "Know you the King of Troy? Our island's magician of that name?"

"We knew him," Widsith said.

"One of his sweven was here," the thin, decorated man said. "It warned us the boy would be coming, and would need protection until his next stop."

"Have you control here?" Widsith asked.

"I carried out orders delivered to the quarries, that is all, and perhaps chose thy faces or gave thee other features in times past. Features, not histories. I know my mandate, and my limits."

"What is that in the krater?" Kaiholo asked, pointing at the dark mass.

"Oh, it is dead, alas," the man said. "Died many a month ago, but before it died, covered itself, as the Old Ones do, to shield its visage from those who must carry it to the plain of jars — but also not to offend Hel. It was once a great and noble Crafter. Fear of it has kept the eastern armies away from this krater, but not for long, I think."

"I am looking at it," Kaiholo said, squinting sideways. "Will I go mad?"

"Not whilst it is cloaked," the old man said. "Nor will you ever comprehend its power. Look upon your tales, your histories, and give thanks to this one — and of course to Queen Hel."

"Where are the armies now?" Widsith asked.

"Likely not far," the old man said. "Did you send the drakes to harry them?"

"No," Widsith said. "Our drakes have yet to join us."

"Well, they should come soon. The armies of the Sister Queens, what is left of them, may their stories curl and burn, are trying to camp a few miles away."

From the other side of the krater cut the twang of a crossbow, and a sharp hum all too familiar to Widsith. The old man was shoved forward and blew the breath from his lungs. He dropped to his knees, and then collapsed, a bolt buried deep in his back.

A double handful of men in rusted armor ran from behind the cloaked shape in the krater, bolder by far than any from this land, Widsith thought. They were followed by two mounted on horses also in armor. Together, they warily ascended the curve of the krater toward Kaiholo and Widsith, and one removed his helmet and cowl to show his face.

"I know thee!" the grizzle-bearded man growled at Widsith. Five of the soldiers surrounded them, and the other five moved around the dead krater garden behind them, silent as cats, vanished into the dry foliage, and then returned with Reynard and Valdis. It appeared they thought they had taken only one prisoner, for Valdis was little more than a wisp, sticking close to the boy.

"This one was on the other side, spying," the eldest soldier said in Spanish, delivering Reynard to his master.

"I know thee as well," the bearded man said to Reynard. "But do not remember thy name. Dost thou remember Cardoza, boy? And thou, old sailor! Art thou amazed I still live?"

"I had so hoped," Widsith said. "I served long with thee, and know thy mettle."

"Thy face I would know through the ages! Where are the others?" Cardoza asked. "Where are those who command drakes?"

Two more caballeros rode up, lances raised, and addressed Cardoza in Spanish. Widsith translated. "They say they returned to the town of the old church and looked for others, but found no one. The town is empty."

The High Tent

THE JOURNEY to the camp of the Sister Queens, set up within the woods and pastures bordering the chafing waste, took less than an hour. Reynard saw that no cultivation had been done here for many a year, nor were the woods harvested. Did the krater city's inhabitants need to eat or build?

Daylight was bright and the sky still clear, and the smoke from the camp's fires rose and spread gray and brown, hazing the sky ahead. The Sister Queens still fielded thousands of soldiers, and likely there were servants from the cities near as well—captives, informants, slaves.

As the Spanish and Cardoza prodded their captives along and through the camp, men and a few women emerged from the tents, all carrying swords, many wearing resin-soaked cloth plates, sheets of raw iron, armlets of bronze: a style of armor other than that worn by Cardoza's men.

And beyond their tents and fires rose line after line of great machines, machines designed to fling rocks and fire and to erect fighting towers — to lay siege and destroy.

None appeared to have been used.

Widsith walked beside Reynard and said, "Look at their faces! This land doth not play by their rules or their tools." His eyes seemed to seek Valdis, but could not find her. "Thy shadow plays with other shadows. What is her plan?"

"I wish she would flee and save the others," Reynard said. "The old servant at the krater —" he began, but Widsith held up his hand and looked down as if in prayer.

"The one who laid out my life, thou mean'st? Who worked with the Crafters to spin a long and varied history, to judge our souls, and to make the worlds I would be interested in seeing?"

"The one who died," Reynard said.

Cardoza was riding far ahead, stopping to consult with other soldiers, some dressed in colorful robes, others carrying longswords and bows, along with crossbows of Spanish design. All were weary, hoping to gather their strength as they rested.

But strength to fight what, or whom?

"If he was my story master," Widsith said, "and I have no reason to doubt his word, then my history is soon at an end. One doth not with impunity meet one's own smith, not on this island."

A great gray and white tent rose into the dusk, lit from inside like a paper lantern filled with fireflies. Outside the tent, cots had been made and arranged to care for hundreds of wounded, and another stretch of ground took as many dead tied into their shrouds. Many soldiers and guards formed rings around the tent, a few fires scattered among the lines, and servants in rags, of all ages, sharing out food and water.

"Did the blunters get away with Nikolias and Calafi?" Reynard whispered to Widsith.

"I doubt they moved far," Widsith said. "They have yet to receive their drakes. This battle is far from over."

"These have already felt the wrath of drakes," Kaiholo said. "They do not look ready to face more."

As Widsith and Kaiholo and Reynard passed the dead, they felt the chill breeze of Valdis cross their path, to tell them, and only them, she was still near. Reynard wondered how she would justify spending her time here — if she ever needed to justify anything. Her presence somehow reassured him, however, but he could not say why he felt such, other of course than her being a weapon, which she could certainly be, if Calybo relieved her of other duties.

Kaiholo made several signs to the servants, but got back no response, other than veiled glances. "Those who attended the Crafter have been sent to the east, methinks," he said.

An older man, almost as old as Widsith had once been, came up to meet them beyond the cooling ground. He looked at Reynard and scowled as if seeing a ghost. In heavily accented English, he said, "I once had fewer years than thee!" and pulled up his sleeves to show some of his many scars.

"Was that a cabin boy from the galleon?" Reynard asked Widsith.

"Yes. Not many still here, still alive. I saw fewer than twenty Spanish soldiers."

Another group of soldiers, in the armor of the Sister Queens, and several women in ochre gowns, emerged from the tent and surrounded the captives, examining them with feverish, or perhaps drunken, interest.

The eastern soldier and four of his fellows ushered Kaiholo, Reynard, and Widsith away from the fire and into the large tent through a half-hidden, draped entrance. Inside, many layers of striped gray and white fabric separated the airy rooms, these thin and current-ruffled walls rising into the heights, where lanterns swung slowly from long chains, casting a fitful, shimmering light without shadows.

Reynard could no longer detect the presence of Valdis, and felt the lack acutely.

"This way," the first soldier said. All had the wear and tear of battle on their clothes and armor, especially on the resin-soaked plates, cracked and chipped. One soldier had the stump of a missing arm wrapped in a bloody bandage, and seemed paler and perhaps weaker than the others, but still vigilant.

"We have no drakes," the leader said as he walked beside them, the others on the outside. "But we still have our courage. We would face you with our bare hands when the Queens are finished."

The one-armed man held out his stump. "The courage of the east, not the sorcery of the west!" he said, his voice hoarse.

Up a flight of wicker stairs, not unlike the stairways in the seed-cage city, and through more translucent drapes, they were led into the throne room of the Sister Queens.

The thrones were empty.

The Sister Queens

WHERE ARE THY DRAKES, men of the western shores?" a soft voice asked. They turned to face two standing women, of medium height and comely, identical of feature, with long, flowing straw-colored hair, standing shoulder to shoulder. The figure on the left had extended her right arm forward and held a cane. The figure on the right seemed to keep her shoulder behind that arm, so close were they.

Reynard glanced at Widsith, who nodded with startled fascination.

Beneath their black gowns, the Sister Queens were joined at their hips — actually joined, it seemed, by a ribbon of flesh and perhaps bone. They were flanked by four other women, all in eastern armor, all stronger and taller than the Queens and fiercer of mien, and Reynard wondered if these were Anakim, like Kern.

But what irresistibly drew his eyes were the Queens, who seemed completely at ease in their proximity, their rule — their identity.

"We have faced those drakes often, and suffered — but where are they now?" asked the Queen on the right.

"Have they passed their season and lie on some mountain, rotting?" asked the Queen on the left.

"You killed their masters," Kaiholo said to both, making Reynard flinch with his boldness. In England, he could not imagine addressing royalty so directly, and clearly this pair was of such a power — of such a royal heritage. Kaiholo finished, "Never wise when the season is still upon them. And for those who split and fly near the end of the cycle, it is still their season."

"How many more of these monsters are waiting to protect you?" asked the Queen on the left. Reynard could detect by her expression that her role sat more lightly upon this sister, and the other took things with a heavier heart.

"We have come to find those who need our stories," Widsith said. "We are filled with sorrow to find them killed or enslaved. Where are the Travelers and servants being taken?"

"We are happy to receive thy stories," the Queen on the right said. "We can even convey the best to those whom we have taken, mostly, to live in comfort on the eastern shores, or to be returned to the lands we have rid of war and the monsters who once filled these kraters. But you will never finish your tasks, for those monsters are dead or dying."

"Of old age," Widsith said. "They were mostly dead before you began your conquests!"

The Queen on the left followed her sister's words with "Out of curiosity, we have left two of the monsters alive. Their servants seem willing to help our scholars, if we do not kill them."

"Can you kill them?" Reynard asked.

"We have sought warriors who can look upon their evil and not go mad. But we have not yet killed them."

"The shrouded one in the cathedral city seems safe enough," the left Queen said.

"But to be sure, we have not been allowed to look at that one, ei-

ther," the right Queen said with a prim expression. "For thousands
of years, the Isles of the Blessed have suffered under the tyranny of
the one who invited these monsters, and gifted them with the sole
guidance of human destiny. To end the reign of Hel, we planned our
journeys in the west and destroyed those villages that still send men
across the oceans, that still support and report to the cities that surround the monsters. We have leveled all but two of the cities around
the chafing waste. So Hel's time is now ending."

"Are you certain?" Kaiholo asked. One of the tall women reached
out to admonish him, but the Queens raised their hands and the
guard withdrew, still angry.

"I am not sure I believe any of this nonsense," said the Queen on
the left. "I do not believe Hel ever existed, or any great sky people.
My sister and I lead practical lives, guided by study and irrefutable
nature — not by sorcery."

"But the drakes still kill," Kaiholo said.

"That they do," said the left Queen. "But not for long. This, I have
been told, will be their last season." She raised her cane. "Now is
the time to introduce our guests to th'other players. One not of the
west hath sent a figure ahead, made of sticks and perhaps bones —
a bone-wife, we hear it is called, incapable of being driven insane. It
might be able to kill these monsters. Dost ye know of the King of
Troy and his toys?"

"He did not serve Hel," the right Queen said. "Perhaps his toys
will serve the island."

The one-armed Spanish soldier approached a guard and tugged
her down to whisper in her ear. At this, with no further ceremony,
the Queens were guided from their throne room. They walked with
surprising grace side by side, though the right-hand Queen rested
her arm on a guard's outstretched hand.

Widsith and Kaiholo and Reynard were roughly shoved and hur-
ried out of the tent chambers, one of the giants wielding a sword

without much care, out of the tent itself, and across the ground between the wounded on cots and the dead in their shrouds. The great
tent was now surrounded by a frightened, exhausted mob of eastern soldiers, and scattered through this roil, a handful of Spaniards,
though Reynard could not see Cardoza anywhere.

"Where are we going?" Kaiholo asked as they were nudged on by
pikes and spears.

"Where you will not get us killed," said the one-armed soldier
when they were a hundred yards from the tent. He seemed high in
rank, and his wound did little more than slow him down. He carried
a long sword and his aide carried a Spanish crossbow, and they kept
glancing at the sky.

Reynard looked at Widsith, then at Kaiholo. Where would they
be able to summon their drakes? Reynard did not know how that relationship worked, or what summoned whom — or even how drakes
and their masters communicated! He had hoped to have instruction from Anutha, but now his mind was empty both of hope and
knowledge.

The soldiers in their guard urged them one direction, then merged
with another group that poked and prodded them another, until
they all had cuts and bruises from spear points or sword blades, and
no one seemed to have any plan — except to get the captives away
from the tent and to a place where they could be unable to interact,
perhaps, with any drakes.

Came a flurry of confusion among those surrounding them, a
roar of anger followed by shouts of pain — and several great glinting
streaks of shadow over the mass of men and women, along with the
pound of hooves and screams of horses —

"They are here!" Kaiholo called, and was struck by a shield, which
knocked him flat. The one who struck him, a broad, bald, young
eastern man, knelt down beside him, as if he regretted striking such

a blow, but knew not what to do, and almost gently, he lifted the island Traveler as if he would revive him.

Reynard saw this with wonder just before he was himself struck down by the flat of a sword, and three men and a very tall, angry woman stood over him, watching the sky, watching the moving mass of soldiers, trying to find a way to carry out whatever orders they might have been given, but all was tumult, and many were fleeing, trampling, even cutting their way through their fellows —

Reynard saw why through the weaving bodies of panicking troops. The drakes' broad wings reflected light from the camp fires. Beneath the swooping drakes, several horses were being guided by fighters in black with red ribbons tied to their arms, along with others wearing armor he was not familiar with, and still others on black horses swift and vague as smoke — Eaters!

Widsith pushed between his captors and threw himself over Reynard, just as a spear bounced from the hard ground and two swords plunged and stabbed nearby. Reynard was astonished to find he was not hurt, nor was Widsith, but he could not see Kaiholo.

He did, however, see rising over this mass of frightened, desperately fighting men — Andalo! On a horse, and not far from him, visible only at brief moments, other young guards from the wagon, fighting fiercely, killing many, causing even more rage and fear among the easterners . . .

Yuchil was wrong about their not being true warriors!

And then, a great flame rose to Reynard's right, to the west, and he saw the Sister Queens' tent was ablaze.

Now he felt a strange prickle in his thoughts, a hard sort of request — a kind of question, as if an insect would ask questions or set up a strange conversation!

And Reynard knew for the first time what it was to summon his drake, and set it to work to protect him.

The Last Krater City

ANDALO GRABBED UP Calafi and placed her on the saddle before him, then rode toward the Sister Queens' tent, under the direction of Nikolias. Nikolias had supplied him with his own great sword, with a double-edged blade at the slightly curved tip — a saber ending in a scimitar. The girl kept murmuring what sounded like spells or chants, and her eyes had rolled back in her head, showing only whites. As he rode toward and then into the confusion, he did his best to keep her steady and swing his sword at the same time, cutting away easterners who were already in a panic.

And then he felt what Calafi must be experiencing. His eyes seemed to leap up and away from the horse, and to change their very nature — to change color and range, almost to see behind him, and it mattered not which way he turned his head — for these eyes were not in his head.

But like his own eyes, they were looking for enemies — and to clear a path away from the great flaming tent and head them northeast, toward what he saw from the sky, in a different sort of memory and with a different sort of judgment, was another great city beyond the horizon — perhaps twelve or thirteen miles off.

That city meant nothing to this insect judgment. It was important only that it might matter to the partner, the one who now rode behind its eyes and might make demands, which it would be the duty for the animal to anticipate and carry out.

The insect, even without Widsith's judgment, seemed remarkably intelligent, even prescient, and together . . .

As Andalo's horse stamped and reared through the fleeing crowd, a drake dropped among them, wings barely missing him and the horse's head. Then the drake rose again, clutching a screaming soldier.

Another did the same. And another.

Andalo tried to remember all who had been given vials by Anutha. He had been. And Calafi. He felt the young girl squirm and try to flail — and knew that they were both guiding drakes. This distraction barely allowed him to hold on to the reins, and he wondered, with what little thought he had left to afford wonder, whether they might all be better off dismounted.

But he did not dismount. Somehow his drake enjoyed the thought of riding a horse — a novelty it had never known before: an animal that could not fly, ridden by another animal that could not fly!

Widsith had already seen what happened to men in the clutches of drakes, and turned away from the harried easterners to a distracted Reynard, who seemed barely aware of what was happening around him. The boy kept looking through the frantic soldiers, as if seeing with other eyes — and indeed perhaps he was. Widsith wondered why he was not being similarly distracted, aided — afflicted . . .

And then the Pilgrim saw his own drake hover and rise and swing around the great flames, and felt his own eyes exchanged for another's, faster and higher, dropping, plowing with many limbs, pushing aside, clearing the way . . .

For Calybo!

Who wished them to go to the distant city, now visible through the eyes of their highest drakes — a city surrounded by the untended dead, for the Sister Queens had spent most of their army on trying to destroy the men and women devoted to their final Crafter, the final arbiter and creator of the world's history until now.

Widsith stayed close to Reynard, as did Andalo and Calafi. Reynard could not see Calybo or Valdis, or any of the other Eaters he knew were here — could feel just yards away, shadows smoothed into other shadows, moving from corpse to corpse, but to what purpose, the boy had no idea, no insight from the memories that Valdis had willed to him in their brief exchange on that beach on the western shore.

They crossed a field of recent battle, hundreds of dead. Reynard saw the bodies from high, and smelled them as he stepped over them, feet catching all too often on tangled limbs.

Widsith focused away from his high, wheeling drake, and saw not just the Queens' armor, but Spanish plate and crested helms — worn by old or middle-aged men, the last from the galleon, the last of the Spanish to die, perhaps, on this far side of the isle.

But no sign of Cardoza. Or any sign of the bone-wives of the King of Troy.

Reynard thought of the burning candles on their path to this place, and the bag of such candles carried by Gareth. His mind was filled with darting images, suppositions, possibilities — pieces of story not concluded, mixed with so many stories that had reached an end, and he knew not how or why.

The Chafing Waste

They walked for an hour through the dead and again crossed the border of the chafing waste, mouths dry, noses clogged with the dust raised by battle. That dust seemed everywhere, stinging, blinding — as it must have blinded the soldiers and Spaniards and Traveler servants . . .

The distant city finally appeared through a veil. Unlike the great circle of cathedral towers, the dust revealed low buildings arranged — he could see through the eyes of his drake, high above — in four quarters or neighborhoods, cut through by a cross of broad boulevards. At their intersection was a krater, covered by vaulted walls and bridges, with at its own center a circular theater. The drake could not see through the shimmer that hid the interior of the theater, and neither then could Reynard.

"Does anybody know where we are going?" Calafi asked, suddenly waking from her murmuring trance. Andalo echoed the girl's question, louder, that more could hear —

Which Reynard realized were now many, dozens of Travelers and, he saw, Kern, and Gareth, and Dana in their leather uniforms, who had gone around the battlefield, intent on only one thing, ready to sacrifice all to this last part of their journey, with no clear conclusion, only a destination they would not reach, did not wish to reach, for their duty was to deliver Reynard.

Nothing more.

After that, he had no idea what would happen to any of them. Nobody knew, not Valdis, not even Calybo, and certainly not Widsith, covered in white dust, more and more like the ghost he would have become had he not returned to the western shore and Zodiako.

"Move on," Reynard heard from a passing darkness and chill breeze. "Move on!"

Then Valdis rose up before him like a blue flame from an icy fire, but the voice was not hers. Behind her lifted an even darker mass, the Afrique. None of the Eaters were mounted now — only the Travelers and Calafi, who appeared comfortable enough on the saddle before Andalo. Andalo gripped a great sword with one hand and Calafi's arm with the other, but both looked haunted, seeing a little through their own eyes and much through other eyes, trying to make out what might be their end, their fate, or their triumph.

Widsith stayed close to Reynard, as did Kern with his sword almost too long even for him to swing. They stood in a half-circle on a low hump in the salty waste.

"I have something to tell thee, fox-boy," Widsith said. Reynard pulled back from his high perspective, for there was something in the Pilgrim's tone that commanded attention — even a change in his voice, as if he were going back to being an old man, for the moment ... reviving a memory he was not completely sure he could have had.

"What?" Reynard asked, puzzled and irritated at this distraction.

Kern moved away from them, but not so far he could not protect. This talk seemed personal, and he was not sure he wanted or needed to hear it.

"Dost remember I plucked thee from the ocean, not so many weeks ago?"

"I remember an old man who saved me," Reynard said. "An old man who looked twice and then lifted me onto a galleon!"

"*Sí*," Widsith said. "An old Spanish man being returned to his beloved isle on a ship that did not belong to him, and who had no power but persuasion, and very little of that."

"What of it? I am grateful," Reynard said.

"I had rarely seen such a thing before," Widsith said. "When first I saw what was thumping against the hull of the galleon, there was only a broken boat, empty."

"Then you looked again, and saw me!"

"No," Widsith said. "Not even the second time."

"How could that be? I was there, and saw you!"

"I saw nobody the first time, nobody the second time, but then I felt I must look again, and thou tookest shape on the wreckage, like a form drawn by a master on paper — roughly sketched at first, then filled in, features clear, pain and distress obvious — and I recognized here was something new, something that had not been there before ... but was with us now, and most importantly, a sign, for rarely do Crafters thus reveal themselves."

"What do you mean? I was there all along."

Widsith nodded, as if not disagreeing, and both were for a time distracted again by the high vision of their drakes, and stepped apart, separated by Andalo's horse, until Kern reached out to draw Reynard away from the nervous animal.

Both he and the giant fell back, and Widsith joined up with them again. Kern still seemed to be deliberately not listening to their conversation, as if embarrassed by its intimacy — but he glanced at Reynard, then looked off to the dust clouds around the last city.

"I was there, and have been all my life!" Reynard said in a resentful undertone.

"And what was thy name, in this previous life?"

"Reynard."

"And who named thee?" Widsith asked.

"My grandmother, I have been told."

"The color of thy hair did remind me of a fox I once fed in the Philippines . . . or perhaps it was in the Japans."

"My hair is black!"

"The sea, I suppose, had turned it red, though to ponder that puzzle is madness . . . But at that moment, I called thee Reynard. Before this sighting, fox-boy, thou hadst no part in this world, and that I'll swear on all mine ancestors, and all I love, and on thee, whom I have come to love like a son. Before I looked that third time, the wreck was empty."

"I do not understand!"

"Nor I. But a Crafter madest thee at that very instant, scrawny, sea-logged, and thirsty, and allowed me to see it happen. And that is when I began to understand how hard things would go in Zodiako, and across the Tir Na Nog, and how change was upon us."

"You speak foolishness! How is it I have my own memories?"

"That is the way of all made by the masters of history and story. There is no man or woman without a navel, some say, though not all are born of woman."

"But why *you*, returning and eager to get home to Maeve?"

Widsith shook his head. "I have always served Crafters, and I can only assume they wished to reward me by bringing thee into the tale."

Reynard stepped away, around Andalo's horse, and met Calafi's distracted gaze. Andalo had lowered her to the ground, and she seemed to share a strange pain he was feeling — coming so close to the dwelling of the one who might have made them both.

"Fox-boy," she said. "Dost feel that?"

He nodded.

"I have felt it coming since I first looked on thee!" She then said, with a pirouette, "Nikolias tells me the same story — that he and Yuchil found me in the woods, at the cross-trod. Or rather — saw me arrive! I remember much before then — being lost, being found. But are we simply staring into our belly buttons? More important, where are we going to complete our task?"

Nikolias was escorted by Valdis, and behind them, Calybo. Both the Eaters were barely visible.

"We are all ready," Valdis whispered. "The chain will form. We will give all of our stores of time and power, and then be done, and at peace."

"But only fox-boy and Calafi can go into the krater," Calybo said.

"Guldreth said as much to me," Kern said.

This on top of what Widsith had said was more than Reynard could take in. He remembered Calafi saying something about the stores of time he did not contain, that he had not been on this Earth long enough to help save Anutha — and that Valdis would not expend any of her time, nor Calybo's, nor the time of any Eater to that end . . .

He remembered also what the man with the plumed hat had said when he appeared like a specter, rising above the waters that nearly covered his uncle's hoy.

But he also pushed his thoughts back through his life, touching on the memories he had, of his mother and father, of that same uncle, of the towns he had visited, the journeys across the ocean to the best fishing grounds, his uncle's tales about sailing with Hawkins, and all his uncle had taught him about tasting the waters to know where they were, and about the types of fish they could hope to find in different currents and in different regions at different times of the year — and those times in which it was foolish to go to sea at all.

But also his own curiosity, his own hunger for learning and language, that had driven him to approach people in Aldeburgh who he knew would treat a scrawny fisherboy with contempt.

And among those visitors —

The man with the white shadow, who he thought might have greater secrets than any in the nearby towns ... If he were real. If any of them were real.

Those memories must mean he lived and saw and remembered before his uncle drew him out to Gravelines and sacrificed crew, nephew, and boat to resupply the British ships going up against the Armada of Philip and the Duke of Medina Sidonia.

All those memories were vivid and real even after all he had seen on this island, all the monsters and strange beasts ...

Even now that he saw from the eyes of a high drake, gliding out on four wings over the next city, which in many ways was not much more than a wide, low town, like Aldeburgh, like his home village ... But with the streets arranged in a spiral, cut in four, the spiral ever curling into a covered krater.

He looked from his own eyes now, leaving for the moment the drake to make its own decisions.

Nikolias walked beside Andalo, while Widsith stayed close to Calafi and Reynard, and Kern followed them at a couple of paces, so close he could almost reach out to them. These people, his partners in this story, were taking him to that covered place, and they were more than hinting that they could push him into closeness with a Crafter, perhaps not a god, though capable (Reynard might concede this) of creating out of nothing a creature such as himself — but a creature from the stars, from the places studied (or that would be studied) by the man with the plumed hat, or known somehow through other than human experience to the man who cast a white shadow.

"The Queens have sent their last force," Widsith said, seeing through his drake's eyes. Reynard switched his awareness again and saw it as well — a divided force of perhaps two hundred warriors, mostly men, coming at them from both sides as they approached the walls of the city, hoping to cut them off, perhaps kill rather than capture.

Taking vengeance for those who had already died in so many actions around the island.

But the drakes were already sweeping in from above these warriors, braving bolts from more than a dozen crossbows, falling and grabbing with their spiked, razor-sharp legs and scissor-gripping talons, pulling up and carving one after another, while the Queens' warriors shouted and screamed, and finally stopped trying to reach them or block their way —

And the dregs of the Sister Queens' armies broke and ran.

This part of the war seemed to be over.

The Change

REYNARD LOOKED DOWN on the city, on the circular whorl of its houses and streets, and was reminded of the spin of hair on a baby's head — another memory, specific and real! — but his insect side saw paths of flight over competing drakes searching for mates.

Two great roads divided the city. The drake's eyes saw this quartering in its own way, ignoring the straightness as irrelevant, its attention moving sometimes to the sky, sometimes back to the ground — but keeping the horizon always level, angling its head to keep a stable reference to all its twisting, to the stimulus of air passing right wings and left, fore wings and aft.

His drake angled to grab a hapless gull, which it brought to its jaws and devoured on the remainder of its descent.

In the insect's extraordinary vision, wide and tinted with colors he had never seen before, Reynard observed that the city had nearly emptied, and its last inhabitants, the servants of the last Crafter, gathered around the great dome that covered, he presumed, a krater.

But now dusk crossed the sky like a blindfold and he saw only through his own eyes. Kern and Calybo protected his sides as they advanced along the straight road through the city to the center.

A gate of beams carved from thick black wood had been propped open, as if awaiting visitors. This gate led them into an inner sweep of the spiral, and finally to the way that led straight to the krater.

To the west, the dense low clouds were parting.

Reynard's drake finished its descent and landed on a tiled roof-top to his left, a few dozen yards ahead of Reynard, while four other drakes landed on other roofs, and one in the middle of the street, all spreading wide their stained-glass wings and staring down on the visitors with eyes the color of emeralds, topped with dark ruby, glinting in the revealed light of the setting sun.

Dark fell slowly.

Kaiholo whispered something to Kern. From the shield blow, his head was still bandaged.

"Neither we nor the drakes can see the center," Widsith said to Reynard. "Canst thou?"

Reynard looked over the rooftops, beyond the drakes. "Ropes of fog," he said. "From here, they cover something large and high — like the seed city, but split in four."

"You see through the fog!" Kaiholo said.

Kern shook his head. "I see nothing but fog."

Reynard could still feel his drake's strange hunger, like a cord blazing down the middle of its body, a hidden fuse — not just for food, but for any challenge. Drakes lived for battle, among themselves and whoever threatened their partners. They fought for mates to the death at times — and finished their seasons with their beautiful wings tattered, ripped, and chewed . . .

And this they knew. This they foresaw. And they did not care. For none survived more than one season, once they rose from the waters and split their cases and dried fresh new wings in island breezes. Reynard felt a sudden sadness at their necessity and passion.

He looked down the road and saw, at a cross-street to the spiral, the broad stub of a candle burned almost to the ground. This drew him away from thoughts of his drake to the King of Troy, whose season, though much longer, seemed to have also passed.

"Where is it, magician?" he murmured. "Where is your bone-wife now, and what is she doing?"

Kern and Kaiholo walked alongside Reynard and Calafi, protecting them all, and Andalo incidentally.

Kaiholo frowned and backed away as the great Eater appeared. Andalo kept the horse from rearing, and brought it under control, while Calafi laughed.

Calybo seemed more solid and present than ever, and this made him, to Reynard, even stranger and more frightening — like a masque in a village play, a demon's masque. His face swept up on one side, then on the other — as if presenting different emotions on different faces, or even different ideas about faces — a masque made for different times.

"Some Crafters must see the stars to make their worlds," the Eater said. "This may be one. The tower is a tunnel to the sky."

As if in response, the twists of grayness tied themelves in knots like those they had seen before, painful to trace. Reynard could feel a kind of wind pull him in and up toward the knots. Following those knots, he thought, trying to undo them, could cost one his very soul.

Which, he realized, was why the drakes had descended to the rooftops and all faced away from the city's center.

Calybo said, "There shall be newness here for the last time. Servants are angry at the end of their usefulness. But they still have tasks — final tasks. And one such is to arrange the last disks around the compass points of the krater, that they may be finished — the last effort of these islands, and filled with the last faces from the soulstone mines. Now we see."

Calafi gripped Reynard's arm. "I think thou art a brother," she said, and grinned up at him.

The Crafter's Lair

THE FORTRESS that lay over the krater revealed a plan like unto the markings they had seen in other kraters on the way here, empty kraters, including the one that still contained the shrouded body of a Crafter. The fortress supported a cleft tower, like a great stack over a forge, a tower likely open to the sky and the stars, and was surrounded by a great outer wall interrupted by arched openings of dense black stones.

Each opening seemed to lead down a hallway, and none led down the same hallway.

"Seest thou the way of it?" Calafi asked Reynard.

Reynard said, "A maze, I think, like the labyrinth that held the Minotaur." Behind them, a furtive group of twelve men and women, dressed in black-and-white-checked robes and high caps, brought forward four disks and stood, waiting to be given permission by someone, or something, to enter the fortress.

"And where dost thou get that notion?" Calafi asked, her voice high and childlike, but also cutting like a blade.

"From memories not my own," Reynard admitted. "From Valdis, perhaps." He turned his head to find her.

Valdis stepped closer, hands held out as if measuring and judging a great force. "Not my gift," she said. "Some other's learning, or maybe it came with the Crafter's work."

Reynard looked back to the ring of fine black sand around the hard rim of the krater, like the lip of a great bowl that carried a meal none dared eat. He could not see Widsith, could gain no reassurance that the Pilgrim had told him the truth. Reynard felt a vibration that squeezed his heart and made it falter in his chest, that bunched the muscles of his stomach and made him wish to throw up — and filled his arms as well, making him shake as if with palsy.

Calafi looked toward the wall and the nearest arch. "This Crafter is still alive."

Reynard agreed.

"But failing," Calybo said, and made his face clear to Reynard.

"I see only darkness in those doors," Andalo said.

The checked servants carried a disk forward and placed it into a groove before the archway. They then bowed and approached Calybo, and spoke to him in whispers — doubtless one of the few times they had ever addressed an Eater.

"Thou wilt pass through," Calybo said to Reynard and Calafi. "There is a last play, and the disk will lead thee to its heart — and protect ye against truths too strong. I will go with ye."

"Who am I?" Calafi asked. "Who are you? And who are we?

"*We are the next.*"

Valdis seemed to flow up beside them, like a shape of smoke, but then looking very much, Reynard thought, like the young Viking girl she had once been. "We will share," Valdis said. She put one hand on Reynard's shoulder, and the other on the girl's head. Looking into the girl's radiant face, and upon Valdis's night-dark features, Reynard felt his indecision and fear fade.

Andalo brought forth a pile of sticks and bones, donated perhaps by the servants, which he laid before Nikolias. As the second candle took its wick and made a greater brightness, a ragged figure in tatters of old muslin came forward, barely recognizable as a female conjure-shape. It reached down with stick arms and pulled up from the bones and pieces of wood another like itself, and Nikolias removed the fine cloak from his shoulders and draped it around the new construct, which suddenly filled out like a woman, with long hair and fine limbs and a lovely face that glowed in the light of the candle which gave it time to do its duty.

The last servants of the Crafter, who had performed menial duties and sacred duties for who could say how long, had arranged themselves around the krater structure and its tower, most kneeling, some in ornate robes standing, hands over their heads, staring inward and paying no attention to the newcomers.

Nikolias rode his horse forward. One of the servants swung her head to see him, but otherwise did nothing — did not rise from her knees, did not speak.

"They are all Travelers," Nikolias said. "They have been here, all their generations, since Hel brought the Crafters down to the chafing waste." He drew himself up straight in his saddle, then nodded to Reynard and threw a kiss to Calafi. "Yuchil and I wish you all triumph," he said. "That Travelers may continue to carry languages and tales, and to sustain gods, heroes, and mortals for all time to come."

They stepped toward the wall, the disk, the archway. Kern and Kaiholo and Valdis stood beside the disk. Kaiholo made a motion with his hand. Reynard would have to stoop to fit his head through.

The interior of the disk was still dark.

"It is solid," Reynard said. "I would not break it!"

"Stroke the upper rim until it sings," Calybo said. "I will follow."

Calafi curtseyed like a princess and stood beside the newest bone-wife, whose own thin voice now carried to their ears — and though feminine, not unlike the voice of the King of Troy.

"I will go before all and make certain," the bone-wife said. "I'll be first and test the airs, little such as I breathe, but as I do not have eyes, mine eyes will not fail, and as I have not a mind, my mind will not fail, and I'll let ye know whether the Crafter is prepared for the line to come to it before it dies."

"Rub the disk," Calybo said.

Reynard held out his hand and stroked the top of the disk, rubbing with two fingers. The sound was muted and blunt. He then touched his fingers to his tongue, moistening the tips, and tried again.

With a slight pressure, the disk began to vibrate, then to sing!

"It is opening," Calafi said. "Can I try next time?"

The bone-wife shivered away some leaves and dust, drew tight her black garb, stooped very low, and entered the disk first. Reynard kept rubbing as Calafi passed through, and then Calybo, and finally, Valdis.

When the Eaters passed through, the disk's tone changed.

"Keep to the left at every turn," Kern advised Reynard. "Many such mazes are in the histories of the giants, and that is always the way to the inner chamber."

"Many times I have riddled mazes with Asian emperors," Widsith said.

"Many times?" Kaiholo asked.

"Three times, actually," Widsith said. "And each time, I failed. A poor Minotaur!" He gripped Reynard's free hand and squeezed. "I envy thee, fox-boy."

The drakes left behind sang a sad humming noise and shifted on their perches, making roof tiles fall to the ground and shatter. Their connection with their masters was now ending, and they wished only to fly off and die on the southwestern shores.

Andalo took another candle from Gareth, lit it, and handed it to Reynard, who now passed through, following Calafi, and heard a rustle of sticks.

The Line Passes

THE BONE-WIFE STOOD in silhouette before them, sticks visible through the gap in the coat. Beyond her, the dark outer wall of the maze gleamed with veins of green fire.

"The airs are suitable," she said. "This way!"

Reynard lit the new candle with the stub of the old, and proceeded, Calafi close behind ... and the Eaters on each side, as if to protect them.

They followed the bone-wife to the right, then took the first left turn into the krater's winding stone maze.

Reynard held out the candle, but it gave little light. And then, the flame turned greenish, and while it still burned, produced no heat, and cast only its own kind of darkness.

They were in a realm of shadows, and this seemed to suit the Eaters. Reynard could not see them, only their outlines against the fairy lights that drifted now and then through the corridors and around the bends.

"Why go through the disk?" he asked Calafi in a whisper.

She shook her head. "I thought you knew!"

Valdis said, "We are in the Crafter's last working, and when we are done here, we will pass through the disk again." There was hope in her voice, but Calybo said nothing.

The deeper they went into the maze, the more the fairy lights resembled childers — but taking on the characters of male or female, their faces acquiring features as well, and growing in number. The corridors were thick with gently glowing figures.

"We stop here for a moment," Calybo said.

Calafi watched the glowing childers with a happy smile. "Was I one of those?" she asked. Nobody could answer. Nobody knew. Reynard wondered as well.

"They gather to act on a Crafter stage," Calybo said. "I have seen them around the western shore, during storms at sea, and windy days on land — blowing through the forests, immortal until they are cast in a new story."

They had again turned left, and now came to a divided chamber where one side was stacked high with granite slabs, and the other with disks upright on racks, like dishes set out to dry. The bone-wife gestured for them to move forward. Childers flowed from the slabs, until the chamber was uniformly brilliant, as if bathed in bright sun, and they could hear distant voices, perhaps singing, perhaps just expressing marvel.

"Do not look into the disks," the bone-wife whispered. "We are too close to where they were made. And you are already in the only creation you need."

She walked ahead, the hem of her robe swishing back and forth, and Reynard saw what might have been an ankle peeping out from that hem — but it was only the knob of a stick. She stopped them once more, then guided them around another corner, left again — Reynard had lost track of how many times they turned. They were caught up in the flowing currents of childers, all headed into the

turn, gently making their own sounds, but then the four heard another sound from within a deeper chamber — a sound like rushing
water in a great cavern.

The bone-wife pointed to Valdis, Calafi, Calybo, and Reynard.
"You will go on, those who have their own roles to play," she said.
"And once you go, I'll perform my last act of magic, then collapse,
and the King of Troy will find his peace. He bids you now farewell."

Valdis and Calafi took hands and walked into the next passage.
Calybo held out his hand for Reynard. The Eater's eyes grew into
distant caverns, showing a single star —

Calafi tugged Valdis after her and offered him her other hand, in-
sisting, grasping, squeezing.

And Reynard was not afraid.

He took Calybo's hand.

He had a sense of what might happen next.

And so did the strange girl.

"'Twill be fun!" she said.

They now strung out in a line, hand to hand, and entered the biggest chamber yet — topped by a great darkness, an ill-defined space
filled with swirling lights that illuminated nothing in this world and
cast no glow on the center of the krater, the center of the bowl that
served up history . . .

And madness.

Reynard saw the Crafter. It had no eyes, yet he was sure it saw all.
It possessed no limbs, yet spun away great ropes of gray mist that
rose high into the tower — mist made of childers, Reynard thought,
but could not be sure of anything. He looked up beyond the ropes of
mist . . . and saw a brilliant green star framed by the opening at the
top of the tower.

"We have stored up all our time waiting for you," Calybo said.
"Valdis, touch the young one. Young mistress, touch Reynard."

"I have him," Calafi said.

Now Calybo raised his head like a wolf, and howled forth that dreadful sound Reynard had heard on the beach when the great Eater, just beneath the stars, had renewed the Pilgrim after his long voyage.

The Crafter now spilled out of the krater and flowed around them like a huge wave crashing, then changing to a great forest growing all at once, and the Crafter surrounded Calybo, absorbed him within greater shadow, Reynard thought he saw, and the little girl again served as a conduit for this chain.

He felt his insides fill with stars.

Green stars.

In the greater darkness, his head and heart brimmed with horror and exaltation. He did not see what became of Calafi, or of Valdis, or of Calybo. It seemed he was about to receive a gift — a very dangerous gift, on top of all the other dangerous gifts piped or funneled into him through that chain of hands.

For an instant, he saw a wide black face, a woman's face, mostly, with eyes the color of a full moon, and quite beautiful, but far more terrifying in her way than the Crafter. That face, for that instant, rose above them all — and he felt and heard Calybo's voice die, and saw him turn into gray ash — empty of all, depleted.

One just beneath the sky, now made stuff for mud.

This was the only time Reynard ever saw that great dark face with moonlight eyes, and for that he was glad, and glad that he had seen so little of her.

The krater and all beneath the tower was empty, and the stone walls of the maze had collapsed, leaving only marks where they had been.

After a moment of utter, tingling shock, accompanied by a whirlwind of voices, he realized what he had been tasked with — his part in the last play — and what he would spend many lifetimes doing. Lifetimes passed through to him by the Eaters, with their fragmented memories, their knowledge in jumbled confusion, but at times ...

Still affecting. Still guiding.

Which was the way Queen Hel had designed them, and the duty she had assigned to them. She must have known all along, if time meant anything to such. But her design, her circumstance, gave Reynard no more choice than being a fisherboy — less, actually.

He pushed up from the smooth, cold stone, and smelled the last humidity of a great storm. The Crafter was covered with a broad shroud, a single figure spreading and drawing it down so that nothing of the frightful corpse of the ancient being could be seen. This was the final task of the magician's bone-wife. And when it was done, she collapsed into sticks and ash and dust, and never again was such a candle seen, here or anywhere else in the world, or a sorcerer as great as Troy.

Reynard walked away from the center, to find his way back, straight out to the arch this time. He looked into the disk, looked up and around the disk, and saw gray storm and falling rain beyond, but through the disk itself — a ray of sun.

Calafi stood behind him and gripped his hand with hers.

"Let us go see," she said.

And she led him through.

Once again, he had to stoop to pass.

And on the other side ...

"Back to the beginning!" Calafi called.

Nikolias and Widsith waited outside the archway, and all the others, but the disk stayed dark, and nobody came forth.

"Where are the Eaters?" Andalo asked.

"Silence!" Nikolias admonished. "They have done what they were made to do."

"And what is that?" Bela asked.

"If we see the boy again . . ."

"I do not think we will," Widsith said.

"Nor do I," Kern said. "I feel very strange!"

"Thou art very strange!" Kaiholo said, and patted the giant's lower arm with false assurance, for he felt very strange as well.

"We are finished on this island," Nikolias said. "All the Isles of the Blessed are finished, and will become other.

"With this boy, in all his charge, a new age now begins."

Widsith saw through the old Traveler and all his companions. Then he held up his own hand and saw through that as well.

He saw grass and a lovely country.

England and No Home

THE ISLAND looked completely different. The sun spread itself over green rolling hills, dotted with sheep and small stone houses and fences, and the fall weather was chill, but there was not yet snow in the air, so he and Calafi hiked over the hills, following the sun until they had to rest.

They found clean hay in a loft in a vale that smelled of the sea. "It is that way, I think," Reynard said, but Calafi could hardly stand and they were too tired to finish the journey this day, so they hid in the barn and piled hay over themselves to try to keep warm.

"No childers anywhere!" the girl said, then clung to him and instantly fell asleep.

As exhausted as he was, he could not sleep yet. He seemed to be taking count of all the ways he had changed since he passed through the disk — but could not, nor could he remember what had happened in the great maze, or who had led him there and what they had given him.

But when he closed his eyes, he saw a field of green stars radiating all around, and knew that something had happened, something had changed him.

And he had to return home.

The next morning, an older woman found them in the barn while she was bringing feed to chickens, and without saying a word, she left some bread and closed the door on the barn, for she knew their times had been hard and did not feel right to disturb them.

They awoke and ate the bread and drank from a stone trough green with moss, and resumed their walk to the shore, which was only a few miles away, through the vale.

Calafi said out loud, "Fortune to those so kind."

Reynard wondered what the girl's blessing would bring for the generous giver of bread.

Calafi held his hand like a sister. "We have many lives now," she said as they crossed a boulder-strewn beach.

"How do you know?" Reynard asked.

"I remember someone gave us time. I remember not who it was, but they gave all they had, and so now we have many lives. And so much time to ponder them all!"

"Memories," Reynard said.

"We are too new to have such memories," Calafi said. She looked across the beach to waves on the shore, and squinted. "Who is that?"

A young woman walked on the beach, white-blond hair streaming in the ocean breeze, her black gown pulled against her legs, and her eyes, brilliant green eyes, saw them, and they slowly approached one another, filled with caution. Then they began to remember a little. Who they all were, if not what they had all been through.

"I have been given my freedom," the woman said.

"I see that," Reynard said.

"Hel gave me my freedom."

"Who is that?" Reynard said, and Valdis smiled.

"Someone I once knew," she said, a little puzzled. "Along with others who served."

A boat was out on the water, caught in a patch of bright sun, and Valdis waved, and curious fishermen from the far north brought their old boat to the shore, gently nudged its bluff bow onto the sand, and asked them what they were doing here in sheep country.

Clearly, they were charmed by Valdis, and she was charmed by them. And so they carried their strange passengers to a fishing village in Norway, and Valdis said this was where she would stay.

Somehow Calafi came upon a purse filled with silver coins, and they paid for a coach to take them to the south, to a larger city, where that same purse bought their passage to England.

White Shadow

CALAFI FOUND the country lanes fascinating and studied with rapt attention the flowers, for somehow they had skipped a winter and a heavy snow, and were now in glorious spring.

They had little money for inns and transportation, and Calafi came up with no more purses, but neither seemed to mind sleeping out under the stars, though they went hungry often enough, and became beggars of a kind.

"Are you my brother, really?" Calafi asked, studying him as they lounged under a hedge and waited for the summer day to grow a little cooler before they moved along.

"I do not think so," Reynard said.

"But if we have no father or mother, perhaps we can be brother and sister?"

"I suppose," he said.

They heard the rumble of a wagon along the lane and peered out to see a tinker's cart, jangling with every bump, pulled by two horses and trailed by a rider on a hefty roan — a rider wearing a long black coat, very like someone they both remembered — in part.

The rider, a tall elderly man, stopped where they were hiding and said, "Is it safe to pass here? No roving gangs or mean spirits?"

Calafi came out, smiling and happy, and the back flap of the wagon opened, and a thin white-haired woman looked out.

"Be ye hungry?" she asked them.

Days later, the wagon rolled on with Calafi, who had decided this was where she belonged.

Reynard and she parted with some tears, but determined they both had to find their ways, for where they had come from no longer existed.

Reynard never found Southwold, nor any village quite like it, nor any who knew his family — though Aldeburgh was still there, and prospering as more and more ships were made. There had been more Spanish invasions, but England had survived and now seemed on the edge of prosperity as her ships sailed the world and brought news of riches and goods.

Reynard worked on farms and in towns, shoeing horses and tending flocks, and one day, herding sheep through a village near York, saw a man with a thick, grizzled beard — a handsome man, though blind and with a kind of lightning-strike scar from forehead to chin. The man was begging on a side street, and Reynard dropped a coin into his filthy hand, and said only one thing:

"Cardoza?"

"Aye, the very same, a poor vagabond master, late of the sea, and who art thou?"

Reynard backed away and pushed his sheep on, and wondered if sometime soon he might find another man of some acquaintance — a man he knew only as Pilgrim.

◆ ◆ ◆

When Reynard took a coach to London, he had saved enough coin to pay for a small room in the garret of an old, leaning house, and here he ate bread and water and hoped to find more work.

But on the street, one middle-bright day, as the summer was coming to an end, he saw entering an alley a figure he recognized instantly: a man in reverse. A man with a white shadow. He waited for Reynard in the narrow lane, in a stray beam of sun bounced from a high, angled window.

This man summoned him to come close.

"Time to begin sharing thy gifts," said the man with a white shadow. "Hast thou found th'one named Bacon? Francis Bacon?"

Reynard said, "I have seen him remarked in passing. I think he lives nearby. And more like him!"

"Then go to them. Many crave the touch of stars that thou dost carry."

Reynard held out his hands, beseeching the strange man. "There are so many in London alone!"

"You were given much time."

"But I cannot visit them all!"

"There were six other islands. All sent forth chalices like thyself, backwards and forwards, across many years. After London, go south to Italy, to Padua, where more await. Wherever thou goest, find those who speak the new languages that giveth humans mastery, and share thy stars with them all."

"And what will they do?"

"They will see, and describe, and measure, and faster than light or spirit, the world and beyond will fill out, and the new will take charge. Give them a touch of the glory of the Seven Isles. Give them a touch of what once was.

"Call it Genius."

Acknowledgments

With thanks to Astrid, my constant provider of balance, to my diligent and tireless editor, John Joseph Adams, and to David and Diane Clark, careful and wonderful readers.

For help with my languages, I owe a debt of gratitude to Kathy Wellen, Judith Bosnak, Richard Curtis, and most especially to Kathleen Alcala.

Any errors that remain are of course my own.